Deeply in You

By Sharon Page

DEEPLY IN YOU

BLOOD CURSE

BLOOD FIRE

BLOOD SECRET

"Wicked for Christmas" in SILENT NIGHT, SINFUL
NIGHT

BLOOD WICKED

BLOOD DEEP

BLOOD RED

BLOOD ROSE

BLACK SILK

HOT SILK

SIN

"Midnight Man" in WILD NIGHTS

Deeply in You

THE WICKED DUKES

SHARON PAGE

APHRODISIA

KENSINGTON PUBLISHING CORP.

www.kensingtonbooks.com

APHRODISIA BOOKS are published by

Kensington Publishing Corp.
119 West 40th Street
New York, NY 10018

All Kensington titles, imprints, and distributed lines are available at special quantity discounts for bulk purchases for sales promotion, premiums, fund-raising, educational, or institutional use.

Special book excerpts or customized printings can also be created to fit specific needs. For details, write or phone the office of the Kensington Special Sales Manager: Kensington Publishing Corp., 119 West 40th Street, New York, NY 10018. Attn. Special Sales Department. Phone: 1-800-221-2647.

Aphrodisia and the A logo Reg. U.S. Pat. & TM Off.

eISBN-13: 978-1-61773-093-1
eISBN-10: 1-61773-093-9
First Kensington Electronic Edition: July 2014

ISBN-13: 978-1-61773-092-4
ISBN-10: 1-61773-092-0
First Kensington Trade Paperback Printing: July 2014

10 9 8 7 6 5 4 3 2 1

Printed in the United States of America

ACKNOWLEDGMENTS

Many thanks to my editor, Esi Sogah, for her enthusiasm for *Deeply in You* and the Wicked Dukes series. Many more thanks for her insightful comments and keen editorial eye. She pushed me to make this book better and better. Also, I am very grateful to the entire team at Kensington who are knowledgeable, fun, and wonderful to work with.

Thanks, as always, to my terrific agent, Jessica Faust, of BookEnds, LLC. And I have to give hugs to my "writer support group," my friends and critique partners. Of course, thank you to my family for putting up with a writer in the family, though at least there are some fringe benefits (like signed books).

Dear Reader,

I'm thrilled to introduce you to my brand-new series, The Wicked Dukes. Deep in my heart I've always wanted to write a sexy, emotional Regency romance with a governess for a heroine and a naughty, rakish duke. It's one of the best-loved tropes of romance, and I've been dying to create my very own special governess and duke.

In *Deeply in You*, Helena Winsome is not just a governess; she also must spy on the *ton* and gather scandals for her gossip column in her half brother's newspaper, which she writes as "Lady X," in order to protect her family from poverty. When she is persuaded to spy on the gorgeous Duke of Greybrooke to prove he is a traitor, she must get close to this very roguish duke to learn his secrets. Tempted by the disapproving but innately sensual Miss Winsome, Greybrooke cannot resist seducing her into his deliciously wicked world. He is my favorite type of hero—a wounded hero who is also passionate and protective.

While I've loved writing paranormal romance, I've had a huge amount of fun returning to the naughty Regency world that I first wrote about in *Sin, Black Silk,* and *Hot Silk*. I hope you enjoy!

Sharon Page

1

London—May 1819

If a governess's wildest fantasy was to take shape and come to life, he would look exactly like the Duke of Greybrooke.

From her vantage point on a bench in Berkeley Square, Miss Helena Winsome surreptitiously studied the duke as he vaulted down from his glossy black carriage with effortless grace. A tall beaver hat added a foot to his already remarkable height. A three-tiered greatcoat fell from broad shoulders and swung open as he walked to the front steps of an imposing town house, giving her a glimpse of trim hips and long legs. His tailor must sew his trousers to him, for they fit like a glove over his muscular thighs.

Unmarried, with a fortune and stunning good looks, Greybrooke was the catch of the year. He had been the catch of the last five years. No lady had snared his heart and tempted him into marriage. But it was said that matrons and widows ardently pursued him for the chance to grace his bed—even just *once*—and delicate maidens fainted in Hyde Park when he smiled at them.

Sensible Helena had scoffed at the gossip, even as she absorbed every detail. How could a gentleman's smile render a woman unconscious? She had encountered many handsome, young men in her years as a governess to the *ton*'s families, and never once had she swooned at the sight of one.

She squinted, trying to see more.

Would the duke notice her peering at him? The risk of capture made her pulse pound with thrilling nerves. If he saw her looking, what would he do? Come and reprimand her? It would be more likely he would give her a scoundrel's knowing smirk from across the road, then ignore her.

At least she had one thing in her favor. He would never suspect a nondescript governess of being a spy.

She withdrew opera glasses from a pocket in her skirts and flicked them open. Other governesses and nurses strolled through the park, pushing perambulators or holding the hands of small children. The sun-soaked square was busy on this delightfully warm May afternoon. But she had chosen a quiet corner near the street, and she sat on a bench ensconced beneath a large oak. No one looked in her direction.

Her three young charges were sitting on a blanket on the grass beside her—Lords Michael and Timothy played with a ball; Lady Sophie had her nose buried in a book; and their young aunt, Lady Maryanne, sat with them, braiding colored ribbons by the feel of their textures. Although nineteen, Maryanne was still very childlike because she was blind. Helena looked after her too, for the girl had been without her sight since fourteen.

Helena also had a pram, and it was positioned in front of her, which gave her something to hide behind if necessary. If the duke glanced her way, she could quickly turn her attention to fifteen-month-old Lord Edward, slumbering happily amongst his blankets. She had offered to bring Edward since it was Nurse's afternoon off, and he made her look even more innocent. What spy would bring a baby along?

Helena put the glasses to her eyes. They let her magnify detail, and she trained them on the duke.

Her breath evaporated in one swift whoosh.

It wasn't as if she hadn't already watched him whenever she could for the past three weeks, after taking a week to settle into her post as governess to the duke's sister, Lady Winterhaven. But each time she saw Greybrooke, her skin would grow dewy with perspiration, making her uncomfortably hot beneath her corset.

How she now understood the term "loose woman," for she yearned to take off her dress and tear her stays open, she felt so heated.

It must be nerves that made her feel as tense as an overwound clock. Yet she had taken quite a few risks in her pursuit of scandals, and she'd never experienced anything quite like *this* oddly anxious feeling before.

Before mounting the steps to Lady Montroy's house, Greybrooke paused to survey the street around him, perhaps to ensure that Lady Montroy's husband wasn't returning to the house early.

His action gave her a full view of his face.

Of full, wide lips that looked scandalously sensuous on an Englishman. His cheekbones were as striking as the Pennines or the cliffs of Dover—high, sharp, and beautiful, with deep wells of shadow beneath. Beneath his hat, his hair was a tumble of coal-black waves. She couldn't see the color of his eyes, but his thick black lashes were unmistakable. That fringe of pure black gave his eyes the arresting quality that robbed her of breath.

Perhaps she could see why less wary, wise, and knowledgeable girls fainted.

His Grace strode to the front door, rapped sharply, and the door opened. A young footman bowed, and the duke disappeared inside.

Helena folded her opera glasses and stowed them away. Her heartbeat galloped, and no amount of controlled breaths could slow it. Ever since she had been given this assignment one month ago, she'd discovered that one could not watch the Duke of Greybrooke and escape unscathed.

For the last three nights, she'd *dreamed* about him. She, the most pragmatic, practical woman in England; the one governess in the country who did not harbor any fantasy that she might catch a rich man's eye and be whisked from her mundane life to blissful happiness.

But the fantasies her mind invented at night—

About lush caresses she didn't even know she knew anything about, until she had experienced them in scorching, thrilling, naughty dreams.

Stop this, Helena.

She must remember the reason why she was watching the Duke of Greybrooke in this clandestine manner. This was not one of her usual missions, where she was working to unearth a scandal for her column in her half brother's newspaper—her very popular column, *Lady X's Society Papers*. She was here to learn everything she could about the duke's habits and his schedule. Here to find out where he went, whom he met, and when he was regularly away from his house. All information she required so she could devise a plan to get the proof she needed.

Proof the Duke of Greybrooke had been a traitor, a spy for Napoleon during the war.

But she was *also* a governess. She had tucked a book at the bottom of the pram, and now she took it out. She motioned the children to gather. "It is time for a story."

"Not yet!" Michael, the oldest boy, the heir to the Earl of Winterhaven, got up and ran to her. He clutched the cricket ball he'd been tossing to his brother. "Winnie," he said, using his nickname for her, "will you play ball with us first? Timothy is too young to throw. His nose runs all the time."

Four-year-old Lord Timothy tottered up, rubbing his nose on his sleeve.

She laughed. "You, young man, have a handkerchief." Helena drew out the square of linen and pressed it to the boy's small nose. "Now, you must blow."

But Timothy sucked in, then coughed.

She coaxed and blew her own nose, but she could not get the little boy to do it himself. Michael proudly showed that he could do it, and she praised him.

"Of course I can do it," he said seriously. "I have to learn how to be a gentleman, for I'm going to be the earl. I'm already a viscount."

Michael already bore a title—a courtesy title—and he reminded his siblings of it several times each day.

"A gentleman also behaves with some humility," she gently pointed out.

"No, they don't." Michael shook his head, his golden waves tumbling around his face. "Uncle Grey says they don't. He tells me I am going to break hearts when I'm big and that I have to be prepared for the adulation I will eventually receive."

"Oh, he does, does he? That is very wrong of him. A gentleman should not break hearts. That is the behavior of a scoundrel."

Uncle Grey was the Duke of Greybrooke—and the reason she had sought out employment with the duke's sister and brother-in-law. As governess, Helena could hear the servants' gossip and discover all sorts of information about the duke—including the fact that his most recent paramour lived on Berkeley Square.

Her thoughts strayed to the duke. In her mind's eye, she followed him into the house.

Was Lady Montroy, his lover, waiting for him in her bedchamber? Helena could imagine the duke making his way up the stairs to her ladyship, his long legs taking the steps two at a time.

He would grasp his cravat before he reached her door, yank it open with one tug, bare his throat. Dark stubble would shadow his jaw, and when the countess kissed him on his neck, she would taste his clean skin and smell the exotic sandalwood that imbued his soap, and he would gather her in a passionate, scorching kiss—

But would they do *it* in the countess's bedchamber? What did people do exactly in clandestine affairs? From studying scandals and love affairs and naughty seductions for the newspaper, Helena knew, in general what couples did.

But how did they actually go about it? How could a woman share a bed with a husband and a lover and not be crippled with guilt? Did they perhaps steal moments of passion on a settee in the drawing room? On the pianoforte bench? In the garden, hidden by the roses?

What would it be like to have a handsome gentleman roll on his back on the soft grass beneath fragrant roses and pull you on top of—?

Be sensible!

Lurid descriptions sold newspapers. Helena knew that from experience. But such thoughts were not appropriate here in the park, when her duty was to her four charges and Lady Maryanne.

"No, we will have reading first," she said firmly. She left her bench to sit with the children on the blanket. It proved a challenge in her snug corset and skirts, but she managed it. As Timothy, Michael, and Sophie sat and Helena opened the book, she took one more glance at the countess's house. It towered four stories tall, fashioned of deep red brick. Elegant and sedate, the house gave no hint at the sinful happenings taking place inside.

The duke usually remained there for exactly one hour—he appeared to be a gentleman who lived by a schedule. Something Helena understood but hardly expected in a careless rake.

She had wondered if this might prove to be a good time of

day to search his home. The only problem was servants. The duke was unmarried and lived alone in his enormous mansion on Park Lane, but he had dozens of servants.

She read a chapter, with Timothy cuddled up to her left side and Sophie sitting on her right. Michael, who wanted to behave like a gentleman, sat at the edge of the blanket with his back erect and his shoulders straight. Lady Maryanne sat demurely at the other end, her walking stick resting beside her legs.

Helena paused to begin chapter 4 when, across the street, a window shot up with a rattle of its sash. A female scream of fury exploded over the square. "You wretch! I've given you everything and you cannot leave!"

Helena jerked her head up. The children gasped and strained to see. The duke was leaving the house, jauntily sauntering down the front steps. His cravat was untied, his blue-black hair tousled and falling over his eyes, and he carried his hat in his hand.

Michael hopped up from the blanket. "It's Uncle Grey!"

Above the duke, white curtains fluttered in the open window. Suddenly, blond hair tumbled out—long, curling tresses of golden hair, falling like Rapunzel's locks. The fairy-tale image lasted only a moment, for the Countess of Montroy leaned forward, revealing her face—scarlet and contorted with rage. "Seducer. Scoundrel. Wretched sod! You made me believe—you told me—I hate you!"

Helena was transfixed, stunned by the countess's terrible behavior. The entire square could hear what was happening. Now everyone knew about the woman's scandalous affair with Greybrooke. The only one who paid no attention was the duke, sauntering toward his carriage—

Michael. Panicked, Helena looked around her. Michael was *gone*. No, he was *there*—running along the winding path, racing toward his uncle . . . and the street. Helena scrambled to her feet, but before she took a step, she spun around and gave orders. "The rest of you stay here. Lady Sophie, watch the others, watch Lord Edward in his pram."

Sophie paled—at nine, she was young to take charge. But there was no other choice.

Then Helena ran. Her feet flew over the path, but an eight-year-old could sprint terribly fast. Her heavy skirts flailed around her legs, threatening to send her tumbling.

"Michael, stop now!"

Her command only made him run faster.

Lungs burning, she sprinted as she would have done as a young girl, when she used to chase her brother. When Michael was within arm's reach, she released her grip on her skirts and lunged, wrapping her arms around the boy. She whisked him off the ground, hugging him tightly.

Still gasping, she plopped her charge back on his feet. Even when out of breath, a governess must be stern when necessary. She wagged her finger. "Michael, you mustn't run away like that—"

He pointed past her, at the countess's house, and gasped, "Look, Winnie!"

Helena whirled around, pressing her hands on Michael's shoulders to keep him trapped. The countess had leaned out of her window again, but this time she clutched the sides of a large, white pot—a *chamber* pot—and she held it over the duke's head.

"Your Grace!" Helena bellowed it across the street, which was utterly improper. But she was a governess, accustomed to thwarting disaster before it happened, and she could not simply ignore a mess in progress. "Your Grace, above you! Look up!"

The duke did just that, and with a cry of fury, Lady Montroy turned the chamber pot upside down. Liquid flew downward, and the heavy pot slipped from her grasp. Greybrooke leapt nimbly to the side, landing with a panther's grace at the edge of the street. The fluid—it was too impolite to name—

spattered on the sidewalk. The porcelain pot hit the cobbles beside the duke and shattered to pieces.

The duke looked up—but not at his furious lover who retreated from the window with frantic speed. He stared at her. Helena.

Magnetic, even with the distance of the street between them, his gaze captured hers. Slowly, like the spill of sun at dawn, his gorgeous, full lips curved into a devilish grin. She could do nothing but gape at him, her practical half-boots stuck to the spot.

Dimples. Rugged lines that bracketed his mouth. A wicked sparkle in his expression. She couldn't break his spell. All around, there was a buzz and blur of people—a throng of curious onlookers, drawn by the shouting and the smash of the pot.

The Duke of Greybrooke bowed to her in a sweep of elegance. In full view of the busy Mayfair streets that bordered Berkeley Square.

People turned to look at *her*. Spies were supposed to disappear into the woodwork, not induce the entire world to stare.

The duke straightened, nodded to her, his smile still in place. He turned toward his carriage.

Helena's heart fell faster than the chamber pot. What had she been *thinking*? She'd failed impetuously, foolishly, miserably. When the duke was about to be soaked and brained by a pot, she hadn't been able to keep silent.

How could she find proof about the duke now? After this, he would notice her if she was within a mile of him.

If she didn't find proof, her family would be ruined.

"Uncle!" Michael jerked forward, bringing her thoughts back from panic. His slim body twisted out of her grip. In her anxiety over the duke, the pot, and her mistake, her hands had slackened on the boy's shoulders.

Like a streak of lightning, Michael shot forward, toward the street.

In a heartbeat, his slim figure vanished between the people who milled on the park's path—ladies, gentlemen, nurses, and governesses, all watching Lady Montroy's house expectantly, as if waiting for her ladyship to return with something else to throw.

Helena ran. "Michael, stop!" she shouted, even though the words would be nothing more than a warning to him that she was on his heels. So many people mobbed together, she could not see beyond shoulders, trousers, bonnets, and skirts.

Please let Lady Sophie have obeyed and kept the others safely on the blanket.

"Please stop that boy!" But the crowd was engaged in the drama on the street, the drama of a duke. Finally her shouts got attention. People turned to her, but no one stopped the small boy who threaded easily around their legs.

She elbowed and pushed, and did everything a proper servant should never do—

She ran on madly, and finally she saw him, almost at the entrance to the street. From the side came clattering, clanking, and horses' wild snorts.

A carriage hurtled down the road, horses flailed by the coachman. It barreled up the street, traveling far faster than it should.

"Uncle!" Michael shouted, blind to everything but the duke. He was going to run in front of the horses.

"Michael, no!" But it was too late. The child jumped off the sidewalk. She couldn't stop him, but if she got to him before the carriage did, she could throw him clear.

Sick with terror, she launched into the street. Rattling filled her ears. Horses whinnied and a man shouted. Hooves scrambled on the cobblestones. But Helena focused only on Michael, who stopped dead in the street, frightened by the noise.

Her boot snagged on her hem. Her feet stopped abruptly, her body didn't. She tumbled forward, but she was so close to

Michael she could grab his coat. Grasping fabric, she shoved him ahead of her—

Long legs suddenly appeared—long legs in black trousers. Strong arms clad in gray scooped Michael off the road. The color gray was all she could see; it whirled around her like fog. A hand gripped her dress and pulled her roughly. Fabric tore, her hip smacked against the cobbles, then her rump bumped over the uneven ground as she was hauled away.

Next thing she knew, she sat upon the sidewalk, staring into emerald eyes framed with black, curling lashes.

The Duke of Greybrooke. He held Michael securely against his chest. Black leather gloves covered the large hands that both cradled the boy's small bottom and splayed against his back. The duke laughed down at Michael, who had his arms wrapped tightly around Greybrooke's strong neck.

"You gave us a bad scare, my young gentleman." His voice was husky. "You had no right, young Michael, to run away from your nurse."

"Governess." The correction fell off numb and trembling lips. Why had she said that? It didn't matter. His Grace had saved Michael's life. Had saved hers.

He had swooped down like an angel, carrying her and Michael to safety.

"Your G-Grace—" Her voice wobbled and broke.

A white linen handkerchief appeared in front of her. The duke crouched in front of her, with Michael seated on his bent knee. Sandalwood tickled her nose, an exotic scent that suited the duke—rumor said he behaved like the sultan of an eastern seraglio.

"Calming breaths," he instructed, in a rich, deep baritone that flowed like silken, melted chocolate. "You have had a bad shock."

"Thank you, but I am all right, Your Grace. I must take Michael to the others. Make certain they are safe too—" Trying to propel up to her feet, she tipped to the side. The duke's strong hand caught her by the waist. One quick jerk pulled her to him, then he set her back on her bottom.

"Do not move too swiftly, my dear." The duke paused and planted a kiss on the boy's head. Beside Michael's guinea gold hair, the duke's tresses were black as jet, and in the sun they had a sheen of indigo blue. "Are you all right, lad?"

As the boy nodded, the duke said to her, "As you've gathered, I know this scamp. He is my sister's son, Michael, and you appear to know me, but I am at the disadvantage—"

"I am Miss Winsome."

Another roguish grin. She should be immune to them by now, but no, she experienced a shivering sensation that rushed down her spine and throbbed low in her tummy.

His green eyes twinkled. "You certainly are."

As if he were a disobedient charge, she said briskly, "It is my name, Your Grace. My name is Helena Winsome. I am governess to your nephews and niece."

"Then you must be far more stoic and indestructible than you look. Those three will bring any woman to her knees. The last governess was built like a pugilist, and even she hung up her gloves after two months."

"Raising children is hardly a battle. But, yes, I am quite strong and capable, Your Grace."

"Indeed. You certainly acted swiftly to save me from the chamber pot. Next time you'll know to hold onto this one tightly in a park. Take him to Hyde Park and you might end up having to swim in the Serpentine to catch him."

Her cheeks heated. She must be blushing with humiliation. A bit tartly, she pointed out, "Your Grace, I am never careless with my charges. Unfortunately the incident with the chamber pot distracted me from my duties. I assure you I will never make such a lapse again. Now, I must go back to the children. I do believe I can stand up now."

"Of course, Miss Winsome." Taking her hand, he helped her to her feet. For a breathtaking moment he lifted her hand toward his lips. She swayed on her feet in surprise.

"I must thank you for rescuing me," he drawled.

He was going to kiss her hand in public.

A good governess did not make an embarrassing scene about a harmless touch. She would accept it with stolid disapproval, then ensure she nipped the problem—or the seducer—in the bud.

A mere half inch before contact—

With an audacious wink, he released her hand, and she almost toppled over from the sudden release of tension.

"Show me the way, my dear," he said casually. "I'll carry this little scamp."

Perching Michael in the crook of his arm, Greybrooke walked at her side as she led him toward the blanket. He took long, easy, prowling strides. He made her think of a male lion—a predator in command but one gentle with his young.

The duke was not at all what she expected. From gossip, she'd learned he had more paramours in a year than most men did in a lifetime. He broke hearts without guilt. He was supposed to do things in the bedroom that made the gossiping matrons blush scarlet, shut their mouths, and fan themselves. Helena ached to know what he did that was so scandalous and forbidden it stopped gossip in its tracks.

Now, she simply couldn't reconcile the man walking at her side with the man she was supposed to investigate. He was leading her back to the children, for heaven's sake, studying her with concern, as if he expected her to suddenly crumple to the ground from the shock.

Today, he'd proven himself a hero. She had not expected to find a decent man within the scandalous duke. But she had.

Could such a man have betrayed his country? Did such an idea make sense?

"I'm glad Miss Barrow left," Michael put in. His slim arms were around his uncle's neck. "She was loathsome. Miss Winsome is jolly fun."

The duke slid his gaze slowly over her. "I can imagine quite a bit of jolly fun could be had with Miss Winsome."

To her embarrassment, she blushed again. She should be made of sterner stuff. "Yes," she said firmly. "Good, decent, respectable fun."

"Uncle Grey!" Lord Timothy leapt up and jumped on the duke's leg, clinging to his elegant trousers. Lady Sophie led Lady Maryanne by the hand and gently put the older girl's hand in Greybrooke's.

Helena saw the duke wipe the corner of his eye as he beamed down at Lady Maryanne, his young sister. She knew he was deeply touched. He bent to kiss her on her smooth, blond curls, then easily swept slender Maryanne into an embrace with his free arm.

Helena patted Sophie on her shoulder. The duke caught her eye. *Thank you,* he mouthed.

What was he thanking her for? Still, she did the same thing in return to him.

"All right, you lot," he growled. He released Maryanne and set Michael down. "You must go and listen to Miss Winsome now. I have to go by my club, my wee angels."

"Gather your things from the grass, children," she directed, which gave her a few moments alone with the duke. But she could hardly ask: "Did you sell secrets to the French? You must tell me if you did. If you lie, I shall make you sit in the corner."

Surely there must be some way to learn something. The duke was strolling away. If she could make him stay just a little longer . . .

She launched forward desperately and touched his arm.

"Your Grace, you really should be more circumspect in your affairs."

He halted. His good-natured expression vanished. He stared at her with cold eyes, and her heart sank. "Do you have a lesson to teach me, Miss Winsome?"

"Your reputation . . . I mean, it is said you . . . well, Michael said that you have advised him to learn how to break hearts. As you experienced with Lady Montroy, that is a rather dangerous thing to do."

"Indeed," he said, and nothing more.

Could she make him reveal something? "What happened to make her so upset, Your Grace?"

"Greybrooke. And the answer is simple."

The duke leaned close. Helena breathed in his heady scent again—rich leather, a dab of exotic spicy cologne, the warm fragrance of sandalwood. His voice became a husky whisper of heat across her ear, making even her toes quiver.

"Lady Montroy was willing to entice me with the pleasures I enjoy most," he murmured. "I tied her to her bed and flailed her bottom with a riding crop. But I found the enterprise was not as delightful as I had hoped. Getting what I wanted from the dear lady did not make me any more interested. She already bored me. So I ended our relationship."

Her eyes felt as large as saucers. "A r-riding crop?" She didn't ever spank children.

"You didn't expect me to be honest? Then why ask the question, love?"

He touched the bare nape of her neck, just below her bun, making her gulp. Lightly, his finger stroked down. Shivers raced down her spine. She flinched and tried to move away, but his hand rested at her waist, stopping her. "I rescued your charge, yet you wish to chastise me over my personal affairs."

She had wanted him to talk, but sense warned her not to antagonize him. "I am sorry. I had no right—"

"True, but I need a new mistress. You are intriguing, lovely, and accustomed to meting out discipline. Don't you ever wonder what it would be like to submit to a gentleman who wishes to discipline you? I would love to see you on my bed, completely bound, utterly at my mercy."

She tried to talk but squeaked instead. Then she gasped, "This is scandalous. You cannot say such things to innocent women. Your behavior is shocking and appalling . . . and wrong!"

"I don't think I was wrong at all, Miss Winsome. I am right about what you want. That's why your cheeks are so pink. On the surface, you are very proper and good. But I suspect, deep in your soul, you would like to be bad."

"I would not." She pulled away from his hand and planted her fists on her hips. "I know what scoundrels do to foolish women who fall for their repugnant propositions. You would ruin me in a heartbeat and it wouldn't matter to you in the least."

His gaze bored in her. His green eyes seemed to glow. "If I were to make you my mistress, I would give you a king's ransom in return. A house, gowns, carriages, jewels. All you would have to do is be my submissive. I would tie you up and show you unbelievable pleasure—orgasms that would make you melt and beg—and reward you with a settlement that would keep you in luxury for the rest of your life." He paused. Repeated, "*If* I were to make you my mistress."

"I cannot listen to this. I must go, Your Grace. I must take the children home."

His gaze flicked to his nieces and nephews. The children had almost gathered up everything. Lady Sophie led Lady Maryanne to help her.

"Of course." His deep baritone rumbled over her. "But tonight, while you are asleep in your small room, on a bed that I assume is not very comfortable, I want you to imagine what it would be like to be bound to a bed with a soft, thick mattress and silk sheets. Then imagine a gentleman's mouth tasting you, everywhere—"

"Stop *this*."

The children were returning. "Come," she said hurriedly to them. "Hold hands and we must hurry back home." She planted one hand on the pram's handle and pushed, clasped Lady Maryanne's hand with the other, and walked swiftly as the children trotted behind.

Now she knew the Duke of Greybrooke was no hero after all. He had boldly propositioned her—a decent, respectable governess.

Or had he? Biting her lip, Helena glanced back. The duke was watching her, stroking his chiseled jaw, frowning. When he saw her head swivel, he lifted his hat in a gentlemanly farewell. His lips quirked in a smile, and his eyes glittered with amusement.

Had he just been teasing her because she'd chastised him?

It didn't matter, did it? She'd discovered from gossip that Greybrooke was arrogant, licentious, and without any moral compass. Now she could imagine he was capable of anything.

Perhaps even treason.

2

A woman in a corset, tied up, positioned on her hands and knees, with her naked derriere sticking up in the air. Normally this erotic scene would have him hard, intrigued, and ready to play.

Not tonight.

Damian Caldwell, the fifth Duke of Greybrooke—known as Grey—sighed. He rose from his engulfing black leather chair, which stood in front of the raised dais like a throne. He prowled to Ruby, who awaited him, positioned for his pleasure on a throw of purple velvet. She squirmed with anticipation.

Red-haired Ruby had her wrists and ankles bound with black leather straps. Her cheek was on the velvet surface, her pale bottom sticking out toward him. She wore a corset of black silk, laced tight to mold her generous curves into a sensual hourglass shape. Her breasts spilled over the cups, her rouged nipples squashed against the velvet.

She was waiting to be spanked.

He should be planning exactly what carnal game he wanted to play here, in the private domination room in this exclusive club, the House of Exotic Desires. He should not be thinking of Miss Winsome. But he could not seem to drag his thoughts away from her.

Grey strolled to Ruby and tapped her lightly on her ass with a riding crop. "Apologies, my dear. My heart is not in the game tonight. You deserve a more attentive gentleman to spank you."

Her soft voice was partly muffled by the velvet, as she said desperately, "No, Your Grace, it's you I want tonight. No other gent makes me feel what you do." Her full breasts moved with her deep breaths. "You can make me come even before you touch me with the crop. I don't know how you do it."

He laughed gruffly. "You are charming, Ruby. On any other night, flattery would get you everywhere. But not this one, alas."

He dropped the stiff-handled riding crop to the floor. Crouching, he helped Ruby to sit up. Her creamy breasts jiggled, her rouged nipples stuck out toward his mouth, but his cock did not even pulse.

He had struck up a regular appointment with Ruby because she submitted to his every desire. He liked to fuck hard, to take his pleasure to the edge.

So why was he so intrigued by Miss Winsome? A gentleman didn't do the things he enjoyed with a prim, dutiful governess.

But it appeared his standing arrangement with Ruby was to come to an end. Lovely as she was, she no longer captured his interest.

Swift motions of his fingers undid the leather strap that bound Ruby's wrists together. "You might as well rest, my dear, before your next client."

Panic glinted in her large brown eyes. "Please do not leave, Your Grace. Mrs. Gull will think I've done something to displease you."

"I will make it clear the fault is with me, not you." He glanced around the domination room, with its chains and selection of whips, cat-o'-nine-tails, and riding crops. "I will ensure she knows it was your willingness to play these games that has encouraged me to be a regular patron."

Ruby frowned. "You will come back, won't you?"

"My dear, I have not made future plans." Though he smiled down at her, his tone was cool, autocratic, and impersonal.

Ruby's lips trembled, but she was not as foolish as the Countess of Montroy. She was too tough to heave chamber pots. "I will do my best to please you, Your Grace. I will do anything you want."

"I have been very pleased with you, Ruby. Do not look so unhappy. Your obedient service will not go unrewarded."

He would reward her with a pretty bracelet—with a few delicate rubies to match her dark red hair. A trifle to him, but it would delight Ruby, and she had pleased him for many months.

With that, Grey left the club. He had no intention of returning home—too many memories there and all of them bad. He avoided his home as much as he could. It was rare that he even slept there. He visited it only to change his clothing or partake of the occasional meal.

He commanded his coachman to take him to a dull, staid environment in which he could think in peace: the smoking room of White's.

A half hour later, Grey was reclining in a leather club chair, a decanter of port on a side table, a tumbler of the liquor in his hand.

A vision continued to haunt him: Miss Winsome with her hands bound in front of her, her head thrown back in pleasure while he slowly brought her to ecstasy by tapping her nipples with a crop.

Damnation. With submissive Ruby, his cock had remained asleep. *Now* he was rock hard. Over a sexual delight he could never have.

"Since when do you spend the evening at White's, Grey? No luscious female to dominate tonight, or did you decide you no longer wanted to have chamber pots hefted at you?"

Grey recognized the voice speaking behind him—one hoarse and raspy from the time the man had spent as a prisoner of war in Ceylon. "I'm thinking about acquiring a new mistress," he casually said to the Duke of Caradon, known to friends as Cary since he'd held the title from the age of five.

"Ah." Tall, blond Cary settled into a wing chair near him, a glass of brandy in his hand. "Who is the new lady?" he asked. "Or should I ask whose wife she is?"

"She's unmarried and innocent."

A brow rose on Cary's world-weary face. "Not usually your taste."

"This one is unique. And she is a governess."

Cary jerked so abruptly in midsip, brandy flew out of his glass and splashed his face. "An actual governess who gives lessons and straps bottoms?"

"Yes, that sort of governess."

Concern etched into Cary's face. "Uh, Grey—"

"I know. A respectable virgin is off limits for a man with my tastes. But there's something about her. Even her name is a temptation—Miss Winsome. What interested me most was that I rescued her before she and my nephew were run down by a carriage, and after I did, she told me off."

"Sounds like hell. Why then the fascination?"

"The truth? I don't know," Grey admitted. "I suspect it's because a woman with spirit is more intriguing to command." He finished his drink, set it down. "Anyway, I can't have her. Ruining an innocent is not something I intend to do. Miss Winsome is far too sweet and naïve to be introduced to my sexual tastes."

* * *

Spotted near Berkeley Square yesterday, very near the home of the Countess of M———, the Duke of G——— came within inches of adopting a new style of headgear. Fortunately, your devoted correspondent believes this new fashion has little chance of becoming all the rage. And rage was the operative word when a certain incensed lady flung a chamber pot through an open window, aiming at the handsome head of a certain rakish gentleman—

With a groan of frustration, Helena dropped her pen in the inkwell. Did she dare recount the duke's near brush with the chamber pot in Lady X's column? Would he then realize Lady X had to be someone who witnessed the event? Or would it be more suspicious if she didn't report this scandalous bit of news?

Greybrooke was one of several eligible dukes this Season. Never—in the history of England, it was claimed—had there been so many handsome, wealthy unmarried dukes at one time. The print shops carried many cartoons of slavering young ladies desperate to snag a duke, any duke. In her column, Helena had first dubbed them the "Dazzling Dukes." But just before the edition had gone to press, she'd realized her mistake. "Dazzling" was a word used by a naïve young woman with hopes of love. A sophisticated woman such as Lady X would bestow them a name that would sell newssheets.

Thus she called them the Wicked Dukes.

Lady X would certainly know about a scandal involving a Wicked Duke. She must give the story to Will to be printed—

Downstairs, she heard an echoing bong. One o'clock in the morning. Helena snuffed her candle and threw on her threadbare cloak. It was time to sneak out into the night and meet the man who was forcing her to spy on the Duke of Greybrooke.

Out the rear kitchen door, across the garden to the gate, then a headlong run down the mews with her cloak streaming back. On the street, a carriage waited, and she hurried up its steps, firmly shutting the door behind her.

The carriage lurched off, leaving the shadows of the mews for the glow of the street flares on Mount Street. Two men sat inside, illuminated by the lamps. One was tall, thin, cadaverous Mr. Whitehall, the man from the Crown who had a skull-like face, had deeply shadowed wells for eyes, and was bald beneath his beaver hat. The other was her half brother, Will.

Whitehall leaned forward as she took a seat. "Do you have it? Have you got proof that Greybrooke is a traitor?"

Helena glanced to Will, who sat at her side. She really considered Will a brother, since Mama had been widowed, then remarried when Helena had been two. She and Will were very much alike in looks, since they looked like their mother, but not at all in temperament. She was cautious and careful; Will threw caution to the wind and believed all would work out. But their lives had been filled with things that hadn't "worked out."

Hope was written all over her brother's handsome face, as well it might, since it was his secret gambling that had gotten them into this mess.

She faced Whitehall, who glared down his beak of a nose with penetrating black eyes. "No, I do not yet have any proof."

After she had agreed to this "mission," as Whitehall called it, he had arranged meetings every third night, held in this carriage so they could have privacy. She had to sneak out of her employers' home, but she was certain no one noticed her slip out the kitchen door, then go across the yard to the rear mews.

"I expected results by now, Miss Winsome." Whitehall turned to her brother. "I could have employed a courtesan to get into his house. Some trollop with a big bosom would have done better than your sister, after you assured me she would succeed."

Will looked a bit shocked, but he assured quickly, "My sister will find the proof. There is no one better than Helena at ferret-ing out secrets."

"I will find it." Helena spoke coolly. She held her ground with dukes and earls—she had her rules for the raising of chil-dren, and she would not break her rules even at her employers' command. She refused to be intimidated by Whitehall, even if the man did hold the futures of Will, their newspaper, and their younger sisters in the palm of his hand. If Will's gaming debts were not paid, their family would be destitute, the newspaper gone, everyone cast into a gruesome, prison-like workhouse. Whitehall had promised to pay those debts, if she found the proof he needed. "But I want to know why you believe he is a traitor, Mr. Whitehall."

Whitehall stiffened. "It is enough that I know he is."

"From a very brief encounter with the Duke of Grey-brooke, I learned he is a charming scoundrel and a man with very lax morals. At that moment, I did think him capable of be-traying his country. But since then, I have changed my mind."

"I am not interested in your personal thoughts, Miss Win-some. I thought that was clear when you accepted this assign-ment. You have a job to do, for which you will be generously paid."

She pursed her lips. "I do not do any task blindly, Mr. Whitehall."

"Helena, don't," muttered Will. His handsome face was pale with worry.

But she had to. There was something very wrong. The duke had been bold and naughty. But now that she'd had a chance to calm down, she realized Greybrooke had been deliberately teasing her.

"Greybrooke saved his nephew's life, snatching him up be-fore he was hit by a carriage," she said. "The duke obviously adores his niece and nephews. Would such a man be willing to destroy *their* country?"

Will put his hand on her arm. "Helena, we must do as Mr. Whitehall asks."

"But what if we cannot find proof because he is innocent?" she asked. "Will you still save my brother from his gaming debts?"

Pure panic flashed in Will's eyes. Icy cold radiated from Whitehall's small eyes. "There is no doubt you will find evidence, Miss Winsome, because Greybrooke is guilty."

"But why are you certain?" she pressed. "The duke does not seem to have been impoverished or indebted, so he did not need money. He appears to have no interest in politics."

"Secrets," Whitehall said. "There are secrets over which a man can be blackmailed to do anything."

"Goodness, I've heard nothing about any scandals like that in Greybrooke's life. I know there are rumors about his father's death. But that would not make a duke betray his country."

"The Duke of Greybrooke has secrets, Miss Winsome. It is your job to find them. And if you do not succeed quickly, your family will lose everything."

Whitehall rapped on the ceiling—a signal the carriage was to return to the mews.

"What you need to do, Miss Winsome, is get into the duke's house. Search for letters. Diaries." Whitehall's eyes glittered coldly. "Remember: One of the most expedient ways to get into Greybrooke's house is through his bed."

"The world must be coming to an end. My brother is out of his bed in the morning."

Ignoring his sister's playful sarcasm, Grey went to Jacinta, rested his hands on the back of her chair, and lightly kissed the top of her head. She twisted in her seat, her hand on her rounded belly. A stack of folded letters sat in front of her on the blotter of her writing desk. Rain beat against the windows, but a fire crackled in the grate, giving his sister's morning room cheery warmth. Two lamps were lit on the desk, casting a halo of gold around her honey-blond hair.

Deep warmth always flooded his heart when he was with his sister and her family. Carrying her fifth child and growing close to her confinement, Jacinta glowed. She also wore a suspiciously devilish smile.

Batting her long lashes, she struggled to look innocent. "Did any ladies try to brain you with a chamber pot on your way here, my dearest brother?"

"Fortunately not," he said. "As for being your dearest brother, I am your only brother. You only call me 'dearest' when you're up to something."

She tipped her head to the side, widening her green eyes. "Grey, I am not doing anything wrong. I am simply writing invitations."

Damnation. "What sort of invitations?"

"I am planning a ball—my last before my confinement. I must decide which of the year's eligible ladies I should invite."

"Your husband should forbid you from such taxing entertainments. I have a good mind to have a word with Winterhaven myself. He should be taking better care of you—"

"My husband does take excellent care of me. He knows how much this means to me, and because of that, he's allowing me to do it without complaint. This ball is for you, my wayward brother. Since you are here, you can help me."

"Help you do what?"

"Choose eligible young ladies. You will be dancing with them, so you might want to have a say in which I invite."

He cocked a brow. "Isn't that like an executioner asking the prisoner to pick the means of his demise?"

"Hardly a demise! It is time you married, Grey. You are a beloved uncle, but you must want children of your own. Heavens, you are almost thirty."

"I'm not thirty until December, my dear sister."

"Thirty is the age where most gentlemen recognize it is time to fill their nurseries."

A tea tray sat on a low table near Jacinta. He poured her a fresh cup and handed it to her. "Seven months. I still have seven months," he pointed out.

"Well, you must begin your search—oh, I just felt a kick. Grey, give me your hand. I am sure this one must be a boy too, for he has the strongest kick I've ever felt."

She reached for his hand, and he let her guide his hand to her tummy. A bump pushed up from her stomach and hit his hand. It moved across her belly like a sea serpent gliding across the water, then disappeared.

He stared. "My god, was that—?"

"The baby's foot, I believe." Jacinta smiled up at him.

It stunned him. What would it be like to be expecting his own son and to play with the baby's little foot? To discover his unborn boy had an admirable kick?

God, he couldn't let his thoughts go there. "Where are the children, by the way? With their governess?" He asked it as casually as he could.

Jacinta nodded, obviously not fully listening, for she was running the tip of her pen along her list of names and frowning at them, with her other hand on the bulge of her tummy.

He should stop this latest bout of matchmaking. He had a very good reason for not marrying: He had no interest in trying to pretend to be a normal, noble English gentleman for an innocent young wife.

"Hmmm, what?" she murmured.

"The children and the governess. I asked if they were upstairs."

Jacinta tore her attention from her list. "Yes. It is raining today, so Miss Winsome is giving them lessons up in the nursery."

* * *

"I wish I'd had such a delightful governess when I was young."

Deep, silky, male—the voice startled her, and Helena spun around to find the Duke of Greybrooke leaning against the doorway of the nursery. His broad shoulders, clad in dark blue superfine, spread across the width of the opening. Then he stepped inside, and he seemed to fill the whole room. Framed by the children's things—small chairs, desks, dolls—he looked all the more large, strong, and male. "Good morning, Miss Winsome."

"Did you wish to see the children?" she asked, busying herself with picking up fallen wooden blocks so he wouldn't see the blush that leapt to her cheeks. She pointed to the doorway at the opposite end of the playroom—the room assigned for lessons, with three small desks and chairs. "They are working on their lessons right now, but I suppose an exception could be made—"

"Exceptions are always made for dukes, my dear. But I wished to speak with you."

"Shh." She straightened and put her finger to her lips. Tried to look calm, though her heart pumped wildly. *Riding crops. Tying her up!*

But Whitehall's warning rang in her ears. If she did not succeed quickly, her family would lose everything.

She crooked her finger for him to follow her into the children's bedroom. "We must not disturb the children," she admonished softly as she pushed open the door.

He put his hand over hers on the knob. His fingers were long. Even through his leather glove and her thin cotton one, the warmth of his skin seared her.

Watching the children to ensure they stayed at their work, Helena led the duke into the nursery room, and stopped in between the two rows of neat little beds.

Even this—just being alone with him in this room—could

see her cast out of her job without a character. A few moments alone could ruin her forever. But she had to take the risk.

The moment she closed the door behind her, he clasped her hand and turned her, and before she had a chance to be prepared, he raised her bent fingers to his lips. "Beautiful hands."

She tried to pull her hand free but she couldn't. He gently brushed his mouth over her fingers. A jolt, like a strike of lightning, leapt through her body from her hand. "How can you know? I'm wearing gloves."

He kissed each finger, making her shoulders quiver with the sheer thrilling sensation rushing through her. "I love slender hands that are small and nimble. These hands dry tears, wipe noses, show children how to form their letters and numbers. These hands forge futures, and that is more than mine have ever done. The only useful thing my fingers have done is tweak nipples and stroke cunnies until ladies scream."

"Your Grace." Her tone was one of severe reprimand. But his words about *her* hands had been so sweet, she was stunned.

"All right, my dear. I won't say anything naughty. Disappointed?"

His index finger rested on her chin. He lifted it slightly, and she tipped her face up. Then she realized she'd obeyed him, and she jerked back. But now she couldn't stop looking at his eyes. They were the most beautiful green—this close she could see that his irises were emerald but rimmed in gold, like priceless jewels in a precious setting.

His lower lip was lush and full, softening now into a seductive pout.

"Why did you come here?" she said desperately.

"I came to apologize. But I have to admit, there is something about you that goads me into behaving like a devil. I know I should keep away from you. My tastes are too dark for a sweet, innocent woman like you."

He spoke as if she were the one in the wrong—for simply being decent. "I take it you mean the riding crops and spanking? I cannot imagine what such things have to do with love affairs. Your tastes are too—too inappropriate for *any* lady, I think. Really, Your Grace, should you not try to behave your—?"

She stopped. Her tongue had raced away on her. To save her family, she was supposed to flirt with him. To get into his house, she must encourage him.

"You've done it again. Insulted me and yet intrigued me." A slow smile came to his lips, and as it lazily unfurled for her, she felt her knees wobble. "Now you see my problem. You should be untouchable for a man such as me—too proper, too respectable, too decent. Yet I have to have you. At any price."

Fear gripped her. She was supposed to agree! She always remained in control; she was always in charge. But that was far easier with children and not a fully grown, immensely powerful duke.

"W-what if I am not for sale?"

"Aren't you? I would be willing to give you the world, my dear. A house of your own. One for you to keep after our affair ends."

"You told me that before." She stepped back. " 'A house, gowns, carriage, jewels,' you said. Why would you spend so much just to have me?"

The duke followed, moving close to her again. Her quick breaths flooded her senses with his masculine smells—that heady scent of bergamot, a subtle spiciness, the earthy aroma of leather.

"I wish I knew," he said softly, a wry look in his eyes.

She planted her hands on her hips. "I think I know. You are piqued because I've refused you. You are like a child who desperately wants what he cannot have. But if I gave in, if I said yes, you would quickly become bored and cast me aside. But I could not just forget you. If I were . . . with you, I would care about you. You would give me a house, but it would be a place for me to hide within. My heart would be broken, my reputation ruined. I would lose everything."

She'd spoken the truth. She hadn't *meant* to. Yet Greybrooke appeared undeterred. He appeared to respond to disapproval.

"But imagine lifting the lid on a velvet box and finding a necklace of diamonds within," he murmured. "Dozens of them, sparkling like stars. Imagine me lifting them from their cushion and laying their cool weight against your skin." Briefly his fingertips brushed over the expanse of her chest below her neck and above the modest neckline of her gown, skimming there, before he moved them away.

Even through her sensible wool gown, his touch burned.

"I would drape you in diamonds and rubies, emeralds and sapphires, and those trinkets would be yours. Did you intend to be a governess for the rest of your life? I offer you freedom."

"You offer me a gilded prison." She must stop arguing. She must say yes. But she . . . couldn't. There had to be another way to save her family.

"I know why I want you, Miss Winsome. It's because you are strong. In character, I think we are equals."

Equals? "You're a rakish duke with all sorts of land and power. I'm a governess. You can live a libertine's life. I have to ensure I never do anything improper. We are not at all equal."

"You think you are superior to me because I'm naughty and you are good."

"No—"

"Let me change your life, Miss Winsome." Another step and his broad chest filled her vision. On his ice-blue waistcoat, dragons were embroidered in fine thread—dragons in battle.

She retreated, but the backs of her legs bumped a small bedframe, and she had nowhere left to go. "I do not want to change my life, Your Grace." But this sparring with him was thrilling.

"So the promise of enough wealth to keep you for a lifetime

is not enough? I have to admit, I admire that about you, even though it frustrates my plans. I have never met a woman who would not be convinced with enough jewels."

"Those are things that would be lovely to have. But there are other things I would want. A husband, children, love. Even just one night with you and I could never have those." Selfish—she was terribly, horribly selfish, for she didn't want to throw away her hopes for those wonderful things. If she became a mistress, she would lose those things forever. Yet if she didn't sacrifice herself, her three half sisters would have no chance of ever marrying, of ever having families.

"No one has to know." He sounded sinful as the devil.

"I would know. I could not lie to a husband. I *couldn't*."

The duke sat on Michael's bed, which gave a creak of protest at his weight. With lightning speed, he grasped her hand and tugged, and she lost her balance. Clawing at the air with her free hand, she couldn't stop her fall, but the duke caught her and planted her derriere on his lap. "You are irresistible," he said.

His thighs were rock hard beneath her rump. She struggled to stand, but he held her wrists and kept her clamped upon his legs. Gently he let out a breath, and it played a merry dance along the sensitive skin of her neck.

"You are incomprehensible," she hissed. "I am refusing you, yet you seem to find that attractive. But the answer will always be no. And you must let me *go*—" Her voice rose with panic. What did he intend to do to her? It was one thing to play a game with him, another to be ruined. "If I'm caught here, with you, I'm ruined. If the children s-see—" Her voice wobbled. She didn't want them to see. They thought her good, but if they saw her on Greybrooke's lap and were told to think badly of her, they would.

To her surprise, he released her. Lifted her and set her on her feet.

"I do not want to get you in trouble or hurt my niece and nephews," he said softly. "You can trust me to be careful."

"Thank you." She didn't know why she was thanking him. But there were men who shredded governesses' reputations and didn't care, as long as they got what they wanted.

Her chest lifted with fierce breasts.

"What about pleasure?" he asked. "You don't want to live your entire life without knowing desire. Have you ever climaxed, Miss Winsome?"

She had no idea what exactly he meant, but it sounded naughty. "Your Grace, stop this at once."

He walked around her, but he did not hold her or trap her. She could just walk past him, but her legs felt strangely shaky and she could not seem to make them move. If she ran, he might follow. What she must do, she reasoned, was stand still, let him make his seduction attempt, then show it did not affect her at all.

"You are luscious, you know. No matter how severe and horrible your dress, I can detect the beautiful curves beneath. Your body was made for sex. To deny it is more than just sinful—it's a crying shame.

"I would devote myself to your pleasure," he continued. "I could spend an afternoon playing with your delectable breasts. Stroking them, then sucking your nipples. Imagine lying on a messy bed in a sun-filled bedroom, letting me suck on your tits until I make you come."

A dozen emotions exploded at once. Languorous delight at the thought of lying on a bed with no work to do. Shock at the crude word. A spike of desire at the image of his sensual mouth all over her breasts.

And under it all, struggling to be heard: the voice of good sense.

"I like to take a lady's seduction slowly, angel," he murmured. "I'd like to tie you to a bed and lick your cunny for hours, building you to climax again and again, but not letting you get there. Until I finally let you explode in an orgasm that makes you scream the house down."

She could barely breathe, and she closed her eyes. As for her heart—could hearts race so fast without exploding?

Something stroked her lower lip, sending a shower of sparks through her body. She smelled leather and knew he'd brushed his glove-clad thumb across her mouth.

That was just one little *touch*. Imagine a kiss.

Imagine more!

"No."

The word came out as such a croak, she thought it was a groan of the house. No, sense still existed inside her and it was clamoring to get out. "No," she said, more fiercely. She pulled her hands free of his. "No. I can't. I won't, Your Grace."

She expected to see fury in his eyes. Instead, a slow smile curved his sensual mouth. "So I can't tempt you with steamy sex and abundant luxury?"

"I want to be decent. You must leave me alone." As soon as she said it, she winced. She was not supposed to demand he leave her alone.

"I'm afraid I will not do that. I want you," he growled. "Wrong as it is—sinful, dastardly, unforgivable as it is—I have to have you."

3

After three days of rain, the sun finally shone again. Thank heaven, for children cooped up for so long turned into wild savages. Helena herded the children—the boys and Lady Sophie—to Berkeley Square. Warmth and abundant rain had brought out all the May blossoms, and she was reading from a book entitled *Improving Stories for Children* when she sensed the children staring at something behind her, mouths gaping, eyes like saucers.

A young footman, with white wig and emerald and silver livery, stood behind her. He bowed with extreme correctness. "Miss Helena Winsome? I have for you a message from His Grace, the Duke of Greybrooke."

With that, the lad thrust out a letter sealed with a blob of scarlet wax.

Startled, she took it. The footman bowed again, swiveled on his heel, and marched away.

No longer were just the children gaping in curiosity. Dozens of people watched her.

"It's from Uncle Grey," Michael declared. "Why would Uncle send you a letter?"

Helena made it a rule to never lie to children. Sometimes, of course, one could not give the literal truth. "I do not quite know," Helena said, keeping her voice admirably calm. Excitement—and fear—warred inside her.

After the Duke of Greybrooke had declared he had to have her, he had left without another word. Three days had passed where she had not seen him. She was desperate to do so. Because she had to learn his secrets, of course.

"It must be a love letter," Sophie declared. She dimpled. "Uncle Grey must have fallen madly in love with you when he saw you! Perhaps it is an offer of marriage."

"Silly," said Michael scornfully. "Dukes don't marry governesses."

They certainly did not. With no letter opener, Helena carefully tore the page around the seal and unfolded the thick paper.

Scarlet rose petals tumbled out, showering over her skirt. Timothy scrambled over to grab as many as he could, which spurred Michael to compete. After shooing the boys away, she finally took a look at the duke's letter.

Beautiful watercolor drawings surrounded the edges of the page. At the bottom was a lovely rendering of a stream, a meadow, and a dark-haired man like Greybrooke feeding plump strawberries to a blond wood nymph clad only in leaves. The nymph looked just like her.

Surely Greybrooke hadn't drawn this. It was remarkable. It had to have been the work of an artist. . . .

Wait, one leaf did not quite cover the lady's breast, and a rosy-pink nipple peeked out. Helena felt her cheeks turn pink. That breast and nipple looked exactly like hers.

He couldn't know what she looked like *there*. He must have guessed at the size of her breast, the nipple and its coloring must have been just luck as well.

Shocked, she looked down at the elegant handwriting. It was a poem.

It would be a ribald verse, of course. One that would make her blush from her hairline to her toes, she expected. She sighed, squared her shoulders, and began to read.

Only to discover she was wrong.

The duke hadn't penned naughty rhymes after all. The verse was lovely, all about the wonder and knowledge she imparted to children.

He must have hired a poet to write something touching and sweet and beautiful. For her.

Timothy peered at her. "Miss Winsome, you've turned every color in the rainbow."

"No, she hasn't, silly. She's not gone green or blue," argued Michael.

Timothy stuck his tongue out at his brother. "She's been white, red, and pink. Maybe she will go yellow and green."

"It is a love letter, isn't it?" cried Sophie. "It's making you blush."

"Nothing ever makes Miss Winsome blush," said Timothy. "I've tried."

"Uncle Grey knows how," Michael said.

Uncle Grey knew quite a lot of things. She did not believe the words truly reflected how he saw her. This was a scoundrel who caused women to tip chamber pots on his head—who had said bold, naughty things to her. Who had claimed it was unpardonable that he wanted her.

She could not reconcile that man with this one who had so cleverly understood what would touch her heart.

She had to remember that nothing he said was real. It would be so easy to preen and believe she had captured the duke's heart with her good character, or her quiet beauty, or her kind heart.

But she would never forget her sister Margaret, and all the wonderful things Mr. Knightly told Margaret when they'd all believed Mr. Knightly intended to marry Meg. But all those things had been lies spun to convince Meg to go to his bed and he'd ruined her.

That afternoon, while the children napped in the nursery, Helena wrote a letter of her own. She folded the poem, tucked it within her letter, and sealed it with a blob of wax. Having a few minutes to herself, she took it and the countess's letters and popped out to post them.

As she walked back to Winterhaven House, she was consumed with one question: Could she keep Greybrooke's interest while not allowing him to seduce her?

Nothing was brought to her in Berkeley Square the next day. Worry nipped at Helena's heart. What if she'd offended Greybrooke by returning his poem?

Perhaps she should have kept the poem, which would have given him hope and encouraged him to approach her again—

"I'm hot!" Michael's whine broke in on her thoughts.

It was unseasonably warm for May today. A tug at her sleeve—it was Lady Maryanne. Gazing blankly ahead but wearing a wistful expression, Maryanne whispered, "It's been years since I've gone to Gunter's for ices. I miss them so! It's so cold on your tongue and it can make your head hurt with the pure iciness of it! But then it melts away and it tastes sweet, and sometimes like fruit. Could we go?"

"Could we?" Timothy echoed.

Lady Maryanne possessed green eyes like Grey's, huge with dark lashes. But her hair was as golden as her sister's, Lady Winterhaven. With an oval face and full lips, she was beautiful.

Maryanne's blindness had been a tragedy, but Helena wanted to give the girl as much normalcy as she could. Maryanne had been spoiled, had learned to give in to tantrums. In just a month,

Helena had made great progress with the girl. She had insisted Maryanne go out to public places, and her plan was working.

Helena opened her reticule. If the children shared two treats, she might be able to afford the ices. It would take her mind off her failure with Greybrooke. She nodded. "We shall go."

Soon, she herded the children to a table in the shop, praying she did have enough money. But the moment they sat, enormous bowls filled with every flavor of the famous ices were brought to the table.

Panic hit her. She couldn't afford this!

An elderly footman came forward and bowed to her. "With compliments of His Grace, the Duke of Greybrooke. He spied his family within and wished to present them with a treat."

Helena's heart wobbled. He had come to her rescue again and done something wonderful for the children. "That was very generous and kind, but it is a bit too much of a treat," she said in her governess tones. Then through the window that looked out to the street, she spotted Greybrooke. His roguish grin speared her. He nodded. To her? Why?

Not to her. His footman came forward once more and presented her with a small, black velvet box. "This is for you, miss. From His Grace."

Heart pounding, Helena pried open the lid, just a little, for she didn't want anyone else to see. She frowned. It looked like a ring of clear, sparkling ice. . . .

Heavens, not ice. Diamonds. A bracelet of them. The glittering fire in the box came from the most precious gems imaginable.

The jewels winked at her from the gleaming gold setting. Gunter's shop seemed to tip and tilt around her, like the blob of ice from Timothy's cup that was sliding across the table. Timothy put his tongue to the table and licked up his wayward lemon-flavored ice. Normally, she would check him at once for such bad manners.

But no words could come out.

All she could do was stare into her box, opened less than an inch. All the glitter dazzled her. She must have looked so stunned that she finally took Sophie's attention away from her treat.

"Miss Winsome, what are looking at? What has Uncle Grey sent you? Is it another letter?"

"It's nothing." She snapped the lid shut. She didn't dare put it on the table. Children could move quickly when they wanted to look at something they were not supposed to. "Just something silly. Of course, though he is trying to tease me, I cannot accept it."

"Why not?" Sophie frowned.

"Your uncle is playing a joke, but it is not proper for me to take a gift." Not a gift like this. Clutched in her hands was a king's ransom of diamonds. They were worth more money than she could imagine. More than she would ever see in her lifetime.

What would it feel like to have dozens of diamonds sparkling around her wrist? Would they be heavy? Blinding?

Madly, she wanted to take them out and try them on. She wanted to keep them, so sometimes she could fasten them around her wrist and dream—

Really, what was she thinking? When would she have the need to drape herself in diamonds while wearing sensible wool gowns and herding children?

But they could be sold for a fortune. . . .

No, she must send them back. At once.

The footman left, and the children devoured their treats. The afternoon passed in a blur. It was as if the diamonds weighed five hundred pounds. They were all she could think of.

The problem with the diamonds, she discovered, was she could not send them back by the post. What if they got lost? She had to wait until the children were napping, then she slipped out and walked the few blocks to Greybrooke's house, which was on Park Lane, opposite Hyde Park. A priceless gift had to be returned in person.

The duke's house was swarming with servants, as usual. But the duke was not at home.

Grey opened the box, tossed it on his desk. The bracelet spilled out and landed on his blotter. He glanced up at the young footman. "This was my gift to the lady. A gift that was not to be returned," he growled. "You should not have accepted it from her."

The young man swallowed hard. "She took it out of a wicker basket, pushed it into me and told me to tell ye, Yer Grace, that she couldn't accept anythin' so valuable, and she stalked away."

"Stalked?"

"Er, I think that's the word, Your Grace. A sort of angry march like me mum used to do when I got into trouble."

Grey picked up the jewels, fingering them. They were damned exquisite. How many women would not be tempted by such a gift? There couldn't be many, but Miss Winsome was one.

He grinned. Never had he known a woman so stubborn. He'd tried appealing to her heart with poetry, for he guessed there was something behind that firm, practical exterior she showed the world. He'd tried blatant temptation.

On to his next plan of attack: finding the wanton inside Miss Winsome.

He dropped the jewels back into the box. "I have another piece of jewelry on order for Miss Winsome," he instructed the footman. "Fetch it from Bond Street tomorrow morning. My usual jeweler."

This was the most unique piece he'd ever had made. It had cost a king's ransom, but it would be worth it.

*   *   *

While the children had biscuits and milky tea at eleven o'clock, Helena tidied up the lesson room. She frowned at a box that sat upon the desk in which she kept her notes on the children's studies. It had not been there earlier, when she'd gathered the children at the table to eat.

To the winsome Miss Winsome, the card read.

Greybrooke was unconscionable! How had he got this gift here? Instinct jerked her gaze to the doorway, but it was empty. Could he have brought it himself and she hadn't noticed?

Her stomach lurched. What if he'd asked one of his sister's servants to bring it to her? How could *that* be explained?

Was this a clue he really was a spy and a traitor? He obviously liked intrigue and games.

She knew he was as daring with his own skin—according to gossip he'd been involved in a half dozen duels.

Helena undid the ribbon and pried the lid off the box.

A note on a cream-colored card sat on top. His crest and title—the Duke of Greybrooke—were embossed in gold. Across the card, in a bold hand: *Meet me tomorrow at 2. Hyde Park.*

Tomorrow was her afternoon off. Greybrooke must have learned that from his sister. Or one of the children. Sinking her teeth into her lower lip, Helena lifted the note.

Beneath was a pair of bracelets. Capturing one with her fingers, she took it from the box. The other came with it, for a thick gold chain connected them. They were gold, set with rubies, diamonds, and emeralds. She fiddled with them, for they seemed to have a moving part.

A part that clamped around the wearer's wrist. Helena glanced at the door, ensuring the children were still at their table, eating biscuits. Her heart beat faster. She opened one hasp, then put it around her wrist. Velvet lined the metal where it touched her skin. She had seen men in chains before—prisoners—and these were very much like . . .

Grey had sent these glittering, costly *shackles* to her at his sister's home.

This was beyond shocking.

Helena slapped the shackles back in their box. She was furious. The duke could ruin her reputation without her ever having done one scandalous thing. She could not keep playing this game with him. He was going to do something so shocking she would lose her place and her future—

But to save her family, shouldn't she be willing to give up everything?

Waves rippled across the Serpentine. The breeze whipped the ribbons of Helena's bonnet around her face. Ribbons were the one luxury of a governess. A gentleman silhouetted against the sun strode toward her, across the grass. Helena's heart leapt, her palms went damp with sudden nerves—

No, this couldn't be the duke—this man wasn't as tall, as broad shouldered, as imposing. Shading her eyes, she saw blond hair beneath the hat, the lanky frame, the face so very much like her own. A face that looked ragged and pale.

"Will!" She hurried to meet him. "What are you doing here?"

Will peered down at her, his eyes pained. "I followed you from your house. I had to know if you were meeting the duke." He clasped both her hands. "You are going to do this, Helena, aren't you? You aren't going to let all of us be ruined. We'll lose everything. We'll be thrown in debtors' prison or sent to workhouses. I'm pleading with you, sister—"

"Will, I can't do this," she broke in.

"Helena, you must! You promised me you would. You promised Whitehall. Why can't you?"

She pulled her hands free, fished the duke's latest gift from her reticule. "That is why!" She opened the box. "That is the sort of man he is. He wants a shocking, experienced courtesan. I cannot do this."

Swallowing hard, Will stuttered, "H-he gave you this?"

"Yes! He's been trying to woo me with presents, but I have given them back. Poetry. Diamonds. And this scandalous thing, which I am going to return to him *now*. At first, I viewed it as a game, but it is not a game. He is not a man to be played with or trifled with—"

"You returned his gifts? Helena, this means he wants you. He's fascinated with you! It's exactly what we need. All you have to do is lead him along enough to get into his house to search it. It's the only way we'll find proof. Letters. Or a journal."

"I thought I could play with him, keep him intrigued, but this game could ruin me."

"Helena, we have to get into the duke's house," Will croaked. "There's no other way unless the duke believes you will be his mistress. Dear sister, please, I'm desperate."

Oh no, she was not going to accept this. She jabbed her finger into her half brother's chest. "We are *all* desperate. I am desperate, for I am playing games with a gentleman who could ruin my entire life at any moment. Your gambling debts are the cause of our desperation, not my refusal to become the duke's mistress. You are trying to make me feel at fault, but the fault is not mine. I will not forget that."

"But you are the only one who can make this right, Helena. I tried to do it myself, but I've only made thing worse." Will brushed his forehead, and she saw sweat had beaded there. Something had happened to make him afraid . . . or he was afraid to tell her something.

Her heart dropped to her toes. "How have you made things worse?"

Will rubbed the back of his neck. He looked at everything but her.

"You gambled again, didn't you? You promised you would never play cards again!"

"I didn't play cards. I played hazard—a game with dice."

"Will—" She was furious beyond words. "You knew what I meant. Substituting dice for cards doesn't make a difference!" Nausea roiled in her tummy. "How much did you lose?"

"Two thousand."

Oh God. She wanted to scream. Two thousand more. "Why? Oh, for heaven's sake, Will, why did you ever think more gambling would solve the problem?"

"I thought my luck had to change."

"These places aren't about luck! They fleece foolish young men."

"Some men win, and win enormous amounts. These places can't cheat men—no one would go. There are rules about that sort of thing."

She rolled her eyes. "Why couldn't you have stayed away?"

"I don't know. I can't, Helena. It's like the way some men need opium or liquor. I seem to crave it. But Whitehall will make it good. I'm sure of it. He'll clear away the additional debt."

What was it that obsessed Will with such places? She could make him promise to stay away, but she knew he would promise and vow and give his word of honor—then he would completely ignore his vow. How could she keep him away?

"Helena, I don't want to put you at the risk of ruin. There has to be a way for me to acquire the money—"

"No!" Not more disaster. Will was right. She was the only one who could fix this. She took a deep breath. "No, I am going to do it. I *have* to do it. I will get into the duke's house, no matter what it takes. I will save this family. And you will never gamble again, Will."

At once he brightened. "I won't, dear sister, I promise—"

"I am not interested in promises. I will make *certain* you never do it again."

"How?"

"If you really intended to never gamble again, it wouldn't

matter to you, would it?" In truth, she had no answer, but she knew how to bluff. Crossing her arms over her chest, she marched away from Will, toward the Rotten Row—the stretch of sand track upon which gentleman loved to race upon their beautiful steeds.

She caught her breath. A huge, pure white horse thundered along the row toward her, long powerful legs consuming the ground, hooves throwing up sand. Astride the massive animal: the Duke of Greybrooke.

Greybrooke rode like a god. He lifted off the saddle, supported on his strong legs, his thighs bulging in riding breeches. His tail coat flew out behind him, his hat remained firmly on his head, and he looked every inch the duke. Spotting her, he slowed the horse to a canter, then a walk, and he reined in at her side.

Helena looked up at long legs, a broad chest, a dazzling smile, and insolently wicked green eyes. Pure white collar points touched the bronze skin of his throat, where dark stubble graced his strong jaw.

She knew what she must do. Agree to become the mistress of this handsome, dangerous man.

He lifted his hat. "Good afternoon, Miss Winsome." He spoke in such a cool, careless way, even she would believe this was a chance encounter and he was utterly indifferent to her. Then he leaned over, eyes bright, and murmured in his deep baritone, "Meet me over there, behind that grove of trees and near the lilac bushes, where we will be away from curious eyes."

With that, he straightened, gave a slight shake of the reins, and his mount trotted away.

She shivered. What she was about to do was wrong, sinful, and was against every principal of propriety she'd vowed to embrace. Yet she gazed at his broad back and thought—

I could touch him. If I become his mistress, I can touch his beautiful shoulders and his strong back and—heavens—his chest. All her wicked fantasies could be hers.

That was the real danger, wasn't it? The danger wasn't entirely about him, it was also about *her.* About wanting a fantasy, when the reality wasn't seductive or enticing at all. In reality, she would end up cold, lonely, devastated.

Helena followed. She had no other choice after all.

It wasn't yet the fashionable hour for members of the *ton* to stroll in the park. But there were gentleman riding, along with governesses and children who had come to picnic and play. She casually made her way across the grass toward the trees, as if she were idly passing her time.

She reached the bushes, where she paused. Something hard and warm caught her by the waist. Suddenly she was pulled into an open space in the middle of the lilacs. Helena uttered half a scream before she came to her senses and swallowed the rest. She spun, and faced the duke and frowned at him as if he were a disobedient child. "You scared me out of my wits, Your Grace."

Sunlight spilled through the canopy of leaves overhead, dappling him with light. Beneath was a floor of soft grass and fallen petals. It was like a secret grotto. "This—this is convenient."

"It's a clearing made by couples sneaking in here for quick, erotic encounters."

And he knew about it. She opened her reticule and fished out the sparkling shackles. As she dangled them in front of him, he held out his hand. "I take it you have come to return them."

"N-no." Her voice wobbled, and she searched for strength. "I came to find out exactly what you wish me to do with them, Your Grace." Taking a deep breath, she held up her arm and fastened one around her wrist.

It closed with a sharp click. Then she let her tongue play over her lips innocently as she gazed up at him. From doorways, she had watched enough balls to know how ladies flirted. She had never been so daring in her life.

The duke's eyes glittered at her, reflecting the sunlight that filtered between leaves. He let out a ragged breath. Deep lines bracketed his mouth. Astonishingly, he looked as if in pain. "Let me show you."

He captured both her hands, holding her wrists together. With a snap of metal, he secured the other shackle, binding her hands together.

She tried to pull her hands out, tried to pull them apart. Of course she couldn't get free.

Helena expected him to do something. Kiss her. Touch her. Take the advantage in some way. Instead, he folded his arms over his chest. He made no move toward her. She stood, with her bound hands clasped to her bosom.

"I want you to understand what I am offering you, Miss Winsome. And what I will demand of you. You will receive a house of your own in town, one for you to keep after our affair ends. Furnished, with a full complement of servants. You will receive jewels, which are, again, yours to keep. Carte blanche at the best modistes in London. At least two vehicles including a closed carriage and a barouche for you to tool around the park. Horses, of course."

He threw it out so casually, this fortune he was offering her.

"All I ask in return is you accept that our sexual pleasures will be enjoyed on my terms."

She lowered her shackled hands. She had no idea where to put them. How bizarre this was to have her hands bound in the park that she associated with picnics and playing with paper boats in the lake. "What exactly does that mean, Your Grace?"

"It means you must go into this arrangement trusting me completely."

"And I am not to ask you questions? No, Your Grace I cannot do that. I cannot trust blindly. It is not in my nature to do so. You must tell me what you want from me." She could *not* agree without knowing.

He stroked his jaw with his black-gloved hand, obviously considering.

She swallowed hard. Why wouldn't he just tell her? He'd already hinted at enough wicked things. Why was he not speaking now?

Nerves took over. She needed to have her hands free. She didn't like relinquishing control; she was too used to being in charge. "At least release me. You said we were equals. I don't feel that way when my hands are bound." She said bluntly, "Poetry, diamonds, and shackles. I have to contemplate what that says about you, Your Grace, if those are examples of life as your mistress. You ask me to give up *everything*, and you won't tell me what it is you plan to do to me."

The duke moved close to her. He plucked a key from his pocket, then bent to free her hands. This close to him, her quick breaths flooded her senses with his masculine smells—the heady scent of spice and the earthy aroma of leather. The shackles opened, then he dangled them from his index finger. "Trust, Miss Winsome. I require it, and if you agree to our arrangement, you agree to give it."

"I'm afraid to . . . to launch into this. I'm, well in truth, I'm terrified. Could we . . . could we do this slowly?"

"All right, Miss Winsome, I agree. We will go as slowly as you desire. Should I speak to my sister tonight?"

"That quickly?" Panic made her squeak. "How could I leave Lady Winterhaven now? She's enceinte!" But she had to do this quickly. She had to get into his house at once—

Then she realized: If she were to become his mistress in truth, she didn't need to spy anymore. If he gave her all those things, she could pay the debts and save her family.

"All right. I will wait until you have been introduced to my preferences. Until then, Jacinta does not need to know."

She felt so guilty, for Lady Winterhaven was a kind employer. But she must either become his mistress or continue to be a spy to save her family.

"I promise I will do nothing that will hurt you," he said gently.

She hated the idea of not knowing what she was walking into. But she said, "All right." Then she thought of Will's gaming, and suddenly she had a brilliant idea. The duke was notorious for his gambling, though he usually won, or at least never lost more than he could afford. "I agree to trust you—blindly— but I have a condition. My brother is addicted to gaming, and I must stop him."

She had a different last name from her half siblings, so none of the *ton* families realized her brother had a newspaper. She could not tell Greybrooke who her brother really was. "He's lost a fortune at these places. He promises me he'll stop going, but he still does. Is there any way I could stop them letting him through the doors? He has no money anymore—surely, if they knew, they wouldn't let him gamble."

"If you wish, I can put the word around the hells. Give me his name and I will make sure he is not welcome at any of the tables."

"You would do that? It would mean so much to my family." But how could she do it, without giving her brother's name?

"It would be a delight to rescue you, Miss Winsome."

"Could I tell them myself? I don't wish to put you to the trouble."

"You want to go to gaming hells and ask them not to admit your brother." He looked startled.

She swallowed hard. She needed a plausible lie! "I—I've been a dutiful governess for years. I've never had any adventures. I've seen so much passion and desire and excitement, but I've never had the chance of any myself. Not even a kiss. I've never been kissed. I've wondered what all these wicked things and wild places are like. . . ."

"So you want to see a gaming hell to see what lures your brother?"

That made sense! That gave the perfect excuse for her determination to go. "Yes."

"Your wish is my command," Greybrooke said easily. "Can you sneak out of the house at night?"

"Yes. I can get out through the kitchens and though the rear gate. I will meet you at the bottom of the mews, at the street." It meant she could spend time with him, and not in a bed. Wearing shackles.

"At midnight." Glinting, his emerald eyes met hers. "At midnight, your adventure begins."

4

Midnight came with echoing rings from a distant clock but no sign of Miss Winsome in the mews. Grey checked his pocket watch while his harsh breathing filled the silence of his carriage. Even waiting for her, he was rock hard with arousal.

Normally, when he desired a woman, it was in an indifferent way. One bedmate was much like another. A momentary flare of excitement and interest, one quickly sated. Certainly, he had never sat with his forehead pressed to the window, cursing the passing minutes.

For a rake, this strange obsession should be a warning sign. Instead, it fascinated him. It captured his thoughts, took charge of his mind, helped him forget. Oddly, this game of seduction took his thoughts away from his hellish past even more than sex did.

He peered into the gloom as if he could make Miss Winsome materialize by sheer force of will. His heartbeat quickened as a figure walked out of the shadows toward him.

Damn. His anticipation deflated. Light from a street flare fell on the person and revealed a slightly battered beaver hat, a man's long coat, and boots.

Grey uttered a ripe curse beneath his breath and lifted his fist to the ceiling, ready to rap on it, a signal for his coachman to drive on. It appeared his feisty, intriguing governess had lost her courage—

The thighs on the young man jiggled. Plump, shapely, those thighs strained the fabric of the breeches. This was no lad. It was Miss Winsome in men's clothing.

Grey pushed open the door and reached out. Clasping Miss Winsome's hand, clad in an oversized men's glove, he helped her up the steps. His footman's impassive stare faltered for a moment, showing surprise as her voluptuous bottom moved past him, up the steps.

"That will be all, Trim," he growled. The servant bowed and closed the door.

Before Miss Winsome could sit down, Grey caught her by her rounded hips. "Turn around."

When she stared at him in surprise from beneath the brim of her black beaver hat, he rotated her so her arse faced him. She wore a tailcoat of blue—in the fashion of several years ago. The tails jutted out, following the two lush gloves of her rump. "Darling, are you really trying to make people believe you're a man?"

She tried to turn, but his firm grip prevented her. Her golden waves had been ruthlessly pinned down beneath her hat. She must have flattened her pretty tits with banding.

"I am going to a gaming hell," she said. "Are they not solely for gentlemen?"

"No, there are females there. However, not dressed as you are."

"You mean *ladies* go there?"

"Prostitutes, Miss Winsome. In very little clothing."

"That was what I thought." She twisted to face him, arms folded over her chest. "I am not going to go in that sort of disguise. And I must be disguised. If anyone were to recognize me, it would be disastrous for Lady Winterhaven."

"True." He would face the wrath of Jacinta for that. His carriage lurched off, and he held her hips so she would not fall. He was going to have to figure out how to have her as his mistress without having scandal taint Jacinta's family. Seducing her governess into becoming his mistress would be exactly the sort of scandal that Lady X would write about.

"Could I sit down, Your Grace?"

He should allow her to do so, but having her full, rounded derriere at eye level was too much fun. "Did you raid my brother-in-law's wardrobe? Though, considering he's over six feet tall, I can't see how you managed to make the stuff fit you."

"The clothes belong to my brother."

Her brother possessed the clothing of a gentleman. Intriguing, when she was a governess.

"Please, could I be seated, Your Grace?"

He loved it when her voice became stern. "Of course." The carriage rounded a corner and she swayed, and he chose that moment to draw her onto his lap. Her bottom landed hard on his thighs—warm, soft, luscious. He would love to introduce her to sex from behind, with her hands and ankles bound, where he could slam against these two perfect pillows with his groin, driving his prick deep inside her.

Having to seduce a woman slowly was a new experience for him. Miss Winsome was a challenge.

He was also learning that Miss Winsome liked to challenge him. He suspected she liked challenges, period. Why else would she have taken the job with Jacinta's children? His nephews had a demonic streak that drove nursemaids and governesses away, like he had always done. As much as he hated it, he was like his father; his nephews were like him. Maryanne's blindness unnerved most servants. Most governesses had no idea how to communicate with the girl or how to deal with her tantrums and frustration.

But Miss Winsome did. She had taken those trials in stride. And in only a month had made remarkable progress with Maryanne.

"Even in gentlemen's clothing," he said softly, "you are still extraordinarily beautiful."

She did an admirable job of looking repressive at his compliment, but she was on his lap, and he felt things she didn't even know she had to hide. Little squirms and twitches.

"I suspect you would say something flattering even if I'd appeared in a sack, Your Grace."

"You could make a sack seductive, Miss Winsome." He let his breath brush her ear. Her answering shiver went through her, down to her derriere, which quivered on his thighs.

"In gaming hells," he continued, "it is customary for a man to have his female companion seated on his lap."

"I do appreciate your help, Your Grace, but I am not attending this place as your particular female companion."

"So that's your plan with your disguise. Not just to protect your identity, but to keep me to my vow of allowing you to select the pace of your seduction. I can't sit you on my lap when you're dressed as a man. You are a very worthy opponent, Miss Winsome."

"Do you consider your mistresses as opponents?"

He rubbed his jaw. "I wouldn't have said so, before meeting you, angel. But now that I look back, I suppose I have. Before you, it always has been easy."

"Are you annoyed that I am not making it easy?"

He threw back his head and laughed. "No, I admire it about you, just as I admire your clever wits. I promised to take my time, and I always honor my word. But if we're having this much fun before we're even in bed, imagine, my sweet, how superb the sex will be."

Those words echoed in Helena's head at the same frantic rate as her breathing. One quick breath in: *how superb the . . .* One desperate breath out: *sex will be.*

She had flung herself from his lap across the carriage to the opposite seat.

It hadn't been fear that sent her leaping across the carriage. It had been *panic*. Margaret had told her, miserably, how physical desire had made her lose all good sense. It had been lust—powerful, overwhelming lust—that had got Margaret in such trouble, that had cost her half sister her life.

And Helena had felt a dizzying spurt of it when Greybrooke had said those words.

She didn't know what to do. She was supposed to become his mistress without knowing what he meant by "his terms." And deep in her heart, she didn't want to be . . . ruined.

The carriage stopped. The duke gracefully jumped down from the vehicle to the sidewalk in front of the gaming hell. She waited for the footman to lower the steps, then hastened down and joined Greybrooke. As she reached his side, his posture changed. He leaned back slightly, his stance more aggressive. He was standing with her as if she really was a male. He exuded power and sensuality as he did. As a female, she was overwhelmed with awareness of him.

"Black's is the best gaming hell in London," he drawled.

She looked up. The tall town house almost disappeared into the night. Its exterior was simple. Closed drapes covered the windows. The address hardly looked elegant and sumptuous. But carriages with beautiful crests lined the street in a parade of obvious wealth—wealth about to be removed. "Best from whose point of view?" she asked wryly.

He inclined his head. "Point taken, Miss Winsome." He strode up the front steps.

Panic flared, and she chased him to the front door. He knocked, and she whispered fiercely, "You can't call me that here."

He appraised her, brow quirked. "All right. I'll think of something else."

"*You* will? Shouldn't I be the one to choose my assumed name?"

"My dear, I'm the one with the experience in wicked places."

The way he said it . . . suddenly she felt as hot in men's clothing as she did under her stays.

She couldn't protest anymore—a man's face appeared at the door's grille. He saw the duke and admitted them instantly. Bald, six and a half feet tall with a huge chest, the servant did not speak a word, but Greybrooke allowed the man to divest him of his greatcoat, then handed over his tall hat and gold-tipped walking stick.

The servant turned to her. She had only Will's tailcoat, but the man pointed to her hat. Obviously, he did not speak.

Instinctively she grabbed her hat—to hold it on. It hid her hair. She couldn't give it up.

Greybrooke gave a discreet shake of his head, and the doorman retreated. She had worked in *ton* families, but it amazed her to see the duke's innate power. He could command people without even uttering a word himself.

What would happen once a man accustomed to such obedience got her alone in his house?

A second servant hastened forward from his post by a closed set of double doors. Wearing an immaculate black coat along with a snow-white cravat, shirt, and waistcoat, the man bowed to Greybrooke with the bearing of a ducal butler.

"It is good to have you here this evening, Your Grace. Your usual table for faro? Or is it to be hazard, Your Grace? I acquired a crate of a most excellent French vintage and have reserved it in anticipation of your visit."

Greybrooke's teeth flashed in a teasing grin—one intended just for her. Helena's stomach gave a little flip-flop.

"Champagne tonight, Melman," he said casually to the servant. "Allow me to introduce my youthful cousin, Mr. George

Caldwell, down from the country. Caldwell, this is Melman, the major domo of this establishment and the reason Black's is the most famed gaming house in London."

"Thank you, Your Grace." The major domo bowed to her. Then, as he straightened and he studied her face, his brow shot up. Bother. Apparently she didn't make a sufficiently convincing male.

"Is Black here tonight? I require a word with him."

"Of course, Your Grace. I shall take you to him at once."

The major domo whisked them through gilt-encrusted doors and through the gaming rooms—some were bathed in the golden light of chandeliers, other were shrouded in gloom. They mounted a sweeping stair and were shown into a massive, elegant parlor. It could have been the drawing room of Winterhaven House. Melman knocked discreetly on a pastel blue door. He returned in moments. "Mr. Black is honored to meet with Your Grace and Mr. Caldwell."

"Oh, but I thought—I thought I could speak to him alone."

The duke's dark brow rose. Of course she'd made him suspicious. "It's just that it's a private family matter, Your Grace," Helena said hurriedly in a false deep voice. "And my brother does not know of your involvement. . . ."

"I understand, cousin," Greybrooke growled. "Allow me to speak to Black for a moment. Then you may go in. At that point, I guarantee he will grant you any request you make."

How could he be sure of that? Her heart thundered and she paced. Did she give this man the truth—admit she was a female? Greybrooke returned and held the door for her. "Smile at him, admit you've dressed as a man on a dare, and Black will eat out of your hand."

She had faced peers of the realm and told them how to improve their behavior with their children—she could face a gaming hell owner. Especially with the duke nodding encouragement. "You could not fail to charm him, my dear."

"I'm not a great beauty."

The duke's brows shot up. "My dear, you are stunning."

She blinked. But there was no teasing smile—he was being honest. The Duke of Greybrooke thought her stunning?

"Outside and in," he murmured.

Squaring her shoulders, she went inside the offices of Mr. Black. The man behind the desk looked like a pugilist. Gleaming bald head, heavy square jaw, nose cocked off to the side, narrow, fierce eyes. But as he looked up from his papers and saw her, Mr. Black leapt up and gave a beaming smile. "My dear, Greybrooke has told me about your troubles—I will be honored to help you. Give me the name of your brother, and I will have the word passed around London. Your brother will be discreetly turned away from all gaming establishments. It will be done so he will have no idea that you had anything to do with it, my dear."

She could not quite believe it. "My brother is William Rains." Then she requested awkwardly, "Please do not tell His Grace who my brother is."

"Rains—the newspaper man?"

She nodded. "But I've been a governess, and I would never find work if the *ton* feared I had a connection to a newspaper."

"Interesting." Mr. Black scrubbed his jaw, which was shadowed in much black stubble. "Perhaps, in return, you could help me. Favorable accounts of my establishments in the papers. And discretion guaranteed for my patrons?"

She nodded. "Oh yes, I promise. I must thank you from the bottom of my heart, sir. You have spared an entire family—"

"Thank Greybrooke, miss, not me. He made a plea for your case—and an offer I could not refuse."

"What kind of offer?"

"To encourage his wealthy peers to frequent my club, especially the ones who tend to lose."

She left his office, closing the door behind her, to find Greybrooke pacing by the fire. He met her with concern. "Did he agree?"

"Immediately. You made him an irresistible offer. Thank you, Your Grace." He had indeed rescued her.

"It was no trouble," Greybrooke said dismissively. "Now— did you wish to begin our pleasures?"

"Oh!" She swallowed hard. Would he really give her time? Would he expect her to go to his bed in return for his help— maybe even tonight?

She should let him take her to his home. But she was nervous. She needed to stall for time while she gathered her wits. "I would like to see more of the gaming club."

His brow quirked. "I could give you a climax first, my dear. Then we could gamble."

"Oh, Your Grace, I really wish to see it now. You must remember I'm a governess and I always go to bed early. I'll fall asleep at the gaming table if I wait too long."

He moved closer to her, and she could focus on nothing but him. He towered over her, his black hair in fashionable disarray—it looked how it would if her hands had run through it. She was so wickedly tempted to touch him. . . .

"I've been aroused for you all day," he said softly.

Those words made her melt, even as they made her panic. She didn't dare touch him. It would be like unleashing a predatory lion, she feared. "Please, Your Grace. This is—it is too fast for me. I am sorry but I'm just not ready."

"Not ready for an orgasm?" His eyes twinkled.

Hers opened wide. "Oh, heavens, no."

He laughed gently. "All right. Follow me."

Apparently gentlemen liked to play cards in gloom—the light of two candelabras barely cut through the shadows. Helena blinked until she could finally see.

She gasped in shock.

Half-naked, buxom women were draped all over the men. One female had her bodice pulled down to reveal her whole plump breast. The nipple sitting on top was as red as a robin's breast. Her gentleman was idly—and openly—pinching her nipple.

"Why do they have such vividly colored nipples?"

The duke's brows shot up. "They use scarlet cream to heighten the color."

Oh dear. She hadn't meant to speak out loud. "Oh—er, I thought maybe women with bright red nipples tended to become strumpets."

Greybrooke smothered a laugh. "Come along, cousin. The cards are waiting for us."

Broad-shouldered and tall, the duke moved easily between the tightly spaced tables. He had such presence that men promptly made room for him, despite being in the middle of games with large piles of money on the tables.

Greybrooke selected a table that included a pair of gentlemen. He drew out a chair, sprawled elegantly on it, and motioned to the one across from him. "Sit, Caldwell." Introductions were made swiftly. Their opponents were the beefy Earl of Brace, and his partner, Viscount Deverell: tall, slender, blond.

Champagne was brought to their table by Melman, who yanked out the cork with a resounding pop. He filled flutes, placing them around the table. A fresh deck of cards was laid in front of Greybrooke.

"This should prove entertaining." Greybrooke split the deck. "This will be George's first attempt at whist."

Deverell and Brace nodded, impassive, but she saw the gleam of anticipation in their eyes. At a table behind them, a man suddenly moaned, "Damnation, I'm *ruined*." His chair scraped, and he staggered toward the door. No one appeared to care.

How could they be so cavalier, so heartless . . . so ruthless?

Luxury and excess surrounded her—in polished wood, exquisite art, extravagant champagne. She should feel anger at the men that owned places like this—who had made all this wealth on the back of naïve young men like Will. But she understood them. They had a living to make, just like she did. It was *Will* who made her furious. How had he faced these merciless gentlemen and believed he had even a chance of winning?

Greybrooke dealt with controlled flicks of one hand. The cards fell swiftly, and when he was finished, she stared at the ones in front of her.

"Wagers first," Greybrooke said, picking up his own hand.

She had no idea how to play whist, and they were playing for money. What happened when she caused the duke to lose? Would he expect her to pay? Unless—

Unless her debt to him was going to grow and grow.

"The wager is a night with a half dozen ladybirds of their choice," Greybrooke said.

She made a choking sound—and quickly took a long sip of champagne to cover her shock.

Bother, she'd drunk *half* of it. At once.

"You're blushing, Caldwell," murmured the duke.

She pushed her glass away from her as if it were the devil. The last thing she should do was get drunk.

Cards flew quickly. Helena had played hundreds of games with children, and she caught on promptly, following the duke's lead. After several hands she could understand how he played—not in a wild or daring way, but aggressively, as long as he was confident he had the cards to back his strategies. With a quiet word to Melman, he replaced her champagne with water. She was thankful. Their opponents downed glass after glass of alcohol, seemingly without effect.

Ruthless play and hard drinking. Her brother had been *far* out of his league.

Greybrooke threw down his last card, winning the trick and that game. Leaning back in his chair, he winked at her, then gazed over her head and crooked his finger. She knew he was up to something devious, but she coolly looked over her shoulder.

A large bosom heaved into her face. Two fleshy mounds the size of watermelons wobbled above the low neckline of a crimson velvet gown. Helena looked up into the childishly pretty face of a dark-haired girl with a button nose, plump cheeks, and large blue eyes. The girl giggled her name, which sounded like Ellie, and suddenly her voluptuous bottom settled on Helena's lap. "How handsome you are, Mr. Caldwell!" Ellie grasped Helena's hand and plopped in on her huge left breast.

She was touching a girl's bosom. What in heaven's name should she do?

She glared at Greybrooke. He looked as if butter wouldn't melt in his mouth.

"Sorry, Ellie. I have to play my cards," she muttered, trying to make her voice sound gravelly. Ellie giggled and wriggled her bottom.

Helena bit the inside of her cheek. She was definitely going to *spank* Greybrooke after this.

A blonde plunked down on *his* lap, legs spread, skirts hiked up to reveal plump legs and stockings.

A strange pain spiked through Helena's belly as she watched the girl—then watched Greybrooke put his arm around her. It felt suspiciously like jealousy. Which was foolish! The duke caught her eye and winked again.

She couldn't even tell Ellie to leave. No normal male would unseat a beautiful, voluptuous young woman from his lap.

Viscount Deverell began the game. Helena peered around Ellie, who kept jiggling in the most distracting way. It was awkward, but she was determined not to give the duke the satisfaction of seeing her shocked. She tried to play her cards coolly, except she couldn't even see them for Ellie's jutting bosom. She threw down a diamond instead of a heart, costing them the point.

Greybrooke cleared his throat.

"Ellie, my cousin has never fondled a woman's nipple. Perhaps you should tutor him in what you like."

Ellie obeyed at once, and the girl dragged Helena's hand to her breast again. A firm point of a nipple jabbed against Helena's palm.

Her head was swimming with the embarrassment and scandal of this. *Oh, Greybrooke,* she thought, *I will get my revenge on you.*

It took all the daring she had in the world, but she bent over and quickly put her lips to the swell of Ellie's breasts. The girl squealed with delight.

Greybrooke's cards shot out of his hands and landed on the table. "Damnation," he muttered. He gathered up the cards and the viscount dealt again.

She squeezed Ellie's right breast the next time, stroking the pert nipple through the girl's dress, and Greybrooke played like a man with no wits. They lost three games in a row.

This time she smirked at Greybrooke.

His gorgeous green eyes narrowed. He paid no attention to the woman on his lap. His gaze was fixed on her—not even on Ellie, but on her. He watched her every movement.

Winning at this game of revenge gave her confidence. She played much more brilliantly, and she and the duke won again. It was a true battle now—she was matching wits with the duke. She watched his every move. Now she realized he was giving signals. A quirk of his brow, a twitch of his lip, the way his fingers rested against the back of his cards. She could tell, without words, exactly what he was thinking. Finally she played a card, and Greybrooke drawled, "I believe that's it. The match is ours."

Ellie squealed and clapped her hands. "Now, then, you can come upstairs with me!"

"Upstairs?" Helena echoed.

"To one of the bedrooms."

"Not now, I'm afraid." Her voice came out far too high and squeaky. She coughed and tried again. "His Grace is going to . . ." She searched desperately. "Introduce me to hazard."

But Ellie was not giving up easily. The huge breasts slammed hard against Helena's flattened chest. Puckered lips pressed hard against hers, and Ellie—sighing, moaning, and wiggling her tongue—kissed her passionately.

She sat, stunned, while Ellie's tongue slid between her lips and the girl gave her a wet, shocking, open-mouthed kiss.

Her first kiss. And it was with a woman who thought she was a man.

It was a scorching kiss, but she wished, madly, it was the duke kissing her.

"Very persuasive, Ellie," Greybrooke drawled. "I'm sure you'll coax young George into bed."

That brought her to her senses. Helena put her hands on the girl's shoulders and firmly propelled her back, breaking the molten contact between their mouths.

Gruffly she said, "Not tonight."

"Oh, gentlemen never want to kiss!" Ellie pouted. She flounced on Helena's lap, crossing her arms across her chest, sticking out her lip.

"Dramatics will not get you your way—" Helena broke off. She'd sounded far too much like a governess. She threw a withering glare at the duke. Mouthed, *You are in trouble.*

Greybrooke leaned back in his seat, trying to look innocent—he was the most disobedient boy in a man's body she'd ever encountered. Then he cupped his hand against his courtesan's ear and whispered something to her. The girl pouted, but she got off his lap, then she hauled Ellie to her feet and the two of them left.

Greybrooke slanted a glance toward their opponents, the earl and the viscount.

Relief flooded.

"Congratulations," Greybrooke threw out. Then he gave her the most devilish of all the smiles he'd given her, and all her instincts went on alert.

He stretched, and said casually, "Now you can look forward to a night with a half dozen whores. All determined to please your cock in whatever way you desire."

Helena choked on his blunt words. But she had to continue to play his game. "I cannot wait," she said, in her false deepened voice.

"Can you not?" His gazed burned into hers. "Neither can I."

He was daring her. She certainly had gotten his interest. Now she had to keep it. "What if what I desire to play with the ladies is a good game of cards?"

Deep, low, his sudden gruff laugh washed over her.

Defiantly, she muttered, "Or perhaps I could share a large bed with all of them."

He sucked in a sharp breath.

"Since I'm a naïve, innocent buck from the country, Greybrooke," she said, keeping her voice as deep as she could, "what would you suggest I do in bed with six buxom ladybirds?"

His finger skimmed around the inside of his collar.

She almost danced a jig when she saw him blush. Just as when she'd made him drop his cards, she had actually shocked him—and he was a man who gave shackles as gifts.

Boring his gaze into her eyes, he growled, "I'm afraid to disappoint you, for we won't collect on the wager tonight. You wanted to play hazard, as I recall. One of the most destructive games."

Lifting his head, he told the Earl of Brace and Viscount that he intended to collect upon the wager at a later time. The two men rose, bowed, and withdrew. The moment Greybrooke stood, Helena did too. He strolled around the table to her, then he bent and murmured by her ear, "This night has been delightful. I am enjoying every moment with you."

He said it as if it surprised him.

* * *

A young viscount kissed his closed fist, then cast something down the table. Two dice tumbled, rebounded off a barrier at the end, and landed to show their black spots.

Helena turned to Greybrooke. He stood beside her at the table, so close his thigh brushed hers. Even through layers of fabric she felt a sizzle of heat where they touched. At first she thought he'd stood so close to unsettle her. But she saw no twinkle in his green eyes, no smile playing at his sensual mouth. She could recognize moods in children. Anger rolled off the duke—anger that did not seem to suit this silly game.

"How can this be the most destructive game?" she whispered. "They are just throwing dice."

Greybrooke pointed to the man throwing the dice, who brushed perspiration from his forehead. "The point is, cousin, this game is pure chance. Logic can be applied, but men become addicted. They believe the next throw will be the one that wins. Fortunes are lost this way."

"Have you lost a fortune?"

"I play games that require skill, not luck. My father, however, was not as circumspect."

She admired the duke. If only her brother had been so circumspect. But Will was impetuous and eternally hopeful. He had probably hoped the next card or the next roll would change his fortunes. But thanks to this man, she no longer had to fear her brother would lose more at the gaming tables.

"Your Grace, I beg your pardon." Melman had come up behind her and the duke.

Greybrooke stepped aside with the servant. The major domo spoke in such low, confidential tones she could not hear a word. To eavesdrop, she would have had to have squirmed in between them.

Helena watched Greybrooke's face. His full lips thinned into a hard, angry line. Whatever the interruption was, it infuriated him. He gave a curt nod. "I will come."

He turned to her. "A moment, cousin." With no more explanation, he stalked away.

This must be important—it could be a critical clue to whether Whitehall was correct and the duke had sold secrets. But to chase after him would look too conspicuous.

Or would it? She muttered words about too much champagne and the retiring room, but everyone watched the dice. No one paid any attention to her.

She threaded through the crowd. For the Duke of Greybrooke, people stepped smartly aside. No one moved to give George Caldwell room. But in masculine clothing, she was agile, and she reached the far side of the hazard room just as the duke disappeared through a shadowy doorway.

If she followed, would he spot her? She had no choice but to take the risk. When she reached the door, though, Greybrooke was gone.

A man's voice said, "Good evenin', Yer Grace. So delighted ye came to meet me."

Mocking in tone, the voice had come from the end of the hallway. With a quick breath of relief, Helena crept down. There was a door ajar, but as she got close, the door shut firmly in place. Bother!

She slipped into the room beside, thankfully empty. It proved to be a small parlor. A window at the end of the room let in silver-blue moonlight. Quickly she looked out, her heart soaring. It overlooked the rear yard and was on the ground floor. If her luck was in, Greybrooke's room would have a window and it would be open enough for her to spy.

Helena slid up the sash, hopped out. Thank heaven for trousers. Greybrooke's room was also a drawing room, but larger, with glass-paned doors leading to a small terrace.

Her work in seeking scandals for the newspaper guided her. She knew to creep along the wall. Then, with her back against the brick, she peeked through the door. The low fire illuminated two men. Greybrooke, who stood with his back to the terrace door, hands fisted. The other man—

She recoiled, stunned. It was a monster's face. A gargoyle, not even human.

Heavens, it was a mask. She'd been startled by a child's oldest trick: to put on a mask and try to frighten people.

The man wore a devil's face, within the hood of his cloak. Whoever he was, he'd wanted to ensure he wouldn't be recognized.

Smash!

Greybrooke's fist slammed into the frame of the door, rattling glass. Helena had to coax her heart back down into place.

Greybrooke's angry punch had unlatched the door. He stalked back toward the masked man. Holding her breath, she snaked out her hand and opened the terrace door about an inch.

"If you 'urt me, Yer Grace, the information I've got gets published for all England to see. Don't think ye can escape this by killin' me. I've planned for that." The man's voice was confident, mocking.

"You want more than can be paid."

"I don't think so. Think the reason you're here is proof I'll get what I want. I'll be a gentleman and keep my price the same. Two thousand."

Greybrooke gave a harsh laugh. "You'll be back for another two thousand as soon as you've run through that."

"Ye can afford it, Yer Grace."

"Who in hell are you?"

The man laughed roughly. Yet, like his accent, it sounded forced, as if he was playing a role. "I'm not going to tell ye that, Yer Grace."

"Damnation," the duke growled. "You will get your two thousand, but it will take me time to acquire the funds. Meet me in two nights in Hyde Park. Midnight. Then you will get your money."

"Double-cross me, Yer Grace, and ye'll be reading about it in the newssheets. What a pretty scandal it would make."

Greybrooke took a menacing step forward, but the masked man laughed. A cackling laugh. "Don't think I haven't taken care of meself. If I die, my associate sends everything to the newssheets. You wouldn't want 'er to pay the price for yer anger, would ye?"

The duke looked like that now—as if his restraint would snap and his body would explode in violence. "Leave her alone, damn you," the duke said. He took a step toward the man, who took a quick one in retreat.

"Bring the money as ye've promised two nights from now, and ye needn't worry about reading the story in the newssheets, Yer Grace. But of course, I know ye will honor your word. Since ye're such a gentleman." Chuckling, the man turned and walked away.

Helena stared at his back, covered by the swaying cape. Firelight reflected on the sinuous slither of it. She would not have turned her back on the furious duke.

Indeed, Greybrooke lifted his fist. Then he drove it, with a growl of rage, into the top of a delicate table. The inlaid wood surface broke with an ear-shattering crash. That must have been painful for Greybrooke, but he didn't even wince. He smoothed down his hair, straightened his cravat, then left the room.

But she now knew Greybrooke was being blackmailed.

5

"Does this mean the duke is being blackmailed because he was a traitor?"

The carriage rumbled off and she faced Whitehall, who sat opposite. This time she had met him without Will and told him what she'd overheard.

Her heart hammered madly as she waited for his opinion.

"Or he is being blackmailed over the secrets that led him to be a traitor." Whitehall leaned forward, a tall beaver hat covering his dark head, but the shadows made his face look even more skull-like. His black eyes burned into hers. "Did you get into his home? Did you find diaries or letters?"

"N-not yet." Greybrooke had been nothing but a gentleman when he'd returned to the hazard table. He had ended their night, had taken her back to the mews behind the Winterhaven house, had not even pressed a kiss upon her. He'd apologized for being distracted and had promised her a more dazzling evening tonight. After all, she knew tomorrow night he was supposed to meet a blackmailer. "But I convinced him last night to bring me to his house tonight."

She shivered with nerves, but also with anticipation, remembering how she'd convinced him. She had asked for one kiss. To see what it was like, to see if she was ready to give him more. One kiss to be given to her in his home.

Greybrooke had agreed on one condition: He was allowed to choose where he kissed her.

When she thought about kissing him, she felt a hot, intense thrill. Then her sensible voice berated her for being heady with desire for a man who was being blackmailed and could be a traitor. At the very least he was . . . danger personified.

"Do not waste this opportunity," Whitehall said coldly. "You must find out the reason behind the blackmail. You must try to learn the secrets he is hiding. It could help us get at the truth and prove his guilt."

But it would have to be something personal. Something perhaps dangerous. "Do we need to actually know what his secrets are? Isn't it enough if we can find out he did commit treason?"

"Miss Winsome." Whitehall's grip tightened on his walking stick as if he were restraining his temper. "You find out the *ton*'s secrets so you can publish them in Lady X's scandal column. Why do you balk at this now, when it is for the good of your country?"

"He did a—a kind thing for me. It was one thing to expose his crime if he is guilty. But it's quite another thing to hunt for private secrets that are none of my business."

Whitehall glared at her. "Are we finished then, Miss Winsome? You no longer want to continue serving your country and you are willing to let your family be destroyed by your brother's debt?"

She took a deep breath. "I cannot do this anymore. I don't want to spy on the duke and his family. I have another way to pay my family's debts."

Whitehall's hand snaked out. He grasped her wrist, squeezing tight. "How, Miss Winsome?"

"Please, Mr. Whitehall. This hurts—"

He began to bend her hand back.

She gasped, the pain excruciating. "If I'm going to have to become the duke's mistress, I can use the jewels he will give me to pay the debts."

Whitehall lessened the pressure on her wrist slightly. "You are not walking away from your obligation to the king, Miss Winsome. We could easily destroy your brother, regardless of his debt. His newspaper could be ruined. We can completely ruin your family. As for you—if the duke were to find out you have been spying on him over treason, do you really believe he would want you?"

"You're going to force me to do this with threats?"

"Yes, Miss Winsome." He gave a ruthless smile. "Until I get what I want."

Lifting the hem of her cloak, Helena mounted the steps, feeling like the heroine of a horrid novel.

She had thought Greybrooke was dangerous. But Whitehall had proved he was the real danger.

The duke's door opened before she even reached for the knocker. A footman bowed with perfect respect, and the door quickly shut behind her.

She held onto her hood, which she'd tugged low to hide her face. She was the one in disguise, knowing she was facing ruin. But the duke was the one with the truly perilous secrets. If he really was a traitor, he had been willing to see young soldiers—his own countrymen—die in battle. And she was walking into his house alone.

Churches were built to make you feel awed and insignificant. The duke's foyer made her feel like the tiniest woman in the world. It blossomed round her like a fairy land.

A domed skylight let moonlight glimmer on the pure white marble floor. Pink marble columns soared, topped with leaves of gilt. The coved ceiling was painted like an Italian church, with ethereal angels, muscular mortal males, and a ring of clouds that opened to a perfect blue sky. It was painted to look as if it disappeared up to the heavens, and she almost lost her balance as she peered at it.

"Ostentatious, isn't it? My father's idea. It used to make me stagger and fall when I'd stumble in drunk."

The duke. His voice held a throaty intimacy as if he were speaking to a good friend. Helena whirled around. Drawn to the fountain, she had not noticed doorways behind her. In one, Greybrooke leaned against the doorframe, his dark hair in tousled disarray. He'd dressed as though he were meeting a friend—in white shirtsleeves and a gray waistcoat. His cuffs were open too, his hands bare.

For some reason, the sight of his naked hands—the long fingers, the strong wrists, the ridges of veins along the back—was shockingly intimate. She remembered what he'd said: Her hands molded children's futures; his would touch her . . . private place and make her climax.

A soft squeak left her lips. To cover that, she said, "It's breathtaking." A part of her wondered if those whispered words were about him, not his ceiling. "It does make one lose one's balance. This whole room . . . it feels as if I am in Italy."

"You've been?" His brows lifted in surprise.

She laughed. The idea of it: her, impoverished governess, touring the sun-soaked beauty of Italy. That was for young men with inconceivably huge fortunes. "Of course not. It is just how I imagined it would be."

"Indeed? I've toured Italy. I believe a man is just as likely to encounter a lovely, virginal angel in London than in Rome."

"Why would a man want an untouchable angel, Your Grace?"

"For the fun of making her fall, of course."

She gave him a disapproving look—then remembered she

had agreed to ultimately become his mistress and had offered to take the second step in that shocking path.

Her heart beat frantically, pounding out the question: Are you really going to do it?

Although the duke was joking, there was no smile on his lips. The shadows from last night still clung to his expression, in the lines on his forehead and a grim look in his eyes. Of course, tomorrow he had to meet a blackmailer and surrender two thousand pounds. If she didn't find evidence tonight, she knew what she must do. Spy on their meeting in Hyde Park, learn what she could. Then she would have to come back, again and again, until she learned the duke's secrets.

Oh heavens. It was one thing to spy on members on the *ton* to find out about scandals. It was quite another to conspire to destroy people's lives.

"You wished to visit a gentleman's home alone," he said. "I thought it was my duty to make this experience as decadent as I could. We begin with brandy in the study."

Brandy? She couldn't drink brandy—she had seen the effects of it on strong men. Besides, the taste of it made her want to paw the surface off her tongue. But she *needed* to get into his study. It was one place where a gentleman kept his private letters.

The duke put his hand to the small of her back. She stiffened. Not out of fear of ravishment, out of guilt born from lying.

"Relax, Miss Winsome. I promise to be as well behaved as your best pupil tonight." He studied her. "I thought you wanted this. A kiss in a forbidden place—a gentleman's home."

"I do," she lied desperately. "It is not easy to undo a lifetime of learning to be proper."

"If you'd let me, I'd show you how quickly it could be undone."

It was a typical arrogant rake's statement, but it didn't put her back up. She was beginning to believe him.

He offered his elbow, as if he were taking her into supper at a party. He thought he was fulfilling the fantasy of a governess. He had no idea.

Helena expected at least a perfunctory tour as he led her to his study. But Greybrooke said *nothing* about his house. Nothing about the enormous music room she glimpsed, or the massive portraits and exquisite landscapes that adorned every wall. In fact, he kept his gaze focused ahead as if he didn't want to look around him.

Acting the part of dazzled governess, she cooed and gasped over many of the things she saw: life-size portraits; an enormous, gleaming pianoforte; a Chinese vase large enough for a child to swim in; a suit of armor by the stairs. But the harder she played her part, the heavier her heart got.

He only wants to use you for carnal pleasures. She reminded herself of that. It should make it easier to betray his trust, shouldn't it?

Finally he pushed open a door of dark oak, and she stepped into the most important room she needed to see. Greybrooke left her to pour brandy, and she drank in everything.

Books lined two walls. A huge fireplace stood in the center of the third, surrounded by sketches of horses and hounds. The outer wall was a line of windows, overlooking the lawns of the rear yard, and the tall, stone back wall. A desk occupied the corner, placed on the diagonal. She walked toward it as if fascinated by the view from the windows behind the desk. A key rested in the lock of the center drawer. Her heart pounded. So close, but she couldn't open drawers with the duke watching her.

He held out her brandy, poured in a huge balloon glass, the plump curve engulfed by his large hand. "You seem more fascinated by my room than you are by me."

"It tells me so much about you," she said quickly.

He raised his glass. "A toast to my adventurous governess."
He took a long swallow.

She took just a sip . . . and swallowed fire. She coughed.
Sputtered. How did he drink this stuff so quickly? She knew of
course: He'd done it so often he was immune to the effects.

They drank in silence—he with his healthy swallows, she
with dipping her tongue into the fluid like a timid rabbit.

"Come here, Miss Winsome." The burn of the liquor had
turned his voice husky.

She swallowed hard. She knew how to deal with children,
with their titled parents, with her brother. She didn't know
how to deal with dukes to whom she'd promised a kiss—to
whom she'd intimated she would be a mistress.

Once she let him kiss her, there was no turning back.

Inspiration struck. "Not here. I want something more daring."

"Really, angel? You won't even drink brandy."

"I *am* drinking brandy."

"Like a kitten lapping milk, love. Though the sight of your
little pink tongue is arousing."

"You are making fun of me."

"No, I'm not. I'm being honest. Isn't that one of the lessons
governesses teach? To own up to one's sins?"

The brandy made her cheeks feel hot. "Yes. You must have
had a spectacular governess. You seem to enjoy owning up to
sins."

"I do. Sometimes I even make some up so I can admit to
them. Things I've never even had the pleasure of actually
doing."

"You are most definitely making fun of me, Your Grace."

She couldn't quite understand him. Sometimes he seemed so
arrogant and commanding. Other times there was a naughty,
devilish little boy inside him. One who couldn't help but make
her smile.

"No," he said softly. "And call me Greybrooke."

"All right, Greybrooke. I wish to see your bedchamber. That is where I want to kiss you."

Utter silence. Broken only by the lick of flames in the fireplace and the slosh of fluid as Greybrooke drank a long draught of his brandy.

She'd thrown the words out as if he'd goaded her into being daring. In truth, she'd taken this bold step because she actually did need to see his bedroom. Besides, if he were in his bedchamber, *no one* would be in his study. So if she could find a reason to sneak back down here alone, she could get at his desk.

Why did he stare at her without saying a word, with his brandy glass almost tilting over in his hand?

"Your Grace?"

"All right," he said slowly.

"I've never seen a strange gentleman's bed," she said with breathlessness that wasn't all faked.

"Well, I am certainly a strange gentleman. Let's not keep you waiting, my curious angel. Since you express an interest in seeing my bed, do you want to actually see me in it?"

Was he just calling her bluff? He watched her intently.

She said, as coolly as she could, "Perhaps."

"Then you'll be disappointed. I never do anything as pedestrian as have sex in my bed."

What in heaven's name did he mean by that?

Of course she was too shocked and cowardly to ask.

Helena steeled her shoulders as Greybrooke held open the door to the bedroom for her; she'd been in Will's bedroom before, but never in the most intimate room of a man who was a stranger.

There was no hint on the duke's face that he intended to throw her on his bed and ravish her. But surely she might as well have screamed, "Ruin me! Ruin me!" at him the instant she asked to see his room.

Except he'd said, quite casually, he never did his ravishing in his bed.

His bedroom was gold—literally everything in it was gold, gilt, or opulently shimmering. It was like a sultan's room. An enormous bed stood in the middle, surrounded by curtains of gossamer-sheer gold lace. Every piece of furniture was richly stained in a dark red, and decorated in so much gilt, they shone. Gold decorated the fireplace, gleamed in the drapes, reflected firelight from the dressing table mirror.

"This is like a sultan's room."

"Again, my father's taste." He grimaced the way she had when brandy touched her tongue. "I never bothered to change it."

"If you don't like it, why didn't you?"

"I spend very little time in here. Besides, my mother hated it."

He added nothing more, but she understood his meaning—he'd kept the room like this to anger his mother. She frowned. That seemed a petty thing to do, and Greybrooke had appeared to be anything but petty. His mother had passed away almost seven years ago, soon after his father had died. So if he still kept the room this way, he must hold grudges for a long time.

Harboring grudges was a foolish waste of time. Fixing problems, not brooding over them, was what a person should do.

He sighed. Still holding his brandy, he flopped down on the bed. The liquid sloshed precariously in the glass, but didn't spill. Then he sat up on the edge of the bed. "Sit here. Beside me."

The moment of truth. Yet she couldn't think of any plan except stalling and evasion. "I don't know. I think it would be too easy, too tempting, to lean back onto the bed."

"But nothing will happen to you, Miss Winsome."

It wasn't when he teased her that he caught her off-guard, dumbfounded and startled her. It was when he threw out something that seemed to have far more meaning behind it than just the words he spoke.

Why would he not have his intimate relations in this enormous, lavish bed? "Where do you do it, then? If not in this?"

His brows lifted. "I acquire houses for my mistresses."

"You don't have more than one at once, do you?"

"Sometimes, I have done. I don't believe that complication would occur with you, Miss Winsome."

"I should hope not. I thought, since I would be surrendering so much, that it would be exclusive. If you expect it of me, I expect it of you, Greybrooke."

He laughed. "I love to see you sputter with indignation. I promise, then; when I'm clandestinely fucking you, I will not even look at another female. I believe you will capture all my attention." His language shocked her.

Slowly his smile faded and his mouth softened and he looked at her . . . differently. With an expression she couldn't describe. Not lust. Longing? Something that spoke of desire and hunger but in a way that drew her to him instead of pushing her away.

What would it be like to sit on his bed, so close to him? Daringly she took a step toward him. He caught her hand and helped her lower to the soft mattress.

Her bottom sank into pure comfort. She put her hands on the mattress and bounced on it.

A grin broke on his face. "Feel free to bounce, love. Play around. Enjoy yourself."

She stopped and straightened her back, sitting properly.

"Miss Winsome, I think you have a devilish streak also. You fight hard to restrain it, don't you? Now I know how you work wonders with Jacinta's children. You know what the boys are going to get up to, because that's how your mind works."

"It certainly is n . . ."

Her voice faded as the duke suddenly put his brandy on a side table, then lay back on the bed, stretching his arms over his head. Did he think she would lie—?

A white pillow sudden launched through the air and smacked into her side. He'd thrown a *pillow* at her. He sat up quickly, armed with another pillow in a white silk case, grinning at her.

But she had the first one, the one that had bounced off her shoulder, and she clutched it with both hands and swung. It slammed into Greybrooke's face, and he let out a howl of surprise and fell backward. She threw so much of herself into the attack, she lost her balance. Next thing she knew, she had fallen on the bed too. Only she couldn't move, not on the soft mattress, held prisoner by her wretched dress.

Wild laughter bubbled up. Who knew triumph made you feel so exhilarated? So giddy! And such a silly triumph—smacking an unsuspecting duke with a pillow.

"I knew it," Greybrooke growled. "You are naughtier than I, Miss Winsome."

Then he was over her, braced on his arms, limned by the candlelight. Eyes a dazzling green, wickedly mesmerizing. She couldn't look away. She was floating into them. Falling up into them.

He caught hold of her hands and held them against the bed. Capturing her.

"Never, Your Grace." Her voice was a throaty purr, and she almost quaked at the pure eroticism it held.

No one had ever looked at her like this. As if she were the only thing in his entire world.

"Now I suppose you want your kiss," he said, and his beautiful mouth looked softer and silkier and plumper than the pillows on his bed.

Ever since the moment in Berkeley Square when he'd rescued her and leaned close to her, she'd tried not to think of how tempting his mouth looked. Now she wanted to feel what it would be like to have her lips press against his.

One dreamy kiss. A moment of something special, monumental, sweet. She got ready: eyes closed, lips puckered. Her heart thundered.

Time ticked by—she could hear his mantel clock measuring each passing second as if weighing the tension in the room. Why was nothing happening?

The bed creaked. He released her hands and she felt him move. Slowly Helena opened her eyes. He sat on the edge of the bed, his hands braced on the sides.

Confusion bit her. Shock stunned her. Humiliation began a slow burn that ignited in her cheeks, then washed all over her.

He, the most famed rake in London, hadn't kissed her. He'd run away from her.

He looked at her with haunted eyes. "My apologies, Miss Winsome. Kissing is something I normally do not do."

6

His next words stole her breath completely.

"The hell with this," Greybrooke muttered. "I can kiss you, Miss Winsome." Then softly, as if to himself, he bit off angrily. "Damn it, I can do this."

Before she could move, he shifted to her side, leaned over her. This time, he took her hands captive again, but threaded his fingers through hers. His long, graceful fingers dwarfed hers. Green eyes gazed at her, determined but also vulnerable, shrouded by a fringe of black lashes.

That vulnerability froze her to the spot. Helena didn't understand. He was a rake and rogue. How could the prospect of a kiss have made him react this way?

Then his arms dipped, his mouth neared hers, and she knew this time it was going to happen.

Her eyes shut. But he commanded, "Open your eyes," before his lips brushed hers, sending a shower of sparks to dance through her like fireflies.

Her lids lifted and she caught dizzying glimpses of his face. His lashes were half-closed, giving his eyes a languorous beauty. His dazzling pale green irises glowed, brilliant as lanterns. His stubble lightly scraped her skin and made her tingle. His high cheekbones had wells of shadow beneath. And his mouth—his hot, gentle mouth took her lips and coaxed them to open in a carnal and intimate way.

She was speared by shock. She thought kisses were done with the lips closed. They were tidy and polite and spoke of love.

She'd no idea they were so raw and primitive. His lips played with hers, pressing against them, stroking them, caressing them, tugging them.

His back blotted out the light. She could see, even in his coat, the exaggerated vee shape of his back. How powerful and large his muscles must be.

It should scare her, shouldn't it? He was so strong, and she was really his enemy.

But deep inside her, in somewhere primitive and wanton, she wanted his strength. In that deep, hungry place, she ached for him.

He shifted, deepening the kiss. Warm, big, he moved over her, his weight pressing lightly into her. How could it go deeper? But it did. She sank deeper into the cloudlike cocoon of his bed; she was falling up into his glorious, wicked kiss.

Heat bubbled up inside her.

For a governess, this was wrong. For a spy, this was danger. She didn't care. For years she'd been the teacher, now she was learning. Learning how a man kissed. Learning how a woman kissed back. Learning so much, so quickly, it made her head spin.

Kisses weren't sweet. They *weren't* monumental . . . because that would mean one was enough.

Kiss me forever. She cried it desperately in her head.

Then his tongue caressed her lower lip, swept over it and slid inside her mouth.

Goodness!

Her senses filled with his taste: the bite of brandy; the slightly bitter, raw taste of smoke on his breath; the warm, erotic flavor of him. His tongue played with hers, and each stroke of it in his mouth sent a pulse of pleasure through her body.

It was like they were joined intimately. That was all she could think of as he commanded her mouth.

With him gripping her hands, she couldn't put her arms around him like she suddenly wanted to. Fighting her skirt, she managed to hook her leg around his calves, her heel skidding across polished leather.

He'd been right all along. She wanted pleasure. She couldn't deny it anymore. She, the cautious governess who only wanted to help people, wanted to fling herself into this and take every risk she could. She lifted to him, aching in her breasts, aching between her thighs, on fire everywhere.

Then, as if a devil had taken control of her, she whispered into his mouth. Words he couldn't hear. But words that terrified her, even as she knew—*knew* with all her soul—she meant them. *I want you,* she whispered into his hot, beautiful mouth. *I need you. Please. Ruin me.*

Greybrooke eased back from her mouth, breaking the kiss.

Oh no. No! Please, please, please don't stop.

He rose off her, splaying his hands on the bed for balance as he got to his knees, then shifted so he sat on the edge of his bed. His eyes were the ones closed now, his long lashes brushing his sculpted cheeks.

Helena gaped at him, suddenly feeling . . . lost. What had she said? God, she remembered.

Ruin me.

At least she had said it into his mouth, not anywhere he could hear her, but the reality of what she'd been willing to do left her shaking.

But why had he been so reluctant to kiss her? His kiss had been *magnificent*.

His eyes opened. "Did the kiss please you?" His breathing was oddly harsh.

"Yes. I don't understand why you said you weren't ready to kiss. You—you kiss like a god." This is what she would do with a shy or uncertain child. Give reassurance.

But how could she be equating the rakish Duke of Greybrooke with a vulnerable boy?

His deep laugh rumbled over her. But he said, softly, "This is not going to work for me. The sex I desire is quite different from what you've been lead to expect from a marriage bed. I want more than that. I want a deeper connection with you. What I want with you, Miss Winsome, will entwine our souls."

That stunned her. "But—"

"But what, Miss Winsome?"

She had to understand. "But when you left Lady Montroy's house, you seemed as if you did not care about her at all. I would not have said your souls were entwined."

"My affair with her was pure recreation. With you, it will have to be something deeper." He stroked his fingertip over her lower lip. "There is danger in that."

The touch made her mouth tingle, aching for another kiss.

She realized she had not really touched him yet. She—well, she wasn't supposed to, and she'd been afraid of encouraging him. But now she saw that every time she could have touched him, when they'd been sharing a moment of some sort of intimacy, he'd captured her hands so she could not.

Why?

"What danger?" Was he speaking of love? She was not the sort of governess who pretended knowledge she did not have— she was an honest one. "Do you mean love?"

A rueful smile touched his lips. "I'm not capable of it, Miss Winsome."

"How could you not be capable of love? You might not want to fall in love, but you are obviously capable of it. Look how wonderful an uncle you are."

"With children, I am very careful not to let my darkness touch them in any way."

"I thought you were a careless and carefree rake."

"You are the most intriguingly blunt woman I've ever met." He sighed. "Unfortunately, I cannot see you tomorrow night."

She knew why—it was the night he was to meet the black-mailer.

"Meet me at the bottom of the mews at midnight on the night after that," he said. "Before you consent to my arrangement, you must understand exactly what I will require of you."

"Why won't you tell me?"

"I'd frighten you, I fear. Seeing it will help you understand."

It would frighten her? "But you gave me the shackles," she said helplessly. "Surely, if you can do that, you can describe what you want me to do . . ." She took a deep breath. "How could it be worse?"

"From my point of view—" He grinned. "It's better. But still I want you to be an observer with no preconceptions." He stood up.

Suddenly, panic flared. He was going to send her home. This was her chance to search his home, and it was slipping through her fingers.

She had to stall for time. "I have to go to the retiring room," she said quickly. "I have to use the necessary."

Greybrooke had looked amused as he directed her here, to the retiring room attached to his dressing room.

Helena crossed the enormous room set aside for his wardrobes. Six of them lined the walls, each decorated with gleaming gilt and inlaid ivory. A beautiful Aubusson carpet of pale blue and gold covered the floor, and two comfortable wing chairs were placed in the center of the room, which was perhaps as large as all the bedrooms in her family's house put together. One lit wall sconce gave her enough light by which she could see.

Did she dare sneak down to his study? How could she get away with that? It would take far too long. Besides, the key had sat in the lock of the center drawer. If the key was still there, there couldn't be anything important in the desk. Certainly nothing Greybrooke wanted to keep hidden.

Where would he keep incriminating papers, if he had any? Could they be in his bedroom, if not in his study? But she couldn't search it with the duke in it.

Unless . . .

Not unless she . . . let him do things and then he fell asleep afterward. And then, once ruined, she had the presence of mind to get out of his bed and sneak around opening his drawers and his wardrobe.

She couldn't.

Anyway, he didn't do such things in his bed. He'd told her that.

The courtesan, Ellie, had claimed gentlemen didn't kiss. Apparently the girl was right. Helena couldn't imagine why not—her lips still tingled, her heart still pounded, and if she weren't so worried about having to search the duke's things, she would be reliving that delicious kiss over and over.

What was it he really wanted to do with her? And if a man who gave shackles as a gift couldn't describe them, what was it he was going to take her to see?

Helena opened the door, expecting it to be a retiring room. Some light filtered in from the sconce behind her, illuminating a beautiful writing desk. In this enormous house, the duke had a room in which to write, as well as his study. One room for the business of his estates and this one for his personal correspondence, she imagined.

She crafted her column as Lady X on a tiny table in her attic

DEEPLY IN YOU / 89

room by the light of one candle. She had to admit she was envious. Draperies covered the opposite wall, which meant a row of windows let in abundant light in the day.

Now, at night, with only a sconce burning down the hall, it was dark and shadowy in the room. She took tentative steps toward the desk, blocking her own light, reaching out in front of her. Maryanne had to cope with this every day—not for the first time she wondered where the girl found the strength and courage.

One step. Then another. Then . . . *bang*.

Her shin bumped a table she hadn't even seen, and she bit her lip hard to swallow the cry. Not only must she prowl through shadow, she must be *quiet*.

Fortunately, years of going to children who cried out in their sleep had given her at least some capability to function without light. She reached the drapes with no more collisions and drew one back.

Here, by his writing desk, she could smell the unusual scent the duke wore—the hint of cinnamon and bergamot and musk. Did it really linger here, by his writing desk, or was it lingering in her memory?

At this moment, she still had a plausible excuse if Greybrooke caught her—that she'd stumbled into the wrong room. If he found her reading his letters . . . what would she say then?

Her father had been gentlemanly, her mother a lady—a viscount's third daughter. Snooping in desks was so horribly wrong she felt a jolt of pain in her heart. Real spies—the ones who worked for king and country—must never have qualms. She could not have them either.

The blotter surface was empty. A clean quill lay alongside a covered bottle of ink. She turned her attention to the deep dockets of the rolltop writing desk.

One folded letter sat in one docket, the others appeared dark and empty. Helena lifted it out.

Even when she'd uncovered scandals, she never felt so guilty or so wrong. There was good in this too. She had to believe that. A traitor deserved to be punished, didn't he?

In the faint, silvery light, Helena had to hold the letters just inches from her eyes to see the writing. Her heart stuttered as she distinguished the signature: Jacinta, Countess of Winter-haven.

What if there was a clue in one of these. Proof Greybrooke had been a traitor.

She had not thought of that. What if his sister, the Countess of Winterhaven, knew about it?

She quickly set the letter down, as if it were on fire and burning her hand. In her mind, she could see Maryanne struggling to cope with blindness; Timothy valiantly attempting to blow his nose; Sophie reading with serious intensity; and Michael, who was filled with the confidence of an earl already.

What if what she learned implicated the duke and his sister? What would she do?

Taking a deep breath, she lifted the letter back up. She prayed they were innocent and that was why they were kept in an unlocked writing desk. Exactly the opposite of what she should want.

This is for king and country, she thought, and she read the beginning of the letter. Lady Winterhaven did not, as most women did, believe in subtle or gentle openings to her letters. Certainly not with her brother. It appeared she'd plunged right in.

> *I am concerned about Maryanne and I am at*
> *the end of the rope over what to do. The poor*
> *child is consumed with guilt. She is tormented by*
> *fear and she cannot put those horrible events of*
> *the past behind her. You have told me how*
> *admirable you find me because you believe I have*

forgotten, that I have found happiness. Yes, I have found joy, but I will never forget.

There is a way, even when haunted by those terrifying memories, to find happiness. I believe it is love. I believe it would save you. I know it would help Maryanne. She is nineteen now, and she could marry, but while you are strong enough to find love if you want it (you simply choose not to do it), she is too frightened to even try. We must help her. We are both to blame for this. It is up to us to make amends for the damage we did by giving Maryanne her future.

There was one more paragraph: a promise that Lady Winterhaven would craft a list of eligible ladies for Greybrooke.

Two thoughts whirled in Helena's head. What was this frightening thing that Greybrooke and his sister were responsible for? This thing that haunted them all and scared Maryanne so terribly? From what did the duke need to be saved? Could it be treason?

The other thought? Lady Winterhaven was acting as matchmaker to Greybrooke.

Why did that thought even matter? Why did it nag so much, pushing the far more important question away?

Helena hurriedly folded the letter and put it back. Why did he have a desk filled with dockets, yet he used only one of them? Tentatively she eased open the drawers, one by one, and felt around in each well of darkness. In the bottom drawer, her fingers struck a leather cover. She drew the book out.

It was a journal.

Footsteps—she was certain she heard soft footfalls echo on the polished wood floor of the hall. Nerves exploded. She couldn't walk out in front of him with his journal. She put the book back in the drawer, closed it, then she ran to the door—

Bluish moonlight fell in square patterns on the white door in front of her.

The drapes! She whirled, ran back, and pulled the curtain across the window. She fumbled through the dark to the doorway.

There was no one there. No doubt her guilty imagination had supplied the footsteps, but it didn't matter. She had been "in the retiring room" long enough. She had to go back to the duke.

Moments later she stood at the door that connected the dressing room to the duke's bedroom.

Greybrooke had removed his coat. She was looking at him in his shirtsleeves—shirtsleeves that bulged over the muscles of his arms.

He'd undone his cravat, the trailing ends lying against his broad chest. His shirt collar lay open. There was bronzed skin in there, a small vee of it, yet it was like a toy to a child—she couldn't draw her gaze away from that glimpse of tanned skin.

His throat was beautiful. No wonder gentlemen wore high collars, cinched into place with their complexly tied cravats.

She wanted to stroke the duke's neck. After kissing him, she wanted to touch her lips to that skin—bronzed, dark with a light coating of stubble.

Madness!

"Come," he said. "I will take you home. You will meet me two nights from tonight?"

Helena was not sure if it was a question or a command. He really must take her home now. Before she lost all control and surged forward and really did try to kiss his throat. "Yes," she said.

"Good." His voice was a throaty growl. She felt it as if her skin was attuned to sound. She felt it all over. "I want to show you my world, Miss Winsome."

7

"Couldn't you sleep, Miss Winsome?"

Helena bit back a small scream. She spun around, her hands on her hood, to face Lady Winterhaven. She'd intended to slip out in the night, make her way to Hyde Park—dangerous for a female to do alone, but she needed to know why Greybrooke was being blackmailed.

"No, my lady. I thought I would walk for a bit in the back garden, until I grew tired," she lied, hating having to do so yet doing it with calm competence.

She'd showed no competence today with the children. She had spilled milk on the plate of biscuits. She had read one sentence of a book over five times, utterly forgetting she'd said it at all. She had tried to dress Michael in Timothy's coat and had dazedly wondered how he'd grown so quickly.

Her head had been full of Greybrooke.

Lady Winterhaven suddenly stumbled, putting her hand to the wall for support. Helena caught her arm. "Let me help you up to bed, my lady." Then she blinked. Lady Winterhaven was not in her nightclothes, yet it was well after midnight. "You should be resting—"

"Oh, I am like you, Miss Winsome. I cannot sleep either. I've ordered tea to be brought to my parlor upstairs. Would you join me for a cup?"

Helena was startled. And anxious, for she must get to Hyde Park. But she nodded. And minutes later she held a cup of steaming tea in her hand.

Lady Winterhaven sipped, then gave a gusty sigh. "Do you have any idea how many eligible dukes there are, Miss Winsome?"

The very word "dukes" made her lips tingle, as if Greybrooke had materialized out of thin air to masterfully kiss her. She couldn't help it—she relived every wicked moment. The soft, firm tease of his lips on hers. His tongue! He'd slipped his tongue between her lips, coaxing her mouth to open. They'd kissed so very, very intimately. . . . A blush heated her face.

She prayed her ladyship would never guess the reason for her red cheeks. She took a quick breath and stuttered, "S-several. I've read Lady X's columns about the Wicked Dukes."

Lady Winterhaven rolled her eyes. "Yes, that woman certainly does enjoy making sport of England's latest miracle: several eligible dukes who possess fortunes, charm, and brilliant looks. And who are all at ages where they should be seeking brides. I am sure all the other dukes will wed first, but I pray there will be some eligible girl left over for my brother."

Helena's eyes almost fell out of her head. "I've heard the Duke of Greybrooke requires a cane just to beat a path through admiring ladies."

"But he keeps saying no. Eventually, most women give up. They do have to get settled. And Greybrooke is the most unsettling gentleman I know."

How very true that was. Helena was a jumble of heat, nerves, and worried for him. But she was astonished that Lady Winterhaven was discussing this with her. It showed how anxious her ladyship must be.

Then Lady Winterhaven waved her hand. "No, I'm wrong. He's not unsettling, he's infuriating. He is such a good man, but he does not see it. When Maryanne was so terribly ill—the illness that stole her sight—Grey never left her side. He barely slept or ate. He watched over her, bathed her with cool water, fed her broth. He became terribly sick himself and almost died. But he only gave in to his illness when he was certain she was getting better."

"I—I didn't know," Helena whispered.

"Marriage would be the making of him, Miss Winsome. But he's too scared to face that. He's like every gentleman I know—deathly afraid of change. We females survive on shifting sands every day. Men have no idea how to cope."

"Shifting sands?" Why would a countess feel she spent her life in instability? Was her ladyship speaking of treason—that would mean a lifetime of fear, wouldn't it?

Lady Winterhaven had always looked so happy. Yet now there were shadows in her eyes, lines where her mouth was taut and her forehead crunched. As if making a great effort, her ladyship forced a bewitching smile. "I am just being maudlin. I am sure I'll convince my brother to marry, somehow."

"I am sure you will, my lady." But her heart gave a painful pang at the thought of Greybrooke with a lovely, gently bred fiancée. Heavens, what was wrong with her?

"It will have to be a devious plan. He was supposed to attend a musicale with me last night, and he cried off at the last minute—" Lady Winterhaven broke off. Peered at Helena closely. "This is the third time you have blushed while I've been discussing my brother." Her brow rose. "He is not doing anything naughty, is he?"

"No. No, of course not," Helena cried.

"Good. He has never been the type to seduce governesses, but sometimes I worry about him. Even though he is a true gentleman, sometimes he wants to do the most dangerous things." Her ladyship yawned. "I think I will go to bed. Do you wish to walk still, Miss Winsome?"

"Just for a while," she lied. She remembered what he'd said, in the children's nursery, no less. *Sinful, dastardly, unforgivable as it is—I have to have you.* Yet according to Lady Winterhaven, he did not pursue women like her. Greybrooke tied her in knots. She had thought him a simple rake. He was far more complex.

She couldn't help it. She hoped, prayed, yearned he was innocent. She must be impartial, but how could she be?

"I am confident I will get my brother married off," Lady Winterhaven was saying. "But it will have to be a plan worthy of Wellington."

At the reference to war plans, Helena went pale. Lady Winterhaven said the words as a joke. Was that a clue she knew nothing about treason?

"Good night, Miss Winsome."

Helena's thoughts went to the duke as she curtsied to her ladyship.

Greybrooke did not want to kiss. He did not "make love" but had a special club where he went and did wicked things. Was that why he was so determined to not marry?

Cool night air enveloped her, and Helena began her walk toward the door in the rear stone wall as a casual stroll, as if she had no other plan than to enjoy the black velvet of the sky, the whisper of the breeze, the lingering fragrance of a spring garden. A few yards from the house, she lifted her hems and ran. She must get to Hyde Park and watch Greybrooke.

But as she neared the gate, a soft sound stopped her.

Sobs—soft sobs floated through the dark. Her first instinct was to ask who was there, but almost at once she knew how pointless that was. She followed the sound to the corner of the walled-in back garden. A pale statue gleamed in the moonlight, but it was the dark figure in front of the statue who was crying.

"Lady Maryanne?"

Helena's foot bumped something hard. Lady Maryanne's stick, discarded on the ground. She bent and picked it up, then put her arm around the young woman. "Oh, my dear, what is it? Whatever is wrong?" She was certain she knew—the girl must be crying over her lost sight. When Helena first came, she was told that Maryanne used to do it almost all the time. Now, it was much less infrequent.

Lady Maryanne lifted her head. Her green eyes were huge, luminous, her blond hair loose and framing her beautiful, oval face. "Be quiet, Winnie! I don't want my sister to find me out here. As for what's wrong? I'm in love! That's the truth—the terrible, terrible truth." She wiped at her cheeks angrily.

"It can't be so terrible to be in love—"

"It is for me! I can't have him. Do you know what that is like, Miss Winsome? To love someone desperately—to have found one's true love, your only love—yet you can't have him."

Helena's heart twisted. She had hoped Maryanne would find love. She knew it would be the best for the girl. She had feared it would bring heartbreak, but she'd hoped a gentleman would fall in love with Maryanne's breathtaking beauty. "Does he love you in return? If so, nothing should matter—"

"*Everything* matters!" the girl gasped. "Oh, it's not because I'm blind. That's what you think, isn't it? That's what everyone thinks—that no one would have me because I'm blind. But this man doesn't care about that. It's not even because Uncle Grey would never, never allow it. That's not why it hurts so much. It's because I don't want to keep secrets from him. I don't want to lie to him. But if he knew the truth . . . if he knew about what happened . . . Oh God, I would lose his love forever."

Helena hated to do this, hated to take advantage of Maryanne's pain and vulnerability. But she must do it—for her family's sake. "What truth, Maryanne? Is it something that your uncle did? Is it something terrible that Greybrooke did?"

"I can't speak of it. I promised I would never speak of it. I kept my word and I lost my sight." Maryanne laughed—a twisted, choking laugh.

No, she must stop now and calm Maryanne. "I won't ask you anything more. I'm sorry. But I don't believe your love is impossible. Have faith and hope, Lady Maryanne—" She stepped forward, to hug the girl, to use touch to soothe her.

But Maryanne fled. Hands out, she stumbled toward the house. Fearing the girl would fall, Helena ran after her and caught up. "Let me help you to bed," she said firmly.

It was only later, when she had Lady Maryanne safely in bed, when she'd solemnly promised she would say nothing of finding the girl crying outside, that she knew it was too late to go to Hyde Park.

"What are you planning to do, Grey? Shoot him?"

Grey frowned at Caradon, who walked at his side along the Rotten Row, into the shadowy expanse of Hyde Park. He carried two pistols in the deep pockets of his greatcoat, and they bumped heavily against his legs. In his boot was a secreted blade. "Unfortunately I can't," he growled. He explained the blackmailer's threat. "If I kill him, his knowledge will be published in the newssheets. However, if I can make him believe I'm angry enough to shoot him anyway, I may get the upper hand."

"Where's the meeting to take place?"

"Just beyond the trees, near the Grosvenor Gate. Keep to the shadows. I want you to hide when we get close. I'm supposed to arrive alone."

They approached the spot, which was deserted. Moonlight fell on the ground between long shadows cast by the trees. A wind flicked their coats around them. Caradon let out a breath. "So where the hell is he?" he asked softly.

"Not here yet. We're early. Take a position behind the trees over there," Grey directed. Then he went to the arranged meeting spot and stood with arms crossed over his chest. After a while, he began pacing. He was certain the blackmailer would show. He had the two thousand pounds, and the man had appeared smugly confident. But while he waited, his thoughts went back to the moment last night where he'd drawn Miss Winsome into his kiss. He didn't kiss. Ironically, in sex, he liked to keep his distance.

She'd kissed with such innocence, but she had parted her lips to take his tongue into her warm mouth. She'd touched her tongue to his. Every sensual move he'd made to pleasure her, to devour her lush mouth, she had countered.

Kissing her had been sizzling and had given him an agonizing erection. But he'd been cautious through it. Careful. He knew the danger of letting his guard down, of giving in to a woman's touch. He wanted her, but on his terms. Her eager kiss had been a sensual treat, making him think of lush, hot, sweaty sex. But he couldn't let himself be vulnerable with her. Not in any way—

Something moved in the shadows. He had to stop thinking about Miss Winsome. Grey eased his right hand toward his pocket, curling his fingers around the pistol grip. "Show yourself."

Moonlight fell on a stooped figure that shuffled out from behind the trees. The bluish light revealed a lined face and glinted on silvery hair. The elderly man moved slowly, limping on his right leg. "Are ye the Duke of Greybrooke?" he croaked. The voice was weak, raspy, as if the man spoke through a lungful of smoke.

"I am. Who are you?"

"Messenger for the man ye were to meet tonight. I were told to pick up what ye've got and take it to 'im."

Hades, he'd been tricked. His pistols were useless—he had no intention of shooting a lackey. Unless this man was more than that. "Give me your name."

"Don't see as 'ow ye need to know it, Yer Grace."

"Are you this man's accomplice?" At the blank look, he clarified, "His partner."

"I were paid just to be messenger."

"Do you know the man who paid you?"

"Never seen 'im before. In fact, I never saw 'im. 'E met me outside me favorite tavern and 'e wore a cloak and a mask."

"All right, I'll make you an offer," Grey said. "You help me in this and I will help you."

" 'Ow would ye do that?"

"Payment. I could give you enough money to live comfortably. Perhaps you have family to take care of."

"I do, and they will be taken care of, Yer Grace. If I don't do as I've been told, it'll be me daughter and her brand-new babby who'll be 'urt. Please, Yer Grace, just give me the message I'm to get, and let me be on me way."

"This man threatened your family."

The elderly man had blanched white. "Aye. 'E knew me name and told me 'e knows where me daughter and her new babby live. If I don't 'elp 'im, the fiend will 'urt them. Kill them."

A crunching sound came from behind the thick trunk of an oak.

The old man looked terrified. Then glared angrily at Grey. "Ye were supposed to be alone, Yer Grace."

Caradon appeared from behind the tree. "He did come alone. I took it upon myself to follow my friend. Now, enough of your tales. Tell us the name of the man who hired you. I believe you recognized him—you wouldn't be so afraid of his threats if you didn't know who he was."

"The man's frightened, Cary," Grey growled. To the elderly man, he softened his tones. "I understand you've been forced into this. I give you one more opportunity to give me your name. I can help you, your daughter, and her child. This I promise you. I will give no sign you've helped me—you will be allowed to leave here unobstructed, and I will not interfere with your meeting with this man. But give me your name and I will help you."

The man hesitated. Grey had to admire him for wanting to protect his daughter and her babe. A tenderhearted parent would have been a foreign thing for him, if he'd never seen Jacinta and her husband with their children.

"You'll let him walk out of here with two thousand pounds," Cary spluttered quietly.

"I will." He turned again to the old man. "I can provide handsomely for your daughter and your grandchild. I can ensure their safety and their futures."

The man finally nodded. "I trust ye, Yer Grace. I go by the name of Orley."

"You can leave here tonight and finish your errand. I will meet you tomorrow."

"Aye, Yer Grace. I can be found in the Old Nichol."

Grey knew the place. Orley meant the Old Nichol Rookery, between Shoreditch in the north and the silk weaving industry of Spitalfields in the south. He gave the old man the package he was to deliver to the blackmailer. "Then go. I'll find you tomorrow," he promised.

Caradon glared as Orley hobbled off, moving slowly over the sand of the Rotten Row. "Aren't we at least going to follow him?"

Grey watched the old man reach the Grosvenor Gate, then limp along Park Lane. "No, he might be being watched by the blackmailer. I can't take that chance."

"You do realize that tale of his was probably a pack of horse dung and you just let him walk out of here with a couple of thousand pounds. The sight of your pistols might have had him spouting the truth."

"I think it was the truth," Grey said thoughtfully. "Though I have to wonder about a villain who sends an old man, essentially a stranger, to collect two thousand pounds."

Caradon frowned. "What are you being blackmailed over, Grey? You didn't tell me."

"I'm not the victim. I'm doing this to help a lady." Grey began walking toward the gate, boot soles sinking into the grass.

Cary fell in stride with him. "A lady? Dear God, you don't mean Jacinta, do you?" Cary's face rarely showed pain, but it was stark now. "I would lay down my life for her. I lost her to Winterhaven, but I've never gotten over her."

"It's not my sister."

"What other woman would you do it for?"

"Unfortunately that is something I can't tell you, Cary."

"Once you've found this Orley tomorrow, how are you going to find the blackmailer?"

"That I don't yet know," Grey admitted.

"Should we hunt together tomorrow night?"

"Not at night—tomorrow night I have an arrangement. I'm escorting an innocent into the world of whips, ropes, and riding crops."

Cary stared at him as if he were insane. "Not your governess?"

"Yes, as sinful as it is, I intend to introduce the pretty governess to my dark world."

"Grey, you should not do this."

"Afraid I'm behaving like my demon of a father? Maybe I am like him after all. I can't seem to resist her, even if it means corrupting her into darkness."

The house stood at the end of a row of gleaming, new white townhouses in a respectable street on the fringe of Mayfair. Elegant carriages stood along the curb. Gentleman moved through the discreet darkness—the street flare here was not lit—swarming to the house like bees to the hive. Through the carriage window, Helena watched these peers of the realm stride up to the door and disappear inside. Greybrooke sat at her side, his presence truly filling the carriage. He didn't touch her, but his long legs stretched out, his arm rested along the back of the velvet seat. Her quick breaths took in his sensual scent.

"What is this place? A b-brothel?" The word came out shakily.

"A private club." In Greybrooke's deep voice, the words sounded sinful.

The carriage stopped. "Come," he said simply. He handed her down, and in mere moments they were admitted to the inside of the club—the place in which things happened that he wanted her to do but that he would not describe.

He had spoken little since he had let her into his carriage at the end of the mews. For most of the journey, he'd stared out of his window, his eyes troubled, his hand stroking his jaw. It didn't reassure her that he looked as if he were about to face hell.

Finally she'd said, "Your Grace, you look as if you are about to face an executioner."

"It's not about you, tonight, or us, my dear. There was a man I had promised to protect and I was unable to do so. I found him in his rooms this morning, badly beaten and almost dead."

She'd gasped. "But why?"

"That is my private affair. But it represents a failure on my part. A misjudgment. My mistake almost cost a man his life. I do not like it when that happens."

He had spoken so strangely. Distantly, even though he was obviously deeply troubled. Was this related to treason? "But how could you have protected him? Who attacked him?"

"I don't know who did it. But I knew he was in danger and I did not take the right steps. Thus I am to blame."

Goodness, could a man who felt such regret have committed treason? "I should think the blame should be attached to the man who hurt him! Perhaps we shouldn't go tonight—"

"No, this gives me more reason to go," he'd said. "I don't

want to be left alone with my thoughts tonight. Imagining the look in your eyes tonight is giving me something to look forward to."

She'd gulped.

Now they stood inside the foyer, which had walls of crimson silk and patterned lamps that gave an eastern, exotic look.

"The décor is hell," he said casually. "But the sex in here will astound you."

Astound? Helena wasn't certain that was quite the word.

His hands came toward her. She pulled back by instinct— then cursed herself. This was it. Whatever he wanted to do, she must let him. But his fingers captured the sides of the black mask she wore, and he adjusted it over her face until he nodded with satisfaction.

For her introduction to this place, Greybrooke had sent her a package discreetly by one of his footmen. It had contained a slender dress of crimson velvet and a mask of papier-mâché painted black and dusted with gold. Actual gold, that glimmered in the light.

"The black is sensual and exotic against your golden curls," he mused. "It emphasizes how beautiful, full, and tempting your mouth is. There is only one thing missing."

From his pocket he drew a black velvet ribbon, then lifted it and let it stroke across her lower lip. Fireworks shot through her once more, making her gasp. Then a large, cool stone bumped her mouth. The ribbon was actually a choker of black velvet from which one ice-white stone dangled.

Greybrooke drew it around her neck, the velvet tickling her, and he fastened it at her nape. A tiny chain dangled from the clasp, teasing the skin of her neck.

"This is not a diamond," she gasped. "Not a real one. It can't be. It's too large."

"I am a duke," he murmured.

"I cannot accept a gift like this."

"It's part of your disguise, Miss Winsome. No one will believe you are my mistress unless you wear jewels, and they will wonder why I've brought you otherwise. Questions would be asked. The *ton* will be like a hound on a scent to learn your identity. And I do not want to cause scandal for Jacinta."

"I know. I don't want to be a part of a scandal either," she whispered.

A strange sound floated down the corridor. Goodness, it was a moan of agony. She blinked. "Is someone in pain?"

"It is quite likely."

She gaped at his profile.

"What?" Green eyes twinkling, he faced her.

"Why in heaven's name do you come to a place like this? Why do you want to do such odd things if they hurt?"

"The truth?"

"I guess I would like to know the truth."

"The truth is that I don't know. This is what I like, what I enjoy. In here, this is sex at its most addictive. Gentlemen like me are taught to be noble and proper for our whole lives, to watch our language around females, curtail our drinking, control our gambling. A certain amount of vice is acceptable, but only if we stay true to our two vows—noblesse oblige or our unwritten promise to never crack our sangfroid. A place like this, unfettered and raw, where you break rules, where sex is a knife's edge between pleasure and pain, has its appeal."

The duke stopped in front of a set of double doors and opened one. "This is one of the voyeurs' rooms. One intended for group play." Crooking his finger, he coaxed her to look.

A woman had her hands tied to a bar suspended by two ropes. She was naked, but Helena couldn't see much of her figure since she was sandwiched tight between two naked men.

Helena could see the backside of one man. He had raven black hair, like Greybrooke. His buttocks were hard, his haunches sucked tightly in, his legs shaped of muscle—

She was looking at a stranger's bottom!

The other man stood behind the naked female. He was blond, with a graceful build, like a Greek athlete, but all she could see was his bare arm, with bulging biceps, and his power-ful leg. The raven-haired man was built like a laborer, with an enormous back formed of solid muscle, a small waist. His nar-row, tight buttocks looked as if they were made out of rock. He appeared to be pumping his hips forward, his hips slapping against the woman, squashing her rather large breasts. . . .

Suddenly Helena knew what she was looking at, and she turned so abruptly she slammed into the duke's chest. She shut her eyes tight. "I can't watch them. It's private."

"It's not, my dear. There are peepholes on the far wall. Many men are watching them. They are performers, putting on a show to arouse the members of the club."

"It is a show?"

"Gentlemen pay an extravagant annual subscription to be a member of this club, which caters to the *ton*'s darkest desires."

"If it is a performance then they aren't really . . . I mean not in front of people . . ."

"Both men are penetrating deep inside her. She's stuffed full, with two large cocks. They are separated by only the thinnest wall of flesh. All three enjoy being watched—it adds to the pleasure for them. She moans louder, they thrust harder to de-light their audience. There's no need to be shocked."

"There is *every* need to be shocked."

His hand skimmed her neck. Somehow he knew exactly where to touch her to make her shiver all the way down to her slippers. "Not yet. There's more I wish you to see."

"Is this the sort of thing you do? You don't want to share me, do you?"

"No." His eyes twinkled. "I would want to keep you for myself."

She let him lead her, though her legs wobbled like jelly. With her hand in the crook of his arm, she stepped into another room. Into another world.

Candlelight glowed, throwing a soft golden light over stunning things. It shimmered on a black satin blindfold that covered a woman's eyes. Black ropes were wound about her wrists, keeping them behind her, and she was on her knees with her ankles bound.

Behind the woman, a tall gentleman in exquisite clothes, looking like Beau Brummel, lifted a whip. He gave a soft flick of the lash. It landed lightly on the woman's rounded bottom.

The woman moaned, the sound low and throaty and sensual.

The man drew the whip back, catching the lash in his hand. Waiting.

The woman squirmed in anticipation.

The whip snapped again, but still lightly.

"How can she do this?" Helena gasped. "Doesn't it hurt?"

Greybrooke moved close to her and murmured, "He begins slowly. That builds the erotic excitement and the ability to endure more."

"But why?"

"It is about an edge. The knife's edge of pleasure. Sex for many is . . . complicated."

Complicated! Surely that was an understatement. She touched his arm. "But how can she enjoy pain?"

"Some people need it. It is the only thing that satisfies them. And pain can be controlled. Modulated in how it is bestowed."

She met his dazzling green eyes. Her lungs felt too tight to draw breath, and her stays seemed to be squeezing her heart. "You laugh with your niece and nephews and you are a loving brother! How can this darkness lure you to it?"

He frowned. "It's not darkness, angel, it is pleasure. Look at them. Do you think they are thinking about anything else right now? I doubt it. This world makes me forget the past. I like to immerse myself in sexual games. Tie women with silk scarves or velvet ropes. Blindfold a woman so all she can focus on is what she feels and the way I touch her, caress her, or even spank her. I come here to commit all my attention to erotic scenes that give extreme ecstasy. I don't bestow pain, but I might coax a woman to feel carnal agony."

Her heart beat so hard. She wanted to take a knife and slice through the lacing of her stays, for they were far too tight. "But why can't you forget without doing such wicked things?"

He shrugged. "This is far more fun."

"But what is it that you want to forget? What have you done?"

"That I can't say, my dear. You have to take me as I am if you are to become my mistress."

Suddenly the woman let out a keening wail. Her head arched back, loose blond hair spilling. Her lover was pinching her nipples, and the woman writhed against the ropes that held her fast.

"She's coming," Greybrooke murmured, and she tensed at his husky, sensual tone.

The woman cried out, "Oh God. Oh, my lord. Oh yes, yes, yes!" Her cries were desperate and fierce, then they dissolved into sobs. Helena's heart skipped a beat . . . until she saw the look on the woman's face. Pure bliss.

"She—she enjoyed that," she whispered.

"It gave her a remarkable orgasm," Greybrooke said.

Remarkable? Another understatement, indeed. What had it truly felt like? It had seemed to take the woman to the limits of endurance. Yet, as her lover untied her, she glowed in delight.

Helena floundered. The woman had just enjoyed intense pleasure but this seemed . . . dark. She hated to think of Greybrooke being dark. Surely it must be wrong that he preferred these games to gentle intimacy. "I can teach and change children, Your Grace. You said you are not capable of love. You must be. You immerse yourself in vices and in darkness. Well, I believe I can change you."

An amused smile touched his lips. "Do you?"

"Yes, I do."

"You are wrong, angel. But you've seen enough. I will take you home—"

"Could you take me to *your* home?"

His eyes narrowed. "Why, Miss Winsome?"

She wanted to find a way to have another look for a journal and letters. But there was more. . . .

He might claim these things brought him pleasure, but she didn't believe it. "I want you to kiss me again," she said softly.

"So you still intend to be my mistress? I won't change, you know. I have no desire to be different. This is the kind of sex I most enjoy."

"I—I'm willing to gamble, Your Grace."

For a long time, he just watched her with brooding green eyes. She assumed he would refuse to see her again. She had pushed too far, and she had lost.

"Not tonight," he said finally. "The hour is late, and I do not want you to be caught by my sister. Tomorrow night you can try to change me. But if you want to be my mistress, you have to play my games first. We'll try them slowly, gently, and discover if I can change *you.*"

Then he bent, slanted his mouth over hers . . . and kissed her.

8

Grey's carriage rolled past a row of modest, newly built townhouses. Caradon looked out the window, his blond brows lifting in surprise. "Are we visiting your mistress?"

Grey shook his head. "I gave my word to Orley I would protect his daughter and his grandchild. I failed to keep the old man safe from harm, but I will not fail on the promise I've made toward his family. I've moved his daughter and the child into one of these houses, where she is now under my protection."

"Grey, it is not your fault that her father was attacked. You couldn't have foreseen that the blackmailer intended to dispose of the man."

He knew Cary meant to ease his guilt. Cary had been through his own hell, yet he was a good man, a loyal friend who was always concerned for others.

"I should have realized why the fiend chose Orley," Grey said. "He needed a man who would be tempted by a small amount of money, who could be easily intimidated, and who was too weak to fight back when the time came to dispatch him."

"Until this, you haven't known exactly what sort of black-guard you've been dealing with."

Grey inclined his head. "True. Now I do." Cary was fighting to talk reason into him. But he refused to be absolved of guilt.

People who tried to change him were wasting their time. People like pretty, stubborn, determined Miss Winsome.

She was not the kind of mistress he wanted. She challenged him too much. He should let her go and find a more compliant woman. What did it say about him that the challenge of her fascinated him?

Cary was correct: It said something that frightened Grey.

Maybe Cary saw something in his expression, because his friend leaned forward. "You can't continue to pay a black-mailer, not one who is also a murderer. The fiend has to be stopped."

"I know he has to be stopped, damn it. If I were his victim, he would already be dead, I assure you."

"If you tell me who the victim is, perhaps I can help you." Cary's expression changed. A deep hurt showed in his pale blue eyes. "Do you not trust me with the confidence, Grey?"

"You kept secrets while tortured, Cary. I would trust you with my life." It wasn't his secret to share, but Caradon had been a friend since he'd been at school. He'd never had any reason to doubt Cary's loyalty, discretion, or friendship. Cary knew something of his secrets—about the beatings, the punishments. Not everything, but enough.

"He's blackmailing Caroline," Grey said softly.

Cary's brows lifted. "Caroline? Lady Blackbriar? What hold does he have on her?"

"Caroline is enceinte, Cary. But the baby is not Black-briar's."

"Yours?"

"God, no. I would never have an affair with Caroline. I care for her too much, and my tastes are too extreme for her. Besides, she embarked on this affair in search of love, and she knows I could never give that to her. I've helped her keep the secret. She's been extremely discreet."

"Then how in God's name did this blackmailer learn that baby is not her husband's?"

"I don't know," Grey admitted, "but I've tried to find out. It had to be someone with intimate knowledge, and Caro swears she's told no one but me. Blackbriar has her so terrified, she's careful with her secrets." A crippling jolt of guilt hit him. "I wish I could get her out of there," he growled, more to himself than his friend, "away from damned Blackbriar."

"His reputation as a gentle scholar hides a cruel man," Cary said. "But what more can you do to help Caroline? You offered to take her away, to leave your estates and live on the Continent, protecting her, and she refused."

He had been willing to live through the scandal to protect her—Caroline had always been a dear friend. Once he'd seen how brutal Blackbriar really was, he'd vowed to protect Caro.

Grey leaned back against the carriage seat. As a child, just before he was punished, he would feel his entire body grow tense, feel a flood of black rage and coldness come over his heart. He felt the same now.

"I should have removed her by force, whether she liked it or not," he said. "The problem with listening to women is that they too often talk you into doing the wrong thing. She's living in terror that Blackbriar will learn the baby is not his. She believes her husband would even be willing to kill the child in his anger. But she's in love with the baby's father, and she feels she would never see the gentleman again if she ran away with me."

"Why doesn't her lover help her?"

"He's married."

"Hell, what a snake pit of disaster." Cary shook his head.

"Don't judge her, Cary. She was desperate to know true intimacy with a man she loved. I can understand it."

"Can you? You've vowed you will never fall in love. You're not desperate to find it."

"Neither are you, my friend," Grey pointed out, to distract Cary.

The carriage creaked to a stop. "Enough of this," Grey said, getting to his feet. "It's not natural for gentlemen to talk this much."

Grey felt Cary watching him, uneasy, as he took a seat across from Orley's wary daughter in the parlor of the house he'd rented for her. A maid had shown them in. He had sent a small staff from his home to look after the house, including a few female servants and several footmen. He wanted men on the premises, there to provide protection.

The daughter's name was Sally Tate. She'd been married, but her husband was gone and she had no idea if the man were alive or dead. "I think 'e's probably gone to sea," she'd said. Her babe was still at the breast.

"Do yer want tea, Yer Grace?" she asked. Her hair was thick and brown, pulled back in a bun. Though pale and haggard, Sally possessed surprisingly pretty features.

"No, thank you." Grey glanced around. "The house is suiting you well?"

"It's . . . it's beautiful, Yer Grace. Thank ye." Even though she was saying her thanks, she didn't look grateful. Wary was the best word for her. She looked like a kicked dog that distrusted a human's kindness and was ready to bite or run.

Finally words burst out of her. "I still don't understand why ye're doing this for the babby and me."

"I needed your father's help in a matter, and he was worried for your safety." He had explained it all before, when he'd found the woman and her child.

"Mrs. Sims—that was the woman who lived next door to me—she was telling everyone that a gentleman only gets a 'ouse for a woman when she's to be his ladybird. I'm a respectable woman, Yer Grace, even if I don't 'ave much."

Grey cleared his throat. "I assure you I have no evil designs on your person, Mrs. Tate." Out of the corner of his eye, he saw Cary smother a laugh at his choice of words. He felt awkward. "I hope that by keeping you and your child safe, I can convince your father to help me. For that, I believe I will need your assistance."

"But what 'appens to us after that?"

"I intend to help you and your father as payment," Grey explained. He outlined his plan. He intended to put a sum in an account for them in the modest four percents. It would draw a small income that would allow them to improve their lot. "If you were to wish to open a shop, or something of that nature, you come to me, and I will take care of it for you."

Sally looked dazzled. The wariness dropped away for a moment, then it returned. He was not insulted by her reaction. He knew a person who had been threatened and hurt didn't instantly lose fear, caution, and doubt. He knew a black past meant a bleak future—he knew you never left behind the hell you'd come through.

"Is me father going to survive?" she asked softly. "Ye never told me 'ow ye found 'im, or what 'ad 'appened."

For good reason. He couldn't forget stepping into Orley's room, surprised to almost trip over a pile of rags. Only to see it wasn't rags, but Orley's body. Blood had matted the hair and oozed into the shirt. Grey had dropped to his knees, covering his shins and boots with the sticky blood that had pooled on the rough floor. He felt for the pulse, expecting to find nothing.

But Orley was tougher than he'd expected. His fingertips had felt a faint heartbeat. He'd carried the man to his carriage, taken him at once to the London Hospital.

But as he'd suspected, when Orley finally regained consciousness two hours later, the man claimed he had no idea who attacked him. Someone had slipped in and coshed him.

"He will recover," was all Grey said to the man's daughter. "I will wait while you dress and I'll take you to the hospital so you can see him, Mrs. Tate. Please bring the child along. I know that will cheer him up and help give him the strength to get well."

As Mrs. Tate went to fetch her daughter, Grey said to Cary, "When I left Orley at the hospital, I gave the man an ultimatum. I told him I would find his daughter and her babe and ensure they are safe. Now he has to talk."

Cary gave him a wry smile. "He won't talk, Grey. And I know you won't have the heart to threaten him."

Grey frowned. But two hours later he discovered Cary was right, and as Cary had predicted he couldn't threaten a wounded man.

The Duke of Greybrooke leaned back in his chair, lifted his glass of brandy to his sensual mouth. "All right, Miss Winsome," he said, after he'd taken a drink, "tell me how you plan to change me."

Helena had no idea. It had been a bold statement to gain her way back into his house. To buy her time because she must become his mistress, but she didn't think she could *ever* do those shocking things she'd seen at his private club.

She truly believed Greybrooke must be changed. How could he say he was incapable of love? She wanted to find the man inside who was capable of caring and capable of laughter with the children. "If I were to be your mistress, I would want to, um . . . make love in ways that made you happy."

She simply could not believe that those things he liked to do were not wicked. They looked wicked. And naughty. Yes, he said he gave women intense pleasure that way, but . . .

Surely he should want to fall in love and not be naughty.

His eyes twinkled. "Having an orgasm makes me happy. As would watching you have an orgasm, especially if you were tied to a bed."

Her cheeks burned. "I don't know if your love affairs really do make you happy, Your Grace." She remembered passing her parents' bedroom when she was young. She'd heard giggling and laughter through the door. "I know that happy people laugh in bed. No one laughed or smiled in that room."

"In some rooms they do. But you have me fascinated. Your goal is to make me laugh?"

He was making fun of her. Helena lifted her chin, refusing to be cowed. "Yes. I would want to do normal things happy, married people do."

He lifted a glass of brandy, took a long swallow. His action was slow and easy, but she felt his tension. He stroked his chin thoughtfully. "But what if I have no desire to do normal things?"

"You must do! You kissed me and you said it was nice."

"Nice." He smiled. "You do not give yourself enough credit, Miss Winsome."

"I thought we could kiss again. And then do . . . I don't know what happens next."

He shook his head. "You are so sweet I should send you home at once. But I can't. So what would you like me to do after the kiss?"

What would allow her to slip back to his writing desk, where she could look at his journal?

"I don't know. I'm not sure I'm ready to—to lose my innocence."

"I know what I would like to do, my dear. I would like to watch you come."

"Come where?" Then she remembered he had said "she's

coming" when the woman in the club had reached her point of pleasure.

His broad chest moved with a low, gruff laugh. "You are almost too sweet, angel."

"Well, I suppose I am not entirely sweet, for I have figured out what you mean. Anyway, when we kiss, could we do it in your bedroom?"

"To be honest, Miss Winsome, I hate that damned bedroom."

She hated having to try to manipulate him into it. But it was the only way she might have a chance to search. She faced the duke, trying to show only concern, not guilt, on her face. "I know it is because it is your father's room. Why do you despise him so much?"

"I do not want to talk about it. You can't heal me, change me, or teach me, love. But I do want to give you what you want. In return, I ask for one night where you give me what I want."

Was she making a bargain with the devil? Swallowing hard, she said, "When? When do you want that one night?"

"I will allow you to tell me, love."

Oh God. "All right, and I thank you for that, Greybrooke," she said in her firm governess tones. "Now, would you take me to your bedroom again?"

As she stepped into his bedroom, Helena took a longing look down the hallway toward his writing room. All she needed was that journal and this might be all over. She wouldn't even have to be his mistress. . . .

Why did she feel such regret at the thought?

A strip of white fabric flew over her head and fluttered to the ground in front of her. Greybrooke stood behind her, having closed the door, and she was facing his beautiful bed.

Slowly, she turned.

The white thing had been his cravat, and Greybrooke was now working on the buttons of his pale blue satin waistcoat.

"What are you doing?" No strong governess tones now. Her voice was a squeak.

"Undressing. I assume this is how happy married people normally have sex."

"But we aren't going to have—"

"Shh. I know, angel. Not yet. But I do intend to make you come, and just for you, I'm willing to take off my clothes to do it. I'll help you undress also. It won't be fun, lying on the bed in stays and that hellish gown."

The hellish gown was her very best one. Striped blue and gray muslin, with a scooped neckline and snow-white lace trim, and she had worn it rather than the crimson one he'd sent her. Having him dismiss her dress was a reminder of who she was.

She was a governess. He was a duke. A completely complex duke, though, with desires she couldn't even begin to understand.

Greybrooke undid his waistcoat and jerked his broad shoulders to pull it off. Covered in exquisite embroidery with buttons of black jet, it must have cost a fortune. He balled it up, then tossed it aside, and it landed in a heap on the floor.

His shirt clung to him, following the wide planes of his back down to the narrowness of his waist. He was . . . simply beautiful.

He jerked his shirt out of his trousers.

Her eyes bulged. "Are you going to take off all your clothes?"

Fire burned in the green depths of his eyes. "That was the idea. Just you and me together naked. Sweetly so. As you wanted."

He winked. Next thing she knew, he disappeared behind a screen in the corner of the room. His boots landed on the floor with two thuds. His trousers were tossed to rest over the top of

DEEPLY IN YOU / 119

the screen. A garment of white linen followed. Goodness, his *drawers*.

He stepped out, and dark blue silk filled her vision. He had put on a robe, but the silk moved, slid open, and she glimpsed the bronzed skin of his chest.

"You took everything off." She spoke on instinct, stunned by what she saw. Dark hair. Dark nipples. Tanned skin that looked solid as rock.

He was so handsome she was almost speared by his beauty, unable to breathe. A melting smile lit up his face. "You know, I've never taken off my clothes to make love. You are the first woman who will see me naked. If you want to see me that way."

He stepped closer until all she could see was rich indigo silk and tanned skin. Her breathing was ragged, and she felt, if she shut her eyes, her lashes would brush against his chest.

She glanced down. The stream of bronzed flesh seemed to go on forever. At least, it went on until she saw the defined ridge of his hip, and the dark curls of his—

She jerked her gaze upward. "I don't think I'm ready to have you . . . naked."

From above her, his voice flowed over her, smooth and deep. "Another kiss?"

"Yes, that is what I want." Something relatively safe.

He caught her hand, lifted her fingers to his mouth. Gently he pressed his mouth to her fingertips. It was heavenly, but what stole her breath was his gaze. Brilliantly green, his eyes glowed as if he were on fire inside.

His lips brushed kisses to her temple. He was supposed to be a rogue and a scoundrel, yet it was the sweetest thing.

He kissed at the corner of her eye, making her giggle. Then his lips trailed down the bridge of her nose, so affectionately it had her heart fluttering. Her mouth ached, waiting for the hot magic of his kiss.

Instead he scooped her into his arms and carried her to his

bed. Next thing she knew she was lying on it. Greybrooke's strong body was leaning over her, and he murmured, "Can I kiss you a little lower?"

"Lower?" Then daringly, she said, "I think so."

Holding her hand, he nestled his head in the crook of her neck and kissed her jaw. She quivered on the bed. It was gloriously sensitive, his stubble tickling her. Intoxicating and rich, his musky scent swirled around her.

He lifted his head for a moment. "You are a unique woman, Miss Winsome. I respect you, I would not dream of hurting you or doing anything of which you did not approve. It must be the governess in you. Taming me already."

Taming him? She didn't believe it.

He took something out of a pocket in his robe. Brilliant colored light played over her dress—firelight reflected by the bejeweled shackles. Before she could say a word, he snapped one bracelet around her right wrist. It was cool. He captured her other wrist in his hand. Waited.

"You can say no," he said.

Her heart was in her throat. But she was wet and aching between her legs. She whispered, "I won't say no. You can do it."

Just as in Hyde Park, he closed the shackles, binding her wrists together. Helena had to admit—there was something rather thrilling about this.

"Now, I'm going to make you come."

"Oh! Um . . . what will it feel like?"

"I don't know."

Surprise made her frown. "How could you not know?"

"I know what it feels like when I come, but I have no idea what it would feel like for a woman. I've often wondered if women have stronger, better climaxes, because it's such a rare treasure for them."

"What does it feel like for you?"

"Like running a mile, followed by having my heart squeezed tight, feeling as if my cock will burst, having a blinding light explode in my head, then blessed, agonizing pleasure."

"It sounds frightening."

"I suspect you think it sounds wonderful, Miss Winsome, and you want to have one."

"But I cannot have one. Not without ruin."

"I promise I can show you ecstasy without taking your innocence. It doesn't take intercourse to make you come, love. I want to be the one to make you scream in ecstasy for your very first time. Or have you made yourself come?"

She must be scarlet. "No, of course I haven't. That's wrong." Or was it? Compared to what happened at that club, it hardly seemed scandalous. Her hips twitched on the bed. She felt even hotter and achier than before. Then she asked, "Why do you want to?"

"That way, my dear, you'd never forget me."

Reaching behind her, he undid the fastenings at the back of her gown. He slid the arms down past her shoulders, and the snugness of the gown helped to imprison her arms.

She stiffened as he pushed up her skirts and his hand cupped her calf.

"Relax," he murmured. "I won't hurt you." With each word, his hand went higher. His fingers grazed her hip. She bit her lip, closed her eyes, then squeaked as his hand reached the vee between her thighs. His fingers stroked her nether curls.

She'd never been touched there—she only touched herself there with a washcloth when necessary. Yet it was the most remarkable thing. The ache in her belly became a pounding need. If he stopped right now, she'd grasp his wrist and pull him back.

"Look at me, love."

Helena opened her eyes. Her skirts were in a crumple at her stomach. She could see her thighs, her belly, her hips, and the vee of golden curls. Against skin that had never seen the sun, his long fingers were a copper color. As she watched, his fingers slid between her golden curls.

The Duke of Greybrooke was stroking her cunny.

She couldn't quite believe it.

He touched a place that sent pleasure streaking through her. She squealed.

That made him smile brilliantly. His finger rubbed softly against that place, and she almost curled into a ball, it was so intense. She batted his arm with her shackled hands. "Oh goodness," she begged.

"You like that, little one?"

"Yes. No. I think—I think you should stop."

"I don't think you really want me to stop. I never would have expected the formidable Miss Winsome would shirk from a new experience. You have courage. Let yourself enjoy this. What harm can it do?"

He pressed harder, in that secret mystifying place, and she screamed. She hadn't meant to. It just flew out. He grinned as though deeply pleased.

"All right," she gasped. "Do more."

His finger made delicious spirals, and she arched up on the bed. Her body began rocking against his hand. She wasn't doing it. Her body seemed to have taken control, and her wits no longer worked.

Laughing gently, the duke lowered the bodice of her shift, baring her breast. Lightly he blew, and the swift caress of air made her nipple grow hard.

His dark head bent, he captured her naked nipple in his mouth. And sucked.

She pushed against his shoulders, but he didn't stop. He sucked and sucked until pleasure was rushing down from her nipple and slamming into the delight shooting up from his stroking fingers. She panted. She moaned. Her hips arched, pressing her delicate, aching cunny harder against his hand. He obliged, rubbing faster. She clung to his shoulder with her bound hands, not caring that her fingers dug into his shoulder blades. Not caring that both her breasts were bared to him now—they'd popped out as he tugged on her neckline with his teeth.

He sucked from one nipple to the other. All the while his hand stroked and played. She lifted against him, racing to pleasure. At last she was going to know what this was like. For once she was a pupil, she was being taught.

His mouth drew on her right nipple, his fingers ruthlessly pinched the left, and his finger stroked so fast she feared she might burst into—

Aah!

Her muscles went mad, twitching and pulsing. Her wits shattered. She wailed. Oh God, it was—

Wonderful. Pleasure wrapped around her like sunlight, like warm sheets, like sin. Pleasure exploded inside her like streaking fireworks. She gasped "Oh God" over and over until her tongue tangled and all she could do was sob with sheer ecstasy.

Finally the pleasure ebbed away, leaving her limp and boneless.

"God, you are beautiful," he murmured huskily. "You look like an angel when you come."

"I couldn't. I must look a mess."

"You look like a well-pleasured lady."

She *was* a well-pleasured lady. She wanted to forget she must lie to him and search his journal, read his private thoughts. Forget she was supposed to capture this man. This was sexual pleasure and intimacy, and it was so intense and sweet she knew she needed more. Another few minutes of hot, damp bliss. Or an hour. Or a night.

He bent and put his lips to her nipple. For just one kiss, then he looked up, lifting his lips, leaving her on the verge of sobbing with desire. "Enough for tonight, Miss Winsome," he growled. "If you stay any longer, I *will* ruin you.

The duke got off the bed and his robe slid off his right shoulder. While he'd been pleasuring her, the belt of his robe had fallen open. He caught the robe before it slithered down his arm and pulled it up.

But Helena had seen his naked, muscular right shoulder. And the network of healed scars that crisscrossed his upper back.

9

Grey threw himself on his bed. His throbbing erection tented his robe, and he shoved the silk aside. A thread of silvery moisture dropped to his abdomen. Hard and aching, his poor cock couldn't understand why he'd let Miss Winsome go. He glared at it. "She wouldn't play with you even if she was here."

He had to be losing his mind, trying to carry on a conversation with his prick. God knew it never listened to him.

Watching Miss Winsome come while knowing he couldn't do more with her—not yet—had been definitely a knife's edge. This one closer to pain.

He could go to the House of Exotic Desires. Ruby would be more than willing to pleasure him, he was sure. This was London, he was a duke, and there were several thousand bizarre and intriguing ways he could get his satisfaction. He could go to his club and indulge in ropes, spankings, manacles, orgies. He needed the erotic anticipation of thinking up the scene, of slowly, deliberately, carefully taking his partner—and him—to that edge of pleasure.

He closed his eyes, picturing an erotic scene to entice him

while he jerked on his cock. But all he could think about was Miss Winsome, her eyes wide with shock as she came for the very first time. How sweet she'd been when she'd surrendered to pleasure.

When had he ever liked it sweet?

Not until now, damn it.

She was getting under his skin. She *was* changing him. But it was for nothing. He could never have "sweet." How could he deal with a sweet woman when he was filled with darkness? His darkness had nothing to do with his interest in bondage. His darkness was something else. He had fought for years to display it as cold indifference. It was really a hot, boiling pit of anger and distrust and pain.

He wrapped his hand around his shaft. Felt his cock swell beneath his grip. It wasn't accustomed to this. An encounter with his hand was the province of young boys, not of a grown man who shouldn't have any need for solitary sex.

But he needed a damned orgasm to blank out his brain. To make him forget.

Grey gave a hard, ruthless stroke. Fluid bubbled out the tip, soaking the taut head. He rubbed his palm over the crown, lubricating his hand. It didn't take long before the moisture disappeared and his strokes were rough, tugging the skin. More silvery juices came, making his cock slick.

He gripped his balls with his left hand, slid his right hand up and down his shaft. While his one hand pumped, he massaged his balls so they spilled over his hand. With lust driving him, he couldn't think.

He lifted his hips, thrusting his cock into his fist. Pumped faster. Gripped his balls more aggressively.

Then, he couldn't help it: He thought of Miss Winsome's pretty, flushed face as she surrendered to her first orgasm. She had been so deliciously adorable—

His muscles exploded, his orgasm burst like cannon fire. A brilliant white light shot through his head, blinding him to everything but raw, harsh pleasure, and a jet of white shot from his cock, spattering onto his hand.

Grey sank back, his breathing ragged. It hadn't meant anything that thinking of her sweet innocence in orgasm had made him explode. He had to have her on his terms. That way he would protect her from his darkness, by ensuring there was nothing between them but sex and pleasure.

Helena left the children playing on the grass in Berkeley Square and hurried over to Mr. Whitehall, who stood half-hidden by a laurel bush and motioned her to come to him.

"Well, have you read through the duke's journal yet?" Whitehall demanded. He was dressed as elegantly as a gentleman, his hands resting on his silver-tipped stick.

"No, I haven't had the chance." She glanced back at the children, afraid they would notice her absence. And, after Michael's near miss, she was determined to keep her eyes on them.

She wished she had not told Whitehall about the journal. All she could think of was the horrible scars on Greybrooke's back. How awful were his secrets?

"If I am to continue to protect your brother, I need something now." Whitehall snarled, his lips curling back from his teeth. He looked . . . sinister. "What of the girl, Lady Maryanne? You intimated that she knew something. She trusts you. It should be easy for you to coax her to confide. The girl is blind and half-witted—"

"That is not true," she broke in. Her voice shook with anger. "Lady Maryanne is blind, but she is normal and intelligent. But I will not take advantage of her trust."

"You are a damned fool," he snapped.

She turned, ready to stalk away, when Whitehall lurched forward and grabbed her wrist.

Helena stared at his clutching hand, horrified. She tried to wrench free, but he wouldn't let her go. "If you are going to grab me and force me to use a defenseless girl, this is finished—"

"It's finished when I say it is," he snarled. "I hold your family's futures in my hands. We believe Greybrooke was black-mailed into committing treason. It is your job to find out if that is true, and discover the secrets that the French agents held over him. My superiors require details. You will return to the duke and you will find out what secrets he has. This, might I remind you, is for your country and your king. And if rumors travel that your brother is on the verge of bankruptcy, those gaming hell owners will not take kindly to losing their money. You would not want your brother badly beaten, perhaps killed, if they use him to make an example to other debtors."

"Are you threatening Will?"

"You are an intelligent woman, Miss Winsome." Whitehall glared at her—with his pronounced cheekbones and deeply set eyes, he looked like a death's head. "I should think you know the answer to your question is yes."

She struggled to stay calm. "I will do what you want, Mr. Whitehall, but I will not hurt Lady Maryanne. I will get at the duke's journal tonight—no matter what I must do. But I warn you—do not ever approach me again when I am with the children."

With that, she took advantage of his surprise and wrenched her hand free. And stalked away.

It was her afternoon out. With the children safely with Nurse, Helena left Winterhaven House and hurried as fast as she could to her family's print shop on Fleet Street. She was out of breath as she opened the door and stepped inside. She had always loved the clatter of the press, the sharp smell of the ink, the bustle of activity as the men made the printing plates and assembled the pages.

It was so familiar. But she had irrevocably changed.

Last night, she'd discovered what pleasure truly was. She could never go back.

Now she knew—she was going to end up ruined.

Helena stopped and examined her cheeks in the window of the print shop to ensure they weren't bright red. She was about to talk to her brother after all.

She had been young when her mother married Arthur Rains, and she looked on him as a true father. William now used Father's office, a small room to the side of the entry. In there, Father had always been available to take in items of news, deal with his suppliers, trade cheerful witticisms with his competitors. Father had never been a cutthroat man of business. He'd been a happy man, and had spread happiness around him. He'd brought joy to Mother, he'd given them all wonderful childhoods; he had been surrounded by loyal and content workers. It was only after his death that they'd discovered Father had been kind but not careful, and he'd been losing money for years.

Helena pushed down her hood and hastened inside the office. Will sat at his desk. Like Father, he worked alongside his men in the print shop. Today his sleeves were rolled up, and his coat hung on a hook.

"Helena!" Will's eyes showed raw hope when he saw her. "Have you got the journal?"

She hated dashing his hope but had no choice. "It's not so simple," she admitted. "I have to find a way to get away from him long enough to read through it. I don't dare take it. If he discovered it's gone, he's going to know at once it was me."

Will groaned. "I see the problem."

"You aren't still going to gaming hells, are you?" She was sure he was not, because of what Greybrooke had done, but it would look suspicious if she didn't ask.

"None of them will let me through the doors."

She fought not to look triumphant. "That's for the best, isn't it?"

"Yes, it is. However, before you act too bossy, sister, might I remind you that you are late with Lady X's column."

Heavens. She'd forgotten about it entirely.

Will just laughed. "For once I've caught you out."

Seeing the old joy on his face made her smile in return. "I could try to write one."

"There's no need. Whitehall has a plan. He has decided to release information he has about the duke in Lady X's columns. He wants to corner Greybrooke."

"But we don't even know if the duke is guilty."

"Whitehall insists his information is correct. He believes it will force Greybrooke to make mistakes."

"We can't print things that might not be true."

"We have no choice," Will said, and she knew Whitehall must have threatened him. Will rubbed his hand over his chin, looking grave.

Heart in her throat, she asked, "Is there something else, Will?"

"Yes." He looked at the corner of the office, not at her. "It's something I must tell you, but I've been avoiding it."

The floor quaked under her feet. She winced. "Tell me, Will."

"Elise has received an offer of marriage."

Her sister had received a proposal and she did not even know? "Heavens, why wouldn't you tell me?"

"I've had to stall for time. There's the issue of a dowry. We don't have any money. I didn't want you to know because I didn't want to worry you. Or make you do something mad."

Will stood and hit the desk with his fist. "I will break into Greybrooke's house. You can help me—get in there and leave a window unlatched. I'll get the journal. That will give us what we need. We'll satisfy Whitehall, and then I'll be free of debt, and Elise can marry. Greybrooke would never suspect you then. You don't have to become his mistress. It's the perfect plan, and it means our troubles will be over."

But she didn't want to be spared from being his mistress.

Heavens, did she really just want an *excuse* to go to his bed? That was the madness. But it wasn't just that. . . .

"Will, you can't break into Greybrooke's house. You could be arrested. I can find a way to look at that journal. Tonight."

Will grimaced, but she said, "It's all right. I know what I am doing." Then she hugged him, and left, hurrying back toward Winterhaven House.

It was only when she was halfway home that she realized she hadn't even asked the name of her sister's suitor.

All she could think about was Greybrooke.

And she knew the only way she was going to be able to look at the journal was to spend the night. Greybrooke hadn't invited her to come to him. She was going to have to go— whether she had an invitation or not. No matter what the duke wanted to do with her. . . .

She must do it.

"Don't be a damned fool, Orley. You saw your daughter and her child yesterday. They are in a house I've rented and are perfectly safe. I've assigned several of my footmen to act as guards. I've stationed one in this hospital. You have nothing to fear, so tell me who this damned blackmailer is." Grey had refused to be beaten. He'd come back, despite Cary's conviction he would learn nothing.

Orley looked up at him, sorrow in his eyes. "What will 'appen after I've told you and after I get out of this 'ospital?"

"I will provide an income for you and your family." He outlined his plan.

"Why, Yer Grace? What is my daughter to you?"

"Some men spend their lives atoning for a wrong. There was a young woman I didn't protect. My penitence is to help others in need. You have my word as a gentleman that your daughter and grandchild will be protected until this blackmailer is arrested," Grey said. "I will extend that protection to you. Now, the name."

The frail old man clutched the blanket that covered him. "That's the trouble, Your Grace. I don't know who 'e is. It's no lie. He was masked when he met with me. Never gave me a name. You won't 'elp us now, will ye? Now that I can't 'elp you."

Sighing, Grey paced by the bed. "This does not change my promise, Orley. But there must be something you can tell me. Did he say anything that would give a clue? With me he spoke like a Cockney, but his accent sounded false."

"Aye, he sounded like a gent with me. A toff."

"Any idea where he came from?"

Orley frowned, and his lips worked as he thought. Finally, he gave a smile that showed a lack of teeth. "When he left me, he took a 'ackney. I was listening and I 'eard the address 'e gave. Twere on the Strand. Number fifteen."

Grey knew the address. "A brothel." It wasn't promising, but it was something.

His carriage hurtled out of the gates. Brooding by the window, Grey caught a fleeting glimpse of a figure in a hooded cloak hurrying down the sidewalk toward his house. The disguise was good, but he glimpsed a golden curl, and he knew from the determined way she moved exactly who it was.

He rapped hard on the ceiling, a summons for his coachman to stop at once. His footman opened the door, panting. Grey jumped down. He met Miss Winsome, who rushed toward him.

"What are you doing here? I didn't summon you tonight because I have business."

Enormous blue eyes gazed at him. Bewitching eyes.

"I'm sorry." She was breathless, and her tone was throaty, husky, and damned erotic. "I will return to the Winterhavens'. I came because I am ready. Ready to try your games. And once I'd made the decision, I wanted to carry it through."

He shook his head. Her timing was damned inconvenient, but he could imagine Miss Winsome doing exactly that.

If he had her wait for him in his house until he returned, she could change her mind and bolt. Now that she'd come to him on his terms, he had no intention of letting her go. "Come with me." He offered the crook of his arm.

She slid her hand there. "Where are you going?"

"A brothel," he said carelessly.

Her hand jerked free, her fists landed on her hips, and she glared at him under her hood. "A *what?* You're going to be unfaithful to me—?"

The hurt in her voice touched his heart. "No, my indignant governess, my business at the brothel has nothing to do with sex. I'm looking for someone."

"Who?"

"Someone who has wronged me."

"*Who* is it?"

"Enough questions. Into the carriage, Miss Winsome."

Black lace was wrapped around the woman's head like a blindfold, and she was bound hand-and-foot to a metal contraption. The whore twisted her head as a man in a black mask, dressed in the style of a century before, including satin breeches of silver and a frock coat of ice blue, strolled around her flicking a whip.

Grey found he was watching the couple without a spark of arousal. Directed to this room to find the madam, he'd brought Miss Winsome with him. Her eyes were huge and shocked.

"Do you want me to do *that?* Like Lady Montroy and the riding crop?"

Looking around for the madam, he answered, "I said I don't inflict pain. Ever. We would start by tying you up, my dear. I love to devise complex ways of tying a woman up so her movement teases her nipples and cunny, so her every wriggle brings her close to orgasm. But when it comes to crops or spanking, it would be what you want, what you wish to explore. And I would ensure you find it erotic, not painful."

She looked up at him, her face partly shielded by her hood. "I don't know about these scenes, these things. I liked what we did last night."

"I thought you were ready to agree to my terms."

"Could we compromise? Sometimes we will play your games, and sometime we will play mine?"

God, she fascinated him. No other woman had tried to negotiate sex with him. He didn't know what to answer. Deep inside, he wanted to give her what she wanted.

But making love to her the way she wanted—with intimacy, without ropes and crops and games to keep a barrier between them—would make her believe they had love, and he didn't want to build hopes he would only destroy.

Let her go, whispered the voice of logic in his head. *You will only hurt her.*

That startled him, but he saw it was true. He cared about her—

"You are mine, wench," the frock-coated man crowed. "Mine to punish as I see fit. Let me give you a taste."

Grey jerked his head up. He stared at the man's face. The black mask was a strip of leather molded over his nose, with narrow slits at the eyes. The man's chiseled jaw and full lips were revealed. The face meant nothing to him. But triumph and arrogance filled the voice. The man laughed as he gave a flick of the whip, and the lash struck the woman's large, pale rump—a smirking laugh that rose several octaves.

This man was the blackmailer.

Blind rage drove Grey. It would be so easy to grasp the smug, overconfident bastard by his scrawny neck and strangle the life out of him—

He'd taken a step forward without realizing it. The man jerked his head up at Grey's sudden movement. "Bloody hell," the blackguard spat. He turned on his heel and ran, pushing through the crowd of men and prostitutes filling the room.

Grey planted Helena against a wall. "Stay there. Do not move until I return for you."

He took off in pursuit. Chasing a villain through a bondage room proved interesting.

The bastard used his whip to make people scatter. Oddly, people who wanted to be tied up and whipped now retreated from the lash. But as they raced to-and-fro, they got in Grey's bloody way, and he had to push them over torture racks and whipping benches to clear his path.

He managed to fight his way out of the room to the corridor. Shoving back his hair, he peered in the gloom toward the back of the house.

Ice blue flashed at the door to the servant's stairs, and Grey sprinted down the hall. A half-naked woman came out of the room, and he had to jump to the side to avoid her, crashing into the wall. Plaster dust fluttered around him, and she hurried to him. "Sirrah, are ye all right?"

"Fine, my dear." He had to dance around her breasts, for she thrust herself at his chest. Free, he raced for the stairs, pounded up them.

His boots thundered on the wood steps. He rushed out the door onto the second story. Then he heard gasping behind him, and he jerked around. Helena was struggling to rush up the stairs, holding her hems in one gloved hand.

"What are you doing?" he barked. "Stay there." Why in God's name had she followed him?

When he turned back to his quarry, he'd lost the man. "Blast." He ran to the end of the hall and pushed open the two bedchamber doors on either side. In one, a man bellowed, "What in the blazes?" as another man looked up from the same bed. In the other, a woman squealed with shock and fell off the man she rode.

The blackmailer must have cut through a bedchamber to get to a window. It was the only way he could have disappeared so fast.

Behind him, Grey heard whispers of sound: a soft movement of satin, the slight creak of a board. His entire body tensed, and his heart hammered. He knew what it was to be ambushed from behind. To have a hand clamped over his mouth, his hands roughly bound behind his back.

Fighting for calm, he turned and faced the barrel of a pistol.

The frock coated man chuckled gleefully. "Walked right into it, didn't you, Your Grace?"

Grey folded his arms over his chest. He'd grown up facing threats. "Going to shoot a duke in a whorehouse full of witness, you scum?"

In the dim light, Grey couldn't distinguish much of the villain's face. The hair was covered in a powdered white wig. For carnal games, many men came in costume. They dressed as devils, Roman gladiators, and sultans to live out their fantasies and hide their identities. He still couldn't identify the man, though now he knew where to hunt for this bastard. Assuming he got out of this alive.

Slowly, he stepped closer to the villain.

The pistol jerked. The man's arm trembled. "Don't move, Your Grace—"

"Or you'll shoot your source of income?" Grey growled. "I think not." Grey took another step, and as he expected from his last two encounters with this scum, the coward retreated. But cowards could do dangerous things when cornered. He couldn't take the risk that the shaking bugger would pull the trigger.

"Oh, my goodness! Greybrooke!"

The feminine gasp slammed into Grey like a brick. Miss Winsome stood behind the villain at the top of the steps. She clutched the doorframe, frozen. She stared at the pistol, her mouth wide open.

"Get out of here," he roared, but it was too damned late.

She turned to flee, but the blackmailer grabbed her by the arm and jerked her to him. He hauled Miss Winsome like a sack of gravel, yanking her so her back was to his chest and his arm was clamped around her bosom.

Sweat stood out on the blackmailer's forehead, but his nervousness had gone.

The pistol's muzzle moved to rest against her temple, an evil, heavy piece of metal pressing to her delicate skin. Grey had never felt so much pounding pressure in his skull. His heart hadn't raced like this since . . .

Since he'd been a frightened boy. He could handle a threat to himself. But seeing a gun pressed to a woman's head was almost crippling.

Fighting rising panic, he faced the frock-coated man with feigned control. "Let her go, you bastard. She's got nothing to do with this. Release her and you will get your foul money."

A wide grin showed beneath the black mask. "You care about her. That should ensure I get out of here."

"Put this weapon down at once. There is no need to hurt anyone." Miss Winsome's voice wavered, but she issued the command like a governess. Even held tight against the body of an attacker, she fought to be strong. Such courage astounded Grey.

Her wide eyes met his, but she spoke to the blackmailer. "His Grace will let you escape if you put the pistol away and you do not hurt anyone."

She was concerned about the safety of everyone else. "Listen to her," Grey snapped.

But the man snarled at him. "I think not. Not when I'm in charge, Your Grace. This is too much bloody fun."

The blackmailer straightened his arm so the gun aimed at Grey's heart.

Grey relaxed slightly. Miss Winsome was still a captive, but she wasn't about to get shot, even by accident.

The blackmailer took several steps back, toward the servants' stairs. He wouldn't drag Miss Winsome down them. Would he let her go? One way to assure an escape would be to shoot her.

The man twisted to see how close the stairs were. Grey sprinted, and as the man cursed and corrected his aim on Grey's chest, Grey grasped Miss Winsome and pulled her free. He pushed her so she was clear of the line of fire. With a cry, she landed on the floor, while Grey waited for the explosion and the sensation of a pistol ball tearing through his body.

Footsteps pounded on the steps.

The man hadn't fired at him.

Grey was shaking, but he left her on the rug and raced down the stairs in pursuit, reaching the main floor as a pistol shot exploded. Women and men shrieked and moved like panicked sheep, scattering and bleating. Half-naked people ran everywhere, slamming into Grey like a rushing tide. At the back of the house, in a small disused room, he found the frock coat discarded on the floor. The window was open.

He stuck his head out, but the yard behind the house was deserted, the blackmailer gone.

He had to go back to Miss Winsome.

Long strides took Grey through the diminishing crowd. The madam of the house rushed to-and-fro, demanding to know what had happened, begging the men to stay. But a pistol shot meant trouble, and her clients were deserting like scurrying rats.

He sprinted up the narrows stairs, three steps at a time. When he reached the doorway on the upper floor, Miss Winsome was picking herself up, using the wall for support.

Her gold hair had tumbled free, and shimmered down her

back. But other than that, she looked collected and in control. How could she after having a gun to her head?

Then she put her hand over her mouth. Her shoulders trembled. She sobbed but wiped angrily at her eyes, as if she could stop crying if she only brushed the tears away fast enough.

Grey's throat tightened. She could have been killed. Over him.

He reached her, scooping her into his arms.

"What are you doing? Where are you taking me?"

He cradled her against his chest. He had to stop her crying. At least he had to make her forget. In his experience, there was only one way to do it.

"I'm taking you to bed."

Never had she seen a man look so afraid for her. She hadn't been carried in a man's arms before either. Carrying was her duty—cradling a crying child or holding a sleepy one against her shoulder.

Now Helena knew why children wanted to be held. Grey's arms pressed her against his solid chest, where she felt his pounding heartbeat. With his strong arms enveloping her, and her hand resting lightly on his bulging bicep—the first time she was really *touching* him—she felt secure.

This man, who was supposed to be a traitor to his country, had risked being shot to save her.

She'd fought for calm when the villain had held her hostage. Now all her strength seemed to be dissolving away. She buried her face in the warm crook of Greybrook's neck. She was all mixed up inside. He was supposed to be wicked, a criminal. Yet he was gentle with children, loving to his sisters, and he'd rescued her.

The duke kicked the front door of the brothel open and swept her down the steps to his carriage. Inside, with the lamps off, he drew her against his side. His large hand skimmed up and down her arm, stroking her. Cuddled close to him, she drank in his enticing male scent—it made her want to put her mouth to his neck and taste his skin. Tentatively, she lifted her hand and let it rest against his chest—

"I'm going to make you forget this," he growled.

"There's no harm done." It came out shakier than she wished. Then she realized . . .

Oh heavens, she wasn't supposed to *know* he was being blackmailed. Her natural response should be horror. And questions. She sat up. "Who was the man? Why did he attack you? He only pointed the pistol at *me* to frighten you."

Deep inside, a voice whispered, *Why did it frighten him so much unless he cares?*

"A madman, Miss Winsome. I have no idea of his name."

Trying to look shocked and surprised, she gasped, "But he knew you! How could you not know who this enemy is?"

The glow of a street flare fell in the window, illuminating green eyes and a hard expression. "Do not ask any more questions," he said coolly. "I want to keep you from danger. Bringing you tonight was a mistake."

She must be close to learning something, if she could only convince him to confide in her. She snuggled closer, peeling off her gloves. Lifting her bare hand, she ran her fingertips along his jaw, brushing light stubble. "I am not afraid. But I want to know what troubles you."

He moved her hand from his face. "Why do you want to know, Miss Winsome?"

"I care about you."

"I suggest you don't."

She hadn't expected that answer. "Then I want to help you."

Still capturing her hand, he bent to her, kissed her temple, putting warmth where she still felt the cold of the pistol's muzzle. "You want to help me with my troubles? Then let me tie you to a bed and lick your quim until you scream with ecstasy."

* * *

Greybrooke prowled around the bed with the same easy, dangerous grace as a black panther. Helena had seen the magnificent animal once in a menagerie. Lying over the palm of his large, gloved hand: three long, black ropes.

Goodness, this was it. She was going to be tied up, like the women in his private club and the brothel. She began to giggle—a funny, hiccupping sound she tried to hide. Greybrooke had insisted she have sherry to calm her nerves. After two glasses, it appeared her nerves had entirely evaporated. A wild courage had come over her—she was ready for anything he could do to her.

Now she lay on his bed, still fully dressed.

He touched one of the ropes to her ankle, below her hems. It was soft, made of velvet. She watched how focused Greybrooke was on his task as he looped the rope around her right ankle and made a snug circlet. Her slipper tumbled off her foot. Then, using the rope, he gently drew her leg to the side, slid the rope around the bedpost, and tied it tight. She tested by tugging at the black velvet cord, but she couldn't make it give an inch.

It proved surprising thrilling to feel the rope against her skin.

With a ruffle and a whoosh, he pushed her skirts up and a breeze flowed over her thighs.

She had one moment to comprehend that her legs were bare when his warm hands lightly touched her thighs and he parted her legs. Wide.

"Oh," she gasped, forgetting everything but shock, but he ignored her squeak of protest and he wrapped another black rope around her left ankle.

He expertly tied the knot, then stretched the rope to the bedpost and secured it. His eyes glittered. "Something simple for now, angel. I can't wait long enough to get fancy tonight."

The duke caught her hands in his and lifted them above her head. Her breasts lifted, pushing against the cups of her corset.

He twined the last rope around her wrists, binding her hands together. Stretching his back, he slid the rope through a ring on his headboard and tied it.

Then, before she could say a word, he got off the bed and dropped to his knees on the floor. Bending forward, he lightly brushed his tongue over that sensitive place between her legs.

He really *was* doing that wicked thing he'd said.

How could he do this? What did she taste like? She smelled so ripe and aroused, she knew her cheeks were scarlet. This was beyond naughty—

She squirmed wildly against the ropes binding her. Exposed. Embarrassed.

The duke stopped and gazed at her over the golden curls that covered her pubis. "Relax and enjoy it," he said huskily. "Lose yourself in this, love."

It came out soft but firm, a definite command. Then he blew a warm breath over her quim that ruffled her curls and tickled her nether lips. She fell back helplessly on his silken sheets. Pleasure shimmered through her. *Yes, do more. Do anything.*

His tongue went *everywhere*. He licked around her nether lips, his tongue tangling with them, his lips tugging on them. Sometimes she felt a pleasure that made her squirm and grow so wet. Then she'd feel something so intense, she tried to curl up to escape. Too much!

But the ropes kept her in place.

His tongue dove into her, into her wet passage, and she gasped as she felt so slick and full. He went lower, flicking on the bridge of flesh between her quim and her bottom, and each stroke of his tongue made her want to scream in delight.

All her world fell away and there was only this—his mouth on her and everything she felt. She felt like a goddess. She felt adored.

She felt she was going to come.

He settled in to a rhythm, a delicious rhythm that was taking her to bliss, just as his fingers had done. This had to be the most intimate thing possible. Her hips rose to his mouth seeking release. It was there, just within her grasp, and she *wanted* it. More . . . just a little more. . . .

Oh, she thrashed, and bucked, and sobbed, and moaned beneath him. He never stopped licking her, even as she came, even as her hips jerked wildly, even as her body thrust up and she smacked her quim into his jaw. He grabbed her hips, held her steady, and his tongue kept sweeping over her with long, rough strokes.

She came again, the pleasure so sharp and intense she cried out—incoherent babblings of "Your Grace" and "Heavens" and "I can't!" even as she did. She exploded so fiercely in orgasm, she felt as if she would fly to pieces.

It was a maelstrom, and when it ended she was spent, damp, exhausted. She flopped back on the bed. Her arms were sore. In all that thrashing, she'd pulled hard against the rope. Sweat glistened on her breasts. The soles of her feet tingled. Her cunny still throbbed and pulsed.

Her gaze met his. Delight filled his green eyes, and she felt so close to him.

He moved over her quickly and his chest filled her vision— his elegantly, simply tied cravat, his snow-white shirt, his silvery-gray waistcoat. Deftly, he untied her hands. She wiggled her fingers, reached for him, but he moved away to attend to the ropes at her feet.

He didn't like to be touched.

Was that because of the scars?

She should ask about all of that, but if it was part of his secrets, he wouldn't easily give them up. For a fleeting moment, she thought of her sister Margaret. *How I understand why you fell! This is irresistible.*

"Feel better?" he asked gently. "The fault is mine you were put at risk, but I assure you it won't happen again. And don't ask me questions about this business. It's my private problem to solve."

He helped her sit up. Helena knew exactly what he was going to do. Send her home.

She had to find a way to stay. Quickly, she blurted, "I—I want to do . . . um, that to you."

Before she could lose her nerve, she did the most daring thing she'd ever done. She grasped the falls of his trousers and undid the buttons with haste. She slid her hand into his linens, bumped her fingers into his erection. Fumbling wildly, she wrapped her hand around his thick shaft.

His lashes dropped, he took a sharp breath, and her heart leapt as she saw his mouth grow tight with desire. He looked gorgeous. Sensual.

And she knew she was not just doing this because she wanted to stay in his house.

10

Goodness. He was *huge*.

Her fingers didn't meet around his girth. Helena tightened them gently around his erection, feeling the ridges, the prominent veins beneath hot, silk-soft skin. His penis was utterly rigid, pulsing in her grip. Yet the skin was so velvety, she could imagine stroking the full, taut head against her cheek.

She met his heavy-lidded, brilliant green gaze and felt her cheeks get hot. She felt shy, but wild too.

She tried to slide her hand up, but she tugged at his skin. Afraid to hurt him, she skimmed very gently until she reached the end of the shaft and the rounded crown at the base of the head.

"Lovely," he said softly, and her heart tripped at the heat in his gaze. He gave a tense-looking smile, pushed his trousers down to his thighs and his linens down to join them. "Do it as hard as you want," he said huskily. "It's accustomed to taking a fair bit of abuse. I'm never gentle when I do this myself."

"When *you* do this?" She knew men did, but only because they were desperate for sexual release. It was supposed to be sinful. He admitted to it as if it were the most natural thing.

"Sometimes I have to. Especially when pursuing a stubborn governess."

Her heart gave another little flip at his teasing tone. "How could *I* make you do that?"

His eyes sparkled. "I was aroused for you, and it becomes painful for a man after he's experienced several unfulfilled erections in a row. So I closed my eyes, dreamed of you, and pumped my cock into my hand until I exploded."

She didn't know whether to go scarlet again with embarrassment or feel flattered. But he made her feel comfortable. She felt so . . . intimate with him right now.

"Is that how I should do it?" she whispered.

"Fondle the head, love. It likes that."

She did, and he dropped his head back. "That's good. Now slide our hand down the length, bring it back up, and squeeze the head. It also likes that."

He spoke as if it were a part detached from his body. She kept stroking him. His thick lashes shielded his green eyes, but she could tell when she gave a caress he liked—he would take a sharp breath, or moan softly, and his hips would rock toward her hand.

Each time she drew her hand up, fluid bubbled out of the tiny hole at the tip. The head was sloped and smooth, and so swollen, it was taut and shiny. The crown ringed it, then the long tapered shaft fell away beneath it to disappear into the thick nest of black hair.

He was letting her touch him. Playing with his lovely, earthy scented, fascinating "cock" was the first time he had let her do it.

His breathing came faster, more ragged. He must be close to his climax. He made expressions almost of pain, but he muttered, "Good, good," so she knew he must be enjoying it. Watching the agony on his face made her ache in her cunny. She could make him feel like that. It felt . . . special.

But her arms were tired from gripping him and pumping. She had to stop, so she lost the rhythm. And he fell back from the peak.

It happened again and again. Was he getting frustrated? She wanted to give him pleasure and now she felt she'd never do it. She had no experience, no skill. But she couldn't stop now, could she?

His hand closed over hers.

"I'm sorry," she whispered.

"The fault is with me. It takes me a long time to reach orgasm now."

"Why?" It had been very fast for her.

"Unlike you, Miss Winsome, I can only have one. Then I need to rest for a while before another. So I trained myself to delay climax. Now that I'm getting old, I think I was too diligent."

"Old? I thought you were not yet thirty. Oh dear, I can see all your gray hairs." She teasingly brushed his hair.

"What gray hairs?"

He looked so genuinely worried she had to giggle.

"There's only one or two, you know."

He sighed. When he did, his rock-hard cock bounced. "I'm almost thirty. The traditional age where everyone worries about a gentleman, and suddenly tries to push him into marriage and children."

He had told her he had no intention of ever falling in love. But she could not let it rest. "You don't want those things, I know. But I cannot understand why."

She had pushed too far. He reached for his linens and began to draw them up, struggling to push his enormous erection down. She didn't want to go yet. She couldn't go yet.

But it was more than her mission. She wanted to stay with Greybrooke. She didn't want this wonderful intimacy to end.

She knew it was dangerous, but she couldn't resist. She'd never felt so alive, so daring and wild and deliciously wicked as she stilled his hands, bent forward, and kissed the head of his cock.

The skin was moist, dewy, and tasted ripe and earthy. What had he done to her? Things with his tongue. Sticking hers out, she licked the head, washed her tongue over it. Juices bubbled out, giving her a sour taste.

She glanced up. He stared at her in amazement.

She flicked her tongue over the head of his cock, just as he'd done to her private place. She couldn't thrust her tongue into him. What else could she do? He'd sucked her nipples and she'd liked it.

Opening her mouth, she took him inside. Tightened her lips around him and she sucked hard. It took her a while to understand she could draw him in and out at the same time.

"To see you with my cock in your mouth . . . it's the most erotic sight I've seen," he rasped. He tensed. "God, you have to stop—I'm going to come."

He tried to push her back, but she wanted to make him have pleasure. She felt his cock swell, felt a rushing sensation beneath his skin—

He exploded into her mouth.

Shocked, she didn't move. He was coming into her mouth, and she tasted the sour, lush, rich flavor of his seed. It was rather . . . intriguing. It was his, and she liked it. She sucked while he was still shooting.

"No, gorgeous, you have to stop. Too sensitive," he groaned. "I'm too sensitive."

It was so tempting to torture him playfully, but he wanted her to stop, so she did. She watched him have his orgasm while she held him in her mouth. He collapsed finally, his chest lifting with harsh breaths. His cock softened in her mouth. She let it drop out.

It was so intimate, her heart pounded. A little with fear, though she didn't know why.

Eyes glittering, Greybrooke let out soft laughter. He gave her a tug, forcing her to fall on top of his chest. Her breasts were squashed against the firm muscle under his chest.

"Was it . . . good?" she asked shyly.

He laughed again, husky and low. She'd told him couples should find happiness in bed. He had teased her then, but she felt—she felt they had been happy together.

"Beyond good," he said. "Life-altering."

"Truly?"

He pulled her closer and his lips softened, and she knew he meant to kiss her.

She tried to draw back. "You can't."

"Why not?"

When he looked curious and inquisitive, she saw he looked very boyish. Even more gorgeous than usual. She blushed. "I— I was just kissing you down there. I must . . . um taste like you." She was so embarrassed.

But Greybrooke grinned. "I want to taste myself on your lips, angel. It's the most erotic thing I can imagine." Softly, his mouth claimed hers, his lips light and teasing. Showers of sparks raced from her lips, tingling through her whole body.

It was wretched. She couldn't enjoy the kiss. She must think about her mission again. She must calculate a way to get to the journal. Could she pretend to go to the water closet? No, she needed longer than that. . . .

"I'm too sleepy to go home." Simple words, but they implied so much. If she spent the whole night here, there was no returning to the Winterhaven house in the morning, resuming her work as a governess. Staying out all night would get her the sack.

Yet she had no choice.

"You can stay here if you wish. You're mine now anyway."

He said it carelessly, but her heart pattered. She wished—

No, wishing was foolish. Wishing led to disaster. She was only "his" temporarily.

He helped her off the bed. "Let's get you undressed." His hands moved skillfully over the fastenings of her gown, and he drew it off over her head as she stood in the middle of his bedroom. She was breathless. She had never been naked in front of him. Not completely and all at once.

Helena saw her reflection in the cheval mirror. Sensible stockings, plain garters, a simple muslin shift. She looked very ordinary.

"Beautiful," he said.

Her heart almost shattered.

He dropped to one knee. Her heart fluttered as he took off her slippers, the ruched garters, her stockings. "Do you want to leave your shift on?" he asked. "Or do you want to be bared to me?"

A part of her wanted to be wanton and take everything off. But she had to sneak around his bedroom. Wearing her shift would be more practical. "I'll leave it on." How she hated this dual life she had to lead. "For tonight," she added.

He didn't take off all of his clothing. He stripped to his shirt and his trousers, carelessly tossing his coat, waistcoat, and cravat to hang over the corner of a dressing screen.

"I saw your scars the other night when you were wearing just your robe. What—what happened?" It was tactless, but she had no time. She had to learn as much as she could.

He looked up. She couldn't read his expression.

"What do you think happened?"

She blinked. Blushed. "You were struck."

"Yes, by many things."

"Why? Why did someone beat you so cruelly?"

"Why do you think they did?"

He wasn't going to answer directly, she saw. "For punishment."

"Exactly. That's all there is to it. I was punished. Regularly." He pulled the covers down on the bed. "You know, I've never slept with a mistress before."

Grey never slept with his mistresses. Once, when he was young, he'd smuggled a girl into his bed, never guessing that she had been paid to betray him. After that, he kept sex separated from sleep, and ensured he was never in a vulnerable position.

Miss Winsome lay on the other side of the bed.

He remembered how she'd said she'd dreamed of marriage. How she'd said she wanted to do what married people did.

What he was doing was damnably wrong. She was sweet and innocent. He was dark and bitter. Ultimately he would hurt her.

He knew he would be unable to sleep. Not with her, not in this bed. His instincts never let him sleep with anyone else, knowing that in sleep he was vulnerable. "Roll on your side, love. With your back to me."

She obeyed. He moved close to her, pressing his chest to her back, his groin to her voluptuous arse. He wrapped his arm around her.

Hesitantly she snuggled back, cuddling tighter to him. "I like this," she said, her voice soft and sleepy. It was so endearing, it almost broke his heart.

He stroked her hair. The gentle motion should soothe her into sleep. "This is the first time I've slept in this bed," he said. A lie, since he knew as soon as she drifted off, he would leave her. Go sleep on a chair.

Helena woke in a panic. She blinked into darkness until her eyes became accustomed to the faint light thrown by the few coals in the fireplace. She'd gone to sleep with her derriere pressed against Greybrooke's strong, lean body. His warmth was gone.

She sat up. *He* was gone.

Had he left the house? Was he perhaps in his study, drinking?

Pushing back the sheets, she slipped out of bed. The floor was cool, but she padded in bare feet. A soft rasping sound came to her from the adjoining dressing room. She looked in. Sprawled on a narrow daybed was Greybrooke, feet hanging off the seat, arm beneath his head. Fast asleep.

He hadn't been able to sleep in the bed. Or with her. Her heart gave a pang.

Before she went to the writing room, she returned to the bed. Hauled the heavy coverlet from it, dragged it to the dressing room, and arranged it—as best as she could—over the duke. It was foolish, worrying about his comfort just before she betrayed him.

Her stomach literally churned with guilt. They had been so intimate, and when he'd laughed, kissed her, it had been dazzling. Yet she had to lie to him.

What if she found out he was a traitor? What would she do? She didn't know.

And if he was a traitor, would she still feel they had shared something special?

This time her heart gave a twinge of pain.

But she padded silently to the writing room. Inside, Helena opened the curtain as she'd done before. Holding her breath, she eased the drawer open. She did it without a sound and drew out the leather-bound journal.

Her tongue ran over her lips. She still tasted the lush, ripe flavor of Greybrooke's warm skin and his thick white come.

Feeling like Pandora, she flipped open the journal. The paper was beautiful—smooth as silk, pristine white, edged with gold.

It was also blank. Every single page was blank.

* * *

A childhood of being hauled out of bed to be punished had taught him to stir at even the slightest sound. Grey woke and fought the weight pressing on him—

The counterpane. He stared at it, slightly confused, still lost somewhere between the nightmare in his sleep and the strangeness of waking. Why was there a cover over him?

Then he knew. Miss Winsome must have found him out here and had covered him up. He was damp with sweat, his brain fogged from being overheated. But he was cooling fast now and his wits were clearing. He got silently to his feet.

A soft sound came to him. Footstep? A door opening? It hadn't come from the bedroom.

He turned and saw a sliver of blue-white light spilling from his correspondence room. Padding on bare feet, he knew how to move with stealth. He had done it on the day of his father's death, thinking he could get there in time, catch his father, avert disaster, only to be shocked into reality by the explosion of a pistol.

Hell . . .

Reaching the door, he knew the curtain had to be open. Now he heard a soft rustle of paper, and quick breathing. Pushing the door gently, he opened it enough to take a peek.

Miss Winsome, looking like a ghost in her glowing white shift, was leaning over his desk, flipping the pages of his journal. The book had been a gift from Jacinta. She'd thought writing things down would help him to put the past behind him. It would be like saying: *That is done, it is over, you can go on.* Some madness that women believed, Grey supposed. But she'd been so earnest he couldn't just discard the book. He had hidden it in a drawer.

Why in hell was his mistress searching his desk?

After years of abuse, he wasn't capable of hot rage anymore.

His anger was cold, and it moved over him like ice forming on a pond.

But his parents were dead; neither of them had paid Miss Winsome to spy on him. So what in the blue blazes was she doing?

He could confront her. Intimidate the truth out of her, then toss her out on her lovely arse.

Bloody hell, she'd made him laugh with delight. When she'd sucked his cock, he'd felt like he'd touched heaven. He should have known it was all a bloody lie.

She set down the journal. Then she bent, running her hand to the very back of the drawer. Efficient little spy, wasn't she? He knew exactly what she was going to find.

She pulled out a stack of paper, edges curled, tied with a strip of leather. His mother's letters. What was in them? Nothing damning—his mother was too careful for that.

He could put an end to this right now. Or he could play along. Find out who Miss Winsome was doing this for.

Finally she gathered the letters back together. He watched how carefully she did it, obviously ensuring the letters were in the same order. She retied the leather string. It looked as if the letters had never been touched. She slid the packet to the back of the drawer, eased it closed.

She was very good at this, he observed.

She wouldn't have learned anything from the letters—nothing of the real truth of his sick past. Nothing of the secrets he and Jacinta had struggled to hide. All she would have known was that his mother had pleaded with him to forgive her.

Ice-cold anger thrummed in his veins. His heart felt like stone. He could have walked into the room, wrapped his hand around her neck, and squeezed the life out of her.

It scared him because he knew he could have done it, driven by years of fury. He could have killed her because he'd never had the chance to hurt the people who had whipped, beaten, punished him.

She closed the drapes, again taking care to ensure they hung a certain way—the way she must have found them. Grey left his place by the door and sauntered back to the bedroom. He had taken a cheroot out of a box beside the bed when she crept back in.

Even by the dim firelight, he saw her go pale when she saw him. Saw her slight jump backward, and the nervous way her hand went to her throat. "I woke up," she said. "I had to go to the retiring room. You were asleep on the daybed."

"Since we're both awake," he said. "I might as well take you home."

Her hair braided, dressed in her plain white nightdress, Helena padded through the quiet nursery. Moonlight glowed on the children's toys, the wood floor, the tiny tables and chairs. She paused to pick up one of Timothy's toy horses.

Tears welled, and she wiped them away. She loved children. Even when Margaret had died, and Helena had learned that men could be scoundrels, she'd still wanted to have a husband and children of her own. It was too late for that.

A soft whimpering sounded from the children's bedroom. She found Timothy in his bed, his legs moving as if he were running. She bent to his side, soothed him until she broke the grip of his nightmare and he settled into sleep.

She was tired. She went back to her bedchamber. She had a stub of a candle burning, on the small table beside her simple cot. She couldn't go to bed yet. There was something she had to do, and she needed the candle to do it—

"Couldn't sleep, Miss Winsome? Neither could I."

Greybrooke. Not possible. But he was there, sitting on her plain chair. "How can you be up here, in my bedroom?"

"I climbed the stairs."

He had left his carriage at the bottom of the mews and walked her up to the back kitchen door. She'd slipped inside without anyone noticing. She'd assumed he had gone home. "But you'll be caught up here. What if Lady Winterhaven finds you?"

"You're my mistress now."

A flare of panic gripped her heart. "Yes, but we can't be obvious about it."

"Lie on the bed," he said. "On your stomach." From his pocket, he pulled out the black velvet ropes.

Seeing them, she felt her cunny ache. She shouldn't do this. But obediently she lay on her tummy. Her sheets were cool beneath her.

"Put your hands behind your back."

She did as he asked, her heart thumping. He tied her hands together so they were captured behind her, resting near the swell of her bottom. She squirmed, wantonly aroused. Then the duke moved her, lifting her bottom, arranging her on her knees with her bared rump in the air.

Something bumped her bottom. She couldn't really see. Her cheek was pressed against the bed. It felt like a wand, or a fireplace poker.

Her shift was pushed up, baring her rump. She struggled to look back. Greybrooke was moving between her legs, his trousers pushed to his hips. His enormous erection stuck out, hard as a brick, and he was pushing it down. The head of it stroked her derriere.

He slid it between her legs from the back, the shaft stroking her cunny lips, then the sensitive place.

He thrust slowly back and forth, drawing across her throbbing nub like a bow over a finely tuned string. His voice whispered over her ear, his breath warm and gentle. "Does your clit like to have my prick sawing across it?"

"Y-yes," she stammered. She was growing wet. Her juices

must be leaking on his shaft. She felt erotic in this submissive position, her breasts crushed against the bed, her round bottom bared to him. "But, Your Grace, I mustn't make love with you. I can't."

"We're not going to. Not now. But I want you to understand you are my mistress now, Miss Winsome.

His hips shifted, drawing his erection back, then his hands rested on her thighs. He got onto his back on the bed and slid between her legs. Suddenly he pulled her on top of him, her cunny landing on his mouth. His tongue slicked over her— over her clit. He suckled her expertly, while she gasped and whimpered and tried desperately not to moan.

She'd never dreamed of being sprawled on top of the duke. It was scandalous. Wicked. Wanton. But so good, so irresistible, she was melting in pleasure.

His tongue surged in her, teasing her, then flicked over her nub again. Over and over. Her fingers curled and her head lolled on the bed, and all she could think of was how good it was to have his tongue loving her—

Heavens!

She had to bite her lip hard to smother wild cries as a fierce orgasm ravaged her.

He moved back, and she felt his hands at the velvet ties securing her wrists. As he freed them, she sat up. Inside she was filled with worry: Had she been too loud? Had anyone heard her? Lady Winterhaven would be scandalized if she found out what they'd done. Goodness, she was so wicked for doing it in the house—

"Tomorrow morning I will come and break the news to Jacinta." His voice sounded like ice. Moonlight slanted across his face. He had pleasured her expertly, but there was no smile on his lips now. He seemed a different man than the one who had laughed with her earlier. Something about him felt . . . colder.

Something was different . . . was off . . . she didn't know why. "What news?" Helena asked, confused.

"That you are leaving immediately with me. I have a house rented for you. You'll have to say good-bye to the children to-morrow."

"Tomorrow? You want me to leave? I cannot."

"Yes, you can, my dear. You are no longer a governess." With that, he turned and left. Without a good-bye. Or a kiss.

She shivered. He seemed angry. Coldly, brutally so. But why?

If he knew she'd searched his desk, she could understand. But he had been asleep. Anyway, there had been nothing to find.

If he was angry over making her his mistress, why then would he do it? And if he thought she was snooping on him, he wouldn't want her, would he? He would angrily cast her aside.

He had a house rented for her. Tomorrow, she would have to say good-bye to the children. Goodness, she had not thought about that—about the moment she would have to tell them she was leaving.

She couldn't turn back now. Greybrooke might be angry, but she felt like bursting into tears. She wasn't being whisked away happily into a mistress's life. She was afraid, and he—for some reason—was cold.

And it had been for nothing, because she hadn't found any-thing.

There had been a letter from Lady Winterhaven in the un-used journal. It had been simple: *For you, Grey. To write things down. It will make you feel better. It will help you to put the past aside. I promise, Jacinta.*

If only he had used it . . . if only he had put something down on paper. Lady Winterhaven must keep a journal and that must be why she had given one to her brother—

Oh goodness, she was dense.

Lady Winterhaven might have put the truth in *her* journal. And her ladyship wrote everything at her desk in the morning room.

Helena was shaky, confused by her conversation with Greybrooke, but she had to deal with her mission. And she had only tonight to find Lady Winterhaven's journal.

11

"Timothy, that is a superb 'T'," Helena declared. "Your letters are improving by leaps and bounds."

Timothy smiled, then stuck out his tongue as he labored on the "I."

In the schoolroom, she watched Michael and Sophie practice their handwriting in their copy books and helped Timothy with his shaky attempts at printing his letters.

A light rap sounded on the door. Helena looked up to find a young maid breathless in the doorway. "Miss Winsome, Her Ladyship wants to see you in the morning room. At once, Her Ladyship said."

Helena's heart dipped. Either it was about Greybrooke—about being his mistress—or she had not been as careful in reading Lady Winterhaven's diaries as she'd thought.

In the middle of the night, she had used her hairpin to spring the lock on Lady Winterhaven's writing desk and had read her ladyship's journals.

She now knew what Greybrooke's secret was.

She had been able to piece it together from Lady Winterhaven's diary entries, and her blood had run cold as she'd read. Their father had been a monstrous brute. His death had not been an accident, nor had it been suicide. He had been deliberately killed. Lady Winterhaven had not said who had done it, but Helena suspected she knew.

It must have been Greybrooke's father who had punished him, who had left the scars on his back. Greybrooke must have been the one to kill his father.

He'd been so brutally whipped and abused, she certainly couldn't blame him. But from Lady Winterhaven's journal, it sounded as if he had not done it because of the abuse he had suffered. He had done it to protect his sisters.

The punishments had begun when Greybrooke was very young—she'd gathered that from the diary. What would have happened to him as grew up? He would be angry, bitter, hurt. He could become incapable of loving someone, like a dog who was so accustomed to beatings, he snapped at any human. Could all that anger and hurt make him commit treason?

Helena reached the morning room, knocked on the closed door. Lady Winterhaven's lovely, soft voice bade her to come inside.

There, amidst vases of white roses, white orchids, white lilies—flowers brought fresh from greenhouses every morning—stood Greybrooke. His arms were crossed over his broad chest. The raking light struck his high cheekbones and strong jaw, making him look cold, strong . . . and sensual.

Sensual but intimidating.

It felt terrible to stand in front of them, knowing their secret, while they both had no clue she had spied on them, betrayed their trust. She had not yet told Whitehall. She didn't *want* to tell him. This secret was so private, so dangerous and destructive. She feared putting it in the hands of that ruthless man.

"I would like a word alone with Miss Winsome, Grey," Lady Winterhaven said.

Greybrook leaned his hips against the writing desk, a dainty thing of white and gilt. "It's not her fault I seduced her. I pursued her with single-minded determination."

His defense of her touched her heart. Perhaps she was wrong—it wasn't anger she sensed.

"I am not going to condemn her," Lady Winterhaven declared, "but I am thoroughly annoyed with you, Grey, for stealing away the most wonderful governess I have ever had. And I really must speak to her *alone*."

Greybrooke's lips twisted in a frown, but he walked toward the door. As he passed his sister, he said softly, "It's for the best, Jacinta." Then he left.

What did he mean by that?

"Of course he says that," Lady Winterhaven complained when he left. "He doesn't have to hire a new governess. I should make *him* go and find one. A *good* one. Now—" Her ladyship crossed her arms over her chest. "Did you understand what you were doing when my brother seduced you?"

Helena swallowed hard. "I—I did know what I was doing."

"Are you certain? My brother can be very persuasive. One of the maids told me you were looking rather furtive, hurrying out of the house with a box. A gift from Grey, I suppose. What did he give you?"

She could not say *shackles*. Heat raced down from her hairline.

"Hmmm, I should have known it would be something naughty."

"It was poetry. And . . . umm, jewels."

"Grey is very generous. I will say that. But his interest does not last long. That is just the way he is. He usually moves from one paramour to another after a few weeks. Are you certain you wish to surrender your future for something so brief? You are a clever woman, and you could probably live comfortably for life on what Grey will give you. But I do wish you would stay."

Stay? That startled her. She thought Lady Winterhaven would be scandalized. She had expected to be tossed out in haste. "I can't," she whispered. "Not now."

"The children adore you, Miss Winsome. And you have done marvels with Maryanne."

Her tongue was so thick and clumsy, it was hard to speak. "There is nothing wrong with Lady Maryanne. She must be treated as a normal girl, that is all."

"That is very true. However, I still believe you are a miracle worker."

Lady Winterhaven's blue eyes looked upon her with a kindness and admiration Helena didn't deserve, having rifled through her ladyship's writing desk. "I've agreed to become Greybrooke's mistress. I can't turn back now."

"You could, my dear. Just tell me if that is what you want."

But Helena shook her head.

Lady Winterhaven sighed. "I could kick my brother for tempting you away. You will say good-bye to the children, of course."

"Oh!" Goodness, she *would* have to do that. "Oh, yes, of course."

It would break her heart.

"Why do you have to go, Miss Winsome? Couldn't you stay? Did we make you go away because we are naughty sometimes? We do mean to listen and do what you say. Truly we do."

Grey watched Miss Winsome drop to her knees on the nursery room floor and hold out her arms. Michael stood with his small shoulders back, his young chin pointed up, as straight and tall as a man. Beneath his tousled blond hair, his young face was brave. Then his eight-year-old lips wobbled and he barrelled into her arms.

Timothy ran at her and collided with her on the other side

with such force, he almost knocked her over. It spoke of a sorrow so deep, it stunned Grey. Miss Winsome held his little four-year-old nephew tightly and stroked the lad while he clung to her skirts. "I don't want to go, Timothy," she said in a soft but firm voice, "but I have to."

"But why do you have to?" His voice was muffled. "Mother wants you to stay. So does Father. I overheard them talking. They said they would never find another governess as good as you. They thought you were happy here."

The last came out as an accusation. Grey knew young Timothy felt betrayed and saw pain in Miss Winsome's blue eyes. "I am very happy here." She patted his head soothingly. "I adore you, Sophie, and Michael, but something has happened that requires me to take another post."

For a lie, it was a good one. But then, she was very adept at lying.

Timothy began to cry, sobbing into her brown wool skirt, so she drew him back. A soft pass of her thumbs wiped away his tears. Grey's heart lurched and his chest grew tight. When he'd been a boy, no one had ever wiped his tears or held him. Instead, his parents had worked bloody hard to make him cry.

When Grey looked up, Miss Winsome was speaking to Michael. "You are going to go off to school soon, Lord Michael. To Eton. You will have a much grander education than what I can provide for you. I know you are going to be a great success at your lessons. You don't need me anymore. Lady Sophie is to go to school too. And Lady Maryanne is to go out in Society."

"Sophie thought you might be leaving to get married," Timothy declared. "Are you going to marry some day?"

Grey heard her catch her breath. Then she ruffled the boy's hair. "I don't know. Someone would have to ask me."

"If you are not married when I'm grown up," Timothy said, his gaze level and serious for a four-year-old, "I will ask you to marry me."

"That is very sweet." Damn, Grey heard tears in her voice. "But I will be old then."

Timothy shook his head. "You will never be old to me."

She hugged the boy tight. "I was so very, very fortunate to be your governess, Timothy."

He buried his chubby-cheeked face against her neck. "I love you, Miss Winsome."

"I love you, Timothy. I always will. I love Lord Michael and Lady Sophie too. And Lady Maryanne. I shall never forget any of you."

Seeing the sadness on Miss Winsome's face broke his heart.

It infuriated Grey. She had searched his desk, damn it. Why should he care about her when she was lying to him?

"Come, Miss Winsome, it's time for you to go," he said.

The children cried out in protest, but he wanted an end to this. Since she was lying, taking her away from them was for the best. He was protecting them. So why did he feel like the villain?

The town house was so new, she could smell fresh black paint on the railings. The curving row of three-story homes was pure, brilliant white—the soot of London's many fires hadn't yet marred the surface. Rain pattered on her umbrella. Roses grew in boxes at the front steps, a touch of vibrant pink at the end of each tight, green bud.

Greybrooke held out an ornate key. "Your new home."

Leaving Lady Winterhaven's house had felt as unreal as a dream. All she'd been able to think of was the children's unhappiness. The cool key lying across Helena's palm woke her up. Now she was most definitely Greybrooke's mistress, and suddenly her entire life was different.

Escorted by the duke, she went up the front steps. The house was grander than anything she could have ever dreamed to possess. But then . . . what did the neighbors think? This was a respectable street. What would people think when they had seen a woman escorted inside by a gentleman, and then later discovered she lived alone? They would guess she was a mistress. Would it bother them? Would they avoid her, give her the cut direct?

What was a mistress's life actually like? Helena realized she had no idea.

The duke rapped on the door, and it was answered by a plain-faced girl in a maid's dress and snow-white cap.

Helena stepped inside, her half-boots echoing on the marble tile of the foyer. The maid took her cloak over one arm and the duke's great coat over the other, with his hat and walking stick balancing on top.

Then it was a whirlwind—shock upon shock.

Greybrooke knew the house already. He walked with familiarity across the gleaming tile and opened the first door in the foyer. Following him, Helena stepped into a drawing room. A breathtaking room. White orchids filled it. The wallpaper was butter yellow, all moldings painted pure white. A settee of pale blue faced the windows, surrounded by plush-cushioned wing chairs. By the fire stood a dainty feminine chair and a sturdy masculine chair of dark brown leather. She caught her breath— he had chosen the chairs for them both.

Did that mean he intended to spend a lot of time here?

"My secretary has engaged three maids, a lady's maid, a cook, and a groom," Greybrooke said. "However, from here forward, staffing decisions are yours to make. I advised on the decoration of the house, but I want you to put on your personal stamp. Change what you wish."

He named the figure of her monthly allowance, and she almost collapsed at the knees.

"All this just because I—I will be your lover?"

"All this because you do it on my terms," he said.

At first he had sounded matter-of-fact about all this. Now she shivered at a trace of coldness.

From the drawing room, they went to a music room, complete with an exquisite pianoforte. There were entertaining rooms, which surprised her.

"Sometimes I expect to give parties, attended by friends," he said. "I will let you review the kitchens and the staff yourself."

"Of course. Thank you." Her parents had kept a small staff, but even so she knew how to manage servants.

"This is one of my favorite rooms." The duke opened a door of robin's-egg blue and revealed a morning room, positioned on the front corner, where it would be bathed in light on sunny days. She now possessed her own delicate white-and-gilt writing desk. Which brought a crippling spurt of guilt.

You know his secret—what are you going to do?

She didn't know.

He was putting on a damned good act.

Ever since he'd been a child, Grey had never trusted anyone, except Jacinta, Maryanne, and his niece and nephews.

He watched Miss Winsome's face as he introduced her to her house. Watched her with cold anger that he fought to conceal. He saw many emotions: surprise, delight, sadness.

Had she deliberately arranged their first meeting in the park? Was she an accomplice of the blackmailer, hunting for secrets to use on him? Why else search his desk and read his letters?

He was going to seduce the truth out of Miss Winsome, use sex to overcome her defenses. That was his reason for acquiring this house, for behaving as though he just intended to make her his mistress.

She stood at the window of the morning room, looking out over a small rose garden. Tears glittered in her eyes.

"What is it?" he asked.

"I was just thinking of the children. I thought I would be the one who was sad, not they."

Grey's heart lurched. *Damn, remember you can't trust her.* "They loved you very much."

Her hand clutched the edge of the curtain. She didn't answer.

"Miss Winsome?"

She turned to him, wearing a wobbly smile. "I'm sorry. I couldn't say a word because I have an enormous lump in my throat. I will miss them terribly. But I'm sure Lady Winterhaven will find a good governess."

He didn't understand. Miss Helena Winsome was underhanded, cunning, devious. She had manipulated him with brilliance. But the children loved her. With them she had been good, kind, patient. The way she had calmed Maryanne's tantrums was remarkable. How could a woman who lied so easily, who was so damned deceitful, be so good with the children?

It was the same question she'd asked him. Essentially how could he be incapable of love when he was so good with children?

It was time to start seducing her. "Come with me to the bedroom. You can't cry—or feel sad—when you're in the middle of a toe-curling climax."

12

Helena almost sank to her knees at the sight of the huge bed-chamber.

This was hers? This enormous bed with its soaring canopy of rose silk? Pillows and bolsters were mounded upon the bed; the counterpane was rose with gold flowers embroidered all over. Another writing desk stood near the window, and a settee was placed in front of the fire.

"I wanted this room to be sinful and decadent and indulgent. I wanted you to be filled with desire the moment you stepped within." Greybrooke stood behind her, his fingers stroking her neck, then he began to flick open the fastenings of her sensible dress. Shivers tumbled.

"Then, it's up to me to pleasure you," he added.

She didn't know what to say. She quivered, surrounded by his scent as he drew her gown down her body. Muslin skimmed over her skin. Her senses were filled by his nearness. The sight of his hands—the memory of what they'd done—made her legs feel as solid as pudding.

This must be what it was like on a wedding night. The bed

stood in front of her. She knew what must happen. She half wanted it, and half wanted to hide due to tremendous nerves. She'd done naughty things with him. But this was *the* thing.

Greybrooke undid the lacings of her stays with quick, firm tugs.

"What are you going to want me to do?"

His lips skimmed over her neck. Was it possible for skin to catch fire? "Submit to me and enjoy yourself," he murmured.

"That's far too mild a word. I'm all—" A thousand emotions tumbled around in her. "All in a whirl."

"I like making you that way." His voice was sin. His hands stroked through her hair. Heavens, even her scalp felt sensitive and aroused. He took out her pins, then fanned her hair to make it fall down her back in waves.

"Your hair is so beautifully tempting."

His voice was so tempting. Helena kept holding her breath, as if the very act of breathing might make this all dissolve. The vanity mirror showed her the lush sensuality of the moment. She looked wanton in her white stays and petticoats with golden hair spilling loose, he elegant in his dark clothes but snow-white shirt.

He helped her out of her stays, her petticoats, leaving her in her stockings and slippers. Her hands went to her breasts. She wasn't cold—a wonderful fire burned in the enormous, marble fireplace. But she was exposed to his gaze, and it still felt strange.

This was going to be the most intimate moment of her life, and she was falling into that intimacy.

The duke held up his hands. The shackles dangled, jewels reflecting light, dazzling her. She let go of her bosom and obediently she held out her hands. She saw the heat in his green eyes as she bared herself to him.

Oh goodness, once she'd thought of marriage. Of going to bed with a husband, the way one was supposed to. Not this wicked heat and sensuality, not this feeling that all she was made of was desire and sensitive skin and need. The shackles closed around her slim wrists, and the moment they did, she felt a twinge of need deep inside her. Having her wrists bound together in front of her meant something now. It meant delirious pleasure was coming soon.

Greybrooke set his hands on her waist, lifting her. The way he focused only on her made her breathless. A smile curved his lips, and her heart soared. He looked happy. Perhaps his coolness before had been nerves over facing his sister, or concern over the blackmail, or something that had nothing to do with her. She felt a distinct victory at his smile. There, she had made him feel happiness in bed.

Goodness, he was lowering her onto her bed—about the size of a carriage, and so comfortable, it was like sinking into a cloud.

"Hands over your head," Greybrooke commanded.

He had his velvet ties, of course. Oh God, did she want to be made love to, all tied up?

Yes, yes, yes. She was squirming with need at the thought. Greybrooke was going to be in command, doing all the things to her that felt so wonderful.

She thought she'd feel some fear at having sex, at giving up her virginity, but she thought of all the pleasure he'd given her. If he said it would give her pleasure, she certainly believed him.

Soft velvet skimmed over her ankles, and he pushed her legs apart. She watched as he tied the ropes in loops around her ankles, then secured them to the bedposts at the foot of the bed. He tied two more ropes to the columns at the head of the bed.

"God, you are beautiful," he said.

"Are you going to undress?" she asked, breathlessly.

"Not today." He watched her, his head cocked. A wistful look touched his eyes, just for a moment, then vanished, and he bent to graze her nipple. His tongue flicked out, stroking her.

Just the slightest touch to her nipple made an intense tug in her cunny.

His lips nuzzled her nipples, teased them, played with them, while he tied the ropes to her shackles. She was completely tied to the bed, unable to touch him.

At his mercy.

And merciless he was proving to be. Opening his mouth, he took all her nipple inside and sucked. Each tug . . . oh, she literally writhed on the bed with pleasure.

He suckled her nipples, licked them, scraped his teeth across them. Then, daringly, bit her left nipple gently while his strong hand cupped her naked breast.

She froze for a minute—how far would this biting go?—then relaxed as he eased back to licking her nipple. His large hand slid between her legs, stroking her, making her wet.

She ached inside. She felt empty inside. Instinctively she knew she wanted to be filled. Her hips arched up rhythmically. She wanted to press her cunny to his hand. Ease the ache, the hunger for more.

But if he wasn't going to undress, they weren't going to make love—

Greybrooke opened the fastenings of his trousers, revealing his thick, engorged erection. Large. Pointing at her. He got on top of her, braced on one arm, balanced on his knees. He slid something onto his shaft. A slender, almost translucent sleeve. "A French letter," he said. "It prevents my seed from entering you. Prevents us from creating a child."

"Oh. That's rather a good thing." She didn't want an illegitimate child. She knew, from her sister Margaret's tragedy, how terrible that would be.

"I want to make you ready," he said softly. He brushed her sensitive nub with the head of his erection.

She quivered. Tugged at her shackles. "I am ready. I want you."

She was a mistress now. She could have the pleasure she wanted. And she ached for it.

"This will hurt a little, I'm afraid," he said softly. "I'll be gentle. But soon, love, you'll want me to thrust as deep and hard as I can."

His hips shifted. It was amazing—he could direct his cock just by flexing his hips. Her nether lips tugged a little, resisting the big, full head of his enormous erection. Helena held her breath.

She had never felt so close to anyone in her life.

"Relax," he murmured. "Just a twinge, then it will be good."

His cock slid forward, gliding in her wetness. He went in only an inch, and she kept gasping, as she felt his hugeness inside her. Yet her body began to relax around him, and he fit as snugly inside her as if she'd been made especially for him.

Greybrooke's hands settled on her narrow bed on each side of her head. He was bearing his weight on them, and he drew his cock back. Just when she was ready to sob, he thrust gently forward again. Over and over he pumped, going a little deeper each time.

This was her whole world. The sensation of his cock inside her, filling her. She couldn't touch him, but she could fill every other sense. She could look at his gorgeous jawline, his long lashes, his longer body. She could smell his maleness. Hear the ragged edge to his breathing.

"I'm inside all the way, love."

He stayed like that, and she savored the moment, getting used to being filled by him. Working against the ropes, she arched her hips up, just a bit, but it sent his thick cock in deeper.

She gasped.

She wished she could see what they looked like joined, but like this she couldn't see the mirror. She watched his face. Could see in the way his mouth tightened how good it was for

him. She could see everything in his eyes. Lust. Need. Pleasure.
Everything she felt.

Never had she dreamed she would be tied up for her very
first time. Yet it was thrilling to have him in command. Greybrooke's hair was damp with sweat—perspiration she'd caused.
She felt rather wickedly proud.

"Does it still hurt?" His voice was soft as a caress.

"No, not anymore."

Slowly he began thrusting. Long, elegant strokes. Her body
loved it and her hips moved, seeking more.

His strokes sped up, became harder. She pounded up against
him, encouraging him.

"I want you to come," he growled.

He pumped fast, his shaft kissing her aching clit with his
every thrust. He sucked her nipples, kissed her neck, gave her
so much sensation, she couldn't think.

Yes, oh yes!

She felt it coming. Felt her whole body grow tense, knew it
was the moment before everything burst—

She was coming. Coming and coming and coming. Her
body was a slave to pleasure, and she thrust back against him
more, taking herself to the peak again. He seemed to be inde-
fatigable, as if he could be hard forever. As if he could keep
thrusting in her, making her climax until she dissolved into a
boneless puddle of pleasure.

Then he tensed over her. Helena sensed it, even groggy with
her climax. His back arched, his head bowed, and he let out a
soft growl. His hips smacked hard against her, and he stayed
absolutely still.

Goodness, he was coming too.

She was exquisitely beautiful. Her cheeks glowed pink, and
her hair was damp from perspiration. Her eyes were closed,
and she was taking quick, soft breaths.

Grey was gripped with a yearning to give her a gentle, sweet kiss on her parted lips.

Hell.

He braced himself over Miss Winsome and withdrew from her, then he discarded the French letter beside the bed and quickly buttoned his trousers.

This was what he always did with mistresses—when he was done, he left. With Lady Montroy, as with all his other paramours, he kept to a schedule. Many men kept a mistress for company, for a sympathetic ear. He had never done that.

Sure as sin, he could not do that with Miss Winsome.

Grey withdrew a key from his pocket and opened the shackles, releasing her wrists, then he untied her ankles.

His body was spent, exhausted, but he wasn't about to lie down on her bed and take a nap. He'd never given a woman her first time. He'd had no idea how intense it would be, how much it would touch him to know he was her first.

The way her blue eyes had glowed at him as he thrust into her—

He had to forget that. He couldn't trust her. He had to find out what she wanted and why, and to do that he must coax her to trust him.

Even though he'd freed her from her bonds, she didn't move. She looked dreamily at him, obviously as languorous from pleasure as he wanted to be.

"Like your house?" he asked.

"The house?" She blinked, a fetching flick of long, golden-brown lashes. "Oh . . . it's lovely. More sumptuous than anything I could have dreamed of."

"You're my mistress, and I want to shower you with extravagance. After all, we are intimate now."

He watched her flinch. Just a touch. She was keeping secrets, and she was not immune to guilt, he realized.

She sat up, then looked down at her naked body. A blush

touched her cheeks. Now that sex was over, she must be feeling exposed.

Good.

She tried to grasp the sheet, but he caught her wrists and sat on the edge of the bed, preventing her from moving.

"Uh . . . do you wish to do it again?" she whispered.

"Not today. I believe you will be sore after your first time. I will return tomorrow."

"Oh. What should I do?"

"Whatever you wish," he said.

Miss Winsome frowned. "I don't really know what a mistress does. My days have always been so regimented. What is it, as your mistress, I'm to do?"

A laugh escaped him. He'd just made love to her; she was concerned about organizing her day. Then he bit back his grin. Probably she was worried about that because she was spying on him. She didn't desire him or want him. Just like his mother had once paid a girl to go to his bed and betray him, Miss Winsome was probably more concerned about having time to plot against him.

The question: Why?

Part of him was tempted to grab her, scare her a little, get the truth out of her. But he didn't think Miss Winsome could be threatened.

And he couldn't carry through on a threat like that. He couldn't hurt her. He couldn't hurt any woman. He had to use seduction to get at the truth.

"You want to know what to do? This. When I want to make love, that's what you do." Grey paused for a moment. "The rest of the time, you are free to do what you wish. Read. Take walks. Meet friends." He watched her eyes closely. Saw a quick downward glance—he knew how to watch and read faces. She kept her features devoid of expression, but she had not been able to control that tiny sign of guilt.

He wanted her to have lots of freedom. His plan was to have her followed. He released her hands and stood. "This is all for today, Miss Winsome."

That night, Betsy, the youngest of her maids—a poor girl of sixteen who was a bit slow-witted and who had been thrown out of her former places—brought her a calling card. Helena's heart leapt. It must be Greybrooke. He must have decided he couldn't stay away until tomorrow.

Helena stared at the name, her stomach churning. It was Whitehall. Of course, she hadn't escaped him. She wanted to forbid him entry. But she feared what he could do to her family, so she told Betsy to bring him to the drawing room.

"Lovely house," he remarked as he took a seat.

She did not say anything. She did not offer him tea or even a drop of Greybrooke's brandy. "You want to know what I found. I went through his desk, found a journal, but there was nothing written in it. But I'm sure, with a little more time, I can coax him to reveal things to me." She was stalling—stalling for time.

"I'm sure you can, if he's rewarded you with this for tupping him."

She went flaming red. "I will get what you want, but I will not sit and listen to insults. I do not want you in my house. You are to go—"

"Shut up and think of your family. You're no better than you ought to be. But now that you're his mistress, get the truth out of him. I will return in two days."

"It will take longer than that. And there's no evidence on paper. I'm sure of it." It was not quite a lie. There was no evidence of treason in Greybrooke's possession.

Whitehall stood and took a step toward her.

"Don't touch me," she hissed. "I have servants, and if you lay a hand on me I will scream for them to come."

"I don't need to manhandle you to hurt you," he said smoothly. Coldly. "Remember that."

Then he was gone, and she dropped her head into her hands. She could not give this man Greybrooke's secret. She would not.

A message arrived at midmorning, brief and to the point:

I will visit you this evening. Greybrooke.

Having a full day alone, Helena went to see Will. She told him Greybrooke's secret, certain she could trust him. When it came to news, she knew Will had great integrity. She told him of her dilemma. She didn't want to hurt the duke and his family. Will had promised to keep the secret to himself until she decided what to do.

Returning to her town house, she had her lady's maid, O'Hara, see to the filling of her bath. The tub was huge, and it was glorious to soak in it. In her years as a governess, she had to bathe in metal tubs. She had no idea what to wear though. Did she dress for bed? Was that too contrived? What would the servants think?

Though, really, they had to know why she had this house. Still, she had pride and she put on her prettiest gown—the one he'd called wretched.

As soon as Greybrooke came into her drawing room, he lifted his brow. "That comes off."

He held out his hand and led her to her bedroom. Helena expected him to tie her up, but instead he undressed her with efficiency. He took off all her clothes, yet he barely touched her skin. To be so close to him and not be touched made her feel balanced on a knife's edge.

As soon as she discarded her shift though, his fingers skimmed over her naked bottom. She blushed at his caress. She was no longer innocent, but she certainly didn't feel experienced.

"Bend over your vanity table, love," he instructed.

She stared at him, confused. So he clasped her hand and led her there, positioning her the way he wanted—with her hands braced on the marble vanity top, her bottom sticking out.

"You are incredibly beautiful."

Then he took something out from his tall leather boot.

A riding crop.

She flinched, expecting him to strike her. But he caressed the curves of her bottom with it, tracing around and around until her skin became highly sensitive and she moaned.

"Good?"

"Yes," she answered breathlessly. "It is."

Lightly, he tapped her bottom. Then again, in little teasing pats. She focused on every one. Her bottom rippled with each soft strike. Sensation spiraled through her. Then he did one a bit hard, just a touch, just enough to make her truly feel it. He slowly built the intensity until each spank of the crop seemed to vibrate through her quim. Her inner muscles began to clutch, and her clit ached with need.

She was soaked with arousal. Almost in pain with the force of her desire. "Are we—are you—?" She could not quite bring herself to ask if he intended to make love to her.

"You can play with yourself, angel. Make yourself come while I spank you."

"I—oh—no, I can't."

"Yes, you can. There's nothing wicked or naughty or bad about it. You told me yourself that pleasure should make you happy. What I want you to see is that pleasure is not wrong."

He guided her hand to the damp curls between her legs. She felt her sticky wetness. Touching herself there released her erotic smell.

"It pleases me to watch you," he said softly.

Her fingers brushed her nether lips. The sensation made her gasp. She rather liked it. And stroked herself again. Her fingers moved higher, and she found her sensitive nub. Oh yes. Yes.

Then she realized he was murmuring words of encouragement. Telling her how sensual and beautiful she was. His husky words wrapped around her, seducing her into pure wanton delight. He spanked her bottom with the crop, and she arched against each stroke, wildly aroused. She played with herself, stroking fiercely.

"Make yourself come," Greybrooke growled.

And she did. It struck like a fork of lightning slamming into a field. She rocked with it, shuddered with it, sobbed his name. *Greybrooke. Heavens, Greybrooke.*

He bent and kissed the nape of her neck. Glorious kisses that made her almost delirious on top of her climax. Then he stopped kissing her, and she collapsed onto the vanity stool.

He picked her up, carried her to her bed, then gave her a robe.

She held it against her, brushing her loose hair behind her ear. Greybrooke prowled across her bedroom. Strange—the room seemed to be filled with tension.

He then sat on her vanity stool, his long legs splayed out. He hadn't joined with her or had a climax. Instead, he tapped the crop against his thigh, watching her.

"I want to know about you, Miss Winsome. I want to learn everything I can about you."

Oh no! She could not tell him who she was. "I'm a governess," she said simply, aware of his focused gaze. She prayed she looked guileless and innocent.

"You had to be something before you were a governess."

"I was a young woman in need of a future and a position."

Greybrooke's eyes narrowed, and Helena knew she could not evade his questions without infuriating him. Could she lie? She didn't want him to know of her connection to the newspaper, or to have any suspicion she was spying on him. But if she told a blatant lie and he found out the truth . . .

"I don't know who I really am." She *hated* telling more lies, so what she was going to do was twist the truth. "I don't remember my father. He died when I was just two. My mother remarried and had more children—those are my half siblings. Then she died—" Well, she had lost Mama, though much later.

"Who was your family?"

"My mother was a viscount's daughter. But she'd married against her father's wishes and was turned out of his house. When she was widowed, she had nowhere to go."

She had been too young to understand the danger they faced—starvation or a workhouse. Then Mama had met Arthur Rains, and their lives had abruptly changed from disaster to happiness . . . at least until the sadness of losing Margaret, then their mother, then her stepfather. She believed Margaret's death had hurt them both so badly that they had not lasted long afterward.

It had all been long ago, but her chest was getting tight, her throat felt sore.

But Greybrooke might want to know about her stepfather. She couldn't talk about him without revealing too much. "When my mother died, I was sent away. I went to live with one relative after another. So many I don't remember their names. At sixteen, I made my way to London."

Greybrooke got off the stool. Concern drew lines in his forehead and etched them around his mouth. "What did you have to do to survive here?"

"I didn't get dragged into a brothel or anything like that. I became a governess at once."

"You are a viscount's granddaughter."

She supposed she was. She hadn't thought about it, since the man had no place in her life.

Was Greybrooke satisfied? How much did he need to know about her?

She must distract him, so she ran her tongue slowly over her lips. Saw his body tense at the gesture and she felt his awareness. "Would you make love to me now?" she asked.

"Of course," he said gallantly. He stood up from the vanity and strolled toward her bed. He carried something now—there was a spill of color in his hand.

As he reached her, she saw what it was. Four silk scarves.

Hours later, Helena woke suddenly with a gasp and sat up. She had gone to sleep! Were mistresses allowed to do that? Where was Greybrooke—?

She blinked. The duke sat on her vanity stool, a book resting on his knee. She saw the pencil in his hand. "What are you doing?"

"Drawing your likeness, angel."

Curiosity drove her to scramble out of bed and go to see, though first she pulled on her robe. His gaze followed her as she approached, holding her robe closed over her body. He watched her until she came to stand at his side and look down on what he'd done.

"You drew this?"

Greybrooke nodded. "You look very lovely when you sleep. I enjoy drawing, and your beauty was so tempting, I had to capture it." Then he frowned. "Is something wrong with it?"

"Nothing's wrong." It was exquisite. It was her likeness exactly. He had captured her in quick, soft lines. Though she thought he'd made her look prettier than she really was. "It's remarkable. . . . I had no idea you were so artistic."

"You didn't? I think my rope work is highly artistic and creative."

She forgot herself. She gave him a very governess-like look

of disapproval. Then softened her expression quickly. "No one ever mentioned you draw."

"No one knows I do it. My father thought it worthless and effeminate. After all, ladies sketch and do watercolors."

"What about the great male artists?"

"My father believed they preferred the company of other men."

"So you were not allowed to draw."

"Let's say I was discouraged."

She hated that. She believed talent should be nurtured. The drawings gave him pleasure and what was the harm . . . ? Oh! She remembered something. "You made the drawings around the poem you sent." She flushed. "Your depiction of my breasts was shamefully accurate."

His mouth quirked in a smile. "I know that now. It was just a guess at the time. In addition, I decided to bestow you with a bosom I would find remarkably appealing. Funny how you ended up looking just like that."

Helena floundered. He was telling her he had fantasized about her, and apparently she'd lived up to his dreams. He had far outdone the wicked dreams she'd had about him.

"You are sleepy, my dear," Grey said gently. "Thank you for today."

Then he left Miss Winsome. He had plans for his day. He had nefarious reasons for sketching her, but she didn't know it. He wanted to show the picture to Orley. Then take it around the rookery where Orley lived, in case someone recognized her.

But by the end of the day, Grey had nothing to show for his work. Orley didn't recognize her, nor did anyone in Orley's slum.

For Helena, her life as a duke's mistress had truly begun.

For the first fortnight, Greybrooke visited her three times a day. As he'd said, she could spend her time as she wished when he was not visiting her. She went to the museum, to bookshops. She did all the things she did with children, even though she no longer had children to educate and entertain.

Shopping took a great deal of time. She'd had no idea how arduous it really was to be fashionable. Endless sittings for the seamstress who created her new, lacy, exquisite underclothes; measurements and fitting for gowns; purchases of bonnets and shoes. Greybrooke would make a request, and she had to ensure it was filled at once: She bought corsets of red lace and black satin, gossamer-thin stockings with exotic embroidery, garters in scandalous colors.

He either made love to her while she was bound or spanked her with his riding crop, pleasuring her to insanity while he did.

He fixed a swing in the special room, hanging from the ceiling, and when she sat on it, he would tease her quim with his tongue and his lips. She came so furiously she almost let go and fell off.

Within days, she was used to being naked for him. Used to seeing the pleasure in his eyes as he looked at her bare breasts, her rounded hips, her bottom. Each time, he told her she was beautiful. She saw her quim as a wickedly pleasurable place now instead of a place she wasn't supposed to touch.

To please Greybrooke—because she loved pleasing him— she became rather good at sucking his cock. She'd learned to overwhelm him with stimulation. She even played with his ballocks while suckling, which always made him explode.

Every time he came to see her, it was for sex. He never spent the night. Certain nights they dined together. She learned his favorite dishes. He loved fish in light sauces, rare roast beef, Yorkshire puddings, and he had a weakness for chocolate desserts. Even something as simple as a fluffy mousse in a long-stemmed glass brought a look of ecstasy to his handsome face.

She had all the gowns she could desire. She discovered that the stables in the mews held two gorgeous gray mares for her use, and Greybrooke gave her a glossy, jaunty pale blue curricle. She'd never driven one before, but he patiently taught her a few basic skills. Every morning, breakfast was brought into her bedchamber on a silver tray.

And then there were the jewels.

The second day after she had moved into the town house, he presented her with a necklace of rubies. Then he gave her earbobs dripping with emeralds. After that, a diamond bracelet.

Already she had sold one necklace and put the money in an account for her sisters, so her family would be assured of food on the table, new shoes, and clothes. She was going to use her allowance to create a dowry for her sisters. Greybrooke was giving her more than she could dream of spending. Really, how did mistresses end up impoverished? They must spend like drunken sailors, or gamble away their money.

Helena supposed it was sinfully wrong, but she was *happy* as Greybrooke's mistress.

Only two things were making her worry. The first: She had not yet told Whitehall what she'd discovered.

The second? While Greybrooke made love to her three times a day and rocked with climaxes that seemed to shatter him, he never removed his clothes. He always bound her hands so she couldn't touch him. And he always looked haunted, as if he were being constantly whipped by his own secret devils.

Two weeks after he had taken her from Jacinta's, Greybrooke left Miss Winsome's town house in the afternoon and walked toward White's. On St. James Street, he encountered Caradon, who took one look at him and said, "What devil is riding you, Grey?"

He had spent a glorious spring afternoon spanking Miss Winsome in the bedroom. She had moaned and squealed with abandon, thoroughly enjoying herself. Then he had shown her how erotic it was when he took her from behind while she watched in the mirror. Her eyes had been huge as saucers, watching his hands cupping her breasts, then playing with her sensitively.

She had climaxed so hard, she had melted against him.

Cary fell into step at his side as they headed toward White's. "You look like hell, Grey."

"It's my mistress."

"The governess? Is she proving a disappointment?"

"No, she's proving to be everything I've ever dreamed of in a woman. Have you ever had a woman who made everything erotic? She is like that. She even makes eating dinner into a sexual event. She closes her eyes and makes all kinds of seductive little sighs."

"But you are not happy."

The famed bow window was just ahead. "No. I can't trust her. I've had investigators try to learn more about her, but she has not gone anywhere but modistes, bookshops, and the British museum since becoming my mistress. She told me about her past, and I'm trying to verify it. But my men have dug back only to her first post as a governess. I do know she is a liar and a spy, and for some reason I have yet to determine, she was searching my desk. However, I'm having too much fun fucking her to find out why."

Before Caradon could voice the shock that was obvious on his face, Grey noticed the sandwich board that stood on the corner, advertising the latest edition of a newspaper. In capital letters it read: DUKE OF GREYBROOKE SCANDAL. Pulling out his pennies, he bought an edition. The paper was the *London Correspondent*, the paper that featured Lady X's famous column. Grey stared at the front page.

On it was an article that speculated that his father had not been killed in an accident while cleaning one of his dueling pistols. It claimed there was evidence his father had been murdered.

"Grey?"

Caradon's voice came through the buzzing in his ears. He realized the newspaper was now a crumpled ball in his hands. How in God's name had anyone found out?

Had Miss Winsome found out? How? There was nothing in his mother's letters that had revealed the truth. No one knew what had really happened. No one outside of Jacinta, Maryanne, and himself.

No one knew that his father had tried to force himself on his youngest daughter and had been killed by a pistol shot blown through his skull.

13

Helena slipped to the print shop during the day, wearing her cloak with her hood up. She was certain two men had been following her for the last few days.

Had Whitehall sent them to watch her? Or was it possible Greybrooke now suspected her? But how could he—how could he suspect her and make love to her so much?

She had taken care to evade them to come here. Now she dragged Will into the quiet office and glared at him. "How could you have printed that story?" she cried, once the door was firmly shut and no one could hear. "I told you it in the strictest confidence. I haven't told Whitehall yet, and I don't know if I am going to tell him. You shouldn't have made it public. Anyway, we have no idea if it's true. I put it together from hints in diaries."

"I think it's true, Helena. The Duke of Greybrooke came here and tackled me about it. Demanded to know where I'd gotten the story from."

"Greybrooke came?" Her heart wobbled. And fear hit her. "He didn't find out who I am?"

"No, why would he? He denied the story, of course. Said his father's death had been an accident. But why else would he have come, irate, if your story weren't true?"

"But still, why did you print it?"

Her brother paled. "Whitehall forced me—why do you think I did it? It wasn't to sell papers, not this time. Whitehall came, threatening to ensure that the gaming hell men came looking for their money. He threatened to force us into bankruptcy and the workhouses unless I did exactly as he asked. It's his plan to unsettle Greybrooke, to goad him into making a mistake."

"This is wrong, Will. We cannot be a party to this."

"Helena, Whitehall can destroy us if he wants. Destroy our entire family. I don't have a choice."

"Madam, the Duke of Greybrooke has arrived and is waiting in the drawing room."

Helena's heart plunged. Of course, Greybrooke was here—he came every night. But she wasn't ready to face him, not with guilt churning in her stomach.

It must have been awful for Greybrooke to see that headline. Even if he were a traitor, she would never publish his private, personal secrets. Never. Yet that had happened. And she felt sick.

Helena hurried down the stairs, stopped at the bottom to gather her courage. She had always been an honest person. A good person. Now she was turning into the most dishonest person she knew. She prayed her guilt didn't show on her face—then felt guilty that her biggest fear was getting caught. She didn't know what he would do to her.

He had risked his life to nurse Maryanne. He'd revealed how he had protected his sister, Lady Winterhaven. He had saved Michael's life. He adored his family, and that story hurt both him and them.

But if she admitted what had happened—if she told the truth—she would lose him forever, and destroy her family. She couldn't let him think there was any connection between her and that story.

She drew a deep breath, went to the drawing room, and stopped on the threshold in shock.

Greybrooke looked . . . dazzling.

He wore a black tailcoat that must have been sewn on him. It skimmed perfectly over his broad shoulders, tucked in over his narrow waist, and followed the lines of his lean hips. Jet-black trousers made his legs look endlessly long. Snow-white shirt points framed his tanned jaw, his white cravat was perfectly tied, and his waistcoat was ivory satin.

She had to hold onto the door. He looked so . . . delectable.

Goodness, she would love to make love to him. Right now. Undo his trousers and naughtily climb on top of him, and mess up his hair, and rumple his elegant clothes.

She longed to touch him. But she couldn't—and not just because he would not allow it. She felt she did not deserve to touch him.

"Go upstairs and get dressed, my dear," he said. "I'm taking you to a ball."

"A ball?" She gaped at him. "Mistresses do not go to balls . . . do they?"

His lips twitched with a smile. Often he looked like that—that he wanted to grin, but something stopped him.

"It's hosted by Lady Ponsonby," he said. "She is a former courtesan who married the earl when he was seventy-two. She throws very scandalous parties. Husbands and wives arrive separately, and everyone is masked. They make use of the bedchambers, but with other people's spouses."

"Why are you taking me?" she asked, wary. "To trade me?"

"Of course not." The statement came out fast and decisive.

"I have no intention of giving you to any other man. You'll spend your night with me. I have my reasons for going tonight—reasons that have nothing to do with you. I could leave you home to curl up with a horrid novel and a cup of tea, while I go alone—"

"No," Helena said quickly. "I want to go." To attend a ball on Greybrooke's arm? Even if she didn't deserve it, she felt a spurt of excitement. She'd always dreamed of going to a ball.

There was no other man she would want to go with than Greybrooke.

That thought stunned her. She barely heard Greybrooke say, "Then get dressed. I have a present for you afterward."

She hurried upstairs, summoned O'Hara, and threw open the doors of one of her many, many wardrobes. Her beautiful new gowns hung within. She chose a sheath of ivory satin—the cut was simple, with a scooped bodice and a column of a skirt. It was embroidered with gold thread, in a fanciful design of entwined flowers, with pearls scattered over it. O'Hara came forth carrying a pair of ivory silk slippers.

Once dressed, Helena sat at her vanity table while O'Hara deftly swept up her hair, leaving a few tendrils that she curled with her fingers. The maid threaded a rope of pearls through her hair.

She looked like a . . . duchess.

"Oh, I will need a mask." Helena opened a drawer in which she had put the one Greybrooke had given her to wear to his private club. It was dramatic in contrast to her pale dress and blond hair, but she liked the effect. It gave a touch of wickedness.

She supposed she was wicked now.

Greybrooke paced at the bottom of the stairs in the foyer. When he looked up and saw her, he stopped in his tracks.

"You are beautiful," he said. But there was a rueful expression on his face.

He held out a box of gold, tied with a red ribbon. "Nothing spectacular, I'm afraid."

She opened it and gasped. A fine gold chain, so delicate it was almost invisible. An enormous ruby dangled from the end, a remarkable teardrop. Even larger than the beautiful diamond he'd given her.

Greybrooke drew out the necklace, moved behind her. He draped it around her neck. The ruby slipped slightly between her breasts. It reflected shafts of red light.

"Just as I imagined it. Sweetly nestled between your perfect breasts," he murmured.

Goodness, she knew she would think of those words all night. His lips touched her neck, and she gave a breathy sigh, instantly aroused. Needing him. Even though they'd just made love *yesterday*.

"Are you certain you don't want to stay here?" she asked.

He looked surprised. "Waiting will make it more fun," he growled.

Lady Ponsonby had auburn hair and an enormous bosom—it seemed to be a requirement for courtesans, Helena observed.

Worse, the voluptuous, beautiful woman fawned all over Greybrooke the instant they had stepped into her large drawing room. At once, the countess slithered over to him, slid her arm through his, and twined around him like a snake with bosoms.

What stunned Helena was that Greybrooke didn't even notice. His gaze swept around the room constantly as if he were looking for someone else—someone specific.

When he managed to peel her ladyship off him, he led Helena to a quiet corner of the crowded ballroom. Then his lips twitched until finally, as if he could hold it in no longer, his dazzling smile exploded. Leaving her breathless.

"Jealous?" he asked.

"She was like a leech. And she is *married*. Goodness, did you ever have an affair with her?" She pictured—against her will—Greybrooke caressing the woman's generous breasts.

"No, I didn't, love." He cocked his head endearingly, then murmured, "Shall we dance?"

She became aware of the strains of a waltz as Greybrooke put his hand on the small of her back and drew her close. He held her other hand, twining their fingers slowly while he held her gaze. By instinct, her hand went to his broad shoulder.

She'd never waltzed. Never danced. She'd watched from the doorways, with other servants, listening to gossip but never sharing any. Watching and wondering what it would be like—

Greybrooke took a step, leading her with him, and suddenly she was revolving in a sea of people. A sea of shimmering silk, glittering jewels, the striking black of men's coats. She floated with Greybrooke, feeling as if her feet were gliding a few inches from the floor. It was a good thing he was leading, for she was falling into his gaze, and she would have crashed into a column—or a peer.

The duke whirled her around, his movements perfect, correct, yet underlain with a raw sensuality that made her hot under her stays.

"You dance beautifully," he said.

"Then apparently I trip well. You are the excellent dancer. I've never done this before."

His brow quirked. "Never?"

"I've dreamed of balls from afar."

"I hope I meet your expectations in a partner."

"You are a dream," she whispered.

All this was a dream. For one glorious moment, she felt as if he could always be hers. They would be together for a lifetime. They would dance like this someday in the future, with their children grown—he under protest, for married gentlemen hated to be dragged on the dance floor. They would share thousands of precious memories.

Was it so impossible? Men had married mistresses. Grey claimed he never trusted his lovers, but surely what she saw in his eyes was more than just desire? Not love—she wasn't ready to dream of that—but at least trust?

The music stopped, the whirling couples stopped. Greybrooke stopped, and a second later so did she. It was over. And she'd learned one thing.

She wasn't sensible at all. She was filled with hopeless dreams.

Greybrooke grasped two flutes of champagne from the tray of a passing footman and handed one to her. She tried not to gulp—because she was hot, and because she was stunned by her discovery. Greybrooke scanned the crowd again. Subtly as she could, she did too.

The gazes exchanged by gentlemen and ladies across the room could melt ice. Secret, erotic invitations were sent in the way women held their fans. Greybrooke stood beside her.

Sipping the champagne, Helena followed his gaze and froze in surprise. Across the room, a set of double doors stood open. Beyond them was a shadowy corridor. A figure in a black cloak stood there, half-hidden in the shadows. Helena glimpsed pale blond ringlets peeking from the cowl of a deep hood. It was a woman watching Greybrooke.

The figure retreated.

"Excuse me for a moment," he murmured by her ear. "There's someone I have to talk to."

Helena gaped at him in panic. "You're going to leave me alone? In here?"

"I have arranged for a gentleman to look after you," Greybrooke said.

"What do you mean by look after me?"

"To stay at your side," Grey growled. "Protect you and en-

sure none of these wolves approach you." He'd noticed that
every man in the room had taken a good look at Miss Winsome.
In the slim-fitting ivory dress, her figure promised to be a
voluptuous treat. Any man who was breathing could tell she
was beautiful, even in her mask. "The Duke of Saxonby."

"Saxonby! He's one of the Wicked Dukes."

"Ah, Lady X's column." That soured him, as he remembered the article in the damned *London Correspondent*. "Saxonby knows better than to poach on my preserve. Here he is."

Saxonby, known as Sax, approached with long, predatory
strides, but Grey knew the man could be trusted with Miss
Winsome. Sax was twenty-eight, but his hair was pale silver, a
startling contrast to his dark brows and black eyelashes. Sax
was damnably handsome and a thorough rogue when it came
to women, unless the woman belonged to a friend. They'd been
friends since Eton days.

The musicians began another waltz. With an elegant flour-
ish, Sax bowed over Miss Winsome's hand and asked her to
dance.

Grey headed across the floor and passed through the double
doors. He went to the usual room he used to meet Caroline,
Lady Blackbriar; let himself in; and locked the door behind him.

Caroline stood forlornly in the middle of the room. Now
she spun, rushed to him, threw herself in his embrace.

Grey groaned as he hugged her. "Caro, I wish you wouldn't
take the risk of coming here."

She gazed up at him, her eyes huge, deep ivy green, and
filled with the look that always made his heart ache. She looked
at him as if he were the only person in the world she had. As if
she desperately needed him.

She was so beautiful, he understood why the Earl of Blackbriar had pursued her with such determination. Back then,
Caro had believed what the rest of the world did about the
handsome, slender earl—that he was a brilliant poet, sensitive

and sweet. It was only when Blackbriar had her safely tied to him by marriage that he'd shown his true colors, beating and abusing her.

"I'm very careful." Her voice was soft and breathy. Just the sound of it was reputed to drive men wild with desire. But he had always seen Caro as a little sister who needed protecting.

"My husband believes I'm at a musicale performance at a friend's house. Everyone who goes there is over sixty, so it is one of the few things he lets me do. His servants escorted me to her house, as always, and once I'm inside they relax their vigilance. My friend Cynthia always ensures they are distracted by food and drink, then I slip over here. Since she is on this street, it is perfect."

"Do not get overconfident, Caro." He clasped her hands.

"I'm very careful." She smiled almost childishly. She was terrified but also defiant in her own way. "He thinks I'm not clever, but I am. Anyway, I meet my lover here." Her eyes became dreamy. "Finally, I've found love. For a brief few hours, I can be happy—I can love and be loved. That is worth any risk."

"Even now?" Grey asked softly.

"Even now," she said firmly.

Caro had found love, which he never had, and she was happy. Grey believed Blackbriar was vicious enough to kill her if he found out about the affair. Her lover had not come to her rescue when she'd been blackmailed. As her friend, Grey had. In his view, if her lover was too much of a coward to have helped her, he wasn't worthy of her love.

But there was no point trying to make Caro understand that.

"Even though I'm afraid," she said, eyes sparkling, "love is worth it. Someday you'll understand, Grey."

"I'm not going to fall in love, Caro." Nor did he want to talk about it.

"What's wrong, Grey? Is it about the money? I know it is a lot of money—"

"Who could have found out the child isn't Blackbriar's?" He asked the question more tersely than he'd intended. "You said you were careful, so how did this man get hold of the truth? Could your lady's maid have guessed?"

"You asked me this before, Grey. I don't know how anyone could know! I've never said a word to anyone. I've only met him here, using Cynthia as my reason to leave the house."

"Could your maid have guessed you had been undressed and redressed?"

Earnestly, Caro shook her head. "Lady Ponsonby has always provided a maid for me. I would bathe before returning home, for I know there is a scent after making love."

"Caro, if no one could have known, how could you be blackmailed?"

She stared at him, gnawing her lip with her teeth. "I don't know! But you do believe me, Grey? That I've made sure no one found out?"

She looked desperate, ready to burst into tears. He hated the sound of a woman's tears. They reminded him of his sisters', and how he had failed them both. "I believe you."

"I saw that terrible story about your father in one of the newssheets," she said. "It's not true, is it? Your father killed himself. That's been the secret you worked to protect. That your father took his own life."

He hadn't admitted the truth to anyone. Not Caroline. Not even Caradon or Saxonby, his most trusted friends. "He killed himself." Essentially it was true. His father wouldn't be dead if he hadn't been such a sick, selfish, perverted bastard.

"You haven't found the blackmailer yet, have you? You haven't put an end to it yet?"

Her questions speared him with guilt. He'd promised to protect her. "Not yet."

"This is the thing that could destroy me." Caroline trembled and went pale. "If this blackmailer were to go to my husband—"

"That's not going to happen. I'm going to find out who he is."

Seeing Caroline's frightened face, Grey knew what he had to do. He had to get at the truth through Helena. Even though no one had recognized her picture, logic told him she had to be involved with the blackmailer. The blackmailer must have sent her to discover his private secrets, so he would become a victim too.

His cock wanted to believe differently. It wanted to believe Miss Winsome was innocent.

Innocent women didn't rifle through desks.

What he had to do was end this. Find the blackmailer. And Miss Winsome was his only connection.

You care for her too much to frighten her. Or hurt her.

He scrubbed his hand over his jaw. It was true, but he had to push it aside. He couldn't care for her—

"Oh, thank you, Grey," Caro breathed, her face glowing with relief and hope. "Thank you so much. But I must go now. *He* might come to me tonight. I wrote him a letter, begging to see him. Surely he will finally come to me . . ." She hurried to the mirror over the mantelpiece, tidied her hair, and slapped her cheeks lightly to put color in them.

It amazed him she would go from desperate fear to desperate desire in seconds. The "he" was her lover, who had distanced himself from her once she got pregnant. "I'll leave first," Grey said.

He slipped out the door and returned to the main salon. Across the room, he saw Sax, who was pulling on his hair in frustration. Gut tightening, Grey reached Saxonby in a second. "Damnation, you've lost sight of her, haven't you?"

Sax raked his hand through his silver hair. "She sent me to get more champagne, and while I turned to summon a footman, she hurried over to Lady Ponsonby. Said I'd admitted to being madly in love with Ponsy and it was my fantasy to bed her. By the time I managed to break free of busty Ponsy, your mistress has disappeared. Who is she, by the way?"

"That doesn't matter, damn it. What matters is where she is. . . ."

He knew where she was, and Ponsy was here.

With Lady Ponsonby blocking Greybrooke, Helena knew she had only minutes to do something dangerous and bold. She hurried toward the double doors of the salon, where Greybrooke's mysterious woman had vanished—

A man grasped her by the arm. "My dear, accompany me on a stroll? Out to a private balcony. I would enjoy rogering you beneath the stars."

The man was masked and dressed in elegant evening clothes. "Please let me go." Then desperately, she added, "I came with the Duke of Greybrooke."

"Just because he is the horse you brought to the stable doesn't mean you can't take another stallion for a ride."

"But he's my favorite and he's hardly broken in yet," she threw back.

Her retort surprised the man, and she wrenched her arm free. She slipped away, weaving through the crowd filled with the most elegant people of Society.

She blinked wildly as she plunged from candlelight to gloom. A door opened ahead of her and a figure in a black cloak stepped out. Helena rushed forward and put her hand on the woman's shoulder. "I must talk to you about Greybrooke."

Huge, dark green eyes stared at her. The woman was as white as a sheet. "Why? Who are you? Did he send you—did my husband send you?"

"No. I came with the Duke of Greybrooke. He came here to meet you, didn't he? Why?" She had remembered Greybrooke's confrontation with the blackmailer. When they had spoken of a woman Grey was trying to protect. Helena had assumed it must be one of his sisters. It was a hunch, but she asked, "Is Greybrooke protecting you from a blackmailer?"

"Did he tell you? How could you *know?*"

"No, he didn't tell me."

The woman grabbed her arm, her grip strong enough to leave bruises. She dragged Helena back into the room and shut the door. "If you are working for my husband, I will pay you for your silence. I will give you anything you want."

"Of course I'm not. I don't even know who your husband is."

But the woman was too careful to reveal his name. She rested her hand on her tummy, just as Lady Winterhaven did—

"Oh, you are expecting a child."

The woman looked panicked. Helena's stomach roiled. "It's not . . . Greybrooke's child?"

"No! It's my husband's." But the woman was blushing, shaking. It was obvious her words were a lie. "Grey and I have never been lovers, but we have been friends since we were children. Oh, I would have wed him happily when I was sixteen, but Grey refuses to marry. He's been a devoted friend and he's helped me. But I can't tell you anything else. I *won't.*"

"You *are* the woman Greybrooke is protecting from the blackmailer."

"I won't talk about it. You must go!" The woman waved wildly at the door.

It didn't make sense. What secret could the blackmailer have against Grey that endangered this woman too? If it wasn't a love affair, what could it be? Could this woman have been involved in treason?

"You must tell me. Greybrooke has given this man thousands of pounds. What hold does this man have over him?"

Her eyes wild, dilated, the woman rushed to the fireplace and snatched up the poker. She waved it in a sweeping arc. "Leave me alone! If my husband finds out any of this, he will kill me. Do you understand? He will strangle me or shoot me or throw me in the Thames. He will kill my baby and me, and he will enjoy doing it. If it weren't for Grey's protection—"

The woman broke off, holding the poker back behind her head, ready to strike. She choked down sobs, making desperate hiccupping sounds.

"This is something you must know," Helena said firmly. "Greybrooke confronted the blackmailer in a brothel, and the man threatened him with a pistol. This man is dangerous. Perhaps deadly."

"D-did he shoot at Grey?"

"Not this time. But Greybrooke is hunting this man, and if he gets too close, very possibly this villain would kill to save his own life—"

"I had no choice! I wasn't worried about me, but about the baby. I went to the baby's father at first. But he is married, and he said he couldn't help me. I couldn't pay blackmail. I don't even receive pin money. Blackbriar would not even allow me that, in case it gave me the ability to run away. He wants me trapped. I know Grey thinks the baby's father is a coward, and I am beginning to see Grey is right. He used to meet me here, and he never comes anymore. He always has excuses. Even if they were true . . . if a man loved you . . . he would come to you when you needed him, wouldn't he?"

Helena knew she must give the truth. "Unless he was a scoundrel."

The woman sank to a chair. The poker clattered on the floor. "I've been a fool. I was so terribly alone. I couldn't face a future without ever having love. I even tried to seduce Grey—"

The woman broke off. "You look horrified. Grey refused me, you know. He said it would ruin the precious friendship we have. Don't judge me. My marriage is worse than unhappy! I've spent years waiting for Blackbriar to beat me to death. To finally kill me. I live a wretched, awful nightmare. I married a demon. And if he found out my child is not his, he would kill me. I owe my very life to Grey!"

A sharp rap sounded on the door. It rattled. Greybrooke's voice, dark and ominous, sounded on the other side. "Winsome, open this door now or I will kick it in."

Helena turned, but the blond jumped to her feet, hurried to the door, and turned the key in the lock. Greybrooke threw the door open.

He looked from the shaking, beautiful blond to her. "How much does she know?" he asked the blond—the Countess of Blackbriar.

"I—I suppose everything now," the countess said. "But she isn't working for my husband."

"No, I don't think she is." He stalked across the room; his face as black as thunder. Helena gasped as he grasped her arm. He yanked her to him; she fell against his chest.

"I know you searched my desk. Now you're spying on me. Who in hell hired you?"

Her heart leapt in her throat. Greybrooke's green eyes were dark, like a storm-filled sky. How did he know she'd searched the desk? She needed a story—she couldn't give him the truth.

He must have known since before he put her in the town house, before he bought her clothes and jewels, before he took her virginity.

It explained why he had seemed so cold and angry when he had said she would be his mistress. But he had made love to her so many times in so many ways . . . he had coaxed her to trust him to let him spank her and tie her up.

She'd seen him come with her, looking so vulnerable her heart ached. She'd seen him smile at her. He'd sketched her, sharing with her a talent he'd never told anyone about. He'd read to her. He'd given her the very first waltz she'd ever danced. He had asked, in a self-depreciatory way, if he met her expectations.

She'd thought something special had been growing between them. She'd thought that he did trust her. That she had touched him in a way no one else had.

All along, he'd been pretending. Lying to her.

Oh God, why had he done all this if he had known she was spying on him? Her tongue was paralyzed with shock—with guilt.

"You wanted to be my mistress," he growled. "I assume it was so you could spy on me. Well, my dear, you are going to get more than you bargained for."

14

"I am telling you the *truth,* Greybrooke. I don't know anything about the blackmailer."

"You don't lie particularly well," Grey said as he led Miss Winsome up her town house stairs to her bedroom. All the way here, she had insisted she knew nothing.

He remembered the way she had given in to tears after the man had held her hostage. Deep in his soul, he wanted to believe her.

But he didn't trust himself. He used to hope for his parents' love. Yearn for it like a pitiful dog that was constantly kicked, yet kept returning in the hopes it would be patted.

"Please, believe me. I was just being . . . curious. Your desk was so beautiful and I just looked at the things in it. I know it is wrong, but . . ."

She lifted her chin and looked at him with her remarkable self-possession, just as she had done on the first afternoon he'd met her—when he'd scooped her and Michael out of the way of a speeding carriage.

"You wouldn't tell me why you wanted to do naughty things with me," she said. "I wanted to understand you."

"You wouldn't go through my desk to do that. You wanted information, and you wanted to obtain it secretly. That reeks of blackmail."

He hauled her into her bedchamber. The fire crackled in the grate. Candles flickered on an armoire, and the glowing light caressed the curve of her cheek, the graceful column of her neck. It danced across the swell of her breasts, reminding him how round and delectable they were, especially when she was nude and they swayed, bounced, and jiggled. God, he remembered how much fun it was to be in bed with her.

He remembered how beautifully she'd danced with him, how special that moment had been when she'd admitted she'd never danced and she'd looked so unspeakably happy.

Grey's heart pounded. Miss Winsome was his. He shouldn't trust her as far as he could throw her. But he desired her. Wanted her.

"What are you going to do to me?" she asked.

"You're my mistress. You agreed to obey."

Her eyes narrowed. "Not without question. I want to know what you intend to do."

"I want to make love with you," he said.

"*What?* But you know I looked through your desk. You said you didn't trust me."

He had to beat down this desire for her—this desire for more than sex. After the waltz, he'd wanted to dance with her again. He'd had to force himself to leave her to meet Caro. He had to expunge any fragment of emotion for this woman.

"I never trust the women I fuck," he said.

Now she knew the blackmail had nothing to do with Greybrooke being a traitor. He had been protecting Lady Blackbriar. From clues in Lady Winterhaven's journals, Helena believed he might have killed his father. She didn't know exactly what had happened, but he'd done it to protect his sisters.

Greybrooke was loyal, deeply protective.

Even though she had no proof one way or another, she couldn't believe he was a traitor.

But it didn't matter now. He knew she had rifled through his desk, knew she was a liar. He was walking into her bedroom and she didn't know what he was going to do.

He prowled around her. Slowly. "Greybrooke, I can explain—"

"You will. You will answer every question I ask. When I am ready to ask them."

Truly, she was afraid. "How can you want to—to make love to me when you think I'm a liar? Why would you do something so intimate with me when you don't trust me?"

Greybrooke stood behind her. Hours ago, she would have been aroused to sense him so close, to smell his unique male scent, tinged with spicy cinnamon, sandalwood, the rich smoke of a cheroot.

Now she found it unnerving.

"If you do as I ask, I won't hurt you. Cross me and I may lose control, Miss Winsome. When I'm really angry, I'm capable of anything. Ask the men I've faced in duels."

Something black suddenly covered her vision. He had draped a blindfold over her eyes, and he tied it deftly, without even tugging her hair. "What are you doing?"

"Whatever I desire, angel. This is about anticipation." He undid the first button at the back of her dress.

She couldn't see him, but he was so close she knew where he was by the creak of the floor, the whisper of his cheroot-scented breath. She was shaking. "This is about fear. You're trying to frighten me. I don't like this! I don't like not being able to see. I don't want you to touch me when I'm afraid like this. You need to be in control, not for pleasure, but out of anger, or fear, or something. Please don't touch me like this. Please—"

"Stop," he growled.

She heard his fast, harsh breathing.

"I know you have reason not to trust me, but why don't you trust other people? Why do you need me tied up—as if you are afraid I'll hurt you? Is it . . . because of your father?"

"Do as I ask. You don't have anything to fear from me."

Velvet slipped around her wrist. He had her hands together in a heartbeat and tied them with the rope in two pounding heartbeats more. But he stepped back from her. She heard the sound of his footsteps moving away.

His voice came from a few feet away. "You are forbidden to ask questions. I want you to tell me who you really are."

She didn't answer. She feared her chest might burst open so her galloping heart could leap out. What lie could she give him? She could tell him she ferreted out scandals, but that would tie her to the newspaper. And he was furious over the story about his father. Which was worse—to admit she was related to Will or that she'd spied on him to prove him guilty of treason?

"What are you going to do to me?"

"Nothing. Just tell me the truth. Who are you?"

His voice chilled her to the bone. "I told you. I'm Helena Winsome, and I was a governess."

"Why did you search my desk?"

"I—I was just curious." She could hear him move, but she could not see him. She wanted to see the look on his face. Know what danger she was in. Would he hurt her? He believed she had helped to hurt his friend, and given how protective he was—

"Not good enough." His soft baritone growled close to her ear and made her jump on the bed. "Was it to help your partner, the damned blackmailer? To steal from me? What do you want?"

"I am *not* involved with the blackmailer! A man offered to pay my family's debts in return for—for—"

Oh God, she'd said too much.

"For what, Miss Winsome?"

She was too confused to lie anymore. "He said you were a traitor. He is an agent of the Crown."

"That is the most ridiculous lie I've ever heard. I should punish you severely for that, Miss Winsome. But first, I can't resist making you come."

His words stunned her. She'd told the truth but he didn't believe her. He was going to punish her—

His lips touched her neck. He kissed her there, a luscious, sensual kiss that made her tremble. Made her wits melt. Was that what he wanted? To make her so she couldn't think?

But to have pleasure like this—"No, please stop. Not like this. Not with you angry at me, hating me, not believing me."

Greybrooke drew back. "You're correct. I can't do that to you. I can't push you when you're afraid. But if you give me the truth, you will have nothing to fear."

"Please untie me. Take off the blindfold. I need to make you understand." Bound and blind, she was helpless. Was he testing her—trying to find out what she knew because he really was a traitor? Helena expected him to ignore her plea.

But something cut through the bonds at her wrists. Gently, he drew the blindfold up, off her head. She blinked, saw his face.

Pulled back.

Not because of the anger she saw in his face. It was the pain she saw there. His mouth was tight and twisted with it. His eyes projected such agony, she winced.

"You are correct, Miss Winsome. That's not what my games are about. It's not why I play them. Not to cause pain and terror. You were vulnerable, and I had no right."

His admission stunned her more than anything. He had every right to be furious. "What I told you is the truth. A man from the Crown approached me, since I worked for your sister. He told me you are suspected of being a traitor—of having sold secrets to the French during the war. If I found proof you are a traitor, he promised my brother's debts would be paid."

Greybrooke paced on the floor, between her bed and the windows. "He told you the Crown—men who work for the king—believe me to be a traitor? That's ridiculous."

"He seemed quite convinced," she pointed out.

"What was his name? What proof did you have that he is actually an agent for the Crown?"

"He gave his name as Mr. Whitehall. And he didn't give me any proof. I saw no reason to ask him for any. Why would he invent this tale?"

"That, Miss Winsome, I don't know."

Miss Winsome. It seemed so strange to think he had done intimate things to her body, yet he still called her that.

"I assure you it's a lie." He frowned. "You agreed to be my mistress when you believed I was suspected of treason. Were you playing at being a spy, hoping to learn my secrets by fucking me?"

Her cheeks had gone beyond scarlet—they burned so much they actually hurt.

"I suppose I've been a disappointment, since I've given you no proof of my dastardly acts against my country."

"I—I quickly began to see it couldn't be possible. How could you be so beloved by your family if you were the kind of gentleman who could be a traitor?"

"I would expect, in most cases, the family is the last to know."

"Your Grace, I would have thought you would try to convince me of your inno—"

"I am not trying to convince you of anything. I am telling you I'm innocent. That is sufficient."

From her perch on the edge of the bed, she looked up at his profile. "I told you my secret. I answered your questions. Will you answer some of mine? Why do you have scars on your back? Why were you punished so brutally? Was it your father who did it?"

"If your plan was to seduce the truth from me, I wouldn't want to interfere with your cunning plot. You are free to try to fuck it out of me. When I'm about to come, I might be vulnerable enough to give you an answer."

Was he trying to shock her? Scare her? Or—"Are you trying to trick me into doing naughty things to you?"

He gave a soft, rueful laugh. "No, I was angry and I lashed out. Again, my apologies."

"You cannot joke about this," she whispered. "Are you angry with me? What are you going to do to me?"

He scrubbed his jaw, looking so serious Helena swallowed hard. "I haven't decided yet."

A rap sounded on the door, and her heart leapt in relief. "Who is it?" she called. Whoever it was, she was going to let them inside at once.

"I'm so sorry, miss, but he said it's urgent. I was to fetch you right away, miss."

The voice belonged to Betsy. Helena got up, hurried past Greybrooke, and opened the door.

"I know I'm not to interrupt," the girl cried, "but the Duke of Caradon is downstairs. His Grace says he must speak to His Grace—I mean you, Your Grace—at once." She turned to Greybrooke and gave a hurried curtsy. "His Grace—the Duke of Caradon—is in the blue drawing room, miss."

"Caradon?" Greybrooke frowned. "What does he want?" He was already striding to the door.

Helena followed him, hurrying downstairs. But he was far ahead of her, and she reached the bottom of the stairs when she heard him say, "Caradon, what is it? What is so urgent?"

She heard another man's voice, filled with sympathy, answer, "Grey, sit down. I have something to tell you—"

"What is it?" Greybrooke's voice was cold, all the emotion drained out of it. "Is it my sister? Something about the baby?"

Helena reached the door to the drawing room, as Greybrooke left Caradon and was at the door, passing by her, shouting for his carriage to be brought at once.

"Steady on, Grey." Caradon came running across the room. "No, it's nothing about Jacinta. I received a message from Blackbriar's house, demanding that you come at once. Grey—" Caradon broke off. His face was unnaturally pale, his blue eyes grim.

"He's killed her, hasn't he? Goddamn it, I knew it would happen. I knew he'd take it too far, hurt her too much. I'm going to kill him."

She was about to rush after Greybrooke and desperately try to stop him when Caradon went over to him and laid his hand on Greybrooke's shoulder.

"Blackbriar isn't to blame. Caro took her own life. She filled her tea with an overdose of laudanum and drank it down."

"I don't believe it," Grey snarled. "It was Blackbriar. He must have forced the stuff down her throat. He must've found out about her child, and he killed her for it. Now I'm going to string him up by his cowardly balls and make him pay."

15

"I could have saved her." Greybrooke's voice, low and cold, came from the dark shadow in the corner of the carriage. The lamps weren't lit and moonlight flitted inside, sending washes of silver blue over his stonelike expression.

Seated across from him, Helena shivered at the self-recrimination in his tone. The golden-haired Duke of Caradon sat at her side. Caradon had forced his friend to stop and have a drink for the shock. She knew Caradon had hoped it would give Greybrooke time to calm down. Instead, Greybrooke had snatched up the decanter in a gesture of fury and poured almost half the contents down his throat. His ability to down that much brandy had stunned her. It spoke of the depth of his pain.

"You did everything you could," she pointed out. "You tried to protect her as best as you could. You paid the blackmailer and tried to find out—"

"I should have found out who he was and ripped him limb from limb," Greybrooke snarled.

"You were afraid to have the countess's secret exposed."

"And that bit of stupidity on my part cost her her life."

"It was not stupidity," she implored. "You were protecting her."

"What I needed was his name. Then I would have had the ability to rip the bastard's heart out."

She cringed. The carriage was rattling onward. "Are you— are you going to take me home? I can wait in the carriage, if you want to do that later—"

"You are coming to Blackbriar's with me," he growled. "If you are involved with that damned blackmailer, you cost Caro her life."

"I'm not involved with the blackmailer. I swear that what I told you is the truth." She'd thought he'd believed her. Now that he was angry—and had downed a lot of brandy—he seemed filled with suspicion and hatred.

He gripped her wrist ruthlessly.

Caradon put his hands on Grey's rock-hard forearm. "Release her, Grey. You're foxed and you're going to do something you will regret. Explain to me what in Hades is going on."

"Miss Winsome believes me to be a traitor."

Helena's eyes almost started out of her head as Grey leaned back gracefully on the carriage seat and casually made the statement. He acted as if it was a joke, but she saw a twitch in jaw.

"She believes I sold my country's secrets to the French during the war, Cary. Amusing to think I even possessed the secrets of my country."

Caradon said nothing. He seemed to be watching Grey warily, the way one would study a bull as it pawed the ground.

"I have never had political interests," Greybrooke said. "I've done my duty in the House of Lords, nothing more. During the war, I spent my time learning the arts of tying up women and a dozen ways to skillfully use a whip. True, I could have sold those secrets to the French. Miss Winsome, however, needs proof to believe me. Just as I need proof that she is not the blackmailer's partner and is not responsible for Caroline's death."

Caradon looked from her to Grey. "Proving a negative is madness. Let me ensure I have the right of this. This lady is your mistress, but she thinks you committed treason?"

"She was seducing my guilt out of me."

Helena blushed. It was not exactly what she had done, but it would have been what Whitehall wanted. To hear it aloud—spoken to his friend—she was ashamed. "I did betray you, and what I did was wrong and I am sorry. But it is one thing to attack me over this—another thing to humiliate me in front of a stranger."

Caradon's brows shot up into his golden hair and his jaw dropped.

"You are in the wrong up to your pretty neck, yet you chastise me?" Greybrooke growled. "All right, I had no right to hurt you in front of Cary. But what I said was the truth. You did betray me, Miss Winsome."

"I know. But you also let me become your mistress without telling me you didn't trust me."

Caradon shook his head. "Good God, both of you appeared to be spying on each other."

She blinked—it was true and it sounded so ridiculous, Greybrooke looked as startled as she felt.

Caradon frowned at her. "Why did you think such a thing about Grey, Miss Winsome? He would never betray his country. He's the noblest man I've ever known."

"Yes. Out with it, Miss Winsome. Give us the whole tale," Greybrooke said.

Greybrooke sounded playful now. She knew, in truth, he was anything but. She hesitated. Greybrooke sank back more on the cushions until he was in the relaxed pose of a dissolute but beautiful Roman god lounging on a chaise.

He looked relaxed, but energy seemed to crackle from him, as if he possessed an inner lightning storm instead of a heart. Helena knew he was filled with anger and pain.

"Cary, your reassurances haven't helped," he said. "She doesn't want to speak."

Earnest honesty showed in the Duke of Caradon's expression. "Miss Winsome, I cannot believe Grey is anything but innocent. We were at Eton and Oxford together. Grey was the sort of gentleman who would fling himself into another man's battle if he believed an injustice had been done."

"He could have believed it was not just or right for France to lose."

Caradon threw his hands up. "Normally your mistresses are much more pliable."

"She was a governess before," Greybrooke said. "She's not accustomed to her new life."

New life? He couldn't mean to have her stay on as mistress? He couldn't—not after this.

"Miss Winsome is my folly in more ways than one," Greybrooke said. "I should have recognized how dangerous she was when she goaded me into kissing her." He rubbed his hand along his jaw. "Think, Cary. Is there any proof I can have to exonerate me? The only thing I can think of is the most obvious—it should be simple enough to prove this Whitehall is no agent of the Crown."

"That should be effective," the Duke of Caradon stated.

Goodness, why hadn't she thought of that? Desperate to help Will—to save her family—she had taken everything at its surface value.

"Beyond that, Miss Winsome, you'll have to trust me. I am not a traitor."

"And I am not involved with the blackmailer! Please," she added softly, "you must believe I had nothing to do with this. I could never have done anything to hurt you like this."

His eyes narrowed, but the crackling energy seemed to have dissipated. "It goes against every instinct I possess, but I do believe you. Still, I have no intention of letting you go anywhere until I make sure you have told me everything." He stretched out his arm, pushing back the curtain. "We're here. Lord Blackbriar's house."

The horses slowed, the carriage began to turn. Through the window, Helena saw an enormous brick house with few windows lit. They passed between towering gate posts. A man stood on the front step, holding a torch, but as the carriage neared, she saw he wore black trousers and a white shirt, not livery.

"That is Blackbriar," Greybrooke growled. "Do not let his gentle appearance fool you. The bastard used to hit Caroline. He's a coward who pretends to be mild-mannered and bookish but secretly likes to use his fists on a defenseless woman."

She saw pure, harsh pain flit across Greybrooke's face for a moment, and her heart ached. Madness but even now, when she was at risk, she couldn't help but feel her heart flutter at how beautiful Greybrooke was.

The Earl of Blackbriar watched the carriage approach, illuminated by the light of the torch. He had dark brown hair and his face was ... exquisitely beautiful. With his high cheekbones, large eyes, and delicate chin, he looked like a carving of an angel done in marble. Lord Blackbriar was known for scholarly pursuits and his love of poetry. Never once, while she had been collecting the scandals of the *ton* for her Lady X column, had she found out anything sordid about Lord Blackbriar. Yet Greybrooke insisted the man was a monster.

Blackbriar was considered a bit reclusive. Neither he nor his wife attended *ton* events. Now she understood why—he had been keeping his wife like a prisoner.

Greybrooke and Blackbriar locked gazes through the glass. The tension grew so great in the carriage, she thought she would scream. "Greybrooke ... don't do anything rash."

"Lecturing again," Greybrooke said. "I'm afraid I'm too old to listen to governesses."

The cold distance in his words hurt. But she'd lost him, hadn't she? He knew she was a liar.

"Not to worry, Miss Winsome," Caradon said. "I will take charge of Grey. I know this is painful for him, but Grey—" The duke turned to Greybrooke. "I intend to make certain you don't lose control."

"Just this once, Cary, I want to lose control."

The carriage stopped and then rocked slightly as one of the outriding footmen jumped down, opened the door, put down the steps. Greybrooke leapt down. Caradon helped her down the steps as she saw Lord Blackbriar approach. Tears stained Blackbriar's cheeks; his eyes were rimmed with red. Tall, slender, his shoulders shaking with grief, Caroline's husband looked devastated.

He bowed, a quick jerk of his body. Greybrooke returned the gesture.

When he spoke, Blackbriar's voice was deep, haunting—he was renowned for the compelling beauty of his voice when he read his poetry. "In death she is exquisite, Greybrooke," the earl said gently. "With all her life gone, she glows with more beauty than ever before; she possesses an angel's serenity, and she looks as if she is now free, soaring in heaven—"

Blackbriar broke off. His face changed. His mouth twisted, his eyes bulged. He'd gone from grieving husband to a man filled with livid fury. "The hell with it," he snarled. "I thought you would want to see her, you bastard, since you were her lover."

Helena expected rage. But Greybrooke coolly glared down his nose at Lord Blackbriar. "I do want to see her, but I was Caroline's friend, nothing more."

The two men circled each other on the step, like wolves waiting for the advantage. Blackbriar stood three inches shorter than Greybrooke. He had looked slender and bookish; now Helena noticed the wiry muscles bulging under his white shirt.

Blackbriar took a step back. "Come and see her first."

Helena had lost her parents. She knew that after death there was usually a whirlwind of busyness, of things to be done. "Your house is so quiet, my lord," she said, softly.

"The servants have been sent to their rooms under orders not to emerge until I ask for them. I did not want anything to be done before Greybrooke came to see the havoc he has wrought."

"My lord—"

"Quiet. Do not bother to defend Greybrooke to me. Who are you anyway?"

"A lady. A friend," Greybrooke said. "She was with me when I received the news. She came to prevent me from killing you the moment I set eyes on you."

It startled her that Greybrooke was being circumspect about her identity. A kind thing to do to a woman who had admitted she'd spied on him.

Blackbriar sneered. How different he looked when he did that. Helena had seen boys who looked like that. They were petulant, self-important, the type who brooded, who plotted elaborate revenge over the smallest slight. She sensed she had the right idea of Blackbriar, and it matched what Greybrooke had told her. He wasn't a gentle poet at all.

Greybrooke must be in great pain, and she wished there was a way she could take some of the pain from his heart.

The house was large, but the woodwork was dark and oppressive. Greybrooke's house had the luxurious, decadent beauty of an Italian villa; Winterhaven House was all pastels and white mouldings and elegance. This house looked as if it were intended for death.

One wall sconce burned. Blackbriar had stuck his torch in a holder outside the house; inside he'd picked up a candle. It threw light on the stairs as they mounted them, but it didn't ward off the sensation of being enveloped by icy blackness.

They passed down a corridor of chocolate-brown paneling. Blackbriar stopped before a double door of dark oak, pushed one door open.

"Look at what you've done." His voice was blacker, icier even than his house.

Greybrooke strode in, but when he reached the bed, his head bowed and his shoulders convulsed with grief. Helena stole up behind him. Only Caroline's head showed. The counterpane was drawn up to her chin, as if to keep her warm. Her pale blond hair flowed around her, like the gilt halo surrounding a Renaissance angel.

"Caro, I'm sorry." Greybrooke whispered the words, his voice cracking.

Helena couldn't stand it—she gently touched his forearm. Without even looking at her, Greybrooke removed her hand from his sleeve.

Of course he didn't want her touch.

"You should be sorry." Blackbriar came to the bed, and the candlelight illuminated Caroline's closed eyes and pale cheeks. "While my fingers searched in vain for my wife's pulse, my gaze fastened upon this. A note, left on the table by her bed with your name written upon it. Not my name—not the name of the husband who cherished her. Instead the note she wrote— her very last words—were for the damned swine who impregnated her. Who destroyed her."

Blackbriar held out a square of folded paper. *Greybrooke* was written on it, in shaky script.

"The child was not mine, Blackbriar."

"Trying to convince me the bastard babe was mine, Greybrooke? Damned pitiable of you. My darling wife admitted it to me—"

"With your hands around her throat." Gently, Greybrooke drew the gold-embroidered cover back. "With you crushing her windpipe, she would have admitted to anything you asked of her."

Helena's hand went to her lips in horror. Greenish-blue bruises ringed Lady Blackbriar's delicate neck.

Blackbriar showed no expression. "I discovered my wife, the woman I revered and adored, had not been true to me, had betrayed me before providing me with a son. My rage was well justified. No one would deny I had the right to fury because my wife cuckolded me without doing her duty and giving me an heir."

"No rage was justified. Caroline was a defenseless woman, and you attacked her."

"She is my wife, my property—mine to chastise as I see fit. She provoked me with her infidelity, after I showed her nothing but love and devotion—"

"You hit her. I've seen the bruises."

"Did you? My wife claimed that I struck her? That was not the truth, Greybrooke. She came home to me with mysterious bruises. I soon realized she had a lover—a lover willing to use his fists on her. To be honest, I thought you were responsible for beating her. She was so weak she continued to go back for more. I was preparing to call you out—to settle this over dueling pistols—when this tragedy happened." Blackbriar drew up the covers, ran his fingers lovingly along his wife's lifeless cheek. "It is well known you spent much time with my wife. No one would be surprised to discover the child was yours."

Helena was stunned. How would Blackbriar speak with such cool detachment? He claimed to love his wife. He should be distraught. He had been angry before, but that rage now seemed forced. If anything he looked . . . satisfied.

With eerie calm, he said, "Perhaps she did not take her own life, Greybrooke. Perhaps you killed her—because you were tired of paying for her blackmail, because you feared what I would do to both of you when I learned you fathered the bastard she was trying to pass off as mine."

Then Blackbriar smiled with such malicious pleasure, her stomach churned.

Greybrooke's face hardened. "Are you accusing me of murder?"

"Perhaps I am. I was angry with Caroline, but I quickly realized I loved her so much that I would even forgive her this sin. I told her I would accept the child as mine."

"Hell, Blackbriar, I doubt that."

"It is the truth. There's a note on her escritoire. It is from me. After our argument, I left her very much alive. I stormed off to my study where I reflected, where I realized I still loved her and would always love her. I feared she would not open her door to me, so I sent her a note."

"Caro was too terrified to ever lock her door to you, you lying bastard."

Blackbriar spoke in the soft, magnetic voice he used for reading his poetry. "My letter begs her forgiveness for hurting her in my anger. It gives my promise to raise her baby as my own, and my promise that I would never cast her out. My darling wife had no reason to take her own life. But perhaps she wanted too much from you, Greybrooke. Perhaps she was foolishly in love with you—and we all know how you trample women's hearts. Perhaps you wanted rid of her—"

"Damn you," Greybrooke erupted. "You're the killer here. You drove her to this."

"There is no proof of that. All my servants will reveal how devoted I was to dearest Caroline."

"Yes, they would lie for you, Blackbriar. They know you'd destroy them if they did not."

"What do you propose, Greybrooke? A duel here, in Caroline's bedroom, with her body lying on the bed? I would be more than delighted to get my satisfaction here and now."

"You can't," Helena said quickly. She had to stop this.

Blackbriar paused, leaned over, and opened a drawer by the

bed. He rummaged in it, and what he took out made Helena gasp in horror. Blackbriar pointed a pistol at Greybrooke's chest. A smirk of triumph lifted his full, handsome lips. "Get the hell out of my house. The next time I see you, I intend it to be when you are dangling from a noose for murder."

Greybrooke's fists clenched. She would feel the raw fury emanating from him. Dear heaven, he wouldn't face down a pistol while unarmed. Or would he?

"Please, we should go," she pleaded. "There's nothing to be done."

"Making him pay for what he did. That still has to be done."

"You are the villain in this piece, Greybrooke," Blackbriar stated. "You seduced my wife, you got her with child, you drove her almost mad with fear, you killed her. So easy to introduce the laudanum to her tea and force her to drink every drop. I had no reason to destroy my Caroline, to lose her forever. You did—you had the need to protect your arse."

His finger toyed around the trigger. Greybrooke did not even flinch. Helena had guessed the duke had been beaten when he'd been young—it explained the scars. It explained why he would have done anything to protect his sisters, if they had been beaten too.

Had his past made him so hard, so tough, he could face down a pistol?

Her legs were weak. She thought she had courage; this was terrifying. She glanced to Caradon, who stood in the doorway. He waited there, but he looked tense, as if waiting for the tipping point where he would leap into action and intervene.

"Please, Greybrooke." She went to his side, knowing she could not touch him. "You cannot bring Caroline back. Think of your family: your sister ready to give birth, and her children. Think of how devastated they would be if you were killed in a duel."

Greybrooke dragged his gaze from his foe to her. "You do

not play fair, do you?" he muttered. "I can't walk away. I owe it to Caroline."

"She would not want you to die. If she can see you now, she is horrified that what she did is leading to the very thing she tried to stop."

"All right. I won't engage in a duel while you are standing here to nag at me."

"The note, Greybrooke." Motioning with the pistol, the Earl of Blackbriar pointed to Greybrooke's hand. "Read the note, then leave it on the bed. They are Caroline's last words, all that remains of her, and I want to keep them."

Greybrooke unfolded the note. His jaw twitched as he read, then he threw it down beside Caroline's body. "Planning to shoot me in the back as I turn around?"

"No, all I want is for you to leave," Blackbriar said. "I've lost Caroline, but at least I can take solace in the knowledge that you have too."

"What did the note say?"

Lines crossed Grey's forehead. His mouth was a tight slash of pain, his eyes empty and hollow. "She wrote that she couldn't go on. That she couldn't hurt other people. She said she had hurt me by letting me deal with the blackmailer—that I might be killed, and she couldn't live with the guilt. She wrote that the villain threatened to have his partner print the story in a newssheet—"

"A newssheet?" Helena froze. They were walking back to the carriage—Caradon walked behind them, allowing them to speak together privately.

The emptiness left his eyes. Hatred flooded in. "They would have lapped up the scandal, destroying her to sell their penny papers. That was the threat, unless she paid another five thousand pounds. She knew he would keep asking for more. And if the truth was published, it wouldn't just destroy her, it would ruin the child's life. She feared no matter what happened the baby would suffer for her sins. She couldn't bear it."

So she had taken two lives. Hers and the baby who had never had a chance to live.

"I'm so sorry," Helena began.

"You were to seduce me for your spying mission," Greybrooke said coolly. "Don't pretend sympathy for me you don't feel." He bowed to her. So much hate glittered in his eyes, they gleamed like lanterns. "Caradon will take you home. I finally have the clue I need. I can't save Caro anymore, but I can at least get vengeance."

Vengeance? "What do you mean? How?"

"The blackmailer threatened to expose Caro's secrets in Lady X's famed column. I am going to the damned newspaper that prints that column."

"No!" She shouted it without thinking.

He stared at her, his face hard.

"It is the middle of the night. Surely no one is there."

But Greybrooke knew enough to know that was false. "They work in the night to produce early editions. Someone will be there—someone who can tell me where to find the man that owns the damned thing. He must know the blackmailer."

"He might not! The blackmailer could have meant he intended to sell the story to the newspaper. Don't go when you are angry. I'm afraid—afraid you might do something rash."

"Listen to Miss Winsome, Grey." Caradon spoke from behind them—he had caught up. "You can't go around blindly taking revenge. You need to calm down. Take tonight and go home and get some sleep. Don't take action when you are fired with rage."

"Being in my damned home will only fire me with more rage," Grey snarled. "All right, I'll take my delightful mistress home and sleep there."

She gaped at him.

Caradon moved away discreetly, leaving them and reaching the carriage.

"You are both correct," Greybrooke said softly to her. "I am too close to losing control. I'll go in the morning. And right now, I need to make love to you."

That stunned her. Then she remembered what he'd said before, to shock her. *I never trust the women I fuck.*

"I want it simple," Greybrooke said softly, leaning against one of her soaring bed columns. "But I want it to be what I desire. I want to tie you to the bed, with your arms and legs spread wide. If you say no, I will respect that. I will leave at once. The choice is yours."

Her heart twisted at the raw agony on his face. She didn't know what choice to make.

He came to her, bent and brushed a kiss to her throat, his large hands resting on her shoulders. Oh, when he did this, she could barely think. Not of anything but him, large, powerful, male, so close to her. His scent surrounded her.

Her hands moved awkwardly, wanting to reach up to touch him. But she let them dangle at her sides, while he kissed her throat, the swell of her breast and made her tremble and melt.

With his face against the crook of her neck, he murmured, "I need to make love to you. I think it's the only way I can face this pain tonight. You have a special way of taking all my attention, so I can think of nothing but you and giving you pleasure."

"But what about—"

"Don't speak of it. I need you. Now."

His warmth flowed to her. His lips on her neck make her ache for him. "My choice is yes."

"Then lie on the bed, my lovely Miss Winsome."

It was as if he wanted to push the memory of what she'd done away for tonight because he needed to make love so badly. She let him undress her, down to her stockings. She was used to being naked for him, but it felt strange again with her lies hanging between them. Still, she lay on her bed. With efficient moves, he had her tied to the posts quickly, her arms and legs spread wide—but not uncomfortably so.

"Now to torture you," he said.

"Goodness, what?"

The duke kissed and licked her nipples, and sucked hard, making her tug against the ropes. He moved lower, teasing her clit mercilessly with his tongue. Heavens, he meant erotic torture.

She'd wanted him, but doubts and fears began to swallow her. What happened after this? Was he still going to throw her out? Then he was inside her, thrusting in his usual teasing, caressing, wonderful way. But she was too nervous to feel anything.

Helena moaned fiercely, moving her hips as though she was in pleasure. She screamed as if having a climax. His eyes glowed at her wails. For once, he climaxed swiftly, surprising her. Moaning, he bucked on top of her. He made an intense, harsh sound of pleasure. He kissed her cheek, a startling kiss filled with tenderness—how could she deserve that? How did you make up for telling lies? How did that ever go away?

She watched as he grasped his French letter and withdrew.

He hadn't undressed, as usual. He untied her, brought her a robe. Then he did up his trousers, went to the mirror, and straightened his clothes. His distance hurt.

"I have to go now, Miss Winsome. In the letter, Caro said the blackmailer claimed his partner owned the newspaper, the *London Correspondent*. That was his security—that his partner was ready to publish at any time. The same damned newspaper that printed the story about my father's death."

Helena gaped in ice-cold shock. It couldn't be true, could it? Will couldn't be involved.

No wonder Greybrooke wanted to destroy their newspaper. How was she going to stop him?

She was so frightened that she went stiff as a board when he came to her and touched her cheek. Then she saw his eyes—the sorrow in them, the pain—and she put her hand to his. To her surprise he didn't move, he let her touch him. For a while, when they'd made love, sex had made his pain go away.

But it had come right back.

Then he drew his hand back, breaking the contact.

"I've always protected myself by staying in control, by not trusting anyone," he said. "I know I shouldn't trust you, but you are the one woman I want to trust. I can't walk away from you. When I'm with you, making love with you, I forget everything but you. From the beginning, I knew I had to have you. Now I think I might need you."

He bent and kissed her neck.

She almost squirmed with despair. He was admitting to needing her, and she was not going to admit she was Will's sister. She was lying to him again.

16

As Helena put on her cloak and bonnet to go to the print shop, the Duke of Caradon arrived.

The blond gentleman bowed over her hand. "I apologize for calling upon you so early. I must explain to you that Greybrooke cannot possibly be a traitor, but you are on your way out—"

"No, please, you must tell me." She drew him into her drawing room. She opened her mouth to ask if he wished tea, but he cut her short.

"He wouldn't have betrayed his country," Caradon said. "Grey was so broken by years of abuse, so racked with guilt for not protecting his sisters that he couldn't think of anything else. I know it was all he could do to survive."

"Who did this to them? Was it their father?"

"I believe so."

"Why? How could anyone be so vicious? I—I saw the scars on his back."

"Grey won't talk about it much. I was held as a prisoner of war in Ceylon, Miss Winsome, and I believe Grey knew a greater torture as a boy than I suffered at the hands of enemies in a foreign prison."

Horror turned her blood cold.

Caradon's eyes filled with pain. "He was badly wounded. Not just physically, but in his soul. I understand, because I know what it feels like. He doesn't trust anyone because he was betrayed by someone he loved. He won't let himself be vulnerable again. He claims he cannot fall in love because he fears that he will lash out at anyone close to him. He is filled with rage and bitterness that he can barely control. I do not believe Grey would be a traitor. He would never deliberately hurt anyone. He would never do anything unjust, because he grew up suffering injustice."

It made sense. It fitted with what she knew about Greybrooke. His refusal to allow a woman to touch him must be because he associated the touch of someone he loved with danger. He never kissed because his bitterness made him reject anything loving or sweet. It explained the rage that burned inside him.

He was a man struggling. That struggle consumed him. He would never have been a traitor—he was too busy fighting his own private war.

"Thank you," she said to the Duke of Caradon. "Thank you for trusting me with this."

He rose to his feet. "I saw your face as you looked at Grey. It was obvious you care about him. Can you tell me anything more about this man who said he was from the Crown?"

"Only what I told you. He gave his name as Mr. Whitehall." She gave the man's description.

Helena thanked Caradon again, then he left. And she had her carriage brought around so she could speed to see Will.

Untying the ribbons of her bonnet, Helena hurried into the print shop. Will was there, carefully setting letters in one of the plates. His sleeves were rolled up, ink stained his fingers.

"Helena!" Will set down his work. "Have you news?" he asked quietly. "I haven't seen or heard from you for days. Have you found some proof we can give to Whitehall—?"

Helena pulled Will by the wrist to the small sitting room off the print shop and she dropped into one of the well-worn chairs. She loved the place, but could see the signs of impoverishment. Furniture was torn, dented, and scuffed. Walls needed painting and plastering.

She waited until her brother sat down across from her. "Will, has anyone ever approached you to print a scandalous story about the Countess of Blackbriar?"

Will met her gaze with a surprised one. "No, Helena. You're the one who unearths the scandals that keep the *ton* flocking to our newspaper. Why would I need to buy information elsewhere? The only story I had to take was the one Whitehall insisted I print."

That was what she'd thought. But why had the blackmailer threatened Lady Blackbriar with publishing her secret in their newspaper? Why her column specifically?

Will's worried voice broke in on her thoughts.

"She's not related to Greybrooke's treason, is she?" he asked. "That's what we need to be doing—satisfying Whitehall so I can get those debts called off."

"I don't think we will satisfy Mr. Whitehall. I don't believe the Duke of Greybrooke ever betrayed his country. I think Whitehall is wrong."

"You keep saying that, Helena. But Whitehall works for the Crown. They are clever men and they've got their own spies. How would they be wrong?"

"Will, that man may not be who he says he is. He may not work for the Crown. This may all have been a pack of lies."

Will drew out a small silver flask from his waistcoat pocket. Once she would have reprimanded him. Now she said nothing—she understood why he would want a drink.

He took a quick swallow, then slowly returned the cap to the flask. What he said then almost knocked her off her worn chair.

"You're not falling in love with the Duke of Greybrooke, are you? That will lead to nothing but trouble. Helena, you've got to keep a clear head—"

"Good heavens," she broke in. "I have the clearest one of the two of us, Will. I am not in love with Greybrooke, and it is not sentiment that makes me doubt Whitehall. It's logic. The Duke of Greybrooke is not what I thought he was—I thought he was a scoundrel who thought of only one thing. I was wrong. He's intelligent. Loyal. Brave."

"So are successful spies, I expect," said Will, stubbornly. "And you sound like a woman in love."

"I'm not. I have far more sense than to do something as silly as fall in love with a man I can never have. I saw what happened to Margaret. I would *never* lose my heart like that. And definitely no one has come to you with a scandal about Lady Blackbriar?"

He shook his head.

"You definitely were not in a partnership with a blackmailer—to extort money?"

"Of course not!" He looked startled, then appalled.

She could tell when Will was lying. This had to be the truth.

"Why are you so interested in her?" he asked. "Has she done something scandalous?"

"No," Helena said quickly. She could not reveal the truth, just in case her brother did write about it. She looked at Will and saw that his desperate straits had made it so she couldn't trust him anymore. "She's dead, Will. I fear—I fear she took her own life."

"You know something about her."

"There isn't anything to know about her."

"We need blunt, dear sister. If you've got a grand scandal—"

"*No*, Will."

"Not even if it keeps your family from starving?"

It would make a pile of money, she was sure. But she could

not do it. It would hurt Greybrooke, and she couldn't do that. And she could not make money on the back of this tragedy. It would be *wrong*. She shook her head.

Will sighed.

"I need your next column, Helena. It's supposed to run tomorrow. I take it you've forgotten."

She clapped her hand to her mouth. She had indeed forgotten.

But could she write an article? She thought of Lady Blackbriar, so terrified that her secrets would be exposed, she'd taken her own life.

Lady X wrote about scandals and love affairs. Helena had thought she was doing good because she exposed scoundrels. Now she wondered: Had she hurt anyone? Had she left disaster in her wake?

She did not want to do that anymore.

Suddenly a feminine voice cried happily, "Is Helena here?" Feet scampered, and her youngest two sisters, Jane and Louisa, burst into the small sitting room.

Helena was stunned. "What are you doing here? Why are you not in school?" Then her eyes widened so much it hurt. Fourteen-year-old Jane had ink-stained fingers.

Two sets of guilty eyes shifted to Will.

He picked up a rag and began wiping his hands. "We can't afford the fees, Helena."

"We can . . . surely."

"The fees for the school have been raised. We can't pay them anymore."

"But Jane and Louisa must go to school!" Just as Elise, the oldest of her younger sisters should marry. She could make it possible—she had the gifts Greybrooke had given her. They would pay for schooling for another year. Cover the rents for the shop and their home.

"I have things I can sell." Her face flamed—she didn't want her sisters to know how she had raised this money.

"Wait, Helena," Will said. "If we don't give Whitehall what he wants, my debts won't be cleared. We'll need the money for those."

"No! This money is needed for rent, for Elise's dowry, for the girls to go to school."

"I'm duty bound to pay those debts."

"Yet you can easily ignore your obligations to your sisters." Then she felt guilty for snapping at Will. "I know you are afraid of what the men who run those gaming hells will do. But we can't have our sisters toiling in the print shop, giving up their futures."

"We have no choice."

Anger was pointless, and it was useless to point out that these debts shouldn't exist. She had to do something. In her heart, Helena knew Whitehall would prove to be a fraud. She didn't believe she could raise enough yet, even on the jewels Greybrooke had given her, to pay the debts, provide a dowry, and send her sisters back to school.

She had to continue to be Greybrooke's mistress.

She had to ensure she won him back.

Whatever it took.

A door crashed open, and a man roared in anger. Will paled and hurried to the sitting room door. He opened it a few inches, then swung around. "It's not an irate creditor. It's the Duke of Greybrooke."

"He cannot find me here. He doesn't know I'm your sister." If the only way to save her family was to convince Greybrooke to keep her as his mistress, he *couldn't* find out.

Bellowing resounded through the printing room. The clattering stopped.

"In the sitting room, Yer Grace," cried one of the printers, and Helena wondered what threat Greybrooke had used to make him shout it so desperately.

She was too late—she would never get away now. But she

had to keep her wits. She'd spent years in this room, now everything in it conspired against her. She couldn't fit under the worn settee or hope to disappear from sight behind a wing chair. There was only one place . . . sun-faded drapes framed the windows, and they were long enough for her to hide behind.

"Send the girls out," she commanded to Will.

"What in Hades does he want?" Will breathed, staring open-mouthed at the closed sitting room door.

Quickly, she told Will about Lady Blackbriar's final note to Greybrooke: that the countess had taken her own life because she feared a scandal being revealed in Lady X's column of their newspaper.

"Damnation," muttered Will. "Helena, you could tell him— no, you can't. We can't give you away now. Whitehall will never save us then. You've got to hide."

She had to make Will accept her doubts about Whitehall, but now was not the time. "I'll hide, but send the girls away." Heart hammering beneath her stays, Helena rushed behind the drapes and arranged them over her. Boots pounded over the floor. She would come out if Will was in real danger.

All she could think of was what the Duke of Caradon had said. That Greybrooke was full of rage and constantly struggled for control.

From her hiding place, Helena saw Will put his hands on Jane's slender shoulders and had her stand behind him. He pushed Louisa to follow her. "We'll stay together," he said gruffly.

Helena wanted to lunge out and shake sense in him. His sisters shouldn't face Grey's wrath. But of course Will hadn't listened to her. No, he was using the girls to hopefully dissipate the duke's anger.

The door to the sitting room flew open, slamming into the wall with the same explosive force applied to the previous door.

Dust flew up. Jane let out a scream before Will put his fingers to her lips.

Goodness, was this Greybrooke?

Scruffy dark stubble covered his jaw and shadowed his cheeks. His face looked haggard—his cheekbones jutted out sharply, his eyes had purple rings beneath. His clothes were rumpled, unkempt. He must have been awake all night.

It showed how devastated Greybrooke was by Caro's death. He'd been hurt so badly in his past, it broke her heart to see him suffer even more.

Peeking out from behind the drapes, she saw Greybrooke's gaze rivet on first Louisa, who was thirteen, then Jane, who was fourteen. He changed. The anger flaring in his eyes disappeared, replaced by a cool, emotionless expression. She could almost see each muscle tense, and he gained control. He bowed. "I beg your pardon, ladies."

Her sisters gawked, stunned to have a duke apologize. Then, in the same measured voice—which meant danger, she knew—he said to Will, "Send the young ladies out of the room. This matter is between us. It concerns the Countess of Blackbriar."

Greybrooke towered over her brother. He glared down his noble nose at Will as if Will were an insect. Her brother took the girls to the door, sent them out, then returned to face the duke.

Greybrooke accused Will of working with the blackmailer, of being the man's partner.

The words froze Helena's heart. She knew they couldn't be true! She believed her brother. But why had the blackmailer claimed to be partners with Will? Why name their newspaper? It made no sense.

Greybrooke was here, ready to tear Will apart. But Will was innocent. Just as she was certain Greybrooke was innocent of treason. Whitehall was the connection between the newspaper and the duke, and now the blackmailer was connecting them too. Could Whitehall be involved with the blackmailer? Could they use unwitting spies to gather their secrets?

"Your Grace, I assure you I do not blackmail people," Will was insisting. "Nor do I associate with that kind of criminal."

The duke grabbed Will by the throat of his shirt and hauled him to his tiptoes. "You're accusing Lady Blackbriar of lying?"

"She must have been mistaken."

"Why would she accuse your newspaper of being in partnership with a blackmailer if it weren't true? She got your name from the damned criminal."

"He lied, Your Grace."

"I've read Lady X's column. Your paper feeds on scandals and thrives on destroying lives."

Helena winced. It was true. She felt so terribly guilty.

"If I discover news, I print it," Will said coolly. "I don't keep it hidden and use it to be paid blackmail. When I learn about truthful stories, I publish them."

"Tell me the name of your accomplice, this blackmailer. Give me the name of the man who drove a woman to take her life."

"I don't know!" Will's voice rose in panic. "I can't give it to you because I'm not an accomplice to blackmail."

"Goddamn it, you do know. I saw no surprise in your eyes when I accused you."

Oh, dear God. That was *her* fault—because she had come here first.

"I know nothing about a blackmailer," Will shouted, scared now. "You must believe me, Your Grace. I have no name to give you."

Greybrooke picked up a wing chair as if it weighed nothing. He flung it, sending it crashing into a wall. Plaster broke and fell in chunks.

Then he growled in anger. "That, I assume, terrified your sisters. Apologize to them for me. I sympathize with them—

they are innocent victims." The duke lowered his voice. From behind the drapes Helena had to strain to hear him. "I will destroy this newspaper, smash it to pieces around you. I will destroy you, Mr. Rains. It will be my personal pleasure to hurt you, bankrupt you, ruin you. I swear I will not hurt your sisters, but when I'm done with you, you will wish I'd walked in here with a pistol and shot you."

17

"Think, Will," Helena begged, keeping her voice low. "There must be some reason why a blackmailer would use the name of our newspaper."

She and Will were speaking in the press room. Work had stopped, for the duke's rage had frightened everyone. Helena had made a pot of tea to soothe her sisters. The girls sipped theirs with the other workers, while Helena had picked up the chair and brushed up the broken plaster.

Now that she had a minute to think, she was angry with Greybrooke for terrifying her family with his rage.

He had calmed himself in front of her sisters, at least. For *that* she could forgive his anger. She did understand his rage and pain. But . . .

He was vowing to destroy her family based on the word of a blackmailer. A criminal.

She must convince him not to attack the newspaper. Her only solution was for her to stay as Greybrooke's mistress. It was the only way she might convince him to listen to her.

Will drew out his flask, added a splash to his tea. His hand shook.

"I don't know, Helena." He looked hollow-eyed and afraid. "I told the duke the truth. I've got no idea why a blackmailer would claim I was his partner. I swear I would not do something like that. I am a gentleman, not a parasite and a swine."

"I know, Will. I believe you." There was so much she must fix—her sisters must go to school, they must be saved from debt. But first, she had to save their newspaper.

What if Greybrooke wouldn't listen to her?

There was one definite way to prove Will's innocence. She had to find the actual blackmailer.

But if the Duke of Greybrooke had not been able to do it, how could she?

The only place she could think to look was the brothel—the brothel where the blackmailer had taken her as his hostage.

A shiver ran through her. Because this time she wouldn't be with Greybrooke. She would be alone.

"Hello, pretty one." A deep, masculine voice drawled beside Helena's ear, and she almost leaped out of her skin. "Spend the night with me? You've a delectable rump, and my prick would love to feel you squeezing it tight."

Good heavens!

Her heart danced about like one of the drunken courtesans who were sashaying around the drawing room of the brothel. She knew that voice; it belonged to the Duke of Sinclair. The fourth member of the Wicked Dukes she had now met. His hand pressed to her bottom through her skirts. Groped and squeezed! She drew away. "I am not available."

The brothel was indulging in a masquerade, so the men wore costumes, just as they had at Greybrooke's private club. The Duke of Sinclair wore a black cloak embroidered with silver stars, and where they glittered and winked she saw tiny jewels were sewn to the velvet. A tall wizard's cap sat on his brown hair. A mask of gilt and black covered his face from his hairline to his high cheekbones. His wide lips quirked in a smile that hinted at the rude thoughts he was entertaining.

Fortunately she had worn the mask Greybrooke had given her the first time they'd come. She had gathered her courage and put on one of the lovely gowns he had bought her—this one was sapphire blue silk that whispered sinfully as she moved. She'd wanted to look very different from Helena Winsome the Governess.

"Already spoken for?" Sinclair asked huskily. "There's no honor in a brothel, sweetheart, where a man's cock is involved. I'll pay double what you've been offered. Triple, with a few sovereigns extra for you to put in your own pocket."

Primly, she said, "I would not betray my protector. Thank you though, for your kind offer, Your Grace."

He gave a deep laugh, but one not quite as darkly sinful as Greybrooke's laugh. "You sound like a governess, not a whore. And you recognized me? This mask must not be as good as I thought."

"It is perfect, Your Grace," she said hurriedly. She had to escape before he either discovered who she was or took his interest too far. Helena backed away to disappear in the crowd. It willingly swallowed her up. She bumped something and turned to discover she had backed into a man who had a woman kneeling in front of him. Head arched back in ecstasy, the man hadn't noticed. She scrambled away.

Shaking, Helena peered through the crowd, looking for the blackmailer's distinctive mask. But what if he wore a different one? She would wager a fortune he would be in that bondage room—which meant she must go there.

A hand grabbed at her breast, and she darted away She didn't even see who had tried to paw her. Running, she managed to thread through the crowd of half-naked females and lusty males, but as she neared the doorway to the salon, a towering male suddenly filled the space. A broad-shouldered, black-haired man who exuded power like the crackle of a lightning storm.

It was Greybrooke, and her heart wedged in her throat. Beneath her gloves, her palms grew hot and wet. She didn't know where to look. She wanted to both run toward him and run away.

Then two enormous breasts, almost spilling out of a low-cut scarlet dress, blocked her view of Greybrooke. The bosom smacked firmly against his chest. Helena felt her jaw drop. The owner of the massive bosom pounced on him. The woman wrapped one hand around Grey's neck, plastered her voluptuous body to his, and dragged his ear down to whisper in it.

He listened intently, gazing down at the woman. At her breasts, Helena feared. How could any man look away from such generous servings of sensuality? *She* couldn't stop gaping at them.

Had Greybrooke come here for the blackmailer? Or had he come for sex, which he used to keep painful thoughts at bay?

Had she already lost him?

She retreated into the shadows by the wall and watched him. Greybrooke remained at the side of the voluptuous courtesan, but he didn't look at the woman—he surveyed the room, studying the patrons.

Helena's heart gave a strong thump of hope. Perhaps he wasn't here for lovemaking. Perhaps he was hunting, just as she was.

Like her, he was probably frustrated. Everyone in the room was masked. She should go to him, let him know she was doing the same thing—

A tiger's face blocked her view, right in front of her face.

Helena's lurched back, but the tiger lifted her hand to his lips.

At the same moment, the bosomy ladybird escorted Greybrooke out of a doorway.

Blast, Helena thought. She couldn't chase him down and join him now. Perhaps the woman had information. Perhaps his interest had nothing to do with breasts so large a man would need two hands to hold one.

Acrid jealousy ate at her.

She must ignore it. She must stay true to her mission to find the blackmailer. Yanking her hand away from the tiger, Helena hurried out of the salon, charged down to the hall to the bondage room, and stepped inside.

Whips cracked. Riding crops were wielded. Ropes bound courtesans in all sorts of artistic ways, and at least a dozen women were tied to racks or suspended. Masked guests and courtesans already filled the room, and several women were completely, utterly naked.

How could they be undressed in this crowd of people? Was it because they wore masks? No one could recognize them, so that made them daring?

She could never be that daring.

A woman let out a moan beside Helena. A hood covered the woman's head; her hands were bound; and a leather leash, like that of a dog, was around her neck. A man held the leash, and he kept smacking her rump with a riding crop.

This was the sex Greybrooke talked about. Her cunny did ache and throb each time she heard a moan. And the things she saw—thick shafts disappearing into sobbing, appreciative women; bouncing breasts; bottoms in the air; people on all fours—were erotic. But all she could think of was trying these things with Greybrooke. It was Greybrooke that made sex exciting, not the acts.

Helena tried to look around for the blackmailer—

"Come on, tart. I'm lusty and I need to relieve myself. Now. You'll do."

Strong hands gripped her and pushed her against the wall. An ox breathed down on her . . . no, it was a man as big as the beast. He jerked her arms up, pinned her wrists to the wall. His heavy body shoved against her, crushing her. Helena struggled to breathe as he ground his crotch hard against her. The bulge there felt enormous. She let out a panicked whimper—she didn't have enough breath to cry out. Her little sound of distress made the fiend grow bigger and harder in his trousers.

The fiend's hands tugged ruthlessly at her bodice. "Let me get a look at these fat tits," he hissed. Pungent alcohol wafted from his breath. He stank of musty sweat. She struggled to fight him while struggling not to breathe in his foul odors.

Her skirts were being jerked up her legs. She kicked madly but cried out in pain as her toes in dress slippers hit the brute's boots.

"Stop." She sucked in a breath to speak and was almost sick. "Let me go. I don't want you."

"You're a whore. You'll take me and be glad of it. No tart refuses me."

One hard tug pulled her bodice down. A seam tore. He jerked the neckline beneath her shift-clad breasts, forcing them up.

"There." He laughed with cruelty. "That's what I want."

Baring teeth, he lunged at her breast, almost visible beneath the fine muslin. Helena drove her knee up, to slam it between his thighs, but her skirts got in the way. Her blow was weak, only enough to enrage him.

He let go of her wrists. Drew his hand back as if to hit her. She wrenched, pulled, tried to slide down out of the range of his fist, but she couldn't move.

"*Whore.*"

Big as a leg of ham, his fist hurtled through the air—

Suddenly, the huge man soared backward, landing on the parquet floor like a felled tree.

A dark-haired man stood over him. Her savior hauled her attacker to his feet. Stunning, considering the gentleman who had come to her rescue stood a few inches shorter and probably weighed several stone less. But two fast, lethal blows from his fists sent her burly attacker slumping to the ground again. This time the fiend slithered as if he had no bones. His cheek hit the ground, blood spattered. He didn't move.

"Speak to me, angel. Chastise me. Lie to me. I think I know who you are, but I have to make sure."

Helena was staring at the fallen attacker. Heart pattering, she turned. She gaped at a mask painted to look like a wolf's face—a silver and gray wolf. But she knew his voice. Greybrooke! He had put on a mask.

"Chastise you?"

"It *is* you," he said. In the eyeholes of the exquisitely painted mask, brilliant green eyes narrowed. "What in the blazes are you doing in here?"

"What are you doing?" she countered.

"Hunting for the blackmailer," he growled.

Her heart gave a soft, foolish leap. He was not here for carnal pleasures.

"Did you come here alone?" he growled.

"Y-yes," she admitted.

"Damnation, what were you thinking? That man was a moment away from beating you senseless, then raping you while you were bleeding and defenseless. You are leaving. Now."

Greybrooke put a small glass of sherry in her hand. "Are you all right? You were shaking in the carriage."

"Yes. I am all right. Thanks to you."

"You are not to go there again on your own. Do you understand? You will do as I tell you."

Her heart soared with hope for a moment—did that mean he intended to keep her as his mistress? But then she realized he was speaking of dictating her every moment. "I will take your advice."

"You will obey." His voice was curt. He had discarded his mask, and she saw his expression wasn't filled with anger as he commanded her. It was filled with concern.

She hadn't meant to make him worry. But it amazed her that he did.

Groaning, the duke sank onto a wing chair opposite her, drinking from a tumbler of brandy. "I haven't found the blackmailer. Despite searching the stews where Orley lives and lavishing bribe money around. Despite searching that brothel. How could I have failed so badly? How could I have failed Caro?"

Helena stood slowly and walked to him. She wrapped her hand around his glass, eased it from his hand, and set it on the table. Gathering courage, she touched the side of his face gently, fearing he would push her away.

He stiffened, but suddenly he turned his face into her palm, so she cupped his cheek.

The depth of his need speared her.

Finding the blackmailer would save both Will and Greybrooke. But she also had to protect her sisters. To do that, she needed to be Greybrooke's mistress.

She wanted to heal his pain, and she knew only one way to do it, but this was more: She yearned to be intimate with him. In those moments, she felt something special, delightful, wonderful. No matter what they did, it was erotic and thrilling.

She desired him, plain and simple.

No matter what happened, she always would.

"Come to bed with me." She had to be seductive, but she didn't quite know how to do it. Sex had always been on Greybrooke's terms—and he came to her when he wanted it.

What would tempt him?

"I'll do anything you want," she said. "Any naughty, wicked game you want to play. I want to experience *everything.*"

Even as she said the words, a thrill raced through her. Daring words. Dangerous words. But she *trusted* him. She clasped his hand and gave a tug to coax him to follow her to the bedroom.

He didn't move.

Then, his words slightly slurred, he said, "Promise me you'll never go to that club alone."

"I won't. I promise. I *swear*."

In one sudden, fluid movement, he lifted his back from the chair and pulled off his tailcoat. She watched his hands move swiftly down the buttons of his waistcoat, then tear open the knot at his cravat.

The cravat fell into a puddle on his chair arm, and the clothes that had covered his chest lay in a heap on the lovely Aubusson rug. He was bare from the waist up. He crooked his finger to her, and she obeyed. Once she was leaning over him, he drew her down. His mouth slanted over hers. Hot, firm, possessive, demanding.

Then he stopped kissing her abruptly, drawing back. Helena sucked in air desperately. While he kissed her, she'd forgotten to breathe. Steam seemed to coil off her lips.

How much would he let her touch him? Would he stop her?

His bunched muscles flexed as he leaned in for another kiss. She put her hands to his chest, and he stopped. From beneath his disordered jet-black hair, he watched her.

Helena let her hands move over his chest. He was so hot. Hot with desire, just like she was. She felt it—that warm, wonderful enveloping intimacy. She stroked the bulge of his pectorals. Almost giggled with the thrill of letting her fingers touch his nipples—they went instantly hard. She skimmed her hands up to his broad shoulders, ran her fingertips down his arms.

He was letting her caress his chest.

"You're so beautiful," she said.

His hand went down, ruthlessly jerked open the falls of his trousers, and he kissed her again. An open-mouthed kiss that made her almost collapse on him. His hands slid along her shoulders, his fingers coasted up her neck.

She sizzled everywhere.

He grasped her hands. Obediently, she clasped them together behind her back, mimicking being tied up. It would be what he wanted.

But strangely, he immediately stopped kissing her. His chest rose and fell with his heavy breaths. "You'll do anything I want? Are you sure, angel? What I want now may be more than you can do."

She *must* do anything. But she knew now that was an excuse. She wanted to be wicked and wanton with him. She wanted to share something extraordinary.

"Try me," Helena said.

Grey's dark brows shot up in surprise. There was one thing he had not yet told her. "I confirmed there is no man named Whitehall working for the Crown."

He watched her face. Dejection showed, then anger, then something close to despair. "I expected that's what you would find, because I know you could not have committed treason."

He wanted to believe she had been duped. It seemed the most plausible story.

But his gut hammered a warning to him: *Don't trust her.*

So why did he want to haul her to her bed, blindfold her, tie her up, and fuck her in every erotic position he could think of? He could walk out the door and find another woman to be his bedmate in mere minutes. He could find a woman who would not lie to him.

Why did he want Helena Winsome so much?

Ropes wrapped around her wrists and ankles, securing her to the four posts of her bed. A blindfold of black silk covered her eyes. Helena heard Greybrooke prowl around the bed. Then she heard a sound like a swish of air.

"What was that?" she asked, nervously licking her lips.

"Riding crop, angel," he said.

She winced, expecting the strike.

Something gently tapped her nipples—first the tip of her left breast, then the right. The quick, light cold tap sent a shimmering bolt of arousal to her cunny. The cool end of the crop circled her nipples. Making them go hard. Making her gasp.

She heard the whisper of his step. The slap of the crop. Against his hand? What was Greybrooke doing now? Not knowing—when she trusted him—proved very thrilling.

Another cool, long, slender thing stroked between her nether curls. Not his cock, which would be hot. Not the crop, this was too smooth. Gently, he thrust it inside her. It was very thick, stretching her. It touched a special place inside her quim—one that gave her shimmering pleasure. She was close to an orgasm, and she fought to hold it off.

Once he'd told her orgasms were so much more intense when they built to a point that they burst through all restraint.

"Now your bottom," he said.

Behind the blindfold, Helena blinked.

His hand lifted her rump. Warm greasiness slid into the valley between her cheeks. Something touched the opening of her bottom. His fingers, she was sure.

No, not his fingers. This was thicker and smooth. It had to be another wand. He slid the ivory phallus in and out of her bottom, and she moaned in sheer pleasure.

This should be too much—a wand in her rump and one deep inside her cunny.

But it was unbelievably good. She felt on the extreme edge of pleasure. The knife's edge, as he called it.

He lowered her bottom, and that pushed the wand deep inside. She couldn't resist—she began to rock on it. Letting it slide out a bit, then taking it deep. The flared ivory end, cool and smooth, bumped against her cheeks.

"I love to see you like this," he murmured. When he had sex with her, his voice was so gentle. Intimate.

Then he gave the wand in her cunny one slow thrust.

Too much! Her orgasm exploded through her feeble attempt

at control. Bound by the ropes, she thrashed helplessly on her bed, giving into wild cries and moans. On a flood of juices, the wand in her cunny slid out. She wiggled just a bit—

The teasing of the wand in her bottom unleashed another climax. She let it take her, toss her about. She'd never been this slick and wet.

She wanted Greybrooke inside her. Right now.

Was he going to join her? Suddenly Helena heard harsh breaths. They came faster and faster. She wanted to see what was happening. Wriggling her head against her pillow, she jerked the knot of the blindfold up and down.

Greybrooke let out an intense growl.

Was he going to come to bed with her? Get on top of her? Make love to her? She was pulsing inside still, but she wanted more. She ached to feel his cock slide in her while the walls of her cunny clutched madly in pleasure.

An arch of her back snagged the blindfold in her pillow and worked it down.

Greybrooke stood at the end of the bed. His open trousers had fallen to the tops of his thighs. He still wore his gleaming leather boots. His linens were pushed down too, exposing his enormous, straight erection. But she couldn't see much more than the shiny, acorn-shaped head. His hand was gripping his shaft hard, jerking back and forth along the length.

Suddenly he shuddered. His stomach tightened, revealing the muscles like cobblestones. His hand gripped tight. White fluid shot out, pouring over his hand while his hips rocked. His seed, the salty, sour liquid she'd tasted. His eyes shut tight, his breathing seethed between his teeth. He looked in pure agony, but she knew it must be pure pleasure.

He had made her climax intensely. So much so, she was still sobbing. He came so hard, his legs buckled, and he grabbed the bedpost. He released his cock, gasping for breath.

They had touched before, when he'd given her sherry. He'd let her touch him. But for making love, he hadn't touched her.

It shocked her. Confused her.

Why had he not wanted to touch her? Why had he wanted their pleasure to be experienced in the same room but to be thoroughly separate?

She shouldn't care, as long as he wanted her; as long as she could remain his mistress and pawn jewels and support her family. But she did care. Deep in her heart, she hurt.

In front of her, Greybrooke drew out a linen handkerchief and cleaned himself. Then he moistened a towel in a basin of water. Her maid was told to always leave one in the room. He withdrew the ivory wand from her bottom, took away the one that had fallen out of her cunny. She marvelled at them—they were carved to look exactly like male cocks. With soft strokes, he cleaned her, wiping away her sticky juices and the warm oil he'd use on her rump.

Helena wanted to say something, but what? Was he not going to touch her with his hands anymore? But what right did she have to complain, since she'd been lying to him since that first day she'd met him in Berkeley Square. Worse, she was *still* lying to him.

He left her tied up, and he sat on the edge of the bed beside her. Green eyes gazed down on her. "I know I want to keep you, Miss Winsome. But I need to know everything about you."

"You know everything. There is nothing more to tell." She had to divert him from more questions. "Please untie my hands," she whispered. "I want to touch you. May I?"

The coolness of his response chilled her heart. "I will untie your hands, but no touching. As you can see, it's not necessary for pleasure."

18

Grey had watched Miss Winsome a great deal since he'd caught her searching his desk. He'd discovered that when she lied, she made a tiny frown just before the lie came out. It was as if telling a lie hurt her. She'd had that look when she'd said she had nothing more to tell.

She sat up on the bed, and he handed her a robe.

He couldn't let her touch him. Not after what he'd felt when he let her caress his face. Her hand had been soft, gentle. Comforting. For one moment he'd just savored being caressed by her. He'd needed her touch. And he knew the danger of that.

Miss Winsome would try to use caresses to con him, just as his mother used to try to use touch to control him. His mother used to embrace him before and after having him whipped and brutalized. As a child, he'd been too pitiful to reject her hugs, her kisses. Even when he was bleeding, his body screaming in pain, he needed her to hold him. He wanted to believe that her touch meant she loved him and would stop hurting him.

Eventually he realized that it was all part of his mother's vicious game.

Miss Winsome drew on her robe. "You don't trust me, I know. I'm so sorry that I had to lie to you. I had no choice but to do what Mr. Whitehall asked. It is the truth that my brother owed a fortune in gaming debts, and Whitehall claimed that the Crown would pay the debt if we helped him."

"Your half brother, you mean?"

Her head jerked up. He saw the watchfulness in her eyes. "Yes, he is my half brother." She paused. "I hate myself for having lied to you."

"That I believe," he said.

"I wish you trusted me. I want so very much to touch you. I know it is because of your past, and I understand."

Do you? He'd wager she had no idea how his mother used touch to torture him.

"But you tried kissing me, and it worked," she went on. "I've told you about myself. Could you tell me about your past—?"

"No. Do not ask me to speak about my scars or my past, Miss Winsome. Tying you up and listening to you scream with ecstasy helps me to forget it. There's nothing to be served by digging it up. I can't change it. I wear the scars. I don't like to be touched. There's no reason for that to change." Grey paused. "If there is one thing I learned, it's that a black past means a bleak future."

The next morning, Helena returned to her town house from a jeweler's shop, one of the disreputable ones not to be found on Bond Street. She had sold the jewels Greybrooke had given her; everything except the pendant with the sole ruby. But soon it would have to go too.

She sat down in her morning room to pen a letter to Will. In it, she told him she had money—money to be used to send her sisters away to school, to create a dowry for Elise, and to pay bills to keep the newspaper running. Her maid entered and curtsied.

"Beg your pardon, miss. Mr. Rains has come to see you. Should I bring him here?"

He'd come to her. How horrible her first reaction was worry. "Yes, bring him at once."

When she reached Will, he was sweeping his gaze around her lovely morning room, taking in the delicate plasterwork, the rich carpet on the floor, the exquisite Queen Anne furnishings, the white china figurines of doves. All beautiful, all selected by Greybrooke for her. She had no idea how he'd found the time to do it. It stunned her that he had bothered.

She could stay here for a while, as long as she didn't push Greybrooke to let her touch him.

"You've done well for yourself, sister," Will said.

"I only had to give up everything to do it," she said drily.

Will frowned. "Are you unhappy?"

No, that was her problem. She might be tossed out on the street at any moment. But even that couldn't spoil the decadent, delicious thrill of making love in the wickedest ways with Greybrooke. Even if he didn't want her touch . . . when he made love to her she could do nothing but explode in pleasure.

She knew she was blushing. "No, I'm not, for I am now able to help you. I have enough money to put our sisters back in school, to ensure Elise can marry, to keep the newspaper afloat. And *that* is what the money will be used for."

"Of course. The thing is . . ." Will scratched his ear. "I don't want you to be with the duke."

"For heaven's sake, now is a bit too late to want to protect me, Will."

Her brother sank down to the settee. He wouldn't look at her. His hand scrubbed his jaw.

Oh no. "What is it, Will?"

"A maid to the Earl of Blackbriar came to see me. To sell me information about Greybrooke."

"What information?"

"She claims she knows that Greybrooke murdered the Countess of Blackbriar."

Helena gaped at him. "*How* did she know?"

"She says she witnessed the entire thing. The duke forced Lady Blackbriar to write a note. He held a pistol on the countess and forced her to drink the laudanum that killed her. Whitehall came to see me—I told him about this. He insists that I publish this story."

"You can't!" It would destroy Greybrooke. She couldn't let this happen. "We have no real proof. This woman could be lying. And Whitehall is not an agent of the Crown. We've been duped. Oh goodness, Will, why did you tell him?"

At his look of shock, she explained that Greybrooke had discovered Whitehall was a fake.

"This is what the Duke of Greybrooke has told you. Obviously he is going to lie."

"I don't believe he is lying. I think it's the truth. And he would know I can verify it."

Will shook his head. "You are falling in love with him. Your judgment is clouded. Greybrooke murdered an innocent woman and you're in danger."

"My judgment is perfectly sound. I'm not in danger from Greybrooke. He is not guilty. Now, tell me this maid's name." Why had the servant told the lie? Someone must have paid her—or threatened her. Helena felt a spurt of hope. Here could be the clue she needed. Did she dare tell Greybrooke? Or should she question the maid herself?

"What of your next column as Lady X? I need it for print, Helena."

She shook her head. "I had no idea how many people I

could hurt by unearthing scandals. I cannot do it anymore. You will have to announce that Lady X has gone for good."

Lady X might have gone for good, but Helena had to use her skills for unearthing scandals. She watched Lord Black-briar's house for two days, trying to figure out how to contact a maid whose name she didn't know. Today another young maid, in her best bonnet and dress, emerged from the house and walked briskly to the street.

Helena caught up with her, showed the girl the four gold sovereigns she held. She knew Greybrooke used money when he asked questions. "I must speak to a maid in Blackbriar's house.

The young, brown-haired maid looked longingly at the coins, then glanced back at the house like a frightened rabbit. "I can't talk, miss! I'm not to talk to anyone from outside the house."

Helena glanced at the enormous mansion. It looked soulless with drapes across most windows. "No one is watching us. I am certain. What is your name?"

"Clarice. Clarice Witticomb," the girl said nervously.

Helena dropped the coins into Clarice's trembling hand and told the girl the description Will had given her of the maid: red hair, freckles, a large bosom, and saucy impertinence. The sort of maid a scoundrel would have. The maids in Greybrooke's house were older women, Helena remembered. Or were a bit slow-witted or had limps. Women who would have a hard time finding employment elsewhere.

She had wondered why a man as notoriously wicked as Greybrooke wouldn't have filled his home with young, beautiful women. Now she knew why. He was rescuing them.

She dragged her thoughts back to the important issues. "Can you give me her name?"

"It's Mary-Alice. But she hasn't been here in days. She's

going to get the sack—without a reference—when she finally does turn up."

The back of Helena's neck prickled. "How many days has it been?"

"Three days, miss."

That was the day Mary-Alice had gone to Will with her story. Mary-Alice could be in danger. "Do you know where she might have gone?"

"Oh, I have no idea I'm sure, miss." The young maid hurriedly looked down.

"I think you do know," Helena said. "You must tell me so I can help Mary-Alice."

"No, miss, I can't tell you. I have to go!" With that, the maid ran away down the sidewalk.

Helena wasn't going to be able to get the truth from the girl. But she must find Mary-Alice . . . of course it was obvious what she must do.

Talk to Greybrooke. If anyone could dazzle this young maid and coax her to reveal the truth, it would be the duke. But as she walked home, disaster struck.

On a street corner, a young boy in a cap was selling copies of the *London Correspondent,* shouting to passersby to encourage them to buy.

"Murder of a countess! Infamous duke suspected!" the lad shouted. Copy after copy was being snapped out of his hand by gentlemen who threw him their coins.

She had to jostle through the crowd. Having wrestled to put reluctant children at their school desks or into their nightclothes, she could withstand jabs by elbows, and when a man butted in front of her, she elbowed him out of the way.

Once she had her copy, Helena rushed away from the crowd and found the entrance to a mews. She stood there, not caring about the smells and the squishy muck underneath her shoes.

On the front page was a column filled with information given by a "mystery witness" that claimed a "certain" raven-haired duke known for rakish living had strangled a "woman of close intimacy" in a black-hearted fit of rage and passion.

"Oh heavens, Will, what have you done?" she whispered. "No matter what Whitehall threatened, we shouldn't have done *this*."

19

_____

"This time"—Greybrooke's eyes held hers as his footman handed her down from the carriage to join him—"you are to stay by my side at all times. Do not attempt to do anything alone."

Helena waited until the servant discreetly moved back to wait at the coach. She looked at the scarlet door of the brothel and shuddered. She was sick with guilt and fear over the newssheet story. But she must act as she normally would. "The first night, when the blackmailer grabbed me, _you_ left me alone to chase him. Running after you had seemed the safest thing."

"Touché. I made a mistake." He took a deep breath, his voice ragged. "But I have to know you're safe, Helena. I couldn't live with myself if you were hurt. In any way."

If he knew the truth he would not feel so protective. "I do wish it hadn't been . . . here."

"What else did you expect? If there is a dangerous brothel in the equation, it's the perfect place to lure people."

With that, he walked inside and she followed. Through the scarlet door, the shadowy foyer, and into the dimly lit hall, Helena could smell the earthy scent of sex. Her head was filled with raucous laughter, explosive squeals, fierce moans.

Large men were claiming young girls to be their bed partners. A man stared at Helena with a question in his eyes. One scowling glare from Greybrooke and the man hurried away.

Apparently, one look was all it took to convince the man that Greybrooke was dangerous.

That was what frightened Helena. Ever since talking to Clarice, Greybrooke had been cool, in full control. The only moment that control had faltered was just now, when he'd said he couldn't live with himself if she was hurt. What was seething inside him? What would he do? He must have read the newspaper story, and he must be filled with even more rage because of it.

Clarice had willingly told Greybrooke everything, and not because of his anger. The maid had gazed at him as if he were a Greek god, and once he gave her the extravagant amount of five pounds she was like clay in his hands. Clarice told them that Mary-Alice was instructed to go to a house on Curzon Street that had a scarlet door. There she would be given two thousand pounds. A fortune.

Of course the brothel where the blackmailer had threatened them had a scarlet door.

Greybrooke put his hand on the small of her back, a sign for other men to keep away. It startled her because he hadn't touched her when they made love. But here, where she could be in danger, he was touching her to keep her safe.

She didn't want to say anything about his touch in case he did move his hand. Feeling his palm against her back made her feel secure.

"How will we find Mary-Alice?" Helena asked softly. "With two thousand pounds she could have gone anywhere."

"She will prove easy to find." Greybrooke's voice was grim. His hand propelled her farther down the brothel's hallway. "What do you mean?"

"I think she was lured into danger. She has done her job—she gave false evidence against me. I expect Blackbriar has ensured she is now dead."

Helena froze on the spot. "Oh, my God, no!" Sickening fear rose up. "But why?"

"Damnation, I've frightened you. No harm will come to you. I promise that."

"But you're innocent! What does he hope to gain?"

Greybrooke answered softly, "I believe he murdered Caroline. He wants to see my neck in a noose instead of his."

"The man is mad." Fury brewed in her, but she realized she had to keep under control. Just like Greybrooke. The fury and rage he was bottling inside must be incredible.

"Angel, I've known that since the first time he hit Caro. Even before that—when I saw a possessive, gloating look in the bastard's eyes on the morning he married Caro. I've lived around madness my entire life. I damn well know how to recognize it."

His voice was detached, but she heard the pain beneath it. Her heart ached for him.

"Come, Miss Winsome," he said. "I have to find the madam."

The madam was a bosomy woman wearing a wig of ringlets and a lot of rouge. She tucked Greybrooke's bribe into her bodice. "A young lady of that description is upstairs, Your Grace. I received a note, with a generous payment, to secure her in a bedroom. But for the amount you have given me, I will let you see her. She is on the second floor—third bedroom on the right."

With that, Greybrooke murmured to her, "Upstairs." Helena was a few steps behind when he reached the door and threw it open. She caught up and peered around his back—

A young woman lay limply over the bed. Her eyes were

wide open, staring blankly above her. Red hair spilled around her face in a wild tangle. Freckles stood out against the gray-white pallor of her skin.

So did bruises. Purple, black, green bruises ringed her throat.

"You were right," Helena gasped, though she seemed to have no breath in her lungs. "The poor thing was lured here . . . and then . . ." And then some monster had wrapped his powerful hands around Mary-Alice's throat and had ruthlessly squeezed until the girl had died—

Helena's legs lost substance beneath her, dissolving like sugar in water.

Powerful arms went around her. A broad chest pressed against her cheek, and she felt her body slump against warm, solid strength.

"I am all right now. It was just the shock." She wanted to collapse against him completely. Horror made her dizzy and nauseated. But she couldn't just fall on Greybrooke like a limp doll. She had to keep her wits about her—she had to help Will.

She had to help Greybrooke.

Governesses were supposed to have strength, and she was trying to dredge up every ounce she had. But it was only Greybrooke's embrace that was making her strong again.

He didn't release her. His hands stroked over her back. He was touching her to soothe her. Then he turned her, his arm around her waist, and he led her to the door. He shouted brusquely for the madam. The woman materialized out of a nearby bedroom. Obviously she had followed them up the stairs.

"The young lady has been killed." Greybrooke gave commands to the madam, who went pure white. Helena realized the woman was in shock—surely she could not be such a good actress. The madam knew nothing about this.

"Go with her," Greybrooke said to her.

"N-no. I want to stay with you." She had to find courage to face this.

"Angel, I am going to question people. Runners will be here as soon as the madam gets the message to Bow Street. I want to learn what I can."

He was so strong. She felt sick.

"The poor, foolish girl." Tears broke then, soundless tears that ran down her cheeks.

Next thing she knew, Greybrooke was taking her out the front door. He installed her in the carriage. "Wait for me."

She did. She felt too sick to try to do anything. Time inched by, then finally the door was thrown open and Greybrooke swung up into the carriage. He sat beside her. Rapped on the ceiling and commanded the coachman to take them to her home.

Once in the door, all he said was, "To bed."

She wasn't sure if she could bear being tied up. Not now.

When he was helping her take off her dress, Helena whispered, "Are you helping me get ready for bed just for sleep?" She knew he needed sex when he was tormented or haunted by horrible thoughts, but she couldn't do it. What she really wanted was to be held.

"If that's what you want." He let her dress pool around her feet and unlaced her stays. "I won't do anything you don't desire. If you just want rest, you shall have it."

She had no right to ask this, but the words tumbled out. "I know you don't trust me, Greybrooke. I know I did a terrible thing by lying to you. But would you consider—for tonight—staying with me? Sleeping with me?"

He hesitated. Then shook his head. "I can't, love."

When she woke, Helena saw Greybrooke sitting in a wing chair by the fire, the chair turned so he could watch her. "You weren't there all night, were you?"

"I returned to the brothel," he said, "then went to Bow Street. I've only been back a few hours." He groaned as he pushed out of it and got to his feet.

He had spent a few *hours* in a chair watching her? She had done that when children were sick. Not only because it was her job, but because she loved them.

Greybrooke did not love her. Even if a duke could fall in love with a governess—really, what mad fantasy was that?—Greybrooke would never allow his heart to open. He would never let himself be vulnerable by falling in love.

But what did it mean that he'd sat awake and uncomfortable, watching over her?

Then she felt a wave of sorrow over the maid, Mary-Alice. Helena slipped out of bed to dress. She was determined to do something. She didn't quite know what. "Why would Lord Blackbriar have had the maid killed?" God, she hated to think of the poor girl—foolish, naïve, now dead. "Wouldn't he want her alive to give her story?"

"He couldn't trust her to stick to the lie. And since I found the girl dead, he probably thought I'd be blamed. I suspect he forced Clarice to give us the tale she did."

"But how would he know for certain that we would find Clarice?"

"She probably reported to him immediately after you questioned her, Miss Winsome. Then he baited his trap."

"But I can vouch for your innocence."

"You look so sweetly indignant," Greybrooke said with a wry smile. "But you're my mistress. Not an impartial witness."

Helena bit her lip. "But the doorman saw you arrive with me, and that was after Mary-Alice had been stabbed. Your coachman will say he took you to the brothel only the once that night. True, they are only servants, but there would have to be actual evidence to convict a duke of murder. And rather good evidence to wrongfully convict one!"

"Angel, only you could make me smile at a time like this," he said. "Your determination and belief in me is adorable. All I care about is protecting you—and protecting my family."

Did he not care about his own life? "I don't want to be adorable, I want to help you," Helena declared. "He won't get you hanged. I won't let him."

As her maid O'Hara dressed her hair, Helena stared at her reflection in her mirror. She was surrounded by her beautiful house, but she didn't care a fig about it. A pale, haggard face looked back at her. Greybrooke had left her to go once more to Bow Street. She was determined to help him get to the truth, but she feared he didn't care whether he lived or died. He was pursuing the blackmailer for revenge and to protect others, not to protect himself.

She believed him. He didn't care about his own life.

She remembered how she had vowed to change him. She didn't want to *change* him. Not the man who did wicked things to her and made her soar in pleasure. She didn't want to alter one thing about his noble, protective ways. Or muck in any way with the artistic soul inside him.

But she wanted him to be happy.

She wanted to be with him. That was the longing Helena couldn't deny. She had always thought she was sensible, but she wasn't.

She must find what had wounded his heart and soul, and she had to give him the strength to overcome his memories.

Her family's newspaper had helped to hurt him. If she could help him, it would make some amends for that. She was still haunted by guilt over Margaret's death. She would never forget losing her sister.

If only she could find out exactly what had happened to Greybrooke . . .

She wished she had been there with him when he was

young. If she'd been his governess, she would have known what had happened. She would have—

His governess. Goodness, why had she not thought of that?

It took Helena most of the day to find out what she wanted. For her Lady X column, she had fostered relationships with servants in many of the great houses. Fortunately no one knew she had left her post to become the Duke of Greybrooke's mistress. True to his word to his sister, Greybrooke had ensured discretion.

She had gone from one contact to another to learn what she needed to know: A woman named Miss Renshaw had been governess to the duke, Jacinta, and Maryanne. Miss Renshaw had remained with Maryanne until the death of the old duke, seven years ago. After that, Maryanne had gone to live with Jacinta, who had by that time married Winterhaven.

Miss Renshaw had been almost thirty when she had gone to the family, but that still meant she was only in her fifties. Certainly still alive.

Armed with a directory of London, Helena set about finding where the former governess lived. It took an hour, but she succeeded—she found the address.

Putting on her most modest gown, Helena summoned one of the carriages that had been a gift from Greybrooke. And she gave the direction to Miss Renshaw's house.

Miss Renshaw poured the tea. Helena accepted the cup. The rooms were warm, welcoming, furnished with pretty things. "You have a lovely home," she said to the former governess.

Tall, with curling gray hair and lively blue eyes, Miss Renshaw acknowledged the compliment. "It is all due to the Duke of Greybrooke. A year after he inherited the title from his father, he searched me out. The young duke granted me a very generous annuity."

To keep her quiet? The terrible thought flitted through Helena's head. But no, she could guess why. "Had you been left badly off?"

"I—" A flush touched the woman's lined cheeks. "I was dismissed from my post by the duchess just after the old duke's death. I spoke out about things that I . . . did not agree with. So I was turned out without money or a reference."

And Greybrooke had come to the woman's rescue.

Helena had no idea how to trick Miss Renshaw into talking. "I must be honest," she said. "I have come to ask you questions. I am worried about the duke, and about his youngest sister Maryanne. I believe you can help me."

She told Miss Renshaw all about Greybrooke. About how he claimed he would never fall in love. About how he was deeply wracked by guilt and tortured by pain.

"I want to help him," Helena finished desperately.

There was a long silence. Very long. Then Miss Renshaw said, "Who are you to the duke?"

She had to admit it. "I am now his mistress. I was once governess to Lady Maryanne. I am sure you are shocked now, but please help me. Greybrooke is being wrongfully accused of murder, and I fear he is so hurt by his past that he will not fight for himself."

"Yes, I saw the newssheets. The stories about his father. The accusations." Miss Renshaw put her hand to her throat. "I wish to help the duke, but I've kept these secrets a very long time. . . ."

"If you can help Greybrooke, please, please, do so." She was so hopeful, so desperate, all the control a governess should display went out the window. "He is such a good man. He's artistic, did you know? But he hid his talent from his family because his father was so terrible. He's such a wonderful gentleman, and I—" Goodness, she had almost said, "I love him."

She did. It was a glorious feeling, and a deep intense pain, and it was happiness and longing wrapped up together.

She knew she'd revealed her heart to the former governess, and she bowed her head.

"You love him," Miss Renshaw said softly.

With Will, Helena had protested and denied it. But Greybrooke was so wonderful, so sensual, so caring. How could she have done anything else?

With a shaky hand, Miss Renshaw set down her cup. "The tragedy is in what Lady Maryanne did. Before the fever that left her blind. The illness was awful—a sort of spinal sickness. The poor child had terrible headaches. Part of her face was paralyzed, and she could not move her eyes or her mouth on that side. It was the most frightening thing. The poor lamb was delirious. She was in the care of her brother, then; the old duke and his wife were dead. The poor child kept screaming that she had done something evil and this was her punishment. She was tormented, certain her soul could not be saved. The duke—the new duke, I mean, not her father—nursed her as much as I did. He barely left her side. But the illness left her blind."

Helena remembered the secret Jacinta had written about in her letters and the terrible thing Maryanne claimed she had done. She declared softly, "Lady Maryanne has been very troubled."

"The new duke indulged her, I am sorry to say. His Grace loves her dearly, and after she lost her sight, he let her have her tantrums, spoiled her rotten. It did the child no good."

Helena ached to know what had happened, but she feared if she asked bluntly, she would make the woman stop speaking. She told Miss Renshaw of the progress she had made with Maryanne.

The older woman rested her hand on Helena's sleeve. "Then you were a godsend for her, Miss Winsome. That is just what the child needs—firm and loving discipline. She went through—" Miss Renshaw stopped. "Well, I cannot say."

"If it would help Lady Maryanne—and the duke—it would be best to speak the truth."

Miss Renshaw frowned. "I know of some of the things that went on in that house. Very bad things."

"Greybrooke was abused," Helena said. "He has told me about some of it."

Miss Renshaw wrung her hands. "It was horrible. She claimed it was for the boy's own good. But what she did . . . well, I would not want to see my worst enemy endure it."

"*She?*" Helena gasped the word. "Do you mean the duke's mother? His *mother* was the one who imprisoned him and abused him?"

"Yes. It was the duchess. They were both terribly cruel and quite vicious, the duchess and the old duke. I know I should not speak of it, but it makes me so angry. For the sake of those children—Lord Damian, Lady Jacinta, Lady Maryanne—I did not say a word once I was turned out. I kept the secrets. When I was in the home, I tried to defend them, but what could I do, pitted against a powerful duke and a wicked duchess?"

Helena's stomach lurched. "Both parents abused them?"

Good heavens, she'd thought Greybrooke's mother must have tried to help him—or she'd been too afraid of her husband to protect him.

"It was almost like a game between them, to outdo each other in cruelty." Miss Renshaw's eyes narrowed with remembered anger. "The duke—he was Lucifer incarnate. And the duchess insisted that she was doing God's work by whipping the devil out of her son."

"That is terrible."

"It is a miracle those children survived it. Once Lord Damian was close to death, for he had been locked in a metal box and left outdoors in the dead of winter. The child nearly froze. Then he nearly died of illness afterward."

Numbness raced over Helena.

"What had Lady Maryanne seen that was so horrible she thought blindness was her punishment?" Helena asked softly.

"I—I really do not know, Miss Winsome. Lady Maryanne would not speak of it to me. All I know was that it happened at the time of the old duke's death. That was fortuitous—the death of the old duke. It happened before . . . it happened at a time to protect the girls. It hit Lord Damian very hard, though of course he knew it was necessary. Only weeks after the old duke's death, the duchess passed away. I was not sorry to hear of it. The new Duke of Greybrooke is a very good man."

"Yes, he is," Helena breathed. But Greybrooke did not see that. There was more here. Why should Greybrooke feel such guilt?

It happened at a time to protect the girls . . .

"Did his mother and his father abuse their daughters too?" She heard the horror in her voice.

Miss Renshaw nodded sadly. "The father did evil, terrible things. And their mother punished them for it, as if it were their fault."

Helena knew Lady Winterhaven would never allow her to approach the children in Berkeley Square. Not now that she was a scandalous mistress.

She hid behind the leafy branches of a shrub and watched the new governess. Filled with envy, Helena had to admit. The woman was very pretty with auburn curls, and the children looked happy.

No—Sophie, Michael, and Timothy looked happy. Lady Maryanne did not. Greybrooke's young sister sat on a blanket in a circle of her skirts, tearing out fistfuls of grass.

Every so often the young governess would glance at Maryanne and bite her lip.

Envy quickly became a sharp pang of guilt. Obviously Lady

Maryanne had been very upset by her leaving. The young woman was once again sullen, vacant, and childlike, just as she'd been when Helena had first arrived.

The young governess drew out some embroidery for her and Sophie, and the two females began to make swift strokes with their needles. Timothy and Michael played leapfrog on the grass.

Now was her chance. She believed the true secret to Greybrooke's pain lay in the terrible thing that Lady Maryanne had done. She must do the very thing she had told that evil, fake Whitehall she would not do. She must coax Maryanne to tell her the truth.

"Maryanne, it's me, Miss Winsome." The girl, who was several yards away from the others, lifted her head, cocked it, then turned in the direction of Helena's whisper.

"Miss Winsome?" She asked it softly.

"Yes, my dear." The governess was absorbed in her needlework, so Helena slipped out from behind the lilac bush. She hurried to Maryanne and clasped the girl's hand. "I need to ask you some questions. It is important you tell me the truth. Important for your brother's sake. It is about what happened when your father's died."

Lady Maryanne's eyes widened. "Do you know? Grey said I was never to tell. Never." Her fingers curved like claws. Like a frightened animal preparing to fight for its life.

Miss Renshaw's words floated back to Helena. *That was fortuitous—the death of the old duke. . . . It hit Lord Damian very hard, though of course he knew it was necessary.*

Had Maryanne seen her brother kill her father? Was that what had tormented the girl? Keeping that secret? Heavens, the old duke had been evil. Greybrooke must have shot his father to protect his sisters. But she had to know if her suspicions were correct.

"Maryanne, how did your father die? Was . . . was Grey-brooke responsible? I know he was beaten, locked up, and whipped—"

"Father never hurt Damian," Maryanne whispered. "It wasn't Father who did that. It was Mother. Damian had to be punished for being naughty and sinful. Mother wanted to make him good. But she was so very wrong—hurting him only wanted to make him misbehave more. The more she tried to stop him from being terrible like Father, the more he wanted to be bad."

Maryanne tipped up her face, and for one moment Helena felt the young woman could see into her soul. "Father was so awful. I wanted Mother to be good. I wanted to be loved. But there was no escape." Tears brimmed, then spilled to Maryanne's cheeks. "It was my fault. That's why I went blind."

"It was an illness that took your sight," Helena broke in firmly, and she put her arm around the girl's shoulders.

Maryanne shook her head. "I did something terribly wrong and I had to pay for my sin."

"Lady Maryanne, none of this was your fault. You were not bad—"

"Killing someone *is* bad." Maryanne put her hand to her mouth. The words came out muffled. "Mother hurt Damian, but Father said he loved us. He said he loved me, but what he did felt so bad. It made me feel so sick. I knew it was wrong—it was the thing Mother punished Damian for. Young ladies weren't supposed to do that. Father said it was all right, because he would always look after me, but he was lying. It was *wrong*."

"Your father committed the sin. You did not. You were innocent—"

"You don't understand. I should go—our new governess will miss me."

Helena looked. The woman had not yet noticed Maryanne no longer sat on the grass. "It is all right. I do want you to understand you aren't to blame, and that illness was not a judgment. It was just chance, Maryanne."

"Damian said he would claim he did it, to protect me. Damian was going to kill Father to stop him. But then I knew I'd been a coward. It was my responsibility. I couldn't let Damian do it when I should do it. So I—I took one of Father's dueling pistols and threatened him. He was furious. He threatened to beat me until I could not walk, then keep me prisoner. Then he lunged at me and—and next thing I knew, the pistol exploded in my hand, knocking me onto the floor. There was choking smoke and—and then Father collapsed. I'd pulled the trigger. I killed Father." Maryanne jerked helplessly as sobs claimed her.

"It wasn't your fault. Dear heaven, it was an accident. Not your fault." Helena wrapped her arms around Maryanne and cradled the girl securely against her chest. She said every soothing thing she could think of.

"Grey said if anyone ever found out that Father was shot, he would say he did it," Maryanne whispered. "They said in the newspaper that Father was murdered. They know, don't they? But I can't let my brother be punished for what I did! I can't!"

The poor girl. No wonder Greybrooke had vowed to take the blame for it. "Do not say anything, Lady Maryanne. No one knows anything. Greybrooke has not been accused of killing your father. You must keep silent. Please, you must trust me."

The girl nodded. "I do trust you, Miss Winsome."

Helena was shaky with horror over the nightmare Lady Maryanne had lived through. She could not let this ever be discovered. But her investigation of Greybrooke had begun to expose his secrets. Someone was accusing Greybrooke of murdering his own father.

First there had been the accusation of treason, then the story that his father had been murdered, now the accusation about Lady Blackbriar's death. Was Whitehall behind everything? Was he the villain, not Blackbriar?

But why was he trying to destroy the duke?

20

Helena hurried back to her pale-blue curricle. Finding out the truth from Maryanne, when Greybrooke had told the girl to never talk, was a terrible betrayal.

She slapped the reins, and her curricle launched ahead. Driving was still a challenge—she had her horses trotting slowly. Just as she would protect children, she was protecting others from her lack of driving skills.

When she reached her white town house, she turned her curricle over to her groom. As she entered the foyer, untying the bow of her bonnet, Betsy bobbed a curtsy. "His Grace has arrived. He is awaiting you in the blue drawing room."

Helena choked down guilt as she reached the room.

Greybrooke sprawled in a wing chair, long legs stretched out. In his hand was a glass of brandy—he'd ensured her home was stocked with what he liked to drink.

He looked up, his mouth a brutal slash of grim anger. "Where in Hades have you been?"

"J-just for a drive," she lied.

"I've been worried sick about you."

He was concerned for her, and she had been finding out his secrets behind his back.

"The blackmailer has been found," he said.

"Oh, thank goodness." Greybrooke would be cleared and so would Will.

"Don't be thankful yet, Helena. The blackguard's body was dragged out of the Thames."

For a moment she just stared. He drained his brandy, watching her over the glass. Then her wits finally worked. "He drowned?"

"No. He was found in the river, but he was dead when he went into the water. Someone strangled him, then threw him in. Bow Street's magistrate suspects that someone is me." His tones were cool and jaded, but his hand gripped his glass.

First the accusations about Lady Blackbriar, about the maid. Now this. "Does he have any reason to suspect you?"

"You mean—did I do it?" His voice was a low, deadly growl.

"Goodness, no! I mean was it like Lady Blackbriar? Was there supposedly a witness?"

He inclined his head, admiration in his eyes. "Yes. A couple of butchers, heading to work before dawn, saw a man of my description push a body into the Thames." He paused. "Do you believe it?"

He was challenging her. She could see it in his green eyes. "No, I don't. Someone is doing this to you. It must stop!"

A grin came to Grey's lips, but it was a bitter one, as if he were laughing just before a noose was dropped around his neck. "Indeed? You have decided it should stop, have you, angel?"

"Don't make fun. I suppose that sounds silly, but I am fed up with this. I refuse to have you hounded or arrested for something you didn't do."

The fury in his eyes dissolved. "I agree, Miss Winsome. This has to stop, and I have something I didn't have before. Now I know what the blackmailer looked like." From his coat pocket, he drew out a folded sheet of foolscap from the pocket.

"The blackmailer's body was taken to a mortuary in Whitechapel. I went to take a look—it was the first time I saw the villain without his mask. I produced this." He unfolded the page. "It gives us something to show people to find out who he was. I want to connect him to Blackbriar."

It was one of his remarkable drawings. On the white foolscap, a strikingly handsome man came to life. This was the face behind the eerie mask, the face of the man who'd threatened her life. Hatred boiled up, but so did a stronger feeling. A warm, aching, intense feeling directed at Greybrooke, who had *saved* her life.

"I haven't forgotten Will Rains of that damned newspaper either. With all that's happened, I haven't had time to destroy his newssheet. Though he's had time to print more lies."

"He was forced to print those things! I don't believe he was working with the blackmailer. Mr. Rains is innocent."

Greybrooke stared at her in surprise. "How do you know all this?"

How could she tell him without giving herself away? "I—I went to see him. I believed what he told me. We have only the word of a criminal that Mr. Rains was involved. He has younger sisters. Please, Greybrooke, do not destroy him. Please wait."

He hesitated, and her heart lodged so firmly in her throat she couldn't breathe. Finally he said, "All right."

Helena almost sobbed with relief. Will was safe for now.

"I am going to take that picture to St. Giles where the black-mailer met Orley. See if anyone recognizes it."

"We must go at once," she declared.

"Soon. There's something I need to do first."

"What could be more important than clearing your name? Than proving you innocent?"

"One thing." Greybrook set down his drink and stood.

"Making love to you. Something quick. I can't be in a room with you without wanting you. Lean over that table, angel, and let me tie your hands."

Startled, she did what he asked. And made remarkable discoveries.

Who knew sex could be so exhilarating when it was enjoyed in mere minutes? Who knew he could make her come so many times, so quickly?

A quarter hour later, still dizzy from climaxes, Helena gasped for breath as Greybrooke straightened her skirts, untied her hands. She put her hand to her pounding heart. "That was amazing. But should we not go and prove your innocence now?"

He gave a soft, deep chuckle. "Yes, I suppose we should. But first let me fix your hair."

Even on a gloriously sunny day, stepping into the Mast and Sails made Helena think she was climbing into a soot-filled closet. Dirt and grime clung to the windows, extinguishing any hope of daylight in the small room. At the bench tables, men hunkered over tankards of ale. In the corners, women sat in bedraggled finery with glasses of gin in their hands.

"Something should be done about such despair," Helena murmured. After all, she knew how easy it was to tumble from respectability.

She felt Greybrooke's gaze on her. Studying her. Had she said too much? Made him wonder about her past again?

To stop him from pondering—if he was—she asked, "What are you going to do?"

"Speak to someone."

Every female eye had gone quickly to Greybrooke, but he singled out one woman, bestowing his stunning smile. She was middle-aged, her face marred by pockmarks. Wispy gray-brown curls stuck out beneath her gaudy purple bonnet. The woman shuffled away from the man beside her—a heavy-set, balding man—and scuttled toward Grey as he sat elegantly on the bench at her side. He ordered the woman a fresh drink.

Heavens, Helena thought, he was good.

She stayed near the door, watching as he took out the picture. Wariness came to the woman's eyes. Greybrooke's gaze held her captive though.

He drew out several gold sovereigns and dropped the coins into the woman's hand. They fell with a melodious clink. The woman bent close to Greybrooke, cupped her hand to her mouth, and whispered something in his ear. He nodded, then he stood and bowed over the woman's hand in parting.

Helena bit her lip as he prowled across the tavern to her. He had to duck since the timbered ceiling was so low.

"She will probably spend it all on drink," she whispered.

"Agreed. But I cannot force the woman—her name is Mrs. Winslet—to change."

"Sometimes you have to make people change whether they want to or not. I always have to do what is best for children."

"There are some people you cannot change."

Helena knew he meant himself. "I do not believe that." She lowered her voice. "How did you know to speak to her?"

"Last time I was searching here, I was told Mrs. Winslet knows everyone in the stews. Now that I have the picture, she was able to help me. She is supposed to be able to tell fortunes too."

"What did she tell you?"

"Something very valuable. And she told me my future, though I doubt her powers of prognostication."

"Why doubt her?" Though Helena did not believe in any of that—in love she had stopped being practical, but she was determined to stay that way in everything else.

"She told me I was about to fall in love," Greybrooke said.

She gaped at him in shock, then said quickly, "Did she tell you who the man is?"

"Come along, angel."

* * *

He said nothing more about the prediction, nor did he reveal what else the woman said.

Finally, as the carriage rattled down the Strand, Helena exploded, "She gave you the man's name. That's why we're racing so quickly. You must tell me who he is. We are in this *together*, and I want to know."

Greybrooke sat across from her. "I suppose we are in this together. There's no point in trying to protect you. You're too stubborn. All right, his name is Turner, and he's an actor. According to Mrs. Winslet, he's been in several plays on Drury Lane. So we will show his picture around there."

"An actor." She thought of Whitehall, who had not been a real agent of the Crown. "Playing the part of a blackmailer?"

Greybrooke flashed an admiring look. "I wondered that myself."

"But wouldn't it have been a terrible risk?"

"Not if you intended all along to kill him."

She shivered, struggled to make sense of it. "Why would Blackbriar blackmail his wife?"

"If he wanted to make her death look like a suicide, he needed to show she had motivation to take her own life. Escaping blackmail—and ruin—would give a strong reason."

"But if he wants to make it appear that you murdered her, why give her motive to have taken her own life?"

"That's the perverse madness of this." With stunning coolness, he added, "All I can guess is that he wanted me to hang either for Caro's murder or for the blackmailer's murder."

"Why would he hate you *that* much?"

"He was obsessive about Caroline."

"You weren't her lover though. You weren't the father of her child."

"I don't know what Caroline told him—maybe she told Blackbriar I was the father to protect her real lover. Or perhaps she told him the truth and Blackbriar refused to believe it. He told me he believed she was always in love with me. Regardless, it doesn't matter. She was my close friend, and she warned me that Blackbriar had always been jealous of our friendship."

"Perhaps she really did love you."

"She would have had no reason to. I never treated her as anything more than a friend. She wanted someone to give her what Blackbriar refused. Tenderness, kindness. Normal love. I couldn't give her that. I'm more warped than Blackbriar."

She hated to hear him say that. And say it with such cold acceptance. "That is not true. You have a terrible past and you must feel so much rage over it. But that is natural—what child would not be afraid to love and open his heart after enduring pain and torture from both his parents? After being whipped. Put in a trunk, for heaven's sake. Your father was a complete madman and attacked his youngest daughter. I understand why you feel such pain, and why you have all this anger. But it doesn't mean you have to feel that way forever."

Greybrooke frowned. Helena had the suddenly sensation of a wall of ice growing instantly between them. Oh God—she realized what she'd said. . . .

"How do you know about the trunk? How do you know about Maryanne? Who told you?"

Helena knew she could never think of a lie to explain how she could know something so specific, so she told him the truth. "I wanted to help you forget the past."

I wanted it because I have a mad dream that I can be with you. Despite all the good sense I've learned to possess, I fantasize about being with you. About being loved by you.

She certainly didn't let one word of that off her lips. He could draw back from her. Probably leave her in a minute if he knew how desperately she cared.

She took a calming breath. "I found your former governess,

Miss Renshaw. From what she said, I realized what had happened. You are haunted by what happened to you. You are haunted by what happened to Lady Winterhaven and Lady Maryanne. Greybrooke, you mustn't torment yourself. What could you have done?"

"We're here," was all he said.

The carriage had stopped near one of the theaters.

"I'll show the picture." She couldn't sit in the carriage, knowing he was furious. She grasped the picture from his hand, flung open the door, and raced down the steps.

She went from one theater to the next, explaining to people that the man in the picture was a friend of her brother's, that her brother was missing and she was praying this friend could help her. It had become so terribly easy to lie.

Greybrooke watched from the shadows. Helena felt his gaze on her like a burning brand.

Finally, at a theater called the Sans Pareil, which meant "Without Compare," she found a young, pimply lad who was building a backdrop of a Venetian scene, and he recognized the picture at once.

"He's one of the most popular actors here." The redheaded lad hauled off his cap as he spoke to her. He blushed when he looked down into her eyes. "His name's Richard Turner. He plays in all the risky plays. They call them the 'burlettes' or something like that."

Helena knew those plays. Called *burlettas,* they were ribald versions of operettas from the Continent, filled with naughty jokes and scandalous innuendo.

Impetuously, she touched the young man's hand. He puffed out his chest in front of her.

"Thank you so very much. You've been such a hero. I will never forget your kindness."

"You're welcome, miss. What's yer name?"

She gulped and gave him a false one. Then quickly asked,

"Do you know where Mr. Turner would live? I could ask him about my brother."

"He'll be at the theater tonight. I think he lives on Kean Street."

Her heart thudded with excitement—they were getting close to finding who had hired Turner to act as a blackmailer, close to having proof it was Blackbriar, if it was him. But what was Whitehall's role in this? Who was he?

Had Blackbriar really concocted all of this to see Greybrooke hang?

Keeping Miss Winsome behind him, Grey rapped on the door of No. 14 Kean Street, then shoved it open. The place was a rabbit warren of apartments. It appeared there were supposed to have been two residences on each of the three floors, but they had been divided into smaller and smaller spaces, with no logical method of marking the numbers. Neighbors claimed Richard Turner lived in an apartment on the third floor, the last on the left.

He did not like having Miss Winsome with him in what could prove a dangerous place. But she'd insisted on coming. He had seen the strain in her face. Knowing she was hurting so much, he couldn't hurt her more by refusing to let her come.

She followed him down a dingy hallway with a floor that undulated like waves. At the last door, Grey knocked hard. He was preparing to break it down when it swung open to reveal a woman in a filmy muslin nightdress. Her breasts were caught together and lifted, for the nightgown was tight and the neckline was a low scoop. Blinking, the woman focused on him. "Who might you be then?" she purred.

"The Duke of Greybrooke." He arched a brow, looking icily ducal. "Allow me to introduce Miss Smith."

"Yer can't really be the Duke of Greybrooke? Why would you come here?"

"I need to speak to you." He ushered Miss Winsome into the room, forcing the voluptuous blonde to step back and allow them in. The apartment appeared to be one room. There was a cot along one wall, a table and two chairs, and a fireplace in which a kettle hung.

The woman yawned, shoving her bosom forward. Her nipples strained against the muslin.

"Perhaps we should have let the lady put on a robe," Miss Winsome whispered to him.

"I'm not embarrassed to let a handsome gent and a *duke* ogle my assets. I've heard of the Duke of Greybrooke. Ye're one of the most desired protectors amongst opera dancers. Everyone wants a go at him. We're all hoping to be the girl who captures yer interest for more than a month."

The girl threw a smirk at Miss Winsome. "Sorry, love. I'm sure yer will be out on your pretty bottom in a month as well."

He took a quick look at Miss Winsome. That was his reputation. Would it hurt her?

"I was warned about that," Miss Winsome said simply. "Though I think it's quite silly to go from one actress to another each month. Most plays run longer than that."

Grey found he had to smile at her wicked sense of humor. If she was hurt, she was hiding it well. And he found he didn't want to think about letting her go.

Miss Winsome surprised him. She tied *him* in knots. He shouldn't trust her, especially now he knew she had dug into his past, but there was something about her. . . .

He liked to be with her. Being with her made him happier. It was the first time this had ever happened.

But right now, he had to clear his name. He turned to the bosomy, blond actress. "Might I have your name, my dear?"

"Florence Marble, but everyone calls me Flossie. I'd like ye to call me that, Yer Grace."

He needed to question her, so he allowed her to drag him

to one of the dirty, scarred chairs and he sat down. Flossie stood so close to him, her breasts pressed against the side of his head like an overstuffed pillow.

He moved away, having to sit right against the wall.

Miss Winsome lifted a brow. "Are you trying to smother His Grace, Miss Marble?"

He bit back a laugh.

"So sorry, Yer Grace. I forget how generous me bosom is sometimes."

"I'm sure you are always very aware of your bosom," Miss Winsome said firmly. "Miss Marble, even if you steal the duke away from me, do remember you won't have him for more than a month. It will be a hollow victory. We came for your help, and the duke is prepared to be generous if you do assist us."

Despite the seriousness of the situation, Grey had to swallow a laugh.

"How generous do ye mean?" Flossie asked.

"If you cause His Grace to pass out due to asphyxiation, you will never know, will you?" said Miss Winsome. "Now, Miss Marble, I am certain you have a quick and clever brain. That is what we are interested in today."

Flossie straightened away from him. "Yer interested in me wits?"

"Exactly."

Grey could see a look of pride in Flossie's eyes. He shook his head in amazement. Without embarrassment or anger, Miss Winsome had taken charge.

He admired Miss Winsome's cool control. In some ways, her strength made him think of his mother. But his mother had been icy, without any passion and without a heart.

Miss Winsome was kind, noble, and good, and she possessed an enormous heart.

"I will stand while you ladies are seated." He took Flossie's hand. The girl's hand was plump with chubby fingers; very different from Miss Winsome's long, capable hands. Hands that could soothe a child, that could give him pleasure, if he could let her touch him.

"Sit, Miss Marble. And you as well, my dear." Grey put his hand on Miss Winsome's slim shoulders and eased her onto the chair beside Flossie's.

"I will pay you generously for information, Flossie. But you won't tempt me away from Miss Smith."

"But in a month, perhaps ye will be looking for a new lady-bird."

"No, I'm afraid I won't be."

The duke's words startled Helena, and she looked at Grey-brooke in surprise. She had been so stunned, she hadn't realized he was questioning Flossie.

Under his avid attention, Flossie was blossoming. "I do poses in my corset or a scanty gown, Yer Grace. Very popular we are, and we've a fancy French name. The *Voloptuaries Plastiques,* we're called. But I want more than just lying about, acting like a wax figure. I want to sing. I want to be on a grand stage, something bigger than the Sans Pareil, which just puts on a lot of dirty operettas. I want to perform for the Prince Regent."

"I could make that happen for you," Greybrooke said, startling Helena. She supposed he could do that—he was a duke.

"But you just said you wouldn't become my protector."

"No, my dear. What I could be is more of a . . . patron."

Flossie looked blank. Helena explained, "Artists have patrons. They pay so the artist can paint. An actress is very much like an artist."

"Indeed, I am!" Flossie said proudly.

Greybrooke's smile could have turned ice immediately into steam. "You will be a star in the best theaters on Drury Lane, my dear."

286 / *Sharon Page*

Delighted, Flossie jumped up. She embraced Greybrooke. "I've got gin," she declared. "We'll have a toast."

Once Flossie had moved to a cupboard and was searching for her liquor, Helena whispered, "But what if she's awful?"

"Then I lose some money," he answered, his lips against her ear. "Not a tragedy. Besides, she might turn out to be very good. Many gentlemen would pay to see her—she might find a generous protector."

"You are taking care of her, aren't you? Just as you look after children and less fortunates. Just as you've taken care of Lady Maryanne."

He jerked his head toward her. She drew back at the intensity of his gaze.

Flossie was returning, with her bottle of gin.

"We'll speak of this later," he said very softly. In icy tones.

Three teacups were placed on cracked saucers. Flossie sloshed a bit of pungent, clear liquid in each cup. The duke lifted his, toasted Flossie, and sipped. Helena took a little and coughed. Flossie tipped hers back with a quick bolt of her wrist.

Greybrooke set down his cup and leaned against the wall. He looked tall and imposing in the small room. "So, Miss Marble, I will be your new patron and you will have the chance to shine upon the stage," he said. "But I do have some terrible news for you, my dear."

His expression softened. He took the woman's hand. Then told her of the death of Richard Turner. He made it sound like an accident, as if the man had fallen in the river.

"Dickie . . . gone? He must have been set upon by thieves. Wouldn't be that he was drunk—never touched a drop." Flossie's plump face crumpled. Grey produced a fine linen handkerchief and offered it to her. She blew her nose in it with a loud honk.

"I'll miss him so. Dickie was great fun. Always generous

and sweet. Always buying a girl a nice gift. A bit of jewelry or a new bonnet. Not like his friend, Morse. Sour-faced cadaver who was always telling Dickie he was a fool for being so nice to me."

"I'm sure Mr. Turner knew what a treasure he had," Greybrooke said. "What can you tell me about Morse?"

"He's an actor too," said Flossie. "His face looks like a death's head. With his horrible looks, he always plays villains."

Helena frowned. The description sounded like Whitehall. He was grim-faced, with skin that clung to his pronounced cheekbones. If both the blackmailer and Whitehall were actors, they must have been hired by Blackbriar, like Grey suspected.

But if Greybrooke found Whitehall, he would learn who she really was. He would find out she had lied to him. He would suspect she had given those stories to Will to print.

He would throw her out, vow revenge on her and Will—and probably destroy them both.

21

In her bedroom, Greybrooke's hand stroked over her naked bottom. "You have the most voluptuous and beautiful derriere I've ever seen. I want to make you melt with pleasure."

Helena wanted to melt so very much, but she didn't know what she was going to do. He wouldn't be complimenting her bottom if he knew the truth.

Across her bedroom, she could see her reflection in her cheval mirror. At Greybrooke's request, she had stripped completely naked. She had one knee on her bed, her bound hands resting against the bedpost. Her reflected face looked filled with nerves and guilt.

Mad panic told her to find Morse before Greybrooke did. But the man was in league with a murderer—or could be the killer himself. He must pay for his crimes. Lady Blackbriar deserved justice, and Greybrooke hungered for it. If she was the only one in danger, she would tell Greybrooke the truth. But she must protect her family, and she had no idea what Greybrooke would do in anger.

What was she going to do?

His finger lightly teased the entrance to her bottom. Closing her eyes, Helena moaned. Just his touch there made her cunny wet.

Greybrooke would find out the truth about her very soon. Once he knew she was Will's sister, he would believe she was responsible for every awful story Will had been forced to publish.

She wanted to savor pleasure and intimacy with Greybrooke before it was gone forever.

His finger went in just a little. Her little anus seemed to open for him, as if her body remembered how good it had been to take that ivory wand inside.

Helena supposed a clever woman might try to extract every present she could from a duke before she was tossed out on the street. But she was not that kind of woman.

She didn't want him for things. She wanted this delicious, amazing intimacy with him.

His finger slid into her rump, filling her. Her cunny clenched madly as pleasure shot through her. Never had she dreamed this could feel so good. But Greybrooke did things to her she'd never dreamed could be done, and each one made her come harder, made her soar higher.

"So hot and so tight," he murmured. "And I know how to make it tighter."

He left the bed, brought a velvet bag from beside the door. She hadn't noticed it in the shadows. Her hands were already tied together, of course, so she could not open it.

"A new toy for you." The velvet dropped away before her eyes, revealing a long, thick wand of ivory. Rubies were set in the base of it. "I want to make you explode in more pleasure than you can imagine."

"I never even dreamed so much pleasure could be possible," she whispered. This would feel so good, so incredibly good. She couldn't wait.

Watching his hand rub oil along its length, her knees almost collapsed. Sexual desire made her legs weak; they were ready to turn into puddles of liquid with her anticipation.

"Oh, please," she moaned as Greybrooke slipped the wand between her plump derriere cheeks and the slick tip of it hit her entrance.

Slowly, he pushed it forward, easing it in and out, filling her with slow, sensual deliberation.

Then it was in her—to the brim. Each tiny shift of her body sent thrilling sensation through her. She turned a little, so she could see the hilt, with the handle made for his hand sticking out of her bottom. She expected him to start thrusting it.

He didn't. He tied a length of black velvet to the handle. Then he tied that around her hips, capturing the wand deep inside her.

She felt a quick burst of her juices flow from her cunny.

"Tonight, I want to cover you in jewels," he said. Lazily, he brought forward another velvet bag—this one deep green. From it he took out hinged clips. A spray of emeralds and diamonds dripped from each one. "For your nipples," he said.

Heavens, how?

The instant the first clip gently touched her left nipple, both of them hardened.

Greybrooke grinned—a wicked quirk of a smile that made her cunny throb. "I think you are becoming very wanton, Miss Winsome. You're aroused with anticipation."

It was true, but she was a bit nervous. "You are going to clamp those on my nipples? Won't that hurt terribly?"

"They are lined with velvet and designed to tug only a little. I promise I would never hurt you. I want you to enjoy intense sensations everywhere."

He had never hurt her, and she trusted him. Though the intense way he promised he would never do her harm made her squirm with guilt.

She did take a sharp breath when he opened them—they were operated by small springs—and he closed one on her erect left nipple, then on her right. As the clamps settled, the jewels dangled. The weight of them tugged at her nipples, making her nipples feel they were being sucked.

She licked her lips at the sight of her full breasts, decorated with swinging, winking jewels.

He was right. She was wanton. Completely, incurably wanton.

Her quim pulsed with yearning. She was afraid to move, because the slightest twitch could set off her orgasm.

She wanted to make it build.

He had already secured black ropes to the bed canopy. With his strong hands, he used them to tie her. Soon her hands were lifted and suspended.

The mirror reflected Greybrooke. A quick jerk of his hand undid his cravat, and he tossed it aside. His coat came off. She was captivated by watching his muscular arms move as he casually undid his waistcoat, then his trousers. Soon, to her amazement, he was naked.

Beautifully naked. Largely, erectly naked.

In the mirror, she saw him get on his knees on the bed. Her white and silver counterpane made his skin look a lovely, almost coppery shade. He was so darkly gorgeous.

She closed her eyes for a moment. Pain swamped her—not physical pain, but a deep, aching pain in her heart. Inside she was terrified, waiting for the end to come—for him to find out the truth, hate her, throw her out. He would be even more determined to crush the newspaper then. She'd have no hope of making him change his mind.

And when it all happened, she would be left devastated. Her heart broken.

But she couldn't think of any of that right now. She wanted to please him—

292 / Sharon Page

Not because she had to, but because she loved him and yearned to.

His body pressed against hers from behind, pushing the wand deeper into her bottom. If it weren't for the ropes holding up her arms, she would have collapsed in boneless need on the bed. His thick erection touched her nether lips from behind.

She was so wet, his cock so rigid, he slid right into her. His thrusts quickly became hard. Amazing thrusts that teased her quim and went so deep. Then, slowly, he stroked her clit.

She was on an edge of pleasure, and just moments of his skillful, circling motion set her off. She came, thrashing her body because her hands were tied, crying out, "Greybrooke!"

Then he came, his hips banging against hers. In the mirror, she saw the erotic agony on his face. Together they rocked in pleasure. Even though he must be consumed by ecstasy like her, he cupped her left breast and teased her clitoris until she burst once more.

As always, he released her afterward. He went to her dressing room and brought in the basin of water and washcloths.

As always, he tenderly washed her.

He doesn't know that soon, very soon, he will be furious with you.

There was something she must tell him, before he threw her out. "I'm not doing this because I have to," she said haltingly. "I mean, because I need money to save my family. The truth is I love . . . this."

The duke kissed the tip of her nose. The gesture was so sweet, it broke her heart. He had denied it before, but he *could* be very sweet. She had seen it from the very beginning with his niece and nephews. And when he did it like this with her, her heart felt full to bursting.

"Greybrooke—"

"Shh. Time for bed," he said.

* * *

Damn, Grey felt guilty. The sex had been superbly erotic. Afterward, Miss Winsome had the sleepy, sultry eyes and tumbled beauty of a woman who had been well fucked.

Now she was sleeping. Grey pulled on a robe, then walked through the dark house.

He returned to the drawing room and went to the brandy decanter. It had been refilled. He poured himself a drink and sat in the chair, in the dark.

Jacinta was going to throw marriage prospects at him. The scandalous news stories had distracted her, but eventually she would return to her quest of finding him a bride. But Grey couldn't imagine finding a woman he wanted to spend his life with. No gently bred lady would willingly enjoy his carnal games, like Miss Winsome did.

He didn't want to marry a woman and live in a house filled with unhappiness. He didn't want a hellish marriage like his parents.

He wanted a woman he could talk to. A woman he desired. A woman like Helena Winsome.

Greybrooke lifted the brandy, intending to throw the entire contents down his throat at once. He paused.

He didn't want to try to blot out his thoughts with alcohol. Why not? He was alone. He was a duke. His life was a damned mess. Wasn't he entitled to get drunk? The brandy touched his lips, but he set the glass down, having barely taken a swallow.

Miss Winsome would expect more from him than to get drunk. He leaned back on the chair and closed his eyes.

That's when he heard it.

A whisper of sound. A furtive footfall. It had to be Miss Winsome, creeping downstairs. Because she wanted to make love with him again? Or for a more insidious reason?

Damn, he couldn't blindly trust her—

A soft creak came from the floor behind the chair, from near the terrace doors that gave out onto the small back garden.

Thought came quickly, honed by years of waiting for abuse. Miss Winsome would have entered the room from the doorway, from the other direction. It wasn't Miss Winsome, and it couldn't be a servant.

The only reason for anyone to sneak up on him was to hurt him.

"Ye sure the toff's out cold?" said a soft, coarse voice.

There had to be two of them, since there was no reason to ask a question unless there was someone to answer it. Grey remained motionless on the chair.

"Keep your voice down," answered another man in a whisper.

"Why? If the duke drank that brandy, he's asleep now, isn't he?"

"He should be," answered the second man. "There's enough laudanum in it to knock out a horse."

Grey had to remember to thank Miss Winsome. If it hadn't been for her, he would have tossed back his drink so fast, he would now be unconscious.

Miss Winsome—Hades, had these men done anything to her?

No, impossible. He'd left her bedroom only moments ago. These two must have broken into the drawing room and hidden in it, behind the curtains.

But why not attack him in the bedroom? Most nights, he came into this room after sex and drank. These fiends had to know that. Who had told them? Who knew?

Acrid anger blazed through him. Miss Winsome knew—

Damn it. So did most of the servants. Any one of them could have been paid to spy.

"I could slit his throat," whispered the first man gleefully.

"The plan is to make it look like he took his own life. Very few men cut their own throats. A pistol is a much more preferred instrument for a suicide."

To make it look as if he'd killed himself, no doubt this assassin intended to put the pistol to his head and pull the trigger, tearing out his brain with a pistol ball, while he was drugged.

Grey kept his eyes closed, but he made a sighing sound, as if asleep. He was naked under his robe, which meant an annoying lack of weapons. All he had in his favor was surprise.

His heart thudded. But he'd learned how to outwit people who wanted to hurt him. He'd learned to fight fear. Though he let his hands fall limply from the chair's arms as if he were unconscious, he tensed, ready to attack.

He kept his breathing slow and rhythmic. For fun, he let his head fall to the side and snored.

Smell guided him. One man stank of sweat, lack of washing, unkempt clothes. The other gave off a perfumed scent, a slightly flowery scent an Englishman would never wear.

"He's dead to the world," breathed the first man.

"Shut your mouth," hissed the second. "Let's be done with this."

"What of the tart?" The first man made a disgusting moist sound, as if licking his lips.

"We're not to touch her. She's to discover the duke in the morning, with a pistol in his lap and half his head blown away."

Having two assailants was going to make this more difficult. Grey assumed only one had a pistol, since they expected to walk up to him and shoot him in the head. But a knife could still be thrown at him. He would have to move like lightning—

Grey smelled a light whiff of powder, felt the disturbance in the back of the chair as a hand settled on the upholstery. He couldn't wait for the touch of the pistol to his head. Likely the assassin would have his finger on the trigger by then.

Taking a risk, he let his lids crack open a little. A floorboard creaked behind him.

At twelve, he'd begun to change the tables on his mother and her lackeys. Instead of being easily beaten, he'd been able to fight back. His mother had been forced to hire more brutal men to keep him in line, to be able to capture him to beat him. He'd fought to learn to outwit them.

The light in front of him changed as a shadow fell across the moonlight.

Grey surged up, slamming his arm to the side of his head with a quick, sharp blow. His forearm hit the pistol's muzzle and sent it flying. The gun hit the ground and the shot exploded.

Damn, it was of no use now. The thought came as his arm already arced in a punch. His fist slammed into the assailant's jaw, snapping the man's head back. Grey whirled, turning toward the first man as the second reeled backward.

Moonlight flashed on a knife blade as Grey used the chair to propel himself up. The man slashed, but Grey threw his body to the side, so the sweep felt short of his body. Then he kicked, driving his foot into the man's gut.

In a split second, he assessed the second man. Built like a giant: a head taller than him, bald as a billiard ball, thick with muscle. His kick had barely winded Baldy. And the first man was up. Out of the corner of his eye, Grey saw black hair in a ponytail, a small beard, sharp cheekbones. Blood dribbled from a snarling mouth, though the assassin wore a cocky grin.

Grey expected him to draw out a blade, but he didn't. Baldy struck again and Grey feinted, avoiding the thrust. He managed to get in two blows to Baldy's jaw. The man jerked his head. Grey's knuckles hurt and became wet with blood. He'd split the skin on them. His punches had done more damage to him than Baldy.

"Not going to be able to pretend he killed himself." Blackbeard sighed. "Though a robbery will be just as convincing and will end up with the desired result. A duke's death."

Blackbeard's hand moved like lightning behind his back, returned with a second pistol.

"Greybrooke?"

Miss Winsome. Damn, she stood in the doorway. Black-beard swung the weapon toward her. Fear exploded in Grey. He surged forward, slamming his elbow into Blackbeard's throat as he grasped the pistol's muzzle with both hands. A cold sensation ripped down his side. He jerked away from it, aware of a stinging rushing along it, like a flame along a fuse.

Out of the corner of his eye, he saw Miss Winsome run into the room. "Stay back," he commanded her.

Baldy thrust again with his blade. Distracted, Grey felt it hit him but glance along his rib cage. He leveled the pistol at the man. Miss Winsome, refusing to listen to him, ran to the fireplace and snatched up the poker.

A knife hurtled through the air toward Grey. If he ducked, it might hit Miss Winsome. He lifted the pistol, slamming the metal barrel into the flying knife, sending the black clattering to the floor. When he jerked his gaze back to the two assassins, they were racing out the terrace doors.

He took a running step to chase them—

"Greybrooke, you're bleeding," Miss Winsome cried. "You've been cut!"

His entire body seemed to sag and crumple. Next thing he knew, he'd fallen to his knees. He put his hand to his side. Felt the pain, felt the wetness. Miss Winsome rushed to him and dropped to her knees beside him.

"Help me up," he growled. "I have to go after them."

"No, you do not," she declared. "You need to be tended. At once!"

Pain shot through Grey. "Gah. Do you have to prod the wound like that?"

Miss Winsome amazed him. He'd been faced with two as-sassins and she had raced for the fireplace poker to help defend him. She had slung his arm over her shoulders and had tried to lift him. He'd staggered to his feet, using a chair to pull himself up. Leaning on her would have hurt her—and soiled her with his blood—but she had put her arm around his waist, led him to the settee, and insisted he lie on it.

Now he was sprawled on the white-and-blue sofa while she worked on his wounds with sewing needles and tweezers.

At his protest, she did not look up. She focused diligently on her work. "I want to make certain it is clean. I don't want it to become infected. An infection of that sort could kill you. Now please hold still."

Ignoring his groans, she cleaned his wound, her hands moving with efficient grace.

She was determined infection wasn't going to take him. He appreciated that. But it was more—she was trying to help him, heal him with her touch. He'd never experienced this before. It was new. Stunning. Confusion made him growl, "You should not have come into the room."

"They would have *killed* you. They were both armed, and they were vicious brutes."

"I'm accustomed to dealing with vicious brutes."

"You launched at the one holding the pistol," she gasped. "I know you did it to protect me, but he could have shot you. The other one stabbed you because you let your defenses down. You shouldn't have risked your life for me."

"Of course I should have," Grey muttered, irritated. "And angel, half the time I don't care if I live or die. I'm accustomed to violence and abuse. As you know, I lived with it during my younger years. If I died then, what in hell difference would it have made? But it was my duty to protect you."

Miss Winsome gazed at him, stricken. "You cannot truly mean you didn't care if you lived or died."

"Yes, love. It's exactly what I mean. Dying would mean an escape from the memories."

She bit her lower lip, pain in her eyes.

"Do not pity me," he said sharply. "Eventually I learned to fight back. They are dead now."

"But they still haunt you. You have to escape the past. I believe the only way to escape your past is to embrace your future."

Her words pricked him as sharply as her needle had done. "Angel, you have no idea. I told you before—a black past means a bleak future. I can't escape the memories."

Her lips parted, and he held up his hand with a groan. "Enough, Miss Winsome."

"All right. But I can help to heal this." Tenderly, she dabbed at the wound with the moistened cloth. "It's very shallow in some places, thank heavens. But it is quite deep in others. It should be stitched."

There was no stopping her. She summoned a physician, and after the doctor sewed up his wound, Miss Winsome put him in her bed. She gently helped him lie back. She drew up the sheets, then the counterpane. Hell, she was tucking him in. He should protest against the sweetness of the gesture.

But, hell, he liked it. Grey drifted off to sleep, realizing he'd never been tended like this.

Grey woke, cracking open his lids. Faint light bloomed at the edges of the curtains. It was morning, but early. He was aware of two intense sensations. His side ached like the blazes, and his cock was as hard as the iron poker Miss Winsome had swung around last night.

Where was she?

He jerked up in the bed, despite the agony of moving. And relaxed.

She was curled up like a sleeping kitten in a chair she'd pulled to the bed. She'd fished a blanket out, but she must have tossed around during the night and now her bare toes peeped out beneath.

How adorable she was. How tender and caring.

He wanted to wake her, and he knew a mischievous way of doing it. First he got a French letter from the bedside table, then he limped to her. Gently Grey drew the blanket up to her hips. Getting on one knee gave him a jolt of pain, enough that he almost passed out. But the throbbing of his rock-hard cock proved stronger.

He pushed up her muslin nightdress, parted her shapely legs, and put his mouth against her warm cunny. He tasted the earthy tang of her juices. Slicking his tongue over her, he felt her body move beneath him. A soft sigh escaped her. She was still asleep, but her hips moved under him, undulating. He was provoking her into an erotic dream.

Feeling devilish, he licked her clit with lavish strokes. Her hands gripped the chair. Her toes curled. She sighed and moaned. Her lashes began to flicker.

He sucked on her clit.

Her eyes opened wide. But she didn't try to pull away. She moaned. "Oh, I can't stop. Oh! Oh!" She ground her hips to his mouth, then she arched under him. A keening cry of pleasure filled the room.

His cock was ready to burst.

Standing hurt, and the movement tugged ominously at the stitches. He didn't want to tear them; Miss Winsome might send for the doctor again. She was still squirming on the chair and moaning. Coming, but not entirely satisfied yet.

Despite pain, he slid his knee beside her on the chair. Grey pulled on the French letter. He had to push his straining cock down with the flat of his hand. Braced on one hand and one outstretched leg, he got his prick to make contact with her sweet, wet quim. Bending forward despite pain, he captured her mouth in a long, slow kiss. And slid his cock deep inside her.

22

Kissing her deeply, Grey savored the tight embrace of Miss Winsome's scalding hot quim around his shaft. Slowly, he moved with her, letting his groin bump her clit. He loved the way she gasped in delight, the way his thrusts made her eyes glow like blue sapphires.

Then she raised her arms so her hands were behind her head and put her wrists together.

He'd made her into the perfect submissive for him. She did exactly what he wanted. Why did he not want it now?

Last night, he had let her touch him to clean his wound. Let her dig into his flesh with tweezers and a needle. He'd trusted her to do that.

The caring, efficient movement of her fingers on his skin had soothed him. When he'd shut his eyes because it damn well hurt to have his wounds probed, her touch had been like a light in darkness. He'd known she wanted only to heal him.

Maybe he wanted to experience more of her touch. Maybe he wanted to know what it was like to have her caress him when she wanted to give him pleasure.

"Don't keep your hands away from me." The thrusts of his hips slowed. "Touch me."

"Are you sure?" she whispered.

"God, yes."

Her hands settled on his shoulders. She slid her palms along the muscle there. "I've wanted so much to do this. To . . . um . . . explore all of you."

"You have?"

"You are so strong and beautiful. My hands have literally itched to stroke your chest and your back. Even . . . I'm embarrassed, but I really wanted to touch your bottom."

He was surprised. He hadn't thought of her getting pleasure from touching him. Yet he loved caressing her body. He did it to delight her, but he loved the plump weight of her breasts, the velvety beauty of her nipples, the slick silkiness of her cunny.

"You have my permission to fondle my arse as much as you like." Did she hear the catch in his voice?

Even though his cock was deep inside her and they were joined as intimately as possible, Miss Winsome blushed. At once her hands cupped her bottom. Grey sucked in a sharp breath as she caressed his taut ass. Her hands massaged, glided, then her fingers went between his cheeks. A bolt of pleasure hit him. . . .

Good Lord, she was trying to touch his asshole. It shocked him. "Miss Winsome—"

"It feels good when you touch me there. I thought—oh, I'm sorry. I should have asked before taking such a liberty. But I didn't quite know how to put it into words."

Sweet. Adorable. Lovely. Once, if he'd thought about the word "sweet" in regard to sex, he would have wanted to run. Now he wanted more of it. It was like ices at Gunter's, or a delectable pie—a treat that he wanted to enjoy again and again.

He thrust in her, trying to keep his strokes controlled. Bury deep, brush his groin against her to tease her clit, gaze into her eyes. Then draw back, brace his weight against the back of the chair on his arms.

Her hands draped weakly around his neck. Her blue eyes gazed at him as if he were a god. She was giggling. Then moaning. This was obviously what she liked. It was special to her.

After rushing in to save his life, risking her own, didn't she deserve something special?

Grey shifted his hips, and sped up, using the strokes of his shaft to tease her hard clit, then he moved again, seeking, until he was certain by her fierce moan and stunned look that his cock was kissing the secret place inside her pussy. He found the rhythm that made her fingernails gouge into his shoulders.

This felt so intimate. He didn't care that there were no ropes, no games, no exotic situations. He cared for her and he liked being joined with her, and he wanted nothing more than to slickly take her to ecstasy.

He had to go faster, his cock demanded it. His balls sucked up tight, ready to explode.

"Oh, oh, oh!" Miss Winsome squealed. She arched up in ecstasy, and her nails dragged down his back.

The sudden shock of erotic pain hit his trigger. A brilliant light burst in his brain. He came apart, shattering into a thousand pieces. All he could feel was his semen rushing through him.

His hips bucked. His wits melted into come and shot out of him. He was falling—

Grey caught his weight on his hands, gripping the arms of the chair.

Shining like an angel, her golden hair in a tangle of curls, Miss Winsome smiled up at him. Dazedly, with her hair in a tangle, her cheeks pink, her eyes glowing.

"Greybrooke, oh! I—"

"Grey. Call me that. My name is Damian, but I hate the sound of it." Hated it intensely because his mother had used it. "Grey is for friends, Miss Winsome."

"Would you call me Helena? I can't be Miss Winsome anymore. It seems wrong. It makes me feel like a governess, and I'm not one anymore. I want—I want to think we are friends."

"We are more than that." He caught his breath as tears glittered in her eyes. "That, angel, was sex your way. I have to admit—you might be right. This was just as good as my erotic games."

She giggled, which he'd hoped she would. The sound of it touched him even more than tears. He had everything here he believed he could never have. Intimacy. Caring. Laughter.

What in hell should he do?

"I like your erotic games," she whispered. "But now you must go to Bow Street and tell the magistrate about the men who attacked you. They would know you are not to blame for the blackmailer's death."

"Helena, love, that doesn't prove anything. Certainly not my innocence. Someone wants me dead, and for me, that is personal. I will try to find the assassins, but tonight I'm going to the theater. To find Morse."

"Tonight?" Her eyes were wide with horror. "I mean, you are wounded."

"I need to finish this business. They will try again, and I'm putting your life in danger too, Helena."

"Then I—I am going with you."

"Of course you are. I am not leaving you here alone, in case the men attack again."

But Grey knew he was taking her because he wanted to be with her. A mad thought hit him: Could he keep her as his mistress forever? Look at Prinny—the prince had carried out an unlawful marriage with his mistress to show he loved her. Grey had no intention of marrying, nor of falling in love. Why not keep Helena forever and be happy?

He had to smile, imagining a seventy-year-old Duke of Greybrooke, shuffling into the theater with his cane, with Helena, his gray-haired and scandalous mistress on his arm.

Thinking of spending his life with Helena was thinking of

something very much like marriage. Why now? Why did Helena make him want to change?

Two rows of plush velvet seats filled the theater box, and crimson curtains framed their view of the stage. Elegant members of the *ton* filled other boxes, and a mass of people milled in the pit below. Burning footlights cast light on the closed drapes of the stage.

Grey led her to a seat. Helena had never been to the theater. She wished this were just a night where he was taking her to see a play, where they were simply lovers and didn't have to worry about assassins and plots. She wished she did not have to worry about losing Grey tonight, when he discovered the truth.

She wished she would not have to see the pain in his eyes when he learned she lied to him still. It made her heart ache with pain.

She felt beautiful, wearing gold silk. The solitary ruby necklace looked lovely with the gold, and made her skin gleam like ivory.

But all of this was to come to an end. Tonight.

It wasn't her life as mistress she was going to mourn. It was the wonderful intimacy with Grey. She'd never felt so close to anyone—she felt as close to him as she did with her family.

She'd discovered what it was to be in love. She was going to have her heart broken, and it was her fault. Perhaps she should have told the truth before. Once Grey learned she had continued to lie, how could he forgive her, trust her, want her?

He casually rested his arm behind her. His fingers lazily grazed her shoulder. He touched her with ease and familiarity, which made her feel terrible. "You are beyond lovely," he said. "Everyone is looking at you."

Opera glasses were trained on their box. Helena saw male faces tip back, the gentlemen nudging each other. It was true—all of the theater people stared at her. Women whispered to each other behind fans. "They are all looking at me because they want to know who your mistress is. They love scandal . . . and I am one now."

She wore her mask, which hid her identity. But it would never obscure the truth—she had changed. She could not go back to her old life of being a governess, and not just because Society would never allow it. She couldn't go back to a life without love or passion.

When Grey found out the truth tonight and threw her out, any other mistress would simply find another protector. She *couldn't.*

She didn't want to go to another man. She wanted Grey.

"You look worried," he said, looking concerned himself. "Do you have regrets?"

"No—no, I don't have any regrets." It was the truth. But there was one thing she did miss. . . . "I still miss being around children. I don't think that will ever change."

He bent and kissed her naked shoulder—her neckline was scooped so low, her shoulders and upper back were bare. "If you want children, I'm willing to give you them."

She jolted away from his teasing mouth. "You *want* children?"

"They wouldn't be legitimate, but I would care for them. I would support them—they would want for nothing, I promise you." Though he spoke soft and low, she heard every word. It was as if the crowd had vanished.

He bent to her neck, raining kisses from her shoulder to her earlobe. Making her dizzy with yearning. She could have children. But they wouldn't be legitimate.

That would be a stain, one that would judge and hurt them, and wouldn't be their fault. She couldn't do that.

The thought of children with Grey was such a wonderful dream, it hurt so much to give it up.

Grey lifted her hand, and she knew he would brush a kiss to

her fingers. She couldn't bear it—him touching her, spinning a future together that she could not have. "I must be practical, Grey. I couldn't raise children who would face a lifetime of shame for *my* choices."

"What do you want more, angel? Marriage or me?"

"I—I don't know." She wanted both, but she couldn't have both.

The truth was she couldn't have either. She probably had this one last night with Grey.

"Why are there curtains on theater booths?" she asked, to change the subject. "Isn't the idea to watch the stage?"

"Let me show you." Grey moved to the curtains, giving her a glorious display of his strong back, wide shoulders, long legs. He drew the drapes closed. Then he undid the falls of his trousers and shoved them down. They shot to his knees and his cock bounced upward, gloriously stiff.

"We can't do this in the theater!" she gasped in a quiet exclamation.

He turned, eyes twinkling. "With the curtains closed, we can do anything we want."

"But people will hear me moan."

"Thought of that." With a quick flick of his hand, he pulled something black from an inside pocket. It was a strip of black leather with a leather ball in the middle.

"What is it?"

"Trust me and open your mouth."

Helena let her lips part. He put the ball against her lips, holding each end of the strap. He drew it into her mouth. Her teeth sank into it, and it filled her mouth. She couldn't speak around it.

But she was doing this with Grey, which made it erotic.

He adjusted the strap behind her head, until the ball sat comfortably between her lips. She felt creamy between her legs already, just from the gag.

Grey gently bound her hands in front of her—just before he eased down her low bodice and her shift and corset until her breasts popped out.

This was his game, but Helena didn't think of it that way anymore. She wanted it too. She liked both—she liked ordinary sex where she could hold and caress him, and she liked these marvelous games where he surprised her with erotic delights and she was the focus of all his attention. These were now *their* games.

She glanced toward the curtain. Just two strips of velvet kept the gentlemen of the *ton* and their mistresses or wives from seeing the scandalous things she was going to do with Grey.

His fingers slid lightly along the side of her face. "I would love to have children with you. It would be like a family."

Like a family—but he refused to have one for real. She could see raw longing in his eyes, a flash of it before it was gone, swallowed up by the look she knew—the one that looked hot and penetrating and meant he was thinking up erotic games.

He helped her slide off the seat, holding her bound hands. She let him turn her so her bottom faced the curtain and the balcony wall of their box, and her bound hands were placed on the back of the seat.

He pushed her skirts up to her waist, baring her legs, her rump, her cunny. She prayed those curtains really did hide everything as his strong hand slid between her legs, and his fingers stroked her clit.

She moaned, but the ball drank up the sound.

Her cunny was soaked, literally dripping with juices. She knew he would go inside her from behind, his groin would collide with her bottom, his erection going so deep he would touch her womb.

Something rough brushed her bottom. He parted her cheeks and slid two lengths of coarse rope between them. His breathing was fast, but his hands moved steadily. He twined the rope around the tops of her thighs and crossed them over her clit—which was aching, swollen. It felt as if one brush would make her explode like a firing pistol.

He crossed it again, artistically, then drew the ropes around her waist. The tug of his hands on the ropes tightened them, made them scrape along her clit.

Her legs almost buckled. She whimpered with pleasure around the ball, rocking her hips.

He brought the ropes up, then tied them with fancy bows to iron rings attached to her gag. She lifted her head tentatively. That tightened the ropes, sawing her nub with them.

Goodness, she could make herself come just by moving her head. It was a struggle to *not* make herself climax. But she wanted to make this anticipation last.

That was what Grey did. He seduced her with anticipation. He made her yearn for the future—even just for a few minutes of future when he would do naughty, impossible things and gave her blinding pleasure.

Helena moved, the rope slid, and she sagged onto her arms as a jolt of pleasure shot through her. Her quim began to pulse, and she feared she was going to climax before she wanted. She made desperate noises around the ball—

Grey came to her from behind again. His cock nosed between her nether lips and sank inside her bubbling passage in one swift stroke. She felt his legs rock as he drove deep, as if the sudden engulfing in wet heat had shocked him completely.

His hands rested on her hips, holding her steady. He drew back, bracing her, then thrust deep again. He was holding her up more than he was holding her steady.

She pumped back against him, urging him to please her.

Oh, he did. With thrusts that lifted her off the ground and made her feel the deep penetration of his huge member. With tweaks of her stiff nipples, kisses and bites on her bare shoulder. Steam poured out of her dress. She rocked against him, so close to coming—

She needed this orgasm like she needed air.

Wait. He had not paused to put on a French letter.

Panic came too late. Pleasure burst inside her, taking her on a whirling, wonderful dance. God, it was so good. She wanted to squeal and shriek, but the ball kept her from hollering at the top of her lungs and letting the entire theater know she was coming.

Grey withdrew, and she felt his staff bounce up as it came out. He hadn't climaxed. "I want to wait," he said. "I want to balance on a knife's edge of orgasm all night, while I pleasure you. Until we have the chance to track down our quarry."

First he undid the ropes and removed the gag. Then he patted her chest with his handkerchief, drying her dewy perspiration, before cleaning her between her thighs.

She wanted to say something about the French letter, but what could she say? He had promised to look after any children. But he'd said it before finding out the truth.

Still a bit in shock, Helena sank down on a seat. Grey opened the curtains, then sat at her side. He leaned to her, his breath tickling her ear. "I want to keep you as mistress for a lifetime."

The man who never kept a mistress for more than a month was offering *her* a lifetime.

But she would not have it.

The lights of the house had been turned down, leaving only the burning stage lights to illuminate the actors, and they were in the middle of the play.

After a few moments, she gasped, "It's a shocking play."

At her side, Grey laughed gently.

"Well, it is," she said defensively.

A man dressed as a woman with enormous breasts was cavorting on the stage with a man, fooling the "young buck" into believing he was a wanton lady. He was singing a ribald song about having decided it was time to pluck his "flower." The young "man" was a girl dressed up, with a codpiece between her thighs that stuck out at least twelve inches.

"It's meant to be titillating, Helena."

The young "buck" wore skin-tight breeches that revealed every curve of the actress's shapely legs. The men in the audience hooted as she approached the edge of the stage. The actress cupped her mouth, as if about to whisper a secret.

"I am Rosalind," she declared. "It is my intent that the lovely 'Desiree' will actually become the bride of the evil guardian who wants to marry me." Desiree was the man in the woman's clothing. The evil guardian? Had one come on in the first scene, while Grey had made love to her in that scandalously delicious way?

A chubby servant ran onto the stage from the left, bedraggled clothes wafting around him. He looked to the audience. "Me master's angry because he broke his favorite whip on me arse. Where should I hide?"

The servant jumped in the air as if he saw a monster chasing him. When he landed, his trousers fell down. Women in the audience screamed, and men roared with mirth.

A tall, cadaverous man stepped out of the shadows on to the stage. The small orchestra played a piece of music that made Helena shiver with apprehension.

The man wore a tall, black hat pulled low over his face and a gentlemen's clothing. He carried a whip with half the lash broken off.

The servant hauled up his trousers and scuttled off stage, holding them with both hands. The ominous villain strode out to the center. He demanded to know where Rosalind was. The audience booed him.

The villain barked at them all in false rage. He pulled off his hat, but Helena already knew who it would be even before she saw the skull-like face with its jutting cheekbones.

It was the man who had pretended to be Whitehall. She turned to Grey, but she didn't need to tell him. He was already on his feet and heading for the entry curtain to their both. From Flossie's description, he had recognized the fiend at once.

"Stay here," he growled. Then he was gone, the curtain at the back of the box flapping in his wake.

But she couldn't stay there. Grey was racing in pursuit of a man who might be a murderer. Helena ran after him as wildly as she had pursued Michael in Berkeley Square. Equally as terrified of disaster.

With his long legs, Grey was already nearing the stairs that led from the upper tiers of boxes down to the stage level. Helena sucked in desperate breaths. She couldn't give up.

The ruby necklace bounced on her chest and hit her chin as she ran. She passed startled footmen who waited by the curtained entrances to the boxes.

She prayed Grey did not do something daring—and crazy— out of anger.

Holding up her skirts, she grasped the banister and rushed down the stairs. As she reached the bottom, she blinked. One brilliant lamp lit the space, and it briefly dazzled her.

There were two corridors. One led to the main entrance of the theater. Down the other, she heard pounding footsteps, and she followed them. They grew fainter—the distance between her and Grey increasing. Curtains stood ahead of her at the end of the corridor. She plunged through into a dark, quiet space. Brightly painted scenery lurked along the wall. She was backstage, in a room used to keep equipment. Ropes lay everywhere, and she looked around wildly for a weapon. Something she could use to protect Grey.

A fake executioner's axe had been propped against a papier-mâché castle front. It was made of wood, but it weighed a ton. Struggling, she lifted it to her shoulder. Then, wavering with the weight of the wretched axe, she crept through the curtain at the other end.

She stood in another small room filled with scenery, and at that moment the weight of the axe overtaxed her arms. It thudded to the floor in front of her.

While she had no weapon, she certainly had the attention of Whitehall and Grey. They stood near the stack of painted scenes. Grey wore the ruthless expression she had seen on his face when he'd thrown himself at his two armed attackers. His eyes were cold like brittle glass, his mouth distorted in a harsh snarl.

With Grey's height, broad shoulders, and muscular frame, he would overpower Whitehall easily. But as the men paced around in a circle, she saw why Grey didn't attack. Whitehall had a pistol.

"The Duke of Greybrooke. What a delight to finally make your acquaintance." Whitehall's skull-like face turned to her. "And Miss Winsome. I doubt your improvised weapon would have served you. Stand still, you little tart, and don't move. So you did become his mistress. I knew such a beautiful and prim creature would turn out to be a whore at heart."

Helena flinched. She had to *stop* this. She didn't want Grey to find out who she was like this. "Put down your weapon. You will never get away, and if you take our lives, you will be hanged."

While Whitehall laughed, Grey swivelled to meet her gaze. "This man is the one who pretended to be an agent of the Crown?"

"Is that what she said? I sent her to spy on you, Your Grace. She went willingly to help me. Even seduced you to do it."

"You were working with this fiend and with Turner? You lied all along?" Pain glinted in Grey's eyes.

"No, it was not like that! He is lying. What I told you was the truth."

Whitehall laughed—a nasty laugh. "So she gave me up, did she?"

"You knew who he was when you heard Flossie's description," Grey said softly. "But you said nothing then."

And that was the truth that damned her.

"I wasn't sure," she said, "not until I saw him."

But she saw Grey flinch. He hadn't done so when faced with pistols. But he did in the face of her lie. Inside her chest, her heart trembled. She could not stand it any longer. "Grey, I am sorry. I couldn't tell you the truth. Not all of it. I couldn't let you find out about my brother—"

"Doesn't His Grace know that your brother is William Rains, that it was Rains's debts you've been rogering him to pay? He doesn't know you're the famous Lady X?" Whitehall asked mockingly.

This was her nightmare. But she knew what the fiend was doing. Distracting them. Getting them to fight together so he could escape. Did that mean he would not shoot Grey?

Grey stared at her, his face white. "Your brother is Rains? That is how he got those stories—from you."

"No," she began, but Whitehall laughed.

"Her brother assured me his sister was excellent at ferreting out gossip. And she was. She gave the stories to her brother, and he gave them to me. I gave him instruction to put them in the paper—"

"Shut up," Grey barked. He glared down his nose at Whitehall, as if he were the one holding the weapon. "I see now this was set up like a play, by you and Richard Turner," Grey said darkly. "But what was the purpose of this ridiculous farce to have me discredited as a traitor? Why in hell did you murder Lady Blackbriar? I swear I will rip you apart unless you give me the truth."

"I'm holding the pistol, Your Grace. Turner was a damned

fool. He handed over blackmail money to our employer. But I know I can get a fortune out of you, Greybrooke. Wouldn't you like to keep your little sister's sins a secret? You wouldn't want the sordid story of your murdering sister to come out—"

Grey lunged, and Helena screamed, "No, you mustn't. He'll shoot you!"

Grey stopped dead, as if frozen in time. Whitehall, shaking, trained the pistol on him. "I want twenty thousand pounds, Your Grace. Or I shoot you now."

Helena stared at Grey's back. There was a bulge under his neat-fitting blue coat, at the small of his back. He must have a pistol.

"You can't pay him, Grey. It will never stop. It would be better to publish the story about Maryanne." She prayed Grey understood what she was doing.

Whitehall jerked his attention to her. "Shut up, you stupid bitch." Then Grey's hand moved like lightning to the back of his coat. Whitehall swung back toward him and pulled the trigger.

A roar almost burst her eardrums. An explosion of smoke filled the small space. A second shot came. Through the billowing pistol smoke, Whitehall stumbled back. The pistol fell from his grasp as his back slammed into the scenery behind him.

Grey held the smooth mahogany handle of a dueling pistol, and black smoke still swirled from the muzzle. His eyes were like ice, his face cold. Whitehall had shot first, but because she had distracted him, his shot must have gone wide.

Grey's shot had caught Whitehall through the shoulder. The fiend slumped to the ground. "Not going to hang. They won't hang me. . . ."

Something glinted in Whitehall's gloved hand.

"Another pistol," she gasped.

But Whitehall slashed his hand across his own throat in a swift, vicious motion. At once, a dark stain covered his skin and his hand. Dark red blood poured over his arm, down his neck.

316 / *Sharon Page*

His body jerked, and he made a horrific gurgling sound, as if drowning.

Dear heaven, he'd slit his throat.

Helena stumbled toward him, her hands outstretched. Could she stop the bleeding?

Grey dragged her back. Not into his arms, but several clumsy feet backward, then he let her go. "He can't be saved now. It's too late."

She knew it. And they didn't know who had hired him to target Grey. They could guess it was Blackbriar, but they had no proof.

The icy cold in Grey's expression was gone, replaced by pain. "No wonder Rains knew how to harass Caroline. I let you find out about that damned blackmail, and you used it. You told your brother. No wonder you told me to spare that damned Rains and his newssheet."

"I did not reveal anything about Lady Blackbriar," she said softly. "The only thing I told him about was your father's death. That it was murder, not suicide. I made Will promise not to publish it, but Whitehall forced him to do it. Whitehall threatened to destroy our family. He forced me to keep spying on you or he would have my brother beaten to death by the ruffians who work for gaming hell owners. Both Will and I had to do what he asked to protect our younger sisters. You understand that—how important family is."

"You told him about Maryanne, about what happened to her."

"I didn't, Grey," she implored. "I swear I did not. I have never told a soul." That was the truth. She had not even told Will. "I don't understand how Whitehall, I mean Morse, could know."

Grey walked away from her. He flung open a black curtain, and she realized this space was separated from the backstage area. The pistol shots had stunned everyone. Actors, actresses, workers of the theater stood motionless, staring in open-mouthed horror. Now they were moving, hurrying toward them. People began to pour through the opening in the curtain. A potbellied man raced forward, pushing his way through. He saw Grey and gasped, "Your Grace!" Nonsensically, he bowed.

Greybrooke. The whisper rushed over the crowd, as people strained to see the now infamous duke.

"The duke did nothing," Helena cried. "This man was a villain. He threatened the duke with a pistol, and Greybrooke had to fire to protect himself. Then this man cut his own throat."

"We will summon the magistrate," Grey said, his tone cold and aristocratic. "Send someone to Bow Street and fetch some of the Runners. At once." He swiveled and glared at the tubby man, who wore a bottle-green waistcoat and blue tailcoat. "You are the manager here? This man is a murderer."

"Of course, Your Grace." Perspiration gleamed on the man's forehead.

Helena felt raw panic. Grey had shot the man. Would it be believed he did it in self-defense? "What if you are arrested?" she whispered. "People will think—"

"That the rumors and lies they read in newssheets are true?" Frost glittered in his eyes and coated every word.

"My brother would not have tried to ruin you unless he was forced to. He was not working with Turner and this man. I said nothing about your sister. Grey, you must believe me—"

"Why should I, Helena?" He crossed his arms over his chest. No one was moving toward him. Some people were hurrying from the theater—

"I know I did not tell you the absolute truth. But I did it only to protect my family. I did nothing to hurt you, I promise."

"You lied to me." His eyes narrowed, glittering and cold, like emeralds.

She should have recognized the danger in his glare. Suddenly he pushed her back until she was pressed against a panel of scenery. His arms bracketed her head. His chest brushed her bosom, his breathing harsh.

He'd moved her in a position to kiss her, but she knew, her heart plunging, he had no plan to do that. He turned to the actors. "Get out, all of you. Close the curtain behind you."

At the fury in his voice, they obeyed. Leaving her alone with Greybrooke.

"He knew about my sister." His tones were so low, no one else but she would hear. But that didn't make them any less lethal and threatening. "No one knew about that, Helena. How in hell did he find out?"

"I—I don't know."

"How did you find out? Miss Renshaw would not have told you, I know that."

She didn't want to tell him what she had done. "Truly, I never told another soul—"

Slam! His hand smacked the scenery beside her head. "How did you find out? Answer me!"

"I asked Maryanne." Her voice was a croak.

"What?" He leaned closer to her, and she twisted her head away, shaking. She clamped her eyes shut.

"What did you say, Helena?" he growled.

"I asked Maryanne." She opened her eyes, looked in Grey's hard, hate-filled ones. "I thought you had killed your father, but she told me the truth."

"She confided in *you*." He spat the word.

"Of course she did," she muttered miserably. "I was her governess before, and she trusted me."

"You used that against her. You played on the vulnerability of a blind, defenseless girl who has been tormented by vicious memories. God, I despise you. You are not to go near the children or Maryanne—or any member of my family—again."

His words burned through her. "Of course." What else could she say? "I will leave the house. I won't take anything."

"The house is yours to use for a year. I won't throw you out on the street. After the magistrate comes, you are to go to the carriage. Have them take you home."

"What—what about my brother? Don't hurt him because you are angry with me. Please."

Grey said nothing. He walked away, throwing open the curtain. And because he was a duke, the remaining people stepped aside, parted like the sea, and let him through.

She'd betrayed Grey, and that he could never forgive. She'd lost him forever.

23

"Obviously he didn't throw me out on the street. I can't imagine why not." Helena poured tea for Will. She was trying to appear under control, but her throat ached and her eyes felt sore. She had cried all the rest of the night. "I did betray him, and I've done nothing but lie to him. But you must tell me the truth. Did Whitehall ever tell you a scandalous story about the duke's sister, Lady Maryanne?"

Will shook his head. "He said nothing to me. But then he wouldn't, if he was using it for blackmail."

Helena picked up her cup. She had expected as much. But how had Whitehall—or rather, Morse—found out the truth? That was what made no sense to her. She hadn't told him. Certainly Maryanne would not have told him.

"Would you tell me what the story is?" Will looked hopeful.

She almost dropped her cup. "No. You will never print another word about the Duke of Greybrooke or his family. Promise me that, Will."

"But Helena—"

"No! He and his family have been hurt enough by those stories."

"All right, I promise. But what will we do now, Helena? Since Whitehall was a fraud and was actually this actor Morse, there is no way I can pay my debts."

She knew Will was afraid. "There is a way. The duke gave me a spectacular necklace. The ruby is as big as a robin's egg. It must be worth thousands." She would have to sell off everything Grey had given her. Carriages. Furnishings. Anything that she could have kept to remind herself of him.

That was for the best, wasn't it?

She was not homeless. She could stay in this house for a year. But it felt wrong to do so.

But was there any point in standing on pride and leaving, putting herself on the street, just because staying was not the right and moral thing to do?

"What are you going to do? Go back to being a governess?"

She gaped at her brother. Could he really be so dense? It was all she could do not to dump tea on him.

"Do you think the duke will still try to destroy the newspaper?" he asked. "You explained to him that I was forced to print those stories."

"I did, but he was furious. I don't know what he will do." She didn't know what *she* would do. What if he did ruin them in rage? It would be horrible to spend the rest of her life hating him for hurting her family but still loving him for the man he was.

"I cannot just walk away," she said. "A murderer is out there. A person who wants to destroy Greybrooke. I don't think that person will stop, even now."

Was it Lord Blackbriar? Morse had not told them. Blackbriar had paid the man, then if Morse had known about Maryanne's secret, so must Blackbriar.

Her teacup slipped from her fingers, fell to the table. Broke.

Dimly she heard Will cry, "Helena!"

If Blackbriar wanted to destroy Greybrooke for some mad reason—jealously, perhaps—what better way than to use Lady

Maryanne? She had to go to Grey or to Lady Winterhaven and ensure they protected Maryanne.

They probably would not even let her in the door now. But it didn't matter. When she'd been a governess, what did she tell her charges to do? To take action and show courage.

She stood, suddenly aware that Will was sweeping up her broken cup, staring at her strangely.

"I have to go," she said, and hurried to her front hall. She threw on her cloak, snatched up a bonnet, and summoned her carriage, aware that Will was still gaping at her as if she'd gone mad.

If she did nothing and Maryanne was hurt, she *would* go mad. She had not been able to save Margaret when her sister was abandoned by her lover, Knightly. She would not fail in this.

On the way to Greybrooke's home, she bit her lip. How could a man like Morse have found out about Maryanne's secret? No one could have overheard her in Berkeley Square, she was sure of that.

Tackle it logically, she would say to children. Who knew about the secret?

Grey. Jacinta, she believed. And Maryanne.

One of those three had told someone. Could it have been Maryanne? Could Maryanne have confided in someone else innocently, and that person was working with Morse and Blackbriar?

Her carriage turned in at the massive gates. Greybrooke's house loomed in front of her.

Helena jumped down and ran to his door, pounding like a madwoman on the thick oak. Grey's butler opened the door.

"I must speak to the duke. At once!"

The butler—a tall, portly, balding man—lifted his brow. "I am sorry, madam, but His Grace is not at home."

"I know he has said he is not at home to me, but—"

"I beg your pardon, madam. But it is not 'to you.' His Grace has gone to the country."

"The country. You mean one of his estates?" Where did Grey have a house in the country? A duke would have *several*.

"He is the guest of the Earl and Countess Winterhaven." The butler firmly shut the door.

Grey held the bridle of Maryanne's mare, Daisy, and led her around the paddock outside the stables at Winterleigh, his brother-in-law's estate. Dressed in a blue velvet riding habit, Maryanne held the reins in one hand and rested her other hand on Daisy's neck. In the country, spring was blossoming into summer. Flowers bloomed in meadows, and the trees were covered in green leaves. For Grey, it hurt to think that Maryanne would never see that beauty again.

He would never voice that pain. He was always careful what he said around her. She had been much happier after Miss Winsome had come as her governess. Today, she looked unhappy. Not angry, bitter, and hurt, as she had done before. She looked troubled and afraid. Even though riding, with assistance, was something she loved to do.

But when he'd asked her what was wrong, she'd shaken her head. "Nothing."

He knew he had to broach it. "Maryanne, I know you told Miss Winsome about what happened with our father."

Maryanne took a sharp breath. "No—"

"I know you did. I'm not angry. Did you tell anyone else?"

"No," she whispered. "No, I would never do that. I promised you I wouldn't, Grey. I would never break a promise to you. I didn't tell anyone."

"I should have realized you would want to confide this secret. I know it has been hard for you to bear. I want you to talk to me when you are troubled. Don't do something foolish, like trying to run away."

It was one of the reasons they had left London. Jacinta had caught Maryanne putting dresses and her underclothes in a bag. Maryanne would not reveal where she intended to go.

The other reason was the attack on him and his wounds. He'd tried to keep it a secret, but Jacinta had learned of it from his servants.

Grey stopped Daisy. He touched Maryanne's hand. The girl bit her lip, tensing. In some ways she was like a skittish horse. "You're safe with me, Maryanne," he promised. "You always will be."

She burst into tears.

He pulled her off Daisy into his arms and hugged her to him. But he couldn't console her. She was saying something over and over. He couldn't tell what it was for her hiccupping sobs. He held her tighter, put his lips to the top of her head.

Then he heard her words. "I shouldn't be safe. I shouldn't be."

He stroked her back, kissed the top of her head. "Of course, you should be."

"I did something terrible. I can't change that, Grey. I killed our father. I should have hanged for it—"

"Did Miss Winsome tell you that rubbish?" Rage boiled in him.

She shook her head. "Miss Winsome said it wasn't my fault. But even if that's true, you're still supposed to hang for murder. If I stay in England, I'll die, won't I? I'll be hanged."

His anger at Helena dissolved. Helena had tried to soothe Maryanne. "No. Dear God, Maryanne, that will never happen to you. It was an accident. One he brought on himself by threatening you, then attacking you. You didn't know what you were doing."

But she struggled in his arms. Her fists struck his shoulders, her body wracked with sobs.

He had no idea how to calm her. Even Jacinta had no idea. The only one who had ever been able to get through to Maryanne had been Helena.

He should despise Helena Winsome for lying to him. But what he felt was not anger. Just pain and gut-wrenching, heart-breaking regret.

He took Maryanne up to her room. Then Grey took out his gelding, Brutus, and galloped down the drive from Winter-haven's house. Rounding a corner, he reined in hard. A carriage approached, one he recognized. Hell, he had purchased the thing.

Keeping Brutus across the drive, he forced the coachman to rein in. Then he walked his mount to the carriage window.

God, she was exquisitely beautiful. Seeing her was like being punched in the gut. The pain was physical. "What are you doing here, Helena?" he asked icily.

"I came about Maryanne. Grey, I must talk to you privately. Please—it is important."

He should send her away, but the look on her face stunned him. She looked as she had done when she had run after Michael into the street. He swung down off Brutus, handed her down from the carriage.

Do not think that she smells like lavender and roses, and if you were to make love to her she would smell sinfully sweet.

She gazed earnestly into his face. "I am worried about Maryanne. I realized that she might have told someone what happened. Is it possible she could have revealed the truth to Lord Blackbriar?"

"It occurred to me she could have told someone else," he said. "There's something else . . . she feels she should be punished for what she did. She tried to run away, because she thinks she should be hanged if she stays."

"You must convince her that is not true! The poor girl."

"I am going to try." He knew Maryanne would listen to Miss Winsome. But could he trust her?

He wanted to touch her, but he feared that if he did, he would weaken. He would end up kissing her, caressing her, making love to her. And letting her touch him. Damn, he couldn't do it. He couldn't be like he was as a boy, so desperate for someone's love that he left himself vulnerable.

"I still want you. That's the hell of this," he said. "I can understand that you lied to me to protect your family. I can forgive you. But I can never trust you now. That's something about myself that I can't change."

"I understand." She gazed at him with the serene, calm expression a governess would wear. He almost expected her to say, "Very good, Your Grace."

Hell, for one moment he wished she would shake him, spank him on his backside, tell him he was wrong. Why didn't she want to change him anymore?

Obviously, because she saw the truth—he couldn't change. It was too late.

"But—" He broke off. "I may want you to talk to Maryanne. She listens to you more than she listens to Jacinta or me. Will you stay here for a while? Stay in the village?"

Concern showed in her eyes, tugging at his heart. *Damn it, heart, stay out of this.*

"Of course I will," she said. "I will stay at the Swan and Stag in the village."

24

The door of the dining room of the Swan and Stag flew open. Lily, the inn's maidservant, ran in the room and curtsied. "It's His Grace, miss! His Grace has come to see you."

Something clattered. Her knife, Helena saw, for it had deposited a blob of butter on the table. "Greybrooke?" It must be something about Lady Maryanne—

Grey strode through the low door. Lily, clinging to the door handle, bobbed another curtsy.

Helena could see why the girl's mouth was gaping in an enormous "O" of awe.

Grey's towering beaver hat, sweeping coat, and broad shoulders made the inn dining room feel the size of a cupboard. Rain had turned his hair into inky black slashes across his forehead. Water streamed off his coat. Mud spattered his boots, his greatcoat, even his cheeks. He'd ridden to her in a downpour?

He whisked off his hat, revealing the raw, desperate hope in his green eyes. "Is she here?" His words came out terse and hard, a crack of a whip breaking shocked silence. He swung toward the maid. "You can go."

But the poor thing froze and Helena said gently, breaking the frightening spell of his sharp command, "That will be all, Lily. Thank you."

The girl slipped out and closed the door.

It was like a knife in Helena's heart to see him so upset. She took a step toward him, before remembering he would certainly reject his touch. "Who? What is it?"

"Maryanne." His eyes met hers, bleak and desperate. "Did she come here to you? We cannot find her anywhere on the estate. I assumed—I prayed—she'd come to you."

All those damned, desperate prayers—he'd said a hundred of them on his neck-or-nothing gallop to the inn—were for nothing. Grey saw shock and panic in Helena's eyes, and knew Maryanne hadn't come here.

Horror gripped him, weakened him.

Just like it had on that night he'd heard the gunshot in his father's study and he'd gone in and seen Maryanne picking herself shakily off the floor, her eyes wide with horror as she stared at the smoking pistol in her hand. . . .

Next thing he knew, Helena's graceful hands pushed down on his shoulders, as if forcing him into the worn wing chair behind him. "Lily," she called out briskly. "Lily, come at once."

Grey let his arse touch the chair for a moment, then he shot up. "I don't have time to sit."

Helena grasped his forearm. The young servant burst through the door, her eyes wide. Helena said crisply, "Please bring brandy for His Grace. There's been a shock and he needs a restorative at once."

The maid bobbed a useless curtsy and ran off.

"For once in my life, I don't need a drink." Grey crammed his hat back on his head. "I need to go in pursuit of Maryanne."

Helena placed herself between him and the door. Why in hell was she in his way?

"Grey, no, we must think. We'll accomplish nothing if we run about in a mad panic. You are telling me she's missing. We must take a moment to think logically of where she would go. And how she got there."

"She's blind!" He hadn't been able to save Maryanne from his sick and twisted father. He would save her now, goddamn it. "She could be wandering anywhere, damn it. The longer I stand here, the greater the chance she's—" God, he couldn't say it.

Why did Helena look so controlled? He'd always seen her like this with the children. She had been like this in the drawing room when he'd been attacked, and when she'd cleaned his wound. Now her unflappable calm only provoked his rage. "Get out of my way, Helena, or I will make you move."

She flinched, but instead of stepping aside she clasped his wrist. "Did she take anything with her? Clothes? Her hairbrush?"

She was so blasted stubborn. "Yes, she did," he snarled. "She took them in a large carpetbag. I was hoping she'd come to you before she did anything rash and foolish."

"Grey, I don't think she would take her clothing if she intended to . . . do something rash."

"You mean, kill herself." That's what he feared. That guilt had consumed Maryanne and she'd decided to escape it with death. He could barely breathe. It was his fault. He should have protected her.

"She would not have taken her things if she planned to take her life." Helena's hands settled on his upper arms.

Damn it, he wanted her to touch him—he wanted to no longer feel so alone. He was clinging to her words.

"If she's taken that case," Helena went on, "she mustn't be intending to walk far. She has somewhere she intends to go—that's why she's taken clothing."

"She tried it before," he said dully. "Jacinta caught her pack-

330 / *Sharon Page*

ing. But she wouldn't say a word to us about where she planned to go. She wouldn't confide in us."

He sank into a seat, his strength gone. Why had she not talked to him and Jacinta? "It's because I failed her then. She doesn't trust me to help her now."

"No," Helena said. "In many ways, Maryanne is still like a child, for all she is nineteen. It wouldn't be that. It—" She broke off, her forehead puckered as she thought.

"I know how dearly she loved you, Helena, and I thought she would come for help." He met her blue eyes. The caring and honesty she always showed in her eyes made him want to give her the truth. He was tired of secrets, tired of lying.

God, he was tired.

"Part of the way here, I realized I wasn't just coming to find Maryanne—though I hoped to God I'd find her here, having tea with you. I was coming for me. I was coming because you are as special to me as she is, and my sister, my niece, and my nephews. I came because I need your strength and support."

That was the pain of this. He needed her, but the gut instincts he had honed as a child told him he could not have her, he should not trust her.

Helena looked dumbstruck. Then she quickly became brisk, taking on the subtle mantel of being in charge. "Put yourself in Maryanne's shoes," she said. "She is your sister and you were obviously close. What would she do?"

They had all kept their father's horrible secrets about his perversions; they had kept the secret of their mother's whippings. They should have bonded together, three conspirators, hiding a secret that would make their family scorned and despised. But Jacinta and Maryanne had bonded. He had been dark, brooding, angry. Jacinta had stood up to him, but when they'd been young, Maryanne had acted as if he was as bad as their father. . . .

"I don't know." He raked his hand roughly through his hair.

"I just don't see how she could have gotten far. I don't see how we couldn't have easily found her."

"She must have someone helping her."

He jerked his head up. "Who, if not you? She's been kept away from other people—"

"Maryanne was in love with someone."

Shock speared him. How in Hades had she known that but had said nothing?

Helena quickly shook her head. "I don't know who the gentleman is—oh!" Her eyes opened wide. "Maryanne might have confided in him. Somehow Blackbriar or Morse learned the truth from this man. But I don't know who he is. She did not tell me. . . . Is there anyone who would know who he is?" She bumped her fist against her temple as if forcing her wits to work, then looked up sharply. "Maryanne had a lady's maid. Anna."

"Jacinta told me that, and I've already questioned Anna to the ends of the earth," Grey said. "The young woman is upset and sobbing and panic stricken, but she's no help." A terrifying thought hit him. "Do you think Maryanne has eloped? She might have felt the only way she could be with this man was to run away."

"I don't know, Grey. But whoever this man is, he might have helped her. We must find his identity."

Grey felt as powerless as when his mother had sent her burly servants to drag him to the cellar for punishments. Maryanne was either out in the world alone, thus in danger, or with someone who was helping her run away. What kind of idiot would help a blind and defenseless girl run away from her family—from people who loved her? He didn't believe this was an elopement. Maryanne had tearfully cried that her secret meant she could never have marriage. . . .

Damn. Why hadn't he seen this before? Someone was trying to destroy him. Now Maryanne was missing. His instincts screamed she was in mortal peril.

"Perhaps no one helped her," he said, his voice ice cold. "I don't believe she has run away. I think she was taken."

Helena stared after Grey as he ran out of the room. Then she ran in pursuit, through the parlor, the hall, the taproom, and reached the door that let out on the inn's tiny courtyard in time to see him swing up on his horse despite the downpour and gallop up the narrow cobblestone road.

He couldn't search wildly through all of the countryside, trying to find Maryanne. He feared someone had taken her to hurt him. Without thought, he was racing into danger.

But if someone had kidnapped Maryanne, why take her belongings? Helena was certain Maryanne had willingly left the house, carrying her bag. What had happened to her after that?

A white, mud-spattered landau rumbled down the lane, pulled by a pair of snow-white horses. A coachman in dripping tricorn hat and greatcoat sat on the box, and a woman with golden hair peered through the window. Lady Winterhaven.

Helena rushed out, forcing the coachman to rein in swiftly. The horses shuddered and pawed in their tracks, and her ladyship leaned out the window, her lovely face stricken with fear. "Miss Winsome, heavens, take care! You could have been run down. You are getting soaked!"

Lady Winterhaven was right. Helena had no coat and her gown already clung to her, heavy and damp. But Grey was soaked to the skin out of worry for Maryanne, and she knew how he felt. Nothing else mattered but ensuring the girl was safe.

"Greybrooke has just left." Helena rushed to the side of the carriage. "We must find Maryanne, but Grey has gone galloping off with no plan and no idea where to look. He's wild with fear and guilt and I—I'm afraid."

Afraid for him. Afraid he was rushing into danger.

Lady Winterhaven threw the door open. "Come with me, Miss Winsome. We can speak on the way back to the house."

She stepped up into the carriage. The coachman cracked the whip, and the horses took off at a canter. Lady Winterhaven had her hands on her rounded belly, making Helena stiff with fear. Could the worry over Maryanne harm her ladyship or her baby?

The wheels creaked over the cobbles, rattling them. Men working around the old stone buildings that lined the main street tipped their caps as they rolled by. "Damn," muttered Lady Winterhaven. "I hate having to move so slowly. Once we're on the wider road, we can make haste. We will return to the house and get dry clothing for you." The countess's eyes were filled with glum certainty. "Maryanne didn't come to you, did she? I told Grey she would not have done so, for you would have stopped her. Grey knew it too, in his heart. I think he came to you because he's come to trust and rely on you."

"He said something like that. But he said before he could never trust me—" Helena stopped. "I'm sorry, my lady, that doesn't matter now. And do not worry about clothing for me."

"My dear, you can be honest with me. Why are you afraid for my brother? Grey can take care of himself."

Helena frowned. "Grey is strong and courageous and brave, but he's also vulnerable."

At the countess's startled look, she quickly told Lady Winterhaven about the night Grey had faced the assassins. "He told me he did not care if he lived or died. Now I understand why. He is racked with guilt and pain. Now that Lady Maryanne might be in danger, I'm afraid he may take too many risks or do something reckless. We must rescue Maryanne, but I don't want Grey to throw himself into danger foolishly."

"I knew he had been attacked—and I had to learn that from his servants, who had learned of his wound from his valet. I did not know that was how he reacted to it."

"I think Lady Maryanne must have left the house willingly," she told Lady Winterhaven, rapidly giving her reasoning.

Lady Winterhaven caught her breath. "I don't know whether to feel relieved . . . or more afraid."

Helena nodded. "That is how I feel. But whomever she went with, she trusted that person."

"Who would she trust more than her own family?" Lady Winterhaven cried.

She—" Helena hesitated. But this was no time to keep secrets. "She has fallen in love. Once I found her in the back garden in London, in tears." She outlined what Maryanne had said. "I assumed she had a crush on someone. Now I realize she must have been meeting a man. What I don't understand is how she met with a gentleman. She never went anywhere alone."

"Of course she didn't. It wouldn't have been safe," Lady Winterhaven declared. "The only thing Maryanne wanted to do was go riding. And that was just one afternoon a week in Hyde Park."

"Yes," Helena said. Maryanne would go right after luncheon, while it was quiet, for the *ton* do not go until late afternoon. "Which groom went with her?" she asked quickly.

"Our head groom, Dixon. He is one of our most trusted servants. That is the only reason I would let her go."

"Is Dixon in London?" Helena hadn't worked with the family long enough to know their servant arrangements when they left the London house.

"No, he is here. Winterhaven trusts no one else to care for his horses, so Dixon comes with us from the estates to town and returns here with us. But Dixon would not have allowed some man to start up a love affair with her. He was very protective."

"I think we had best speak to him as quickly as we can," Helena said. "Perhaps one of the children knows who this man is."

Lady Winterhaven whipped her head to the side, apprehension in her eyes. "We will speak to Dixon. We will not go to the children unless it is absolutely necessary." Her voice became determined—as ducal as Grey's, and with all the fierceness of a protective mother. "I do not want any trauma or fear brought to my children." Her ladyship rapped the ceiling, urging the carriage on.

Should she reveal that she knew about their family's secrets? Helena's heart ached for Lady Winterhaven. If something happened to Grey or to Maryanne, it would put the whole family through terrible pain. It would break the children's hearts—

She couldn't bear it either if something happened to Grey. Her heart would shatter, and how could anyone live with a heart that was nothing but little bits and pieces?

At first the groom denied everything. Dixon shook his head as Lady Winterhaven asked him question after question. Did Lady Maryanne ever speak to a gentleman? Did she arrange to meet someone? Was she ever left completely alone? Had she revealed she was in love?

"No, there was nothing ever like that, my lady."

But Helena saw the man's hand shake as he tried to groom a large gelding. She stepped into the stall, giving the huge horse a wide berth. She touched Dixon's shoulders. The man dropped the brush and stepped into horse dung.

"You must tell us the truth," she implored. "You must do this. I am sure you are frightened about what will happen to you. But Maryanne could be in terrible danger. So could the Duke of Greybrooke. Maryanne has disappeared, and we fear she has put herself in this man's power. We must learn who he is."

She looked to Lady Winterhaven. "You would not condemn him for keeping Lady Maryanne's confidences if he does the right thing now, would you, my lady?"

The countess nodded. Obviously she understood. They must not frighten the man or they would learn nothing. "No, I would not condemn him."

Dixon leaned against the horse. He looked weakened, older. "She could be in danger, and it is my fault for saying naught."

"Tell us now, before it is too late," Helena urged.

" 'E were a gentleman, right enough. Fancy riding clothes, but not too 'igh in the instep to talk to a groom like me. The gent met Lady Maryanne in Hyde Park. There didn't seem no 'arm in letting them talk and ride together. 'E were a bit older than 'er, though that's just me guess."

"Do you know his name?"

"Never told me. Got the idea 'e was a peer. But I don't know all of them by sight."

"What of his appearance? The color of his hair? His eyes? How tall was he?" Helena asked.

"Couldn't judge the 'eight as 'e were in the saddle. Couldn't see the 'air for 'is tall 'at. Might have been a blondish color or maybe it were dark. 'E always stood in the shadows or with the sun behind 'im so I couldn't see 'im well. And me eyesight is not so good."

Dixon told them the gentleman paid him a small fortune to allow him to ride with Maryanne. The groom watched them from afar—they never left his line of sight. The gentleman kissed her hand several times. On the last time, the gentleman kissed her. He expressed his intention to court Maryanne, claiming the Duke of Greybrooke would never permit Maryanne to marry because she was a blind. "I just wanted to see Lady Maryanne 'appy."

But Lady Winterhaven did not recognize the man from Dixon's meager description. Helena had thought of Blackbriar—he was older than Maryanne. He had been obsessed with his wife Caroline, but had he struck up a friendship with Maryanne as part of his plot for revenge?

"Where is Lord Blackbriar's estate?" Helena asked quickly.

"Lord Blackbriar? He is—was—married. And his estates are far to the west of ours." Lady Winterhaven put her hand to her mouth. Her face paled, her hand trembling. "They must be somewhere on the road. I will catch up to my husband, tell him what we know. If she's eloping, they will be on the road to Scotland."

Helena watched Lady Winterhaven's landau disappear around a bend in the drive. Servants headed in every direction in the search. Every carriage and every horse in the stables had been put into use.

It seemed the most logical that Maryanne had gone to Gretna Greene, where she could marry without her family's permission.

How could Lady Maryanne have left the house alone, then met this man somewhere on the road? Lady Winterhaven believed she had. Helena was certain she must have had help. Maryanne had learned to fend well in the house, but how could she make her way down the road to meet someone? Even if he'd waited right outside, how could she have done it without being caught?

What if she'd had someone in the house help her? It would have to be someone Maryanne could trust. Someone she was sure would never give her away. Not a servant . . .

Goodness, how stupid she'd been. She rushed up to the nursery. Sophie looked up from her book as Helena reached the doorway, gasping for breath. She didn't even need to ask the question—guilt, fear, agony were etched on the young girl's pretty face.

Helena's fingers shook as she swiftly wrote three notes. One to Grey. One for the Earl of Winterhaven and the countess. One to leave with the—

"Who are you and what on earth are you doing writing at her ladyship's desk?"

At the stern words, Helena erupted out of the seat. The

338 / Sharon Page

housekeeper stood in the doorway, a tall, foreboding figure, her brows arched with disapproval. Helena did not know this woman, who looked after the house of this estate.

"I am Helena Winsome and was governess to the children."

"The one who left so quickly?"

"Never mind about that!" Helena cried. "This is about Lady Maryanne! I know where she is, and we must get to her. You must take these. Get one to Lady Winterhaven or the earl, and one to the Duke of Greybrooke. At once! Read this one, and instruct any servants that return what to do. Follow my instructions to the letter." She hurried over and thrust the three folded notes at the housekeeper.

"Where is she then?"

"Borderleau House. It has been rented by the Earl of Blackbriar." This was what Sophie had told her. Helena had done her best to make Sophie believe she was not at fault for keeping Maryanne's secret. Once she had Maryanne home safe, she would try to ease the girl's guilt.

The housekeeper glared. "No, you are mistaken. The house was rented by a gentleman named Mr. Nutall."

"That was the name Blackbriar used. But that is where she is. Please, you must do as I ask."

"Miss Winsome, I think you must be mad!"

"Is that what you will tell the Duke of Greybrooke when it is discovered his sister has run off to get married? How shall you explain that to Lord Winterhaven?"

The housekeeper paled.

"I am going to go there now and try to bring Lady Maryanne home. I am certain I can convince her not to go through with an elopement. The Earl of Blackbriar is a dangerous man. I am now certain he murdered his wife."

The woman gasped in shock. Then she came to her wits. "What shall we do?" she cried. "We must get this to his lordship, but everyone is already out searching for Lady Maryanne!"

Helena hesitated. It was madness to go alone, but she had to move quickly. "We must get it to the earl and His Grace somehow. But I will go right now and see if I can speak to Maryanne."

With every horse out of the stables, Helena had to walk. At least the housekeeper—Mrs. Philpot—and every other servant in the house knew where she was going. She'd thought of bringing some of the female servants, but then wondered what use they would be if Blackbriar was dangerous. The notes were enough. Mrs. Philpot had sent every last person in the house in pursuit of other male servants, whom they could send to find the earl on the road.

She had to be careful. Maryanne was going willingly with Blackbriar, having no idea what sort of monster he really was, but Helena knew to fear him. Had he murdered his wife because he wanted Maryanne? Had he pursued Maryanne from the beginning to get revenge on Grey, since he believed Grey had been his wife's lover?

Surely he wouldn't hurt Maryanne. Surely his revenge involved marrying her, not hurting her.

Helena ran along the track that crossed the field toward the house as fast as she could.

The earlier rain had stopped, but now thunder rumbled again. Thick, ominous clouds had amassed over Borderleau, an elegant manor house that stood about two hundred yards ahead of her. She shivered. The slate-colored clouds had mushroomed into the shape of an anvil. In the distance, gray cloud stretched down to the horizon. A wall of rain was racing toward her.

Mud caked her skirts. Her lungs heaved. Helena half ran down the hill, along a track that Mrs. Philpot promised would take her to Borderleau in the quickest way. She was at the bottom of a small valley that ran between the Winterhaven estate and the Borderleau property, and now she had to climb the lawns as quickly as she could.

The lawns ran along the side of Blackbriar's house. There were thick shrubs that would give her cover. Each step pounded her aching legs now. The last time she'd run like this, it had been to save Michael from the carriage.

It felt like a lifetime had passed since then—for her life had completely changed. She'd discovered passion. She'd fallen in love. She'd lost love.

She had to stop Lady Maryanne from making a choice that would ruin her life. Blackbriar was a beast who had abused his wife, then killed her.

She couldn't let that happen to Maryanne. Helena could see now that Maryanne had been desperate for a love she believed she could never have. It must have been easy for Blackbriar to capture her heart.

Why had he done it? To hurt Grey? Or did he truly care for Maryanne?

Helena raced from a shrub to a clump of laurels. The house was just ahead. Her heart hammered.

It didn't matter if Blackbriar loved Maryanne; the poor girl was in terrible danger. He had loved his wife, Caroline, and he had warped love and turned it into something horrific.

From behind the laurels, she surveyed the house. It looked quiet. Still. No sign of servants, no lights glowing in the windows. Doubt hit her.

She couldn't hesitate now. Acting as a spy had taught her a few things, such as studying a house to find the best way in. Here, it would be through a terrace door. She could try the kitchens, but she no longer looked like a servant. And in her lovely clothes she was no longer invisible.

She hurried across the small lawn, trying to stay hidden behind the laurel bushes. A terrace ran along the west side of the house, facing the valley and Winterleigh, Winterhaven's house.

At the front of the house there was a circular drive and an entrance with a long portico.

Borderleau Park wouldn't be as large as Winterleigh, but it would still be a maze inside. Where would Maryanne be?

"Who might you be?" snarled a guttural voice. It came from behind her, sharp and vicious.

She fought numbing fear and turned—only to face a huge chest. An enormous man towered over her, peering down at her with narrow black eyes. He had a grizzled face. Deep scars slashed along both his cheeks. His clothes were the sort a farm laborer would wear. He looked very much like the giant of a man who had attacked Grey.

" 'Is lordship don't like snoops. Ye've dropped yerself in a 'eap of trouble, missy, seeing as 'ow ye're 'ere all alone. Watched you come over from Winterhaven's 'ouse. Come to find Lady Maryanne, I bet. Well, yer wish is granted. Ye're going to see 'er soon." The man chuckled and gave her a wink—a horrid wink that made her skin crawl.

This beast was not taking her anywhere. But she was not going to wait to debate.

Helena spun, yanked up her hems, and ran. The man laughed uproariously. She tore away like a madwoman. Right now she was running for her very life.

Another man stepped out from behind the bushes. In his hand, he held a pistol. Fat as Friar Tuck, he wouldn't be able to outrun her, but he did not need to. A smirk of triumph reigned on his fleshy face. "Come on, miss. Try to get past me. I do like to watch females die."

Oh God.

25

_____

Ropes secured her arms behind her and kept her ankles bound together. Helena struggled, but she couldn't loosen the knots. Each tug of her arms and legs only seemed to tighten them. And her hands were going numb.

When Grey had tied her up, playfully and for pleasure, it had been *nothing* like this.

She lay on the rug in a bedchamber, a few feet from the bed. There was no fire in the grate—she could have risked burning the ropes. Outside the windows, it was almost as dark as night, and rain pelted the windows.

Her cheek stung. Desperate to get free of the burly man who had dragged her in here, she'd resorted to a child's attack— she'd bitten his arm where it was clamped across her. He'd punched her across the cheek in retaliation. Her head ached from the force of his blow. She'd never been hit before in her life, and her brain felt as if it had slammed into her skull.

How had Grey stood up to constant abuse? Aching every- where, sick with fear, Helena had no idea where a young boy had found such strength. She admired Grey so very much. She understood what a struggle it must be for him to forget the past, to not give in to bitterness and rage. It made her want to help him all the more.

Bother, now was not the time for such thoughts. She had to worry about Maryanne first.

The girl must be freed from Blackbriar's clutches. He was the true monster, and he employed monstrous men.

Tears leaked to her cheeks. She wouldn't give in to them, but she couldn't help crying in fear over what might happen to Maryanne.

She needed Grey. So much for her plans—she wasn't going to be able to take Maryanne home. Unless she got her wits about her, she wasn't even going to get out of this room.

Footsteps sounded in the hallway. Panicking, she gave one more fierce and furious battle against the ropes, straining until she let out a scream of frustration. How could it hurt so much when she got nowhere? She fell back, gasping for breath as the door swung open.

Gleaming black boots filled her vision. Helena strained to look up.

Blackbriar stood above her, smirking. "How delightful. This is fortuitous, Miss Winsome."

"Why?" She'd been such a fool. But at least she had left those letters. At least Grey would get one and he would know where to find Maryanne.

"I thought Maryanne would tempt him to come in pursuit. I thought I would allow him to run about the countryside in a panic for a few hours. Then I would send a note, requesting him to come to me. But now, I have something much more tempting. For you, my dear, are expendable."

Expendable. The careless way he threw the word at her hit her as hard as his lackey's slap. Fear made her body numb. She knew what he intended to do, and she was utterly helpless to stop it. Voice shaking, she accused, "You're going to use me as bait for Grey."

He bowed. "Exactly, Miss Winsome."

"He won't come for me. I'm not important to him."

"He will come for Maryanne, but do not underestimate your charms, my dear. Greybrooke is quite besotted with you, or so I have heard. He will come for you. I think I will arrange a charming scene. There's an old cottage on the Winterhaven estate. Grey will have taken you there—and shot you. He will have killed you in revenge for publishing those stories about him and his family. Then, since he will have murdered my wife, the blackmailer, and you, he takes his own life."

Blackbriar recounted his story with relish and rocked back on his heels as if awaiting her approval.

Horror gripped. "This is utter madness." Anger at this demented man gave her strength. "This is wrong and evil. You have no right to destroy Greybrooke's name, nor take his life. You had no right to take the life of your wife. You certainly have no right to touch Lady Maryanne."

Blackbriar threw back his head, laughing. "You expect me to untie you and let you go because you disapprove. If I were you, I would not displease my captor."

"What are you going to do to me?"

"For now, leave you here."

"Where is Lady Maryanne?"

"She is having a deep and relaxing sleep. I saw no reason to trouble her with sordid details while I take care of her damned brother."

"Why in heaven's name are you doing this? Was it to be free to marry Maryanne? Are you doing this to hurt Grey, or because you want her? He would never have let you have her."

Blackbriar smirked at her. "You are quite clever. Obviously he would not let me marry his sister. And he took my wife from me. When I first married her, I loved her. He had always owned her heart, and he would not set her free. He worked at her until she refused to love me."

"There was nothing between them. They weren't . . . weren't lovers. You are the one who drove her away."

"I did not. I was the most devoted of husbands. But no matter what I did, she loved that careless rake instead of me. Then I met Maryanne." He steepled his fingers, closed his eyes, looked heavenward. "So beautiful and so vulnerable."

"You don't mind that she is—"

"Blind? Of course not." He glared at her. "What sort of pitiable man do you think I am?"

He was a murderer, yet offended by that?

"She is so vulnerable, so sad and wounded. I knew she was suffering under the weight of a terrible secret. She would not reveal it to me. How was I to learn it? I needed to know what it was."

Oh heavens. Now Helena saw how she had been used. It wasn't Greybrooke's secrets she was to uncover, it was Maryanne's.

Blackbriar paced on the floor, hands clasped behind his back. "I overheard your brother in a gaming hell, bragging about the mysterious Lady X and how she could ferret out any secret. I also had a small problem. I was in dun territory a few years ago and was forced to pass along some information for a substantial payment. Unfortunately, the Crown had grown suspicious of my sudden 'good fortune.' I saw that using you and your brother gave me everything I wanted: Maryanne's secret, a scapegoat for treason, a motive for Greybrooke's eventual 'suicide.' Of course, you didn't reveal the truth about Maryanne, but your discussion with her prompted her to reveal it to me. So there would be no secrets between us as we embark on married life."

He smirked. "I really must thank you, Miss Winsome. Now I can help Maryanne. She is growing to depend on me."

Helena saw then what Blackbriar wanted: a woman who

was utterly dependent on him. But poor, vulnerable Lady Maryanne could not marry this violent madman.

"You might as well rest, Miss Winsome. I have to contact Greybrooke and tempt him here. I will not need you for several hours. But you will soon play an important role. You will ensure Maryanne's future happiness. You will be pleased to know that. And you will die with Greybrooke."

She shivered. She had time, now she must think of a way out.

Blackbriar bowed, in a parody of politeness that sickened her. He turned abruptly and marched from the room, slamming the door shut behind him.

His poor horse, Brutus, was soaked to the skin. The beast's hooves were caked with mud, and he had forced the animal to gallop up the roads leading away from Winterleigh. Grey couldn't push Brutus any further.

He didn't believe Maryanne had left by the roads. At every small farm or croft he had passed, he'd asked if a carriage had passed, or a couple on horseback or foot, or a woman alone. No one had seen anything. Servants were combing the woods. If Maryanne and her captor had taken that route, they would have been found. Blind, Maryanne would not have been able to move quickly through the dense woods.

He'd been a fool to rush out without thought. Helena had shouted that to him as he'd run out. She'd been right. He'd wasted precious time, driven his horse to the point of exhaustion.

He forced Brutus into one last trot, which took them toward the stables. In the distance, he could see footmen, maids, grooms searching Winterleigh's grounds—the meadows, fields, woods that surrounded the house.

Maryanne had to be somewhere close. Damn it, she could have been hidden by her captor somewhere on the estate.

He had to believe she was alive. He couldn't face the alternative—

A madman wanted to destroy him, to kill him. The only person he knew who hated him was Blackbriar. He'd found no way to prove Blackbriar had hired the blackmailer or the actor who had played Whitehall, but in his gut he knew the bastard was behind this.

If it was Blackbriar, where in hell had the fiend taken Maryanne? Had he taken Maryanne to use her as bait? That was what Grey suspected. So why hadn't Blackbriar lured him into a trap?

Brutus clopped up the gravel path to the stables. He would shelter the horse, quickly dry him, and use that time to employ his wits. Running around like a madman had done nothing. Helena had been correct—he'd been blindly driven by guilt. He must think. If it was Blackbriar, how would he have gotten to Maryanne? Had he waited until she went outside and grabbed her then? Why hadn't she screamed? Why had no one seen a man kidnap her?

Grey dismounted, led Brutus to a stall. Quickly he removed the saddle and bridle, wiped the animal down, then put on a warming blanket. It took precious minutes, but he could not let his horse suffer for his—

"Yer Grace! I saw ye on the path!" A young lad, one of the bootboys, ran up to him, panting. "I were told to find ye and give ye a message. From Miss Winsome. She wants ye to go to Borderleau 'ouse. Said Lady Maryanne is with a bloke named Blackbriar. Said to warn ye 'e's dangerous. Coo, has Lady Maryanne been kidnapped?"

Helena had gone?

Borderleau was right beside Winterleigh. There were fields between the two properties, also the dense woods that bordered the lawns of Borderleau and would make a good place for him to hide servants. He couldn't charge the house—that would be too dangerous. Looking down at the lad, he said softly, fighting for calm, "Tell as many of the other servants as you can, and send them to the woods on the south side of Borderleau. They must remain hidden. Get word to Lord Winterhaven and give him the same directions. Can you remember all this?"

The boy puffed out his chest. "Indeed I can, Yer Grace."

"Good." Quickly, Grey outlined his plan. Then he sent the boy away. Taking the shortcut to Borderleau across the fields would put him out in the open. As a boy, Grey had come here a few times. Sometimes the Winterhavens had taken him, Jacinta, and Maryanne for summers. They'd treasured those times they could escape their hellish home. And they'd all kept their secrets even when away from home—their parents had trained them well, he thought bitterly.

But because he'd come here as a lad, he knew a secret path through the woods to Borderleau. Grey was running to it, when a horrifying thought hit him. He skidded on the wet ground and caught his balance by slamming against a tree.

Helena must have gone there—she and Maryanne must be Blackbriar's prisoners.

The fear, the guilt, struck him so hard, it was a wrenching physical pain. It made him want to vomit. But he wasn't a boy anymore, who could be frightened into immobility.

Despite the slick ground and pounding rain, he raced like a madman to the path in the woods.

Grey stared down at the unconscious man. Using the element of surprise, he'd taken Blackbriar's lackey from behind, swung the man around to meet his fists. After dragging the unconscious body behind a grove of laurels, he had divested the paid villain of his pistol and a knife. Arming himself was something he'd forgotten to do in his blind panic.

"With my upbringing," he muttered, "I know exactly how

sadistic bastards think. And I know where they position their henchmen."

Screened by the laurels, he assessed the house. Blackbriar wanted him dead, which meant eventually he should have been led to a trap. He must be early. Good.

Keeping out of the line of sight of the kitchen door and windows, he crept to the wall of ivy that ran down the house. It was thicker now, but he sliced it away with the knife. There was a long forgotten door behind it. The door was still unlocked—no one must remember its existence. Grey pushed it open. He had to get Maryanne. And get to Helena—he had no doubt Blackbriar had caught her. She was filled with good intentions, filled with the need to rescue Maryanne, and she wouldn't have watched out for herself carefully enough.

He couldn't lose either of them. God, they had to be both alive.

He didn't even have to use the pistol to threaten Blackbriar's man, who was watching out the partially open kitchen door. A hefty rolling pin sent the man to the floor. He had no mercy for these louts. He remembered the cruelty of the servants in his parents' employ—they did it for money or because they were sick and evil.

Blackbriar was probably keeping the women in bedchambers. Grey made his way up the servants' stairs to the upper floor. He had his pistol ready, but he encountered no one. If Blackbriar had touched them, hurt them—

Rage flooded him. It made his jaw twitch, his heart pound, his hands turn into fists. He wanted to kill someone right now. . . .

"The tart's tied up upstairs. Supposed to be the mistress of a duke. His lordship wouldn't know if we had our fun with her. Wouldn't you like to poke a hole that's been filled by a duke's cock?"

"I don't think you're going to be in any condition to touch anyone," Grey said coldly, stepping out into the hall. His boot drove into the man's crotch, sending him choking and gasping to the carpet. The man was so fat, his stomach hit the floor, and he curled like an oversized cricket ball. "Oooh, I'm dying." He vomited on the rug.

Grey waved his pistol at the second man—the villain Baldy—who brandished a knife. "Drop it," he growled. "Where is she, the woman you were just speaking of?"

Baldy glowered, clearly hating being in a position of weakness when he'd assumed he would get to have the power in this. "The room at the end of the hall."

"And the other lady? Lady Maryanne? Where is she?"

"His lordship's bedchamber." Baldy smirked—Grey knew his horror had been written on his face. "After all, they're going to be wed. His lordship's probably sampling the goods first."

Baldy fell back, hitting the hallway rug like a load of bricks. Grey glanced down at his knuckles. His gloves had split, and blood dribbled from his broken skin again. Fury had given him the strength to knock the bastard cold, but it had felt damned good.

Feeding his rage felt good.

Breaking down Helena's door proved easy. The door splintered around the lock as his shoulder drove into it. He found Helena bound on the floor—

He was ready to kill without thought.

But he had to stop long enough to set her free; to get on his knees and slice through the vicious bonds at her hands and ankles. Her eyes were wide, her skin pale. A green and purple bruise bloomed on her cheek.

Blackbriar was going to die for that. And for the red chafing marks on her delicate skin. For the fear in her huge blue eyes.

"Grey," she gasped. "Thank heavens. I feared Blackbriar would trap you—"

He gathered her into his arms. God, he had done this to her. By dragging her into the sick vortex that was his world, he had damaged her badly. "You brought me here. It was your clever-ness—figuring this out, sending the message through the ser-vants. You are the heroine in this, Helena. I was an idiot, and you were right all along."

How could he ever make this right? He knew that wounds like this—wounds based on fear, horror, terror—never healed. They scarred over but festered underneath forever.

Helena could not quite believe the Duke of Greybrooke had called himself an idiot. And told her she was right.

She laughed for a moment, a wild laugh that became a sob. "Thank goodness you've come. You have nothing to blame yourself for! You wanted to save your sister. You are a good and noble man. Yes, I *am* right about that."

His expression turned grim. "I'm going to find Blackbriar and rip him to shreds." He got to his feet, lifting her with him as if she weighed nothing.

"Grey, you cannot do that. Even with all he's done. He needs to face justice by the law, not at your hands." It fright-ened her. What if he killed the blackguard? Could Grey be hanged?

"After what he's done to Maryanne, I want to see him suffer. I don't want to take any chance he can use his position or his money to escape punishment." His eyes were bleak, his voice like ice. He started walking away from her. "I'd rather you got out of the house, but I need to know you're safe. You have to come with me."

She hurried to catch him. "He won't have hurt her. He loves her. He intended to marry her, and to do so he had to get rid of his wife and get rid of you. He won't have hurt her, not when he wants her to love him."

"He might have touched her. He might have ravished her." He put his finger to his lips, opened the door, and checked the hallway.

Heavens, she hadn't thought of that. What would it do to Maryanne, who was so traumatically wounded by her past, to learn she had made love to by a man who was a killer?

Behind him, when Helena saw there was no one in the hall, she whispered, "No, I don't believe he will do that. He looks on her as a lady. He would be certain they would be wed. I don't think he would do such a thing . . . but we must find her."

"She's in his bedchamber. I don't know where he is. He intended to lure me here. We have to be careful." Grey drew out a pistol, making her catch her breath at his expression. Calculating, ruthless, murderous.

"If he attacks us, I'll shoot him down. Understand that, Helena."

He had turned to speak to her, and she saw a flicker of movement in the gloom of the hall behind him. "Grey," she gasped.

The explosion almost deafened her. Grey was thrown backward against the wall.

Talking to her, he had been distracted. And in that moment, Blackbriar had stepped out of a bedroom and shot him. "Fortunately for me," the fiend cackled, "you left a trail of unconscious men in your wake, warning me you had arrived early. I knew where you would come. All I had to do was await my opportunity. Unfortunately no man about to commit suicide would shoot himself in the chest. I may have to rethink my delightful scenario, Greybrooke."

Shot in the *chest?* Muffling a scream, Helena grasped Grey by the arms. He was struggling to stay on his feet. Blood was soaking into his coat, turning his waistcoat red.

He found the strength to push her away and fell back against the wall. "Goddamn it, Helena," he rasped. "Run. Run for your life. Get out. Get to my servants."

"I can't. I won't leave you to die."

Then she saw something even more horrible. Grey slid a bit down the wall, leaving a line of blood. It was awful, but what made her heart almost stop was a boy's plaintive voice crying, "Uncle Grey? What's happened? You're bleeding!"

There, behind the villainous Blackbriar, stood Michael and Timothy. Clinging to each other and shaking with terror.

26

Already he felt cold, and his chest felt as if four elephants had fallen on it at once. Getting shot hurt a hell of a lot more than being stabbed, Grey discovered. He'd still believed, even with the pistol ball passing through him, even after he'd collapsed against the wall, that he could win this with Blackbriar, but the sight of his nephews drained his hope.

He'd hoped to somehow trade his life for Helena and Maryanne. Now he knew Blackbriar was too much of a sick monster to barter. Blackbriar just intended to kill him.

Hell, he couldn't let a shot take him now.

He had to fight. He'd fought back as a child. He'd found the strength to do it. Now he must find even more strength.

The pistol ball hadn't hit him in the heart. He'd be dead if it had. But it had ripped a hole in the flesh and muscle of his right shoulder. The pain was making it hard to focus.

Timothy shrieked in terror, causing Blackbriar to whirl around on the lad. "Shut up, you noxious brat," he snapped. "If you hadn't insisted on following Maryanne, you'd be home safe. But you are both spoiled wretches, and you'll get what you deserve."

"You monster," Helena cried. "How could you have taken them? They are children!"

"Unfortunately, due to their stupidity," Blackbriar sneered, "the Earl of Winterhaven is about to lose his heir and his spare."

Helena tried to step toward the fiend, but Grey barked at her, "Stop."

Blackbriar had already moved. His arm wrapped around Timothy's small chest; he had the boy clamped to his legs and held a knife to the boy's throat. Grey had his pistol, but they were notoriously hard to aim with great accuracy. He couldn't take the risk of hitting Timothy. Still he lifted his weapon. Already, his arm shook with the exertion. It took all his strength to make his muscles obey his command.

He didn't want Helena in his line of fire as well.

Grey was swaying, his arm almost numb, so he couldn't prop himself against the wall to take aim. How could he shoot Blackbriar without hurting the boy? Blackbriar was laughing at his feeble attempt to save his family.

Just as his father had once laughed at him. His father had laughed at him for crying when he'd been beaten with a riding crop. Laughed at him for not being strong enough to withstand his mother's cruelty.

His family had been mad. But watching Timothy, terrified, his life held in the hands of a madman, Grey felt something snap inside. Why should Timothy be hurt for the sake of Blackbriar? Why should his life be held at risk by a monster who deserved to die?

Helena gasped, "No, Michael. No, you must keep back."

Her soft, frightened voice broke through Grey's dimming thoughts.

He saw Blackbriar jerk around to see what the lad was doing. At that moment, Helena made a slithering motion. Was he seeing things?

No, Timothy made the same motion. Somehow, Timothy

seemed to make himself smaller and thinner, and the child dropped to his knees, free of the knife.

Michael heaved something at Blackbriar, who put up his hand in instinctive defense.

Despite screaming pain, Grey straightened his arm. Took the shot. Blackbriar's chest jerked back, then the fiend toppled, thudding on his back on the carpet.

After that, Grey's legs seemed to dissolve, and he sank to the hallway floor. "Go to Miss Winsome," he shouted at the boys. He wanted them safe, and away from the gruesome sight of Blackbriar's body. He wanted to protect them from horrors that would haunt them—

Everything looked foggy. Indistinct. But he saw skirts swishing toward him. He looked up, despite the pain, and saw Helena hurrying toward him with her arms around both his nephews. Damn, she was supposed to take them away. He forced a smile on his lips. He didn't want to worry them—he loved them so much. The three of them.

"Timothy, good boy," he managed to say. "You followed Miss Winsome's direction. Michael, what did you throw?"

"Nothing," Michael whispered. "I pretended I was throwing something to distract him."

Helena gasped at Michael, "Goodness, you shouldn't have taken such a risk."

"I had to help Timothy," his nephew said staunchly. "And Uncle Grey. And you, Miss Winsome."

"Michael, Timothy . . ." Grey tried to make his voice sound normal. "You are both heroes."

"And you need a physician. At once," Helena declared. "We must get you out of here now—"

"You have to find Maryanne first. There might be other men in here. Damnation, I should not have let myself get shot."

"You cannot blame yourself for that!"

The boys' heads twisted back and forth to face each of them.

Footsteps pounded in the corridor. Dazed, weak, Grey cursed. These might be more of Blackbriar's henchmen.

"Greybrooke? Miss Winsome? Are you there?"

"Thank heavens." Grey heard Helena's voice break on a sob. "It's Lord Winterhaven."

Her face swam in his vision, and he saw how pale she was but how hope had lit up her eyes. Then Grey saw nothing but a fuzzy grayness, as if a blanket had dropped on him. He slumped to the floor.

Grey remembered a lot of things.

Pain. There'd been a hell of a lot of pain. Agony had lanced his shoulder and chest when he'd been moved to a carriage, despite the care with which his brother-in-law and several footmen carried him. Pain hit him with each jolt of the carriage on the road. And again, when he'd been hauled into a doctor's surgery. And when the damned surgeon had poked and prodded his shoulder, had picked pieces of his shirt out of the wound, while Helena insisted the sawbones do a thorough job.

All throughout, he'd drifted in and out of consciousness.

Helena had always been there. Each time he'd awoken, he'd heard her voice. Or caught a fleeting glimpse of her before that gray blanket was thrown over him again. As far as he could tell, she had never left his side.

Finally, as he opened his eyes, he felt he might actually stay conscious for more than a few seconds. Hushed voices reached him. Female ones. Quiet voices in front of him . . . hell, did it mean after all that prodding, after all that pain, after those damned stitches, he was going to die anyway?

No, he wasn't. A few hours ago—or whenever it was he'd been shot—he might have put money on odds against him. Now he felt strong. He had no intention of dying. People depended on him.

He was going to call for Helena, when a woman's voice rose.

Distinctly he heard Maryanne say slowly, "It was all a lie, then. He didn't love me—he used me to hurt Grey. To hurt all those people. . . ."

Grey struggled to sit up. He clenched his teeth against the pain in his shoulder, but he did it. Propped up on the arm on his uninjured side, he could see Maryanne and Helena seated on the wide window seat of his bedroom in Winterleigh.

"I believe he did love you, Lady Maryanne," Helena said vehemently. She wrapped her arm around Maryanne's slim shoulders. "Lord Blackbriar loved you very much. But he had an evil streak within him, and that made him do terrible things. Loving you was perhaps the one good thing he did."

"This is my fault," Maryanne whispered.

Guilt gripped Grey, ready to crush his soul.

"No," Helena said firmly.

Grey's heart filled to bursting as Helena insisted, "This was all his doing and his fault. You have never done anything wrong. You will find a true love. A decent love. This I promise you."

Grey would make this happen. He and Jacinta had kept Maryanne from Society to protect her because she had suffered so much pain at the hands of their father. But she did not deserve to be kept a prisoner. At the moment when he'd realized that he refused to allow Timothy's life to be ruined or forfeited, he'd seen the truth.

He would find a decent man to be Maryanne's husband. A gentleman who would understand she had been a victim and she now deserved happiness.

"Lady Maryanne, your brother is awake," Helena said softly. The glow of delight on Helena's face stunned him as she led Maryanne to his bedside. She wagged her finger at him. "You should lie down, Grey. You will tear the stitches and reopen the wound."

"Then that quack of a doctor can sew it open again. He'll complain, but he'll be happy enough to do it for what I pay him. I'm willing to open my stitches to do this. . . ." He clasped Maryanne's hand and drew her to sit on the edge of the bed. Pain shot through his shoulder, but he didn't care. Awkwardly, since his right side felt as if it had been flattened by a runaway carriage, he hugged Maryanne. How small she was, smelling sweetly of lavender.

"I am so sorry," his sister sobbed, pressed against him. His chest was bare, except for the bandages wrapped around his torso.

He kissed the top of her head. "You have nothing to be sorry for. The mistake—every mistake in this—has been mine. I tried to protect you when you were a girl, and I should have been more ruthless about it. But that's in the past. It is the present and the future that matter. Jacinta and I should have let you live like the young lady you are. We wrongly thought to keep you safe, and all we did was make you unhappy. It is my fault you turned to Blackbriar, because I didn't understand what I was keeping you from: the chance to find love and happiness. That's what I stupidly did to myself. And it was even more stupid to do that to you. Helena—Miss Winsome, I mean—is correct. Things are going to change. You did nothing wrong in the past, Maryanne. You did nothing wrong now. You see the good in people."

"I don't see anything at all," she mumbled. "I can't be like other girls. Won't you be ashamed to have me in Society? I'm blind."

"Not ashamed." He was horrified. "Never. Was that what you thought? Dear God, that was never my intention. I'm proud of you, Maryanne."

His sister glowed at his words. How lovely she was. He prayed there was a gentleman worthy of Maryanne. Now that Jacinta no longer had to worry about finding a bride for him, they could devote their time to finding the right man for Maryanne.

As if summoned by his thoughts, Jacinta popped her head into his room. "I thought I heard your voice, Grey." She hurried in, her belly very round, her hand resting on it. "I've been so worried about you!"

Guilt tried to rear its head. She shouldn't have had to worry about him when she was so close to her time. She shouldn't have had to race around the county, afraid for Maryanne—

No, it wasn't his fault. It was Blackbriar's fault. She looked well. And Maryanne looked so much happier than she had since she lost her sight. His nephews were—

"Michael and Timothy." He met Jacinta's gaze. "How are they?"

"Fine. They had some nightmares the first night, but Miss Winsome sat with them. Last night, they slept soundly. They are young and will recover." His sister smiled at Helena. "Now, I think Maryanne and I will leave the two of you alone."

He lifted his brow. His sister smiled at his former mistress as if they were good friends. That brought a warm glow to his heart. It also made him suddenly nervous.

He knew what he had to do. He cleared his throat. And said . . .

"Wait—the first night? How many hours have I slept?"

Damn, damn, damn. That was not what he wanted to come out.

Helena was tidying things on his bedside table. She poured him a glass of water and put it in his hand. "Hours? You have gone in and out of consciousness for three days. We've all been terribly worried."

Now he saw the dark rings beneath her eyes, the pallor of her skin. "Have you slept?" he asked, guessing that she hadn't. He knew she must have spent hours by his bedside, ignoring her own health. After what she'd been through, her thoughts had been for him.

He was humbled. Hades, he didn't deserve it.

"You haven't asked about your wound. How bad it is."

She spoke slowly, which should make him worry. And it suddenly did. If he was to have a crippled arm, maybe he wouldn't be good enough. . . .

"Is it bad?" he asked. "Does the sawbones think I won't be able to use my arm?"

"No, it isn't bad at all. In fact, Doctor Penworth feels you were very fortunate. The pistol shot did not go through your chest, which I feared it had done. It grazed your shoulder. There was some damage, but he is confident it will heal."

"Good. Helena, there's something I have to tell you."

Ask her. Ask her now.

Damn it, he couldn't. She had stayed up with him over the last three days. But could she forgive him? He had to say something. Had to make her understand what she had done.

The impossible.

She had changed his entire world.

"Do you remember when I told you that a black past meant a bleak future? But now I want to believe that isn't true. Maryanne deserves a future, as does every member of my family who has gone through hell at the hands of Blackbriar. Why should their lives be forever ruined by the actions of a madman? They deserved a life untainted by that worthless scum."

He had always believed he should pay penance for the rest of his life. Now he saw how insane that was. Helena had made him see how insane it was. Why should he pay for the mad actions of his parents?

"I am going to fight to make sure they do," he said. "I don't know how it can be done, but I have to believe it can be."

"This is how," she whispered. "By the strength of love. The thing is, I understand. I have been haunted by my past. My sister died when I was younger. She was seduced, she became pregnant, and the man abandoned her. All along, I've wanted to make men who were scoundrels pay. That is why I wrote the articles as Lady X. My family found a man willing to marry her—an older widower with six children. I told her to refuse, for I knew she wouldn't love him. Then she died in childbirth, alone. If she'd married, her husband would have had a physician attend her, and she and the baby might have lived."

There. She'd revealed her deepest mistake. She had known Knightly was to blame, but for years she had felt guilt. If she had encouraged Margaret to be practical, her sister might have lived.

"None of that is your fault," he said softly. "You wanted her to have love and happiness. Now I understand what you gave up when you became my mistress. You felt that love was the most important thing in the world, didn't you?"

"I was very foolish."

"Not foolish. Helena, you are right. You are right, and I was wrong." He should get down on one knee. Was lying in a bed, looking up at her good enough? "Helena, there is something I have to ask you—"

"Oh heavens," came a cry from right outside the door to his room. "The baby is coming!"

Two thoughts hit Grey at once. His sisters had been listening at the door.

And Jacinta was about to have her baby.

He had no chance to ask his question of great import of Helena, because she rushed out of his room at once to help his sister.

Babies were not born beautiful.

His tiny niece possessed a cone-shaped head that looked squashed flat on one side. Grey had to fight the instinct to fix it, to remold it into a round, baby-like shape. Inside a circlet of lace-trimmed blanket, a red face peeked at him. The nose was upturned, the cheeks heavy, and tiny, dark eyes stared at him before the little face screwed up and a wail filled his bedroom.

"How does someone so small make so much sound?" He

shared a look with Helena. She held the baby—he didn't trust himself to gather his new niece in his arms with a wounded shoulder.

"I have no idea." She giggled. "Does the sound bother you?"

"No, but it makes me wish I could move heaven and earth to make her happy and make her stop."

Helena smiled, which made her eyes glow brilliantly.

"She's perfect," he murmured. To him, she looked like a miracle. Jacinta had begun her labor with the breaking of her waters, and in mere minutes after her pains started, the child had come. His sister's strength had amazed him. And Winterhaven had tried to appear calm but had brought brandy to Grey's room, and had admitted how nervous he was and how much he admired Jacinta. "Marriage," Winterhaven had said, "is the making of any man."

"Not you too," Grey had groaned.

"Lady Winterhaven asked me to bring her to you," Helena said. "Of course, Lord Winterhaven was nervous about letting me carry his daughter."

"I think he would be nervous about carrying her himself." He sighed. "All their children are fortunate to have such loving parents."

He heard Helena fight back a soft sob.

"No tears," he said gently. "Take my sweet niece back to Winterhaven. There is something I want to ask you. I need to be prepared to take action, and the little one—as adorable as she is—will be in the way."

Mystified, Helena returned the baby to the countess's bedroom. Lady Winterhaven put her baby to the breast and nodded with satisfaction. "I hope it works. A helpless, precious newborn is the most dangerous weapon I have in my arsenal."

"A weapon?" Then she knew. Lady Winterhaven hoped seeing the baby might spark Grey to want to start a nursery of his own.

The thought made her heart ache. But he must marry. More than that, he *should* marry. She must accept that she should step aside and allow him to take a bride and fill his nursery. He would be a superb father.

Of course, the thought of him gazing lovingly down at another woman while he cradled their child was heartbreaking.

In the corridor, a flurry of activity began. Servants hastened down, carrying pots of hot water toward Grey's rooms. Curious, Helena followed.

Rain streamed down again, just as it had on the day they had confronted Blackbriar. Helena would never forget that day, for she'd been so terrified she would lose Grey forever. But he'd survived, Maryanne and the children were on the mend after their frightening experience, and Lady Winterhaven had given birth to a healthy baby girl with admirable lungs.

There had been terrifying moments, but also blessed ones. She had almost held her breath the entire time Grey was recovering from the pistol shot. She wanted to see him again to savor having him safe and sound.

A door near his bedchamber was open. A claw-foot tub stood in the middle of the room, surrounded by folded towels. Grey stood in the room, a towel wrapped around his hips while his valet redressed his wound.

"You are having a bath."

"Don't leave," he said quickly. With a wink to her, he dismissed his valet. The slender man looked a bit shocked but bowed and withdrew, leaving them alone in the room—at least until more servants arrived with more water to fill the tub.

"We both are in need of one," Grey said. "You need a good soaking in a hot bath after staying awake for days with me." He flashed a grin. "We would both get done quicker if we share one."

"We shouldn't be so scandalous in your sister's house," she said awkwardly.

"Perhaps. But I can't wait another minute."

Helena had planned to step aside, but she couldn't resist this. Just to have a little more time with him. And in a warm bath? It was the definition of heavenly. "All right."

Grey took her hand and propelled to the dressing room, which contained the tub, then he opened a door that connected to a balcony. A balcony that adjoined this room and his bedroom.

Grey's breath, warm and gentle, brushed over her ear from behind. As she always did, she quivered. She was going to lose him to marriage. Her head accepted it, her heart refused to, and her body . . . her body simply ignored the truth. She just *wanted* him.

"It's so hot and sultry out," she whispered.

"Do you know what I want to do to you?" he murmured. "I can't do it in here. Not while a parade of servants is in my dressing room, preparing the bath."

"Where can you do it?"

He put his finger to his lips. Then he put his hands on his shoulders and urged her to step outside onto the balcony. It was the way she imagined a Turkish bath would be, even hotter in the summer rain than it had been before.

Grey closed the door, a thick towel draped over his arm, which made her curious. Holding hands, they went to the end of the balcony, outside his bedroom, where the drapes were closed. In only minutes, she was wet.

"I want to do this," he said.

With care, he got down to his knees, laid the towel in a thick square, then lay on his back with his head, shoulders, and the wounded area of his chest supported by the towel.

She watched as he undid the towel around his hips. His cock bounded up, looking strong, straight, and eager.

"Are you certain?" Helena asked. "I fear you are going to hurt yourself."

"I'm fine," Grey said. "This time, love, I want you on top."

Lying on the wood deck, he drank in the sight of her. Helena's soaked dress clung to her rounded hips and her tiny waist and cupped her full bosom like eager hands. In her wet clothes, with her hair in soaked waves around her, she looked like a sea nymph—

Hell, too flowery. She looked like a wanton with her gold, wet hair falling around her, her dress plastered to her round breasts and shapely legs. The proper governess wasn't gone; she had just made good friends with the wanton governess.

Helena hiked her skirts up to expose damp legs and soaked stockings tied just above her knees. She straddled him, resting her rump on his groin, squashing his aching erection.

He loved it.

Sliding his hand under her derriere, Grey fumbled with his cock, holding it upright.

Wet hair suddenly slapped his cheeks as Helena leaned forward. Her mouth captured his. Erotic pleasure almost scalded him. Having her on top, refreshing drops rolling off her hair to his face, her mouth playing with his . . . it was heaven.

Making love with the warm rain teeming on them. . . . Funny, he'd never guessed there was anything more heavenly than heaven.

With Helena on top, he was essentially a prisoner. He didn't care. He put his hands at her waist, held her steady, kissed her deeply.

A lifetime of this. . . .

A future of this to burn away the ice-cold fears and guilt and damnable memories of the past. He moved his hand and pressed one finger between her legs through her clinging drawers.

She jerked away from his lips. "I want you, but you deserve more. You deserve to be married."

"I intend to be married," he growled.

She jolted back. "I—I am so glad. But if you are going to find a bride, I can't be—I mustn't be your mistress."

"You are going to be my bride."

"What?"

"I intended to ask you formally after making love to you." He clasped her wrists, drew her down so his lips were an inch from hers. This made much more sense for a proposal of marriage. For when she said yes, he could kiss her.

"Helena, will you marry me?"

"I—oh! No."

She wrenched free of his arms. Clawing at her skirts, she freed her legs from the folds. Befuddled with lust, he still couldn't understand what she'd said. He thought it was "no."

She half rolled, half stumbled off him.

Wait, it *was* no.

Grey moved fast, wincing in pain, and caught her green skirt before it was out of his reach. "Why? Is it because I was such an idiot before? Or is it because I'm so ruined by my past? You know most of it, but I'm willing to reveal anything to you. I trust you, Helena."

He took a deep breath. He never spoke of his past; he'd tried to stow it away in the dark recesses of his mind, like jamming forgotten items in a cupboard. But that hadn't worked. "My mother was the one to punish me. You know that. She hired servants to grab me out of my bed and drag me to the cellar. There, I would be tied up and beaten. And throughout the whole thing, she would touch me. Kiss my head, stroke my cheek, give me all this damned affection. At first, when she did it, I thought it meant my punishment was to end. Eventually I realized the touching was a game to her, some sick way of showing her superiority. My father was never faithful to her, always telling her she was not beautiful or she was too old. She wanted power. I guess that is why I never wanted to be touched. But you changed me, Helena. You made me see how beautiful it is to touch, to love, to share. You showed me the rewards that come from trust and love. I said you could never change me, and I was wrong. I honestly am a changed man."

368 / Sharon Page

She stared down at him, eyes wide. "I didn't say no because of you. Grey, you must see—you are a duke and I am a ruined former governess. How can we marry?"

"We get a license and go to a church and say vows before a minister. That's how."

"I am not—"

"You are more worthy of being a duchess than any woman I know. I love you. Now that you've made me see sense and convinced me to fall in love, you can't expect me to lose without a fight. No one knows I ruined you. You've been masked when out with me in public. Your servants know but know better than to speak of it. They know they would face my wrath if they did. So I'm not letting you go, Helena. I want to spend my future with you. God, say yes. Finally I have a future to look forward to—but it would be empty without you."

"You love me?"

"I've loved you from the first moment I pulled you away from the carriage and you glared at me with disapproval. You are the only woman who expected me to be a better man than I was. Not because you thought I was capable of it, but because you thought I already was that man. You taught me that love has to be enough." He gave her a playfully pouting look. "Don't prove me right, Helena. God, don't prove me right."

She put her hand to her mouth. Her lashes dipped. Droplets sparkled in them. From the rain or from tears?

"Yes," she whispered. "I love you so much. I will not prove you right, Grey. Love is more than enough, and I can't give it up either."

She giggled, and his heart took flight at the happy sound. "You know," she said. "I did have a fantasy—a secret, naughty desire—when I was a governess. And it was you, Grey. My wildest, most wicked desire has always been to be with you."

He felt his chest swell with pride, his heart with happiness.

His cock . . . well, it was already swollen to bursting, eager and ready.

She came back to him, climbed on him. This time she took hold of his cock, positioned it upright, and sank down on him.

God, it was heaven.

"What has always been your wildest and most wicked fantasy?" she asked.

"I don't know about wickedest. But the dream I thought would never come true, the dream I clung to when I was young, was that I would find someone who loved me," he admitted. "Someone who was good, kind, sweet, and perfect. You've always been my dream, Helena. A dream I was too afraid to even let myself have."

She caught her lip in her teeth. She began thrusting on him, and he moaned with pleasure. And relief. He was ready to explode, and he was fighting for control.

Hoarsely, he went on, "Now my dream is to be married to you and start on our enormous brood of children. I want Maryanne to live with us too. She adores you, and I know together we can put her past behind her and give her happiness."

"Yes, we can."

"I hope your brother will accept me, Helena. I forgive him for those stories in the news sheets. It was not his fault. What of your sisters—will they forgive me for my shouting and threats? I will take care of them all, if they will let me. If you will."

"Oh, Grey, they will be so happy. You've made me so very happy." She frowned, but he could see the teasing in it. "How enormous a family are you speaking of?"

"Maybe a dozen children?" Grey lifted his hips, thrusting into her hopefully. "I was thinking of funding schools and homes for blind children, children less fortunate. We could use our position and your wonderful skills with children—" He broke off, then said, "I am so deeply in love with you."

"And so deeply in me," Helena whispered, giggling with joy.

She gazed down at him. She never knew she could be so happy. He'd said she'd taught him how to love. He had taught her that dreams did come true.

"After," she whispered, "If we can be alone, I'd like you to tie me up."

"I didn't think you would want that," he said softly.

"It's something erotic and fun that we share. Something wicked and special. I rather like submitting to your erotic will."

His green eyes blazed. "I'm glad you enjoy it. I love sharing it with you. That's what I want, Helena. To share happiness and pleasure with you."

He thrust wildly into her, rubbed her clit with his thumb, and gave her an orgasm that turned the hot, drumming rain into bursting fireworks.

"I love you," he cried, then he arched up and came too.

And her most wonderful, perfect fantasy of passion and happiness with the Duke of Greybrooke was coming true.

Bells rang from the village church in the village of Winter's Bough, the village near Winterleigh. The entire village had been invited to attend the marriage of Damian Caldwell, the fifth Duke of Greybrooke, and Miss Helena Winsome.

Helena knew the real reason for the excitement brewing among her sisters and the other unmarried females in attendance. Two unmarried dukes were among the guests: the Duke of Caradon and the Duke of Saxonby.

Caradon had insisted she call him Cary, as Grey did. He was the best man. Helena had all her sisters and Maryanne acting as her bridesmaids. To make that possible, Elise and Maryanne walked arm in arm. Both looked breathtaking in their ivory satin gowns.

Helena followed her bridesmaids down the aisle. Will was giving her away.

Grey stood at the altar with the reverend, and the look on

his face as she approached almost made her toss her bouquet and run into his arms.

He looked so happy.

Next thing she knew, she was repeating her vows to Grey. She stumbled over his full name: Damian George Arthur Richard David, but Grey only smiled at her.

Then it was time for those two simple words that promised happiness and told Grey how very much she loved him. "I do." Goodness, she thought she saw a glint of a tear in Grey's eyes.

He gazed deeply in her eyes as he repeated his vows. "I do," he said, huskily. "I do. I do. I do," he mouthed to her.

"By the power vested in me," intoned the reverend in his clear, deep voice, "I now pronounce you man and wife."

They were married! Grey clasped her hand and hurried her down the aisle and through the church doors. They burst out into the warmth and sunshine of a glorious June day. A breeze sent fragrant petals scattering over them.

"I planned that," Grey teased.

"Of course you did," she answered, loving the happy smile on his lips.

He stopped on the steps of the church and drew her into his arms. A hush settled.

"We're wed," Grey said softly. "It seems like a miracle."

Then he leaned in that last inch, and his lips claimed hers. Holding her bouquet, she hooked her arms around his neck, savoring all the complexity of the kiss. There was sweetness, a hint of naughty passion as he teased her with his tongue, and something intoxicating and precious and lasting, that she knew was love. She could feel all of it in his kiss, and she tried to bestow it on him in return.

Cheers sounded, along with laughter, and suggestions that were just a little ribald.

Breathless, Helena drew back. Dizzy from his kiss, she tossed the bouquet. It soared through the air toward Elise and

Maryanne. Then it kept arcing, and the Duke of Caradon had to grab it so it didn't hit his face.

Applause and cheers exploded. And more ribald suggestions.

Grey was taking her toward their carriage that would whisk them away. Her family was to stay as guests of the Winterhavens, then to join them at Grey's estate, which Jacinta—Lady Winterhaven had insisted Helena use her Christian name—said was even more grand than Winterleigh, but also lovely. The sort of home that deserved to be loved.

"And it can be loved now," Jacinta had said firmly. "I feel as if the past has weighed on us for years, but you have shown us all that we must cast it off and be happy."

Now Helena hugged her sisters-in-law.

Grey embraced Elise. "Soon it will be your turn, my dear, brand-new sister," he said. Helena had to put her gloved finger to the corner of her eye. A tear threatened to spill. Grey had been so wonderful with Elise, Jane, and Louisa. They were to all live with him. He had settled a stunning dowry on Elise, enough to ensure she and her husband-to-be would have a secure future. Elise's fiancé, a studious, gentle young man named Anthony Styles, was training to be a surgeon. Jane and Louisa would be starting at the best school for girls in England.

Will stepped forward, and Helena's heart soared as Will and Grey clasped hands, then Grey gave her brother a brief, masculine embrace.

She had been so worried about what would happen between Grey and Will. How could Grey, who found it so hard to trust, forgive him? Will had printed a retraction in the newssheet, had insisted the stories were false, and revealed he had been forced by a villain to print the lies. He had printed an apology to Greybrooke and his family and an apology to the readers of the newspaper.

Will had told her he believed he should close down the

newspaper, since he had tarnished its integrity. He apologized in person to Grey. And he had apologized to her for having been irresponsible. To Helena's surprise, Grey had accepted the apology and had become a financial investor for the newspaper, insisting Will continue at the helm.

Grey helped her into the open carriage. Caradon came forward with the bouquet. "And who did you think should have this?" he asked her.

Helena shared a wicked look with Grey, who said, "It's yours, Caradon. Beware: My new bride and my sister are plotting to fell the Wicked Dukes with matrimony." Then his voice caught and he added, "I hope they do. There is no greater joy than love."

The carriage lurched forward. And Grey drew her into another kiss.

A glorious kiss to herald their future.